Praise for Kendra Elliot

"Elliot never ceases to amaze readers with her magnificent gift for romantic suspense, and book four of the Bone Secrets series is absolute proof . . . fans of mystery will revel in the sheer thrill of uncovering the evil crime."

—*Romantic Times Book Reviews* on *Alone*, 4¹/₂ stars, Top Pick

"Kendra Elliot does it again! Filled with twists, turns, and spine-tingling details, *Alone* is an impressive addition to the Bone Secrets series."

—Laura Griffin, *New York Times* bestselling author, on *Alone*

"Kendra Elliot delivers unpredictable, captivating stories of romantic suspense. With a fascinating mystery and a passionate romance, her latest Bone Secrets novel, *Alone*, kept me turning pages long past bedtime."

—Melinda Leigh, bestselling author of the She Can series, on *Alone*

"Elliot once again proves to be a genius in the genre with her third heart-pounding novel in the Bone Secrets collection. The author knows romance and suspense, reeling readers in instantaneously and wowing them with an extremely surprising finish . . . Elliot's best by a mile!"

—*Romantic Times Book Reviews* on *Buried*, 4¹/₂ stars, Top Pick (HOT)

"[A] thrilling tale of passion and suspense . . . Realistic characters and a frightening plot will keep readers spellbound with numerous twists and turns . . . Wraps up with a love scene that's hot enough to make a polar bear sweat."

—*Romantic Times Book Reviews* on *Hidden*, 4¹/₂ stars (HOT)

"A page-turning blend of romance, thrills, and danger! *Hidden* is a winning debut from a new star in romantic suspense."

—Allison Brennan, *New York Times* bestselling author

"Make room on your keeper shelf! *Hidden* has it all: intricate plotting, engaging characters, a truly twisted villain. I can't wait to see what Kendra Elliot dishes up next!"

—Karen Rose, *New York Times* bestselling author

VANISHED

Also by Kendra Elliot

VANISHED

KENDRA ELLIOT

Montlake
Romance

Text copyright © 2014 Kendra Elliot
All rights reserved.

Published by Montlake Romance, Seattle

www.apub.com

ISBN-13: 9781477823477
ISBN-10: 1477823476

Cover design by Marc Cohen

Library of Congress Control Number: 2014900304

Printed in the United States of America

For all the missing children

Mason Callahan hadn't seen Josie in three months. The leanness of her face and the indentations above her collarbones told him she'd lost weight. In a bad way. Time hadn't been kind to her, and the scabbed sores on her cheeks hinted that meth was probably the new love of her life. There'd been a time when he'd fought a bit of an attraction to the woman. She'd been sweet and eager to please, a pretty woman in a wholesome-country-song sort of way. She and Mason shared a rural background and a similar taste in music that'd made her more enjoyable than his other confidential informants.

But now she'd never work with him again. His fingers tightened on the brim of the cowboy hat in his hand, and he swallowed hard at the sight of her contorted body on the floor of the bathroom in her cramped apartment. Anger abruptly blurred his vision. Someone had taken a baseball bat to her skull. The murder weapon was dumped in the shower, blood and hair sticking to the bat.

"Holy mother of God," muttered his partner, Ray Lusco. The two detectives had spent several years responding to brutal crimes as part of the Oregon State Police's Major Crimes Unit. But this was the first time they'd both known the victim. Josie's murder wouldn't be their case. Their sergeant had assigned it to another pair of detectives, knowing that Mason had worked with Josie several times for information during a prostitute murder case.

Detectives Duff Morales and Steve Hunsinger were the team chosen to find justice for Josie.

Mason would look over their shoulders and ride their asses the entire time.

"You got your look. Now get out of my crime scene," Morales said from the hallway.

Mason glanced back at the man but didn't move. He and Ray were still studying the scene. Josie had broken fingers. She'd tried to protect herself against the bat, perhaps even tried to grab the bat from her attacker. Once she was on the bathroom floor, the attacker had continued to beat her. Arcs of blood trailed up the walls to the ceiling, where the weapon had flung blood as it whipped up for another swing at her head.

"What are the bits of broken green metal by her head?" Lusco asked.

"Earrings. Christmas balls," answered Morales.

Mason silently swore. Did Josie's family expect her for Christmas next week? Did she have family? He'd seen the decorated plastic tree in her living room. A few presents were stashed below, waiting for eager hands to rip them open.

Mason closed his eyes, remembering the last time he'd met Josie at the Starbucks four blocks away. She'd ordered the biggest, most sugary Frappuccino on the menu and talked a mile a minute. Had she already been using meth? He'd assumed she'd been overcaffeinated and lonely. Even prostitutes get lonely for conversation. They'd been an odd pair. The perky prostitute and the cowboy detective. He'd followed her back to her tiny apartment because she had some twenties from a john who was part of a recent big drug bust. Mason wanted to tell her the bills probably wouldn't have prints or aid the investigation, but he went along because she wanted to help and seemed to need some company.

Being in her home had been a bit awkward. He'd been hyper-aware of the intimacy of simply standing in her feminine space. She'd offered him a soda, which he'd declined, but he'd accepted her suggestion that he grab a bottled water from the fridge for the road. Her fridge held water, soda, and milk. Nothing else. What did she eat? He should have known then that she was using drugs instead of calories to function. He'd exchanged her bills for some out of his own pocket and offered her sixty dollars extra. She'd politely turned it down, but he'd tucked the money under the saltshaker on her kitchen counter, and she'd pretended not to notice.

Mason had seen enough of Josie's blood. He turned and pushed past Lusco and the other pair of detectives, avoiding eye contact. He strode into her tiny kitchen. The kitchen was a nasty-smelling pit of dirty dishes and takeout containers. On his previous visit it'd been immaculate.

The saltshaker was still there—part of a set of silver cats—but the money was gone. He scanned the sad room. It wasn't even a room, more like a large closet with a sink and small microwave. He wanted to open the fridge to see if she'd finally added food, but he knew he couldn't touch anything until the crime scene unit had processed the apartment. The kitchen showed cracks in the counters from age and heavy use. Sort of how Josie had always looked. Her cracks had shown in the stress lines around her eyes and mouth. Lines that shouldn't have been present on a woman younger than thirty.

Who slipped through your cracks, Josie?

She'd told Mason she never brought johns back to her apartment. She'd kept a careful line between her work and where she lived. Had she broken her own rule? Or had someone followed her?

"Just another dead hooker," said a voice behind Mason.

He whirled around to find an unfamiliar Portland police officer studying him with sharp eyes.

"Show a little respect," snapped Mason.

The officer smirked, and Mason wanted to use the bloody bat on his head.

"She's been picked up three times in the last month. Twice for public intoxication and once for a catfight with some other hookers. I have a hard time feeling sorry for her," the officer stated.

Mason was taken aback. That didn't sound like the Josie he knew. Why hadn't she reached out to him if she was having problems? He'd smoothed her way out of small jams before. Had she gotten into something she didn't want him to know about?

"Let's get out of here," said Ray. Mason's partner had silently moved to the doorway of the closet-sized kitchen and had probably witnessed the anger on Mason's face.

Mason shoved his hat on his head and moved past the uniform. The officer barely turned to give him room to get by.

"Nice hat," the officer muttered at Mason's retreating back.

Mason ignored him. He didn't mind the occasional jabs about his hat. Or his cowboy boots. He was comfortable with his clothes. Cowboy hats were rare on the west side of the Cascade Mountain range, but when he headed back to his hometown of Pendleton on the east side of the state, they popped up everywhere.

Right now he was upset that he hadn't checked up on Josie. Usually he heard from her about once a month with information she wanted to sell. He hadn't heard a peep from her in three months, and she hadn't crossed his mind.

Guilt.

He followed Ray out the apartment door and down the dark stairwell. They avoided the elevator in the old apartment building. The stairwells might stink of piss, but it beat getting trapped for a few hours in an old creaking elevator. It'd happened twice to other detectives in other buildings. Mason didn't care to share the experience.

He pushed through the outer door into the bright sunshine and sucked in a breath of icy air. It was one of those rare clear winter weeks in the Pacific Northwest when residents dug out their sunglasses and pretended not to need heavy coats. Mason's skin soaked in the sun that'd been hiding behind dark-gray rain clouds for months. He'd nearly forgotten that the sky could be such an intense blue.

A few groups of people clustered on the sidewalk, squinting in the sun and speculating as they studied the four double-parked police cars. The Portland neighborhood was made up of dozens of short apartment buildings and old houses on narrow streets. It was a neighborhood known for its population of college kids and transient adults. No one ever stayed very long. Ray glanced at his watch. "Almost noon. Want to grab a bite?"

Mason muttered that he wasn't hungry as he pulled out his silenced cell phone. He had five missed calls from his ex-wife.

Shit. Jake.

His heart sped up, and he returned the calls with abruptly icy fingers. "Something's up with Jake," he said to Ray. "Robin has called five times in the last half hour."

"Is he home from college for winter break?" Ray asked.

"Robin picked him up from the airport two days ago. I haven't heard a word from the kid except a reply to my text asking if he'd landed safely." His son lived with his ex-wife, her new husband, and their joint young daughters. Mason had planned to reach out to his son this weekend to see if he wanted to go to the next Trail Blazers basketball game.

Just as he expected Robin's cell phone to go to voice mail, she finally answered. "Mason?" she asked.

Almost ten years had passed since their divorce, but he knew from the tone of her voice that she was terrified.

"What happened? Is Jake okay?" he barked into the phone.

"Jake's fine." Robin's voice cracked. "It's Henley. She's missing." She burst into sobs.

Mason's mind went blank. *Henley? Who—*

"Lucas is a mess," Robin wept.

Aha. Henley was Robin's stepdaughter. Mason couldn't remember the girl's age. Early teens? Jake rarely mentioned her, and Mason had met the girl only once or twice. She lived with her mother most of the time.

"When was she seen last? Did you call the police? How long's she been missing?" Mason rapid-fired the questions at his ex.

"Of course we called the police. Clackamas County Sheriff. She's been missing since this morning. She left for school, but they say she never made it." Robin's voice was steadier.

"School's not out for vacation yet?"

"Today's the last day."

"Okay. I'll call Clackamas County and see what's going on. How old is she?"

"Eleven," Robin whispered.

Crap. Mason closed his eyes. "We'll find her."

• • •

Mason shifted his weight from boot to boot as he waited for Lucas Fairbanks to usher him into his home. The entryway of the accountant's suburban house was huge, with a heavy wood-and-iron door that belonged in a castle. And the home looked exactly like the other fifty homes in the suburban upper-middle-class subdivision. Mason had never been a fan of Lucas, but he respected the man for doing a decent job of helping to raise Jake. Robin had always seemed happy once she'd married the accountant.

Lucas had succeeded where Mason had failed. Robin had known she was marrying a cop when she married Mason, but she hadn't understood how hard it would be to always come in second place to the job. Mason had tried to get home at a reasonable time each night, but it was rare. Crime didn't work nine to five, and neither did he. During the divorce Robin admitted she'd spent years thinking of herself as a single parent to save her sanity. It was the only way she could mentally cope with his absences. Otherwise, she was always waiting and waiting. In her head it made more sense for her to never expect him; that way she was never disappointed. When he managed to walk in the door in time for dinner, it was a nice surprise.

Mason followed Lucas into his formal dining room and tried not to gawk at the flashy chandelier. The room was packed with adults. Outside there'd been three cars from the Lake Oswego Police Department, two Clackamas County vehicles, an unmarked police car, and three generic American sedans that indicated the FBI had arrived. Mason scanned the room, searching for familiar faces. He didn't know any of the officers. Robin sat at the table, gripping the hand of another woman, who spoke with two men in suits. Both women had a well-used pile of tissues in front of them. Mason figured the other woman to be Henley's mother, Lilian.

Mason had never seen a slump in Lucas's shoulders. His usual chipper greeting had been severely muted, and he looked like he'd been sick for weeks. "The FBI is sending more people," Lucas said quietly. "I guess they have some sort of specialized team they pull from the other West Coast offices to respond to kidnappings."

"The CARD team," Mason answered. "Child abduction rapid deployment. They take this shit seriously. We all do." He swallowed hard and thanked heaven again that it wasn't his kid who was missing. He glanced at Lucas and felt instantly guilty. The man was staring at his ex-wife as she sobbed on Robin's shoulder.

Mason didn't know how their marriage had broken up. He'd never asked and now it didn't matter. They had a little girl to find. The Oregon State Police would offer resources, but Mason couldn't be one of them. As a family member, he couldn't be an official part of the investigation. But he'd set a plan in motion to get around that rule. He'd already requested some time off. And God protect anyone who tried to tell him his help wasn't needed.

"Tell me what happened," he said in a low voice to Lucas.

Lucas glanced at the two women and then jerked his head for Mason to follow him into the breezeway between the kitchen and dining room.

"Henley has been staying with us this week. Usually I get her one of the two weeks of winter vacation, but her mom asked me to add this extra week while she got some work done. Henley left for the bus stop like normal at about seven thirty this morning. Robin watched her walk out the door. A few hours later, her mom called, asking if Henley had stayed home sick from school, because she was getting automated calls and emails that Henley wasn't at school."

"The school will contact you if your kid doesn't show up?" Mason asked.

Lucas nodded. "You're supposed to call in on a special line if your kid will be missing any part of school that day. I know we forgot once or twice with Jake when he stayed home sick, and so we got a bunch of notifications. It's a good system."

"But it still takes a few hours to process."

"Well, they have to compare the attendance to the sick calls. That's entered by hand. Discrepancies trigger the calls and emails."

"What happened when Lilian called here?"

"Robin assured her Henley had gone to school and immediately called the school to confirm that she was there. I think Lilian called them, too. Henley's homeroom teacher said she hadn't shown up."

"What about the school bus driver? What about the other kids on the bus? Anyone talk to Henley's friends?" Mason rattled off question after question.

Lucas seemed to deflate more. "They're working on all that."

"Wait. How does Henley ride the bus if she doesn't usually live with you?"

"We live in the same school district and have the same elementary school boundaries."

"I didn't know you lived so close to your ex. Has it always been like that?"

"Yes, Lilian has a place about five minutes from here. It's really convenient for Henley. Lilian and I get along pretty well."

"Is she remarried? Do they have more kids?"

Lucas shook his head, and his gaze went over Mason's shoulder as the volume rose in the dining room. Mason turned around to see more people joining the group—judging by the dull suits, FBI agents. Good. No one knew more about child abductions, and the unique skills the FBI could offer to the local police were gold. Depending on its size, a police department might deal with one major child abduction over a decade. The FBI dealt with them monthly. Mason had never seen the CARD team in action, but he'd heard good things.

Mason turned back to Lucas. "Officially I can't join whatever task force they set up, but I can help as a family member. I'll be the family voice for the media and the liaison to the police and FBI. Let me do this for you guys. I've already told work I'm taking some time off. However long it takes to bring Henley home."

Lucas started to refuse, and Mason put a hand on his shoulder, giving the man a little shake. "Listen to me. Your wife and ex-wife are gonna need you for support. You don't have time to deal with the politics of the situation. I know how these guys work. Let me handle that. Everything I find out, I'll immediately pass on to you. Robin, Lilian, and you are going to want to be in the center of the investigation, and that's not going to help."

Lucas's eyes looked bleak. "Will they let you do that?"

"If you back me up. Make it clear you'll step back a bit, and they might be more accepting."

Desperation lurked in Lucas's gaze as he looked into one of Mason's eyes and then the other.

"I don't know what to do," he whispered. "I have to help. I have to know what's going on. She's my *daughter*, for God's sake. I can't just step back and do nothing."

"You won't be idle. They're going to interview the heck out of all of you. Over and over. Everything you can tell them will help, but they're not going to let you look over shoulders in the command center. I'll do that and report back to you."

"Command center?" Lucas's voice cracked. "You think they'll need—"

"They'll set up something within the hour I'm sure. You need to let them do their job. That's going to be your hardest role." Mason frowned as he glanced back at the growing crowd.

He'd originally hated Lucas with a passion, ever since he'd first heard Jake excitedly talk about the man. Lucas was everything Mason wasn't. He'd coached every boy sport in existence, and Mason had never heard a foul word from the man's mouth. Lucas always had a big smile. Until today. Mason had fought the urge to wipe the smile off Lucas's face the first few times he'd met him, believing the man was gloating. But it'd turned out he was one of those rare always-happy guys. Lucas wasn't a faker. It'd taken years for Mason to accept that the man was the real thing.

He couldn't have asked for a better man to help raise his son.

Didn't mean they had to be best friends.

Guilt swept through him again as he remembered all the resentment he'd held against the man. Part of Mason had been jealous that he hadn't created the type of picket-fence family with Robin that she had with Lucas. Now he didn't want to be in this man's shoes for anything.

"Where's Jake?" Mason asked. His son hadn't made an appearance.

"In his room. He was down here for a while but said he couldn't handle seeing his mom fall apart. I don't blame him," Lucas said with a glance at his wife. She and Lilian were still clutching hands but paying close attention to the man speaking quietly with them.

A dizzying need to see his son swamped Mason. "I'll be right back."

He left Lucas behind as he headed for the stairs.

2

5 HOURS MISSING

"Afternoon, Ava."

Special Agent Ava McLane nodded at Assistant Special Agent in Charge Ben Duncan as she stepped into the Fairbankses' crowded dining room. "How's it going, Ben?" The number of bodies in the room was claustrophobic. Everyone talked in low voices as they moved around, speaking on cell phones or in private conversations. Determination and focus filled the air.

His brown eyes met hers, and he gave a small smile. "We're still in the process of organizing everyone. We'll find her."

Good man. Staying positive. It was her personal number-one rule when searching for kids. She blew out a breath and surveyed the room, taking stock of the players. She was one of two Crimes Against Children coordinators at the Portland FBI office, and she'd been the special agent to take the call about Henley from Clackamas County this morning.

Ava's gut had twisted as she'd listened to the county sheriff. She'd known they needed to act fast. She thanked her stars that Clackamas County hadn't dithered about starting an investigation. They'd moved rapidly to comb the school and question neighbors.

The Clackamas County Sheriff's Office had recommended that Henley's elementary school move all the children to the gym for a "fun day" while they did a sweep of the school and the surrounding area. Henley Fairbanks was nowhere to be seen. They weren't certain that she'd even made it to the school bus. Mom and stepmom hadn't heard from Henley, and most of her close friends' parents had been contacted to see if the girl had appeared at one of their homes. Eleven-year-olds didn't simply disappear. They hid, wandered off, or were abducted. Henley's teachers and parents were convinced the girl didn't qualify for the first two categories, and the sheriff's search was rapidly proving them right.

The probability of abduction was growing by the hour.

With these facts in hand, it'd been Ava's decision to request that headquarters activate the CARD team. They'd agreed with her assessment and put the wheels in motion. Six special agents with unique skills to solve child abductions were on their way to Portland from various FBI offices in the western half of the US.

To the FBI, there was no such thing as over-responding when a child vanished. Whether the child had wandered off or been abducted, they didn't wait to act. Waiting cost lives. The FBI reacted as if the worst-case scenario had happened. Ninety percent of the Portland office's special agents were clearing their schedules for the next forty-eight hours to have more feet on the ground for the search. The lines between the official divisions in the office were gone; today, every agent belonged to VCMO, Violent Crimes and Major Offenders. It didn't matter if an agent was assigned to terrorism, white-collar crime, cybercrime, or art theft. Today everyone was looking for a child.

There'd be tons of grunt work. Interviews of every resident in the neighborhood and each adult at the school. Interviews of children. Leads from citizens to follow. Miles of square footage to search. Surveillance tapes to review. And that was just the beginning.

Ben tipped the eight-by-ten photo in his hand so that Ava could see it. Brown-eyed, blond-haired Henley Fairbanks smiled at her from a school photo. She was missing an upper front tooth. Ava's heart contracted.

"Any fights with her parents or bad times at school to make her hide or run away?" Ava questioned, even though she knew it'd already been asked a dozen times.

Ben shook his head. "Nothing has indicated that she's a runner."

"Where do you want me?" Ava asked Ben.

He frowned as he studied her for a second. "Stay close. I'm going to have you talk to the mothers in a moment. Sanford has been speaking with both of them, but their body language is screaming that they don't like him."

Smart women. Sanford was a great agent, but he couldn't establish a rapport with a woman to save his ass. What he believed he projected as kindness came across as condescension. Ava was surprised Ben had let him talk to the women at all.

"He was the first one here," Ben said quietly as if reading her mind. "I knew you were on the way, so I let it run for a while. I think you might relate better to them." He glanced at his phone's screen and his face lit up at a new text. "There's a church several blocks away that's agreed to let us use their conference wing for our command center. Sounds like it'll be perfect. I'll assign Sanford to help set that up. He's had the training for crisis-management coordination."

"He's not going to just walk away from the interviews," Ava muttered.

"Wells is taking notes." Ben dipped his head toward the lean special agent sitting next to Sanford. "He's been listening in for the whole interview. He can get you up to speed."

Ava nodded. Zander Wells was one of those quiet agents who drank in information and facts like he was dying of thirst. His memory and assessment skills were out of this world. He could probably repeat the whole interview verbatim without looking at his notes.

Ava agreed that Sanford's organizational talents were better utilized setting up the command center. Within hours the church's wing would explode from a simple space into a high-tech computer lab. Locating the center close to the victim's homes and school was ideal since Henley had vanished nearby.

Or so they suspected.

Don't assume anything.

Ava studied the two moms. She knew the brunette was Henley's stepmom and the blonde was the birth mom. Both women looked like typical upper-middle-class moms in their thirties. Yoga pants, ponytails, and probably a minivan in the garage. Ben was right about their reactions to Sanford. The blonde scowled at him, and the brunette sat so straight she appeared to have a spine of steel.

Will they like me any better?

A silly female part of her wanted the women to like her, not simply trust her in her role as an agent. For some reason she struggled to form female friendships. She had lots of male friends, but women usually kept their distance. Her fellow female agents respected her and treated her well but never invited her out for drinks. Her blunt-spoken sister had said it was because she was no fun. According to Jayne, she was straitlaced, all about business, and impossible to get loosened up.

Nothing wrong with that.

The mothers were around Ava's age, but they'd both experienced marriage and children. They'd traveled a path that hadn't presented itself in Ava's life. From day one, her path had law enforcement scribbled all over it. In grade school that had meant reading every mystery she could find, like Trixie Belden and Nancy Drew. Later on, that fascination had extended to true-crime novels and a hands-on teen Explorer program at her local police department. College had brought an FBI-as-goal-driven degree. The marriage and children part had never cropped up.

"Sanford." Ben stepped up to the table. "I'm gonna need you to get in touch with Morales about setting up the command center. I want you as one of the crisis-management coordinators."

Sanford looked at the ASAC in surprise and blinked. "But . . ." He didn't finish as he saw the determination in Ben's face. Agents didn't question orders. They went where directed. Sanford glanced behind Ben and saw Ava waiting. Comprehension crossed his face.

Ava could read his thoughts. *Oh, sure. This needs a woman's touch.*

He'd assume he was being bumped because he wasn't female, but Ava knew the issue was his manner, not what hung between his legs.

Sanford looked to Wells and then back at Ben. "Is Wells—"

"I want Wells to stay with his notes and bring Agent McLane up to speed."

Sanford excused himself to the women, stood, and pushed in his chair. He pulled out his cell phone as he silently left the room, not giving Ava another glance.

Ava hoped setting up the command center would heal his ego. That was a big project to manage. She pulled out Sanford's chair and slid into the warm spot. "I'm Special Agent McLane," she said to the two women, meeting each of their curious gazes. "I'm one of the Crimes Against Children coordinators." She spoke in a calm, low voice. Her sister Jayne called it Ava's I-know-what-I'm-doing voice and claimed it made the listener instantly confident in her. Ava didn't do anything special. It was her everyday voice, and it'd bugged her as a teen that she had a lower timbre to her voice than the other girls. The women introduced themselves, and Ava asked Wells to catch her up as she pulled out her notebook. "Let me know if something doesn't sound right to you two, okay?" she asked the women, looking one and then the other directly in the eye. The women nodded in unison.

Ava took notes as Wells covered the women's stories. She stopped him occasionally and asked the women to clarify a few points, but basically Wells recited their stories perfectly. Ava had crossed paths with Zander Wells a few times. He belonged to the cybercrimes division, which would intersect with her cases when children were exploited online. His social skills might be a bit weak, but she knew she could rely on his work.

From Wells's account, Ava confirmed her earlier information. Henley Fairbanks was a fifth grader at Westridge Elementary School. Today was the last day of school before two weeks of winter vacation. Henley had been with her dad and stepmom since Sunday night and had been looking forward to the last day of school. "It's one big party on the last day," Robin had said. "There's no way she would have wandered off. She was so excited to go to school this morning she could barely get to sleep last night. She bounced out the door today." She'd kissed Henley good-bye at seven thirty that morning and watched her walk to the sidewalk and turn east, heading for her bus stop seven houses down. That'd sounded like a short distance until Ava had driven into the neighborhood and noticed its oversized lots and curving streets.

"What have we heard from the kids at that stop?" Ava asked Wells.

"Nothing officially. The school wants the parents present before we question any of the kids."

Ava bit her lip. "What about unofficially? Has anyone just asked them if Henley was there this morning?"

Wells glanced at Duncan, who was deep in conversation with three other agents. "Two of the kids told Clackamas County that Henley wasn't at the stop this morning."

"I knew it," Robin whispered.

"Until we've talked to all the kids that were there, I don't want to state that she didn't make it to her stop. But yes, two preliminary accounts say she didn't make it." His eyes pleaded with the mothers. "Let's not accept this as fact yet, okay? And we're investigating both avenues simultaneously. We could miss possible leads by assuming that she didn't make it to school."

"What about the bus driver?" Ava asked.

Wells frowned. "She says she doesn't remember. A half-dozen kids get on at that stop. Sometimes more, sometimes less. "

"Any parents waiting with their kids at the bus stop?" she questioned.

"Not this morning," Wells stated. "And Henley walks around a large curve in the road right before the stop. There's no line of sight for the other kids to see her approaching."

"Why is no one telling us anything?" Lilian burst out. "So far all we've heard is speculation and secondhand statements from kids. You have to give us more than that."

A tall man Ava had seen speaking with a local plainclothes cop pulled out the chair next to Robin. "I'm Lucas, Henley's dad," he said to Ava. She noticed immediately that he had Henley's brown eyes. He took Robin's hand and squeezed it while leaning toward Lilian. "I don't think they have much to tell us yet, Lilian. But Mason has offered to be the liaison between the family and the investigation. I think we need to let him be the one to deal with them, and trust that he'll keep us up-to-date, instead of us pestering the FBI nonstop to keep us informed."

"Who?" Ava and Wells asked at the same time.

"He's my ex-husband," Robin said quietly. "He's a Major Crimes detective with the Oregon State Police. I think that's a good idea. Mason knows who and what to question. And I trust him. He has time for this?" she asked her husband.

"He says he's taken the time off work, and that it won't be a problem."

"I'm sure he has plenty of vacation time available," Robin muttered.

Ava raised an internal brow at the comment. Were there some sore feelings between Robin and her ex-husband? But Robin had been quick to chime in with a vote of confidence for him to act as a liaison. Ava liked the idea of a liaison for the family, and she knew Ben would, too. Managing a family during kidnappings took manpower. They deserved to know what was going on, but the agency didn't want ten family members asking multiple agents the same questions. A conduit, especially someone in law enforcement, would be ideal.

Would Ben embed an agent with the family? It wasn't uncommon for an agent to move in with the family to help manage their side of the investigation.

"But how long can this last?" Lilian asked, her voice rising. "You'll find her soon, right? Do you really need to set up a command center, and do we need a liaison? She can't be far away. It's only been a few hours, right?" Desperate-mom eyes stared at Ava.

It's been over five hours.

Ava looked directly at Lilian. "We want to catch every opportunity we can. When it comes to kids, we jump into action. We don't wait. That means immediately investigating each lead we get. To do that, we need our resources pooled in one area. It's more efficient. Trust me, we know what we're doing." She ended softly and gave Lilian a sad smile. "I know it's hard for you. You're sitting in here and can't see the fifty agents who've already joined the search at the school and in the neighborhood. And a lot more are on their way." Her heart ached for the parents. The FBI had extensive experience organizing searches for missing children. It was a finely honed set of skills, acquired in a painful way.

"Is someone at Lilian's home?" Ava asked Wells.

He nodded. "Yes, we have agents waiting there and canvassing the neighborhood. She doesn't have a landline, so any phone calls she gets will go to her cell." He raised a brow at Lilian for confirmation. She nodded and touched her iPhone on the table, making the screen light up. Ava caught a glimpse of a photo of Henley. It wasn't the school photo Ben had shown her. This one had been taken at the ocean.

"Do you think there will be a ransom?" Lilian whispered.

Ava shook her head. "I don't know."

Lilian touched her screen again.

"Can I see the photo on your phone?" Ava asked, holding out her hand. Lilian gave her the phone.

Ava studied the little girl splashing in vibrant blue water. That wasn't a Pacific Northwest ocean. "Hawaii?" she asked, choosing the closest tropical vacation site.

Lilian nodded.

The child in the photo still had that thin layer of baby fat that kept her from being mistaken for a middle-school student. This was a child who still reveled in being a little girl. Her bathing suit was Minnie Mouse, and her long white-blond hair hung in braids to her waist.

"Beautiful." Ava handed back the phone. "Does Henley have a cell phone?"

"Yes, but she leaves it at home." Lilian stood up. "Will you excuse me for a minute?"

Ava nodded and watched Lilian leave the room. The birth mom was a slim, athletic-looking woman. Ava knew she was unmarried, but did she have a boyfriend? She heard a door close down the hall from the direction Lilian had gone. Probably a bathroom.

Ava turned her gaze to the couple across the table. Lucas had Robin's hand in a death grip on the table, and the woman briefly rested her head on his shoulder, her eyes closed. Lucas met Ava's gaze, his expression grim.

"The three of you seem to get along fairly well for a divorced situation," Ava prodded.

Robin lifted her head and nodded. "I'd call their divorce rather amicable." She looked at Lucas, who grimaced and nodded.

"For the most part," Lucas agreed. "We put Henley first. That was our agreement from the beginning. When Robin and I started dating, Lilian was already in a serious relationship, so it made it easier to handle."

"Is she still seeing him?" Ava asked.

Robin and Lucas glanced at each other. "No," Robin answered. "That was two boyfriends ago. She's not seeing anyone right now."

"You sound quite certain."

Robin gave a half smile. "Surprisingly, Lilian and I are pretty close. We both love Henley, and we have a lot in common. It wasn't hard to become good friends. She keeps me updated on her love life."

Lucas gave a short nod.

Okay. That has to be odd for him. Ava raised a brow at Lucas. "Worlds colliding?"

He snorted. "It's really all right. It was a bit weird at first, but Lilian and I have evolved into just friends. Our marriage seems like a lifetime ago. It was such a short period in my life."

Ava looked to Robin. "You have two daughters together?"

"Yes, Kindy and Kylie are three and five. I had my parents pick them up this morning. And then there's Jake, who I had with Mason, the state detective I told you about. Jake is a freshman in college."

"Is he away at school?" Ava asked as Lilian rejoined their group.

"Jake's upstairs. He's home for winter break and is absolutely devastated," Lucas answered. "He's tight with all his sisters, but he and Henley have a special bond, I'd say." He glanced at Lilian, who nodded, and fresh tears rolled down her face.

"That's true," Lilian agreed. "Even with the seven-year age difference, those two will talk and goof off for hours. Before he left for college, he'd come babysit, and I think he enjoyed it as much as Henley did. Those two geek out over some of the same video games."

"But there's no blood relation there," Ava added for her own benefit, mentally trying to get the correct parents assigned to the correct kid. *Lucas and Lilian's daughter and Robin's son.*

"It's never mattered. Perhaps they're closer because there is no relation," added Robin.

"Jake gets along with his dad?" Ava asked. "He spends time with him?"

Lucas and Robin nodded.

Ava waited for more.

"Mason's a good dad. He just never had the time for a kid. Before Jake went to college, Mason had him every other weekend," Lucas offered.

Stepdad has positive things to say about cop dad. Ava thought that spoke well of the detective. "Everyone seems to get along pretty well here," she said. "You're not the screaming divorced family from TV." *Almost too good to be true . . .*

"We're relatively sane people," Lucas said after exchanging a look with Robin and Lilian. "No crazies here. The kids come first. As long as everyone has that priority, it works."

"Tell me about Henley," Ava asked gently, looking Lilian in the eye. "What does she love to do?" Ava settled in to the interview, turning up her listening skills as the mother spoke and studying her body language, listening for the words the mother didn't say. Beside her, Wells continued with his notes.

In her mind, the image of the little girl grew piece by piece, gathering life as Henley's mother described her daughter's sunny nature. Ava tuned out the other conversations in the room as she concentrated on Lilian's stories. With each word, Henley Fairbanks became more to Ava than just a picture on her mom's phone.

3

Mason paused at his son's closed bedroom door. He knew his way around the house, but it still felt wrong to be wandering on his own. He'd passed a little girl's bedroom with two suited agents combing through it and stood aside in the hallway as three agents walked past with their arms full of computer equipment. The FBI wasn't wasting any time.

He wondered if Lucas's accounting business would be affected by the sudden loss of equipment. He knew Lucas had an office in Lake Oswego, where agents were probably knocking on the door, questioning coworkers and requesting hard drives. How much work did Lucas bring home with him? Mason figured the accountant had his files backed up somewhere in a database, but it was going to be a pain in the ass to get his work done if the hardware was missing. At least it was December, not April.

He knocked on Jake's door and waited.

Silence.

He knocked harder, and the door finally opened. His son had a headset with a microphone around his neck and a gaming controller in his hand.

"Hey, Dad." Jake stood back, holding the door open as an invitation into his room. Mason sniffed. Jake's room faintly smelled of pizza, and he spotted a few crusts left on a plate on his son's desk. Mason felt a small wave of familiarity; his son still didn't eat his pizza crusts.

Some days Mason felt he didn't know his son. Jake lived primarily with his mom, and Mason had been an every-other-weekend dad for a decade. But right now, he saw the small boy he'd always known. Jake's eyes were red from crying. He'd always been an empathetic kid.

Mason gestured to the headset. "You gaming with someone?"

Jake pulled it off. "Not anymore. I thought it'd be a good way to take my mind off of Henley, but all my friends are asking questions, and I don't want to talk about it." He tossed the headset on his bed, avoiding his father's eyes. The sag in his shoulders broke Mason's heart.

"They'll find her, Jake. The FBI has opened the floodgates. Nearly every agent in Portland is pounding the pavement to search."

His son turned toward him, and Mason wanted to brush the shaggy hair out of Jake's wet eyes. "She's just a kid. A little girl. Do you know what kind of sick fucks take little girls?" His voice cracked.

"Don't swear," Mason automatically corrected. "I do know who those assholes are. *No one* knows better than me the sort of sick people who are out there. But you can't let your mind accelerate to the worst situation. It'll only pull you down."

"No one will let me do anything." Jake dropped the controller next to the laptop on his bed. "I wanted to go talk to the kids at her school, but the cops said I have to stay here."

"They're exactly right. They're taking care of that. They don't need you in their way. Have the police or FBI talked to you yet? They'll want to interview every family member in depth. Probably more than once."

Jake shook his head. "Not really. One guy talked to me for about ten minutes, asking if I had any idea where she might have gone, or if I'd seen anyone hanging around the house in the last few days. I wasn't even up when she left for school. I didn't know anything was wrong until Mom came up to ask if I'd heard from Henley." He sat on the end of his bed, his hands clenched together between his thighs.

Mason had flashbacks of his father when he looked at Jake. Tall, lean, huge hands, and wide shoulders. At eighteen, Jake hadn't grown into his body. His collarbones protruded through his T-shirt, and he didn't know what to do with his long arms. He looked like he needed another twenty pounds to fill out properly.

Jake gestured at his laptop. "I looked it up. Seventy-five percent of kids that go missing are killed in the first three hours. By seven days that's increased to ninety-seven percent." His eyes pleaded with his father. "You've got to help them find her. Can't you call someone? Like an elite tracker sort of guy? Do you know someone, like a mercenary, who can cut through all the red-tape bullshit? I know Lucas would pay whatever it takes."

Mason didn't correct the curse word. He stared at his son. Who did Jake think his father was? Some sort of covert-ops team leader who worked for the state police as his cover? Was Jake's brain so warped by movies and video games that he truly thought that was possible? Mason slowly shook his head and watched the misery deepen in Jake's eyes.

Mason sat down next to Jake, feeling like his legs were made of rubber and his heart was about to split open. "I'm sorry, son. That's not the real world. Our best bet is to let the FBI do what they do best. They know how to look under every rock. I know it feels like nothing is happening, but while we're sitting here talking, there are a hundred agents out there, beating on doors and searching high and low."

"But they never found that one Portland boy. The kid who went missing when his stepmom dropped him off at school. It's been four years!"

"You can't compare Henley to other cases, Jake. Every situation is different. Those guys downstairs won't give up, and they have the best resources for this kind of investigation. For your own mental health, you need to stay positive. It hasn't even been one day. Don't get ahead of yourself."

"How can someone stay positive for years?"

"Look at those three girls in Cleveland who were imprisoned for a decade. Or Elizabeth Smart, who was missing for nine months. There's always still hope as long as they don't find . . ." Mason swallowed hard. He'd been about to say "a body."

Jake stared at him with the eyes of a child who'd just been told Santa wasn't real.

His son was near adulthood, but he still had the soul of a child. He'd always been ruled by his emotions. "Next week is Christmas," Jake whispered. "I bought her one of those pillow pet things. You know, a stuffed animal that folds up into a pillow. She already has five, but she wants more."

"We'll find Henley. I promise you. We'll get her back in time for Christmas," Mason swore to his son. He never made promises he couldn't keep. Never. But he'd just made a promise where he had no control over the outcome.

He felt like a liar.

Jake slumped into Mason's arms and sucked in deep breaths, his chest heaving, and Mason felt the boy's hot tears soak through his shirt to his shoulder. He blinked back his own tears, kicking himself for underestimating his son's attachment to his stepsister. Mason wished he'd paid better attention the few times his path had crossed Henley's. But she'd been a small child, invisible to him, and he'd overlooked her.

Now she had his full attention.

• • •

Mason stopped in the downstairs hallway to catch his breath before rejoining the group in the dining room. His talk with Jake had ripped open in him a deep place he hadn't known existed. Jake had always been a likable kid and hadn't struggled with bullies or sports, and Mason had never needed to protect his son; it was a new experience for him. Jake had weathered the divorce well. But five minutes ago, the emotions Mason saw in his son had destroyed him like nothing else. Part of him wanted to find Henley just to mend his son's broken heart.

Family portraits lined the hall. Mason found the most recent-looking one and stepped closer to study it, his gaze going to his son. Jake looked tall and strong, and pride flowed through Mason which was immediately replaced by a familiar sense of dishonesty. Who'd made Jake the almost-man he was today? Lucas? Mason knew the man deserved some credit, but how much?

The two small dark-haired girls in the happy family picture were mini-Robins. They were painfully young in Mason's eyes, one about three and the other around five. Mason could never remember which one was Kylie and which one was Kindy.

My Lord, he was an ass.

He couldn't keep the girls straight, because it'd been weird to see Robin pregnant with another man's child. So he'd blocked it out, never fully listening when Jake talked about his younger sisters. This morning Robin's parents had taken the girls to their home for as long as was needed, and Mason had asked if Clackamas County was giving protection. If one daughter had been targeted, the others might be, too.

The county had already parked a deputy in front of the grand-parents' home.

Is Jake safe?

Mason had told him not to leave the house. A person who kidnapped an eleven-year-old girl probably wasn't interested in an eighteen-year-old gangly man-boy, but Mason wasn't taking chances or making assumptions. No one knew the motive behind the kidnapping.

If Lucas Fairbanks had pissed off a client who was now seeking revenge, no one in the family was safe.

Mason couldn't see Lucas making anyone angry. The guy was too nice. But until the FBI knew why Henley was missing, law enforcement would stay close to all family members.

He moved into the dining room, the constant flow of uniforms and suits creating a comforting rhythm that returned him to work mode. Work was Mason's comfort zone. Not soothing a teenage boy in his room. Upstairs with his son crying in his arms, he'd felt lost and helpless, uncertain if he was saying what Jake needed to hear. Down here, Mason could get something accomplished.

Lucas caught his eye and gestured to the chair next to him. Mason strode over and pulled out the chair, sizing up the two FBI agents at the table. In the far corner of the room, ASAC Ben Duncan, who was holding court with another agent, nodded at him. Mason knew Duncan from previous cases. He wondered if Lucas had already mentioned Mason's request to be a liaison. If Lucas hadn't, Mason figured Duncan had put two and two together. In his past experiences with the ASAC, Mason had recognized that they were cut from the same cloth. If Duncan were in Mason's boots, he would do what Mason had planned. He was glad Duncan was the ASAC who'd been assigned the case.

Mason didn't know the two agents at the table. The man was well dressed but lean, and his manner screamed *computer geek* even though he took notes on a legal pad. The woman was younger but emanated the authority at the table. Mason had been in the room long enough to realize she was asking the questions and guiding Lilian, Robin, and Lucas through their preliminary questioning. Her clear blue eyes studied him as he sat next to Lucas. She didn't project any of the defensiveness Mason expected in response to his crashing her interview.

"This is Mason Callahan, the state police detective who's offered to be our spokesperson," Lucas said to the woman.

She stood a bit and leaned over the table, holding out her hand to Mason. "I'm Special Agent McLane. This is Special Agent Wells. Thank you for offering to help."

Her voice was low and rich, making Mason nearly forget to take the offered hand. He stood, shook it, and then shook Wells's hand. Mason watched Wells add his name to the notes in neat print.

"You've approved some time off with your commander, Detective Callahan?" McLane asked.

That voice. Before this moment, only voices that sang country music had ever captured Mason's attention. Special Agent McLane sounded like she should be singing some bluesy soul song in a dim bar with a fine whiskey in her glass. He eyed her pressed white blouse, straight posture, and sleek, dark ponytail, wondering if she could sing. Or if she'd ever even stepped foot in a smoky bar. McLane looked more like the type to visit the gym. Or the library.

Mason eased back into his chair and noticed everyone looking at him expectantly.

What had she asked?

"I emailed him. Haven't heard back. I don't think it'll be an issue. Please continue." He gestured at the family members. "Don't let me interrupt your interview."

"Actually I think we're at a good stopping point for the moment. Lilian needs to go pack a bag—she's going to stay here tonight." Special Agent McLane smiled at the woman. "I'll drive you to your place."

Mason noticed Lilian and Robin seemed very receptive to McLane. He wondered what happened to the first agent who'd been questioning them when he arrived. Both mothers had looked ready to fly off the handle while talking with him. Now Lilian and Robin were calm and determined, mimicking Special Agent McLane's attitude. A harmony thrummed among the three women. Somehow Agent McLane had worked a spell.

Mason glanced at his watch. Two o'clock. He should go pack, too. He couldn't be a liaison from his home; he planned to set up camp at the Fairbankses'. Better to be prepared now than have to borrow something from Lucas later.

Wells made a few more rapid notes as McLane and Lilian stood. ASAC Duncan approached.

"You're getting some things from home?" Duncan asked Lilian, who nodded. Duncan's gaze swept the table. "Having you all in one place will make it easier for us. We're setting up operations in a church not far from here, so most of the agents will be out from under your feet. We still have some forensics people in the home, and I'm assigning someone to stay here around the clock. They'll basically be moving in. Is that going to be a problem?" He eyed Robin and Lucas.

The couple exchanged a glance, and Robin shrugged. "We have a guest room, and my mother will keep the younger girls, freeing up their rooms. As long as your person doesn't mind Hello Kitty sheets."

"I don't think Agent McLane will mind," answered Duncan.

"What?" Agent McLane spun around to her boss. "Me? What about Christine?"

"Her maternity leave kicked in last week. Her doctor put her on bed rest for the final two months. You hadn't heard?"

"No. I hadn't," McLane said slowly. She turned back to the mothers and Lucas, an apologetic look on her face. "Christine is our victim specialist. She's usually the one who stays with families during times like this. Her role would be to offer support and help you with whatever you need."

"I think you'll mesh nicely," replied the ASAC.

Mason bit his cheek. The FBI agent hadn't seen that one coming. McLane blinked rapidly, trying to process the apparent curveball the case agent had thrown at her. Would that change her role in this case? Mason wondered how McLane felt about being thrust deep into the family dynamics.

Judging by the look on Robin's face, she was pleased, and Lilian nodded emphatically.

"You're very welcome to stay here," Robin said. "I'm glad they picked you instead of the first agent who spoke with us."

Lilian snorted.

Mason saw Agent Wells's lips twitch as he continued to write on his notepad, and Agent McLane abruptly wiped her face clear of emotion. Mason wondered what he'd missed with the first agent; the man must have been a prince.

6 HOURS MISSING

Ava gaped as she drove past the condo building Lilian indicated and wished she owned a unit. Lilian lived in a fresh new building with Roman-looking architecture. It had a quaint coffee shop and art gallery on the bottom level. The city had decorated for the holidays; wreaths and red bunting hung from the antique-looking street lamps, and tasteful Christmas trees spotted the storefronts. Ava wondered how much Lake Oswego's décor budget was, since they hadn't hung the tacky metal sparkly garland like some cities. It looked like they'd hired a professional designer to get the residents in the holiday mood.

Ava pulled around to the back of the building and got out. Glancing to the south, she realized the upper levels of the building probably had beautiful views of the lake and surrounding hills.

"Nice," Ava muttered under her breath, thinking of her tiny house and its yard with never-ending maintenance.

"I love it," Lilian replied, stopping on the sidewalk. "People always ask why I didn't get a house for Henley, but we aren't yard people. We love to walk the city and visit the shops. The salespeople all know her by name, and there's a great park a few blocks away."

Ava sniffed the air. "Does it always smell like coffee here?"

"Yes! And that scent never gets old."

Ava followed her through a security gate, approving of the keypad and card swipe to enter the condo area. "No vagrants wandering around?"

"In Lake Oswego?"

The woman had a good point. The city in Oregon with the highest per capita income didn't attract bums. If one did decide to visit, there was no doubt they were sent quickly on their way.

An elevator took them up three levels. They moved down a hallway, stopped, and Lilian started to unlock her door.

"Just knock," suggested Ava. Duncan had sent several agents to the condo earlier, and at least one was expected to house-sit for a while.

Lilian stared blankly at her, then nodded and knocked. Ava saw the flicker of sadness that crossed her face, no doubt from having to knock on her own front door. Ava hoped the search inside had been done neatly. Her protective mama bear would emerge if the police had left a mess. She'd taken these two terrified mothers to heart and was determined to keep their days as pain free as possible.

Ava didn't recognize the young male agent who opened the door. They exchanged identification. Special Agent Parek stood back and let the women in. It wasn't unusual for Ava to not know someone from the Portland office. They had nearly a hundred agents, and agents frequently transferred between offices. She'd been in Portland for five years and liked it. She'd hated her previous posting in Los Angeles. She'd missed the changing seasons, and there was simply too much city. Too many people. And too many cars.

She followed Lilian through the luxury condo, spotting a fantastic view of the lake from the formal living room. So far the home didn't look disturbed. Either the police had been exceedingly neat or someone had spent some time picking up. Lilian moved down a hall and stepped inside a bright bedroom. Ava squinted. Three of the walls were neon lime green, and one was hot pink. It was all girl. Lilian slowly turned in a circle, studying everything.

"I can tell they searched," she whispered. "They did a nice job putting things back, but I can tell."

Ava thought it was surprisingly neat for an eleven-year-old's room. At that age, she and her sister rarely saw the floor of their shared bedroom; they had practically used the floor as a closet. Henley's bed was made, and there wasn't a shred of clothing to be seen. Several shelving units held fabric storage bins. They looked nice and neat from the outside, but Ava suspected they were loaded with a mishmash of toys, books, and Barbies.

A poster of an unfamiliar boy band held the place of honor over Henley's headboard. A huge white desk with a hutch for knickknacks overflowed with stuffed animals with huge eyes. A dozen lip glosses and a lighted makeup mirror were pushed to one side of the desk.

"They took her computer." Lilian ran her hand across the white wood. "I'm not surprised. It just seems to leave a glaring empty space on her desk."

Ava stared at the blank spot. Did all eleven-year-olds have their own computers in their rooms? Didn't all the parenting magazines caution against that?

"I had good parental control software on there," Lilian said as if reading her mind. "It kept her from accessing certain websites. Even some websites that I had no problem with."

"Did you ever look at her browsing history?"

"I did at first. But it was all simple stuff. Disney and Barbie and games. I haven't checked in a while." Her voice faded away.

Ava's thoughts sped to Internet predators; she suspected Lilian's did, too. "If there's something on there, our guys will find it. Fast. It'll be the first thing they look for," she said.

Lilian shook her head, staring at the pile of lip gloss. "I should have checked more frequently. But I trusted her to come to me with questions. We talked about what was appropriate on the Internet, and I cautioned her about being contacted by people she didn't know. I know she did some game sites with her friends, but she couldn't really chat with other players. She could only pick from a set of phrases to use, like 'This is fun' or 'Have a happy day.'"

"The FBI will be able to see every site she visited," Ava said.

"I should have watched her better," Lilian whispered. "I let her be on there by herself too much."

Ava didn't like the despair threatening Lilian's gaze. The woman was falling into a whirlpool of self-doubt and blame. "Lilian. Look at me." The woman turned, her brown eyes moist. Ava grabbed her hands and squeezed them. "Listen. You are not a bad mother. Not looking over your child's shoulder every minute of every day does not make you a bad mother. This is not your fault. *Do not* beat yourself up when we don't know what's happened." The woman nodded as Ava spoke, but she doubted her words penetrated Lilian's self-blame.

How does a mother function when her baby is out of her reach?

"Let's get your bags packed." Ava assigned a task, hoping it would shift Lilian's focus. She tugged on the mother's hands, pulling her to the door. Lilian followed and didn't look back into her daughter's room. In the hallway she seemed to snap out of her mood and moved past Ava to her own bedroom.

"It'll just take me a few minutes." She shut the door to her room.

Ava halted in the hall. That was an unmistakable *don't come in.*

This was her new role. As soon as Duncan had said she would be embedded with the family, Ava's role had switched from being an investigator to being a hand-holder. It would have been nice if Duncan had approached her privately about embedding. It was a bit of a dickhead move to pop it on her in front of the mothers. But she would have agreed if he'd asked her beforehand. And Duncan knew her well enough to know that. Still, she'd hide his favorite coffee mug in retaliation for not warning her.

She let Lilian have a few minutes to herself and went to the kitchen. Special Agent Parek looked up as she entered. He sat at the kitchen table, two cell phones, a novel, and a notepad in front of him. Ava avoided looking at the Christmas tree in the living room. The stack of presents underneath made her heart hurt.

"She says they put things back neatly. She seems pretty pleased," Ava told him. He nodded and gestured at a chair at the table. She pulled out the chair to join him. Parek seemed like a quiet type of guy. He was compact, not much taller than her, with kind, dark eyes. "Do you know how the canvass went in the building?"

"Out of a dozen units, only six had people inside. A team is coming back this evening to knock on doors again. The art gallery has a camera system that catches part of the sidewalk out front and another camera on the rear entrance. They had a backup of forty-eight hours of footage, so if Henley somehow made it here, we'll see her." Parek took a sip of a soda, and Ava realized she'd missed lunch. She never missed lunch. She swallowed hard, her mouth dry. She had to eat several times a day, or she suffered severe headaches.

She would eat and sleep this case until it was over. It was the type of case that she had to throw herself into 100 percent, or she'd feel she failed the parents. And failed herself.

She was prepared for the worst, but she would fight for the best outcome for Henley in every way she could. But she wouldn't be out tramping the sidewalks or digging through paperwork on this case. Her hands had been tied on the investigative side. As the fill-in victim specialist, her job was to be there for the family. Not to interview the parents.

Of course she'd keep her ears open . . . and ask a question here and there.

"What do you think of the mother?" Parek asked in a low voice.

"I don't know. I met her a few hours ago, and she's traumatized over the loss of her daughter. It's too early to form any accurate opinions."

But what does my gut tell me?

She'd been watching Lilian's every expression and movement. She'd been analyzing every word out of her mouth. Had she seen anything to make her feel Lilian was lying? Or holding something back?

Not yet.

Her departure in the hallway had been abrupt, but Ava had understood the need for some privacy. The woman wouldn't have much of it until they found her daughter.

"Has anyone stopped by? Any neighbors or friends?"

Special Agent Parek shook his head. "It's been quiet. With the security system the building has in place, I don't expect any friends to drop in. As for the neighbors, I don't know if this is a get-to-know-your-neighbor type of building or not. There's no landline, so no calls, either."

"I'm ready." Lilian stepped into the kitchen. "I didn't know how many days to pack for. Do you think I need more than a day or two of clothes?" Her red-rimmed eyes blinked rapidly, and Ava knew she'd cried as she hid in her bedroom.

There's no answer to that question.

Ava forced a smile. "We can always come back for more."

Lilian flinched, and Ava wished she could have said, "I'm sure that's more than enough."

But that wasn't who she was. She was too damned practical. "Pack for the worst," she wanted to say. She believed in keeping a positive attitude but didn't let it affect the practical decisions that needed to be made.

Prepare for the worst.

You could never pack too much underwear or question too many neighbors. An agent did what needed to be done.

"That doesn't mean we don't expect to find her soon. It's okay to plan ahead." Her voice softened. "Our goal is to find her before you need anything you've packed."

Lilian's throat convulsed as she swallowed. She nodded. "Let's go."

In the car on the way back to the Fairbanks house, Ava asked her if it felt odd to stay in her ex-husband's home.

"Not really. We've done some short vacations together. Like trips to the coast or the water park in Washington," Lilian answered, her gaze on the scenery they were passing.

"You do all get along," Ava stated. "That's rare."

"I guess. The kids all like each other. Even Jake enjoys being with the younger girls. He's a good big brother. It makes it easier when the adults have all committed to doing what's best for the kids."

"What about Jake's dad? Is he around much?" The detective was stuck in Ava's brain. His level of professionalism and almost old-fashioned manners at the interview had impressed her. He looked to be in his late forties, with salt-and-pepper hair and dark-brown eyes. She'd immediately picked up that he was an investigator through and through. It took one to know one.

"Mason? He's a good guy. Just always working. He's married to the job. I don't know how he and Robin lasted as long as they did. I don't see much of him, but Robin says he stays in touch with Jake. She has nothing but kind words for him. I think she almost feels sorry for him. He never remarried and seems to have a pretty solitary life."

Ava understood perfectly.

She felt Lilian's gaze focus on her. "What about you? I don't see a ring. Do you have kids?"

Ava paused. In any other situation, she'd deflect the questions. Her personal life was her own business. But she was facing the possibility of spending a lot of hours with Lilian and the Fairbanks. She needed to appear open to gain their trust. "Never married. No kids. I guess I'm a bit like Jake's dad. Married to the job. But I like it that way." She didn't look at Lilian, whose curiosity filled the car. Did she believe her? Some people thought their life wasn't complete unless they had a significant other.

Like Ava's sister. She bounced from man to man, searching for her soul mate.

"Sounds peaceful. There've been times when—," Lilian broke off, a sob catching in her throat. "Oh my gosh," she whispered. "How did I ever think like that?" She buried her face in her hands and let the tears flow.

Ava knew she'd been about to say there'd been times when she wished she lived alone.

Every mother must have wished for solitary peace during the trying times of child raising. Especially when she was doing it on her own.

Now Lilian had gotten her wish, and she was in hell.

5

7 HOURS MISSING

Mason jogged up his front porch steps, his boots clomping loudly. He considered it a warning to anyone with the balls to break into his house. He was being kind to let them know he was home and saving their asses from being surprised and probably shot. He hadn't surprised anyone in twenty years; he was disappointed when he pushed the door open and discovered quiet instead of a meth head diving out a window. Apparently he had some extra adrenaline to burn off.

He stepped inside, stopped, and stuck his head back outside to scan his wide porch. All quiet.

No dog.

He gave a couple of soft whistles and a "Here, boy."

Still quiet. He mentally shrugged and stepped inside, reaching for his cell phone. He needed to pack a bag and talk to his boss. He hadn't received a reply to the email he'd sent to his sergeant informing him of the shitstorm that'd suddenly opened on Mason's life. He found his boss in his contacts and pressed the "Call" button. He strode down the hall, his phone to his ear, hitting light switches and checking all the rooms. His usual habit upon getting home.

No meth heads.

His home wasn't large. It was just right for a single guy who didn't have time to do yard work and didn't like to clean. He considered the money he spent on a housekeeper and yard guy twice a month the best investment he'd ever made. He grabbed a carry-on roller bag out of his closet and dumped it on the bed. His boss answered the phone.

"Schefte."

"Denny. Callahan here. Did you get my email?" Mason pulled a drawer open and grabbed three pairs of socks. Would he need more?

"I did. That missing little girl was on the noon newscast. She's your ex's daughter?"

"It's my ex's stepdaughter. From her husband's previous marriage."

"She's only eleven," Schefte muttered. "Goddamn the assholes out there."

"Amen. And as a heads-up, you might be seeing me on the news. I'm not gonna let the family step in front of any cameras. I'll handle any public speaking for them. Warn the department the press might be sticking their noses in my business."

Schefte cleared his throat. "Yeah, we'll make it clear you're acting solely as a family member to any press that asks. This is outside our jurisdiction, but you let the FBI know they can ask for any support they need. I've got your schedule covered for the next few days. Morales and Hunsinger can pick up any spillover."

"How are they coming with the Josie Mueller case?"

"Asking lots of questions. She didn't hang out with the cleanest people, you know. They're interviewing people who spend more time on the street than with a roof over their heads. As you can imagine, their stories aren't the most accurate."

"But something keeps coming up," Mason stated. He could read between the lines. Something was being mentioned frequently enough to make Morales and Hunsinger look for clarification.

"Yeah, sounds like a john was hanging around her place. There were a couple reports of a regular visitor in jeans and cowboy boots. And some have mentioned a cowboy hat."

Mason snorted. "You sure they're not talking about me? But I haven't been there in months. Of course, they might have no concept of time if they're using regularly. One of Josie's rules was that she didn't bring johns back to her place. She used one of those motels on Barbur. I guess she could have changed. It's cheaper to use her own place than a motel. I know something was up with her, Denny. She looked like hell this morning; she'd lost a lot of weight."

"Early forensic reports suggest she was using her apartment for *business.*"

"Shit."

"You can't save 'em, Callahan. Especially once they get on the drugs. All they want to do is get money to feed their addiction. When someone like Josie discovers the easiest way is to spread her legs and charge for it, their rules and morals go out the window."

"Yeah, I know. I'd hoped she'd make it. She was a good kid. Just had some bad luck." Mason closed his eyes for a second. He had thought he'd gotten through to Josie. She'd seemed determined to turn her life around. *What threw her off course?*

And why hadn't she called him?

She was embarrassed. She knew you wouldn't approve. So she hid it.

"You taking personal time or vacation?" Schefte asked, abruptly changing the topic.

"Call it vacation."

Schefte snorted. "Since you never take your vacation time, I think you've got more accrued than the entire department put together."

"What would I do on vacation? Sit on my porch and watch people drive by?"

"How about go to Hawaii? Or Vegas for a week? That's what normal people do."

"Too hot." Mason tucked the phone under his shoulder as he dug three T-shirts out of a drawer, rolled them up, and neatly tucked them in the suitcase. Two pairs of identical jeans followed.

"Then take a cruise to Alaska."

"That's what old people do. I'd be bored out of my brain."

"You're not a spring chicken anymore. When's the big five-oh coming up for you?"

Asshole. "I'll always be younger than you." He had a few years before that looming milestone.

"Keep me in the loop. Email me on Monday with an update. For now, I'm clearing next week for you."

Mason froze as he reached for an ironed shirt in his closet. *A week?* Would it take that long?

Schefte was quiet for several beats. "And Callahan?"

"Yeah."

"I hope they find the son of a bitch and bring her home safe." Schefte spit the words.

"You and me both." Mason hit "End" and tossed his phone on the bed, his vision narrowing at the thought of Henley in the hands of a pervert. *Keep her safe.* Please let this be a ransom case. Someone after a piece of Lucas Fairbanks's money. Ransom cases treated their victims better. Their motivation was money. Not something unmentionable.

The doorbell interrupted his packing.

His partner, Ray Lusco, stood on his front porch, his linebacker-wide shoulders blocking the sunlight. "Hey, your dog wants in," he announced as Mason opened the door. A black mutt with a white chest and socks trotted in.

"Not my dog," said Mason.

The dog headed straight for the bowls of dog food and water directly to the right of the door.

"It acts like your dog."

"Not my dog," Mason repeated. He watched the animal inhale the food. He hadn't seen the dog since yesterday, and it acted like it hadn't found anything to eat since then.

Ray stared at him. "When did you get a dog?"

"He showed up a few weeks ago. I feed him every now and then. I don't know if he belongs to someone in the neighborhood or got dumped here."

"Did you call the county?"

"No, I checked all the missing dog sites I could find. He doesn't have any tags. I keep expecting him to disappear." Mason scratched his temple. He didn't know what to do about the dog. What if he took the dog to the county and it turned out to belong to a neighbor?

"You should take him in. Maybe he's got one of those chips."

The dog finished its food, sat, and stared at Mason expectantly.

"He's still hungry." Ray pointed out the obvious.

Mason went to the kitchen and got the bag of dog food from under his sink. He dumped another serving in the bowl, and the dog went back to work. Ray eyed the food bag.

"You act like you have a dog."

Mason scowled at him. "I got tired of feeding him half of my frozen pizzas. This was easier. He hangs around constantly."

"Because he knows you're a softy and give him food."

The dog left some food in his bowl and trotted over to the area rug in the living room, turned three times, and flopped down with a sigh.

Ray's eyebrows shot up. "Holy crap, that dog has picked you. I thought I'd never see the day. You need to take him to the vet and get him scanned for a chip before you get too attached to him."

"I won't get attached to him. I don't like dogs. Too much work. And who's gonna let him in and out all day when I'm at work?"

"Put in a dog door. Your backyard has a good fence. You really need to take better care of him instead of letting him roam," Ray pointed out.

"Screw you."

Ray grinned. "You talk to Schefte yet?"

"Yeah, I'm clear for the next week."

"Shit. Think it'll take that long?"

"It'll take as long as it takes." Mason didn't want to think about it. "You good with the McGregor and Temple cases?"

"Yeah, those won't be a problem. You taking a few days off actually happened at a pretty opportune time." Ray scowled. "That didn't sound right."

"There's no good time for crap like this to happen. I know what you meant." Ray was right. Their case load had lightened a bit of late. People were more focused on the holiday instead of committing major crimes. And it'd been really cold. That always calmed crime down for them. For some reason, people were better behaved when it was freezing outside.

"So you're moving into the Fairbanks place?"

"For now. If this doesn't get resolved quickly, there's gonna be a media storm, and the family needs someone to ask the right questions of the police and FBI. I think they were relieved when I offered to be their go-between. That way they can focus on themselves and not constantly wonder if the investigators are getting shit done. That'll be my job."

"You talk to the FBI already?"

"A bit. Remember Ben Duncan?"

"Yeah, he's a good one."

"It's his case. He's waiting for the CARD team to swoop in, but he's got a hundred pairs of feet on the street already. And he planted an agent in Lucas and Robin's place. That'll help me out, too."

"I don't think the CARD team has been called into the Portland area in four years."

Mason nodded. He and Ray were familiar with the case of an eight-year-old who'd vanished from his school. The boy was still missing.

"There're some similarities there," Ray pointed out. "The school. Divorced parents."

"Yeah, I'm sure the FBI zeroed in on that immediately. Honestly, I don't see it. I think this is a stranger abduction. That case focused on family members."

"Stranger abduction? Those are pretty rare."

"True. But I know this family. None of them would do this," Mason argued.

"You know the birth mom's friends? She's not remarried, right? What about the guys she's dated? There are all sorts of people in their circles that you aren't aware of."

Mason silently swore. Ray was right. He'd let his knowledge of the family narrow his vision of the entire investigation. But it wasn't his investigation; he was an observer.

That didn't mean he couldn't poke around a bit on his own.

"What the hell are you thinking about?" Ray asked. "You look ready to go dig up some graves."

"I'm not investigating this case."

"But you should have a good view of what's happening. Do they have a command center set up somewhere?"

"Yes, there's a church a couple of blocks away. I'm gonna swing by there on my way back and stick my nose in. I want them to get used to seeing me around."

"They gonna have any problem with that?"

"I don't think so. Duncan seemed like he almost expected me to insert myself into the liaison role. As long as I'm not interfering, I think he'll be happy to use me to communicate with the family."

"Who's the agent they embedded?"

"A Special Agent McLane. I didn't catch the first name, but Robin and Lilian seemed very comfortable with her, so that's good if she's gonna be around twenty-four seven. Seems sharp and levelheaded. Ever heard of her?"

"No. Want me to ask?"

"Yes. See what her reputation is. I'd like to know who's living in the same house with my kid."

"How's Jake holding up?"

"Shitty. He's pretty attached to Henley. Makes me feel like an ass that I barely even know who the girl is."

"Of course he's attached. She's his little sister. Doesn't matter that they're not blood. I'm sure they spent a lot of time together."

"He's upset that Christmas is next week."

"They'll find her before that."

Silence stretched out between them. Both men knew there were no guarantees that Henley would be home before Christmas. As the hours slipped by, her chances of coming home grew thinner. Ray looked at the dog on the rug. A soft, doggy snore was audible.

"You should keep the dog," Ray said. "Looks like he's chosen you anyway. They say it's healthy to have a pet around. It's good to have something to take care of, you know?"

"Yeah? Well, who's gonna watch him while I'm gone?" Mason looked expectantly at Ray.

Ray backed up a step. "I can't take him home with me. Jill's allergic."

Mason sighed and looked at the dog. "I'll put something on the porch for him to sleep in and move his bowls out there. My neighbor can dump some food in it. We'll see if he sticks around."

The dog raised his head, looked at Mason, and thumped his tail.

"Looks like you have a new family member," stated Ray. "About time."

6

8 HOURS MISSING

Ava showed her ID to the Clackamas County deputy standing watch at the church entrance. She was pleased that he looked hard at her picture and her face before letting her in. "Follow the hallway to your right. You'll find the room by all the voices," he told her.

She stepped inside the building and was greeted by the sight of four-dozen poinsettias in different shades of red. It was one of those megachurches that felt almost like a huge school instead of a house of worship. It definitely didn't feel like the ornate Catholic church she'd attended as a child. She hadn't set foot in a church in twenty years except to attend weddings, and a bit of guilt flowed through her. It almost felt wrong that the command post had been set up in a house of God, but maybe it would bring some divine guidance to their search.

She turned to the right and followed the hum of voices. Outside, the parking lot was full of police vehicles from local and federal agencies. This case wasn't going to suffer from a lack of manpower.

Her stomach twisted a bit in excitement. The thrill of the hunt. The FBI at full throttle was a beautiful sight.

And she got to sit in the house with the family and hold their hands.

Part of her was flattered that Ben had chosen her to stand in for the FBI's pregnant victim specialist, but another part ached to pound the pavement with the rest of the team. She'd dropped Lilian off at the Fairbanks house, checked in to see if anyone needed anything, and told them she'd be back in an hour. She wanted to see the command center and remind the other agents that she was still part of the case. In the Fairbanks home, she'd be out of sight and out of mind. She didn't want the agency to overlook any contribution they knew she could bring.

The hum of voices grew louder, and she stopped at the door to a giant multipurpose room. Long tables and folding chairs filled the room. Computer monitors dotted the tables every few feet along with miles of dangling computer cords. Agents were seated in front of half of the computers while techs continued to wire the rest of the monitors and equipment. One wall of the room had three huge whiteboards. On one of them, someone had started the timeline. The timeline board was a key element of their investigation. Every incident was noted with its time. Stepping closer she could read "left home for the bus" and the timing of the school's first, second, and third parent notifications among the dozen markers.

Blown-up pictures of Henley and her family were posted with tags stating each person's name and age. Ava mentally called it the player board, since it identified each person involved in the case. She noticed that photos of teachers from Henley's school and the bus driver had been added beside the family photos.

Maps of the city and neighborhood were posted next to the photos. Red and green pins with flags indicated something that Ava wasn't privy to. Yet. She scanned further and studied the start of the lead-management chart. It documented the leads spilling in from the public and to whom they were assigned for follow-up. It had over a hundred and fifty entries already.

She turned back to the room. Someone had created paper signs indicating the area of interest assigned to each group of computers: school, neighbors, media, and police. Ava knew that was just the beginning.

A plainclothes policeman leaning over the shoulder of one of the Clackamas County deputies at the police table turned toward her, and she recognized Robin Fairbanks's ex-husband, the Oregon State Police detective, Mason Callahan. Shrewd brown eyes met hers, and he nodded in recognition. She noticed he had a cowboy hat in one hand and wondered if he would have tipped his hat at her if it'd been on his head. Few people could get away with dressing like that in the suburbs of Portland, but this man made it work. Something about him was extremely old-fashioned, but in a good way. It wasn't the cowboy boots and hat. It was the man himself. He put out a no-nonsense aura, and she got the feeling that he wouldn't be afraid to use his fists or boots in a physical fight. He studied the world around him with a calm look, as if he had seen it all and could size up a situation in a matter of seconds.

With an investigator's eye, Ava studied the man who was going to be her housemate for as long as it took to bring Henley home. She'd noticed in their brief meeting that his eyes rarely reflected surprise, something she'd seen in FBI agents who'd spent years on the job. The job sucked something out of a person, and often it was the part of a person that experienced shock.

In the right person, it was replaced with confidence and logical thinking. In the wrong person, it could be replaced with addiction and burnout. It took a truly evil event to shock even her these days. She crossed her fingers that this case would not turn out that way.

In her brief meeting with Mason Callahan, she'd seen the right things and heard the right things from the people who knew him. But she knew better than to make snap decisions about a person.

She'd reserve judgment for later. She'd interviewed too many patho-
logical liars and pretenders. She'd even grown up with one.

Her personal cell buzzed in her pocket. She pulled it out.

Speak of the devil.

She let her sister's call go to voice mail. If it was urgent, Jayne
would send a text, knowing Ava was slow to listen to personal voice
mails.

Ava and Jayne had wildly different interpretations of "urgent."

No one seemed to have noticed her besides Callahan. She walked
slowly past the boards, eyeing the operation in its infancy. Sanford,
the agent Ben Duncan had put in charge of setting up the center, was
in his element. He was deep in discussion with two special agents
and a Clackamas County deputy, writing furiously in a notepad and
pointing at two banks of unused computers. Ava wrinkled her nose
as the scent of salami reached it. To one side was the cornerstone
of any operation: food. Three coffee urns, two deli meat-and-cheese
trays, and four huge packs of bottled water sat on a long table with
several pink boxes of donuts.

Her stomach churned. She couldn't eat processed food. The lin-
ing of her stomach didn't allow for it. She swore her brain also func-
tioned better when she ate simpler. Her weakness was pizza, and she
paid the price for two days when she indulged.

She approached Special Agent Sanford and his group. He glanced
up and nodded at her. "Hey, Ava." Her spine relaxed a degree. He'd
forgiven her for taking his interviewing position in the home. He
probably thought she'd caught a shit assignment of staying with the
family while he would be in the center of the action.

Her chin lifted a notch. Sanford could never do her current
assignment.

"You need to get some decent food in here, Sanford," she said.
"Or you're going to have a team with severe headaches. Get some
fresh fruit and salads. Ask the deli to bring in some protein that
hasn't been processed and loaded with salt and chemicals."

His eyes narrowed briefly. She knew he didn't order the food, but she felt like getting under his skin a bit. And if she had been assigned to the command center, she'd want a healthier selection. One of the agents chimed in. "Good point. I'm trying to eat Paleo these days. Keeps the brain focused." He caught a glare from Sanford.

Ava bit back a smile and kept walking. She found herself drawn to the computer bank where Callahan and the Clackamas County deputy were in deep discussion about the report on the monitor, a city map with a few highlighted spots. She moved closer and her stomach clenched. *Sex offenders.*

She stopped and stared at their screen, her focus zooming in on the Fairbankses' location. Two dots appeared on homes in the same neighborhood. She exhaled. No doubt those were the first homes where Ben Duncan had ordered agents to knock on doors. Callahan looked up and met her gaze.

"Both offenders were home when Clackamas County knocked earlier today," he said. "They even agreed to a search. Nothing turned up. They've expanded the search and even sent special agents back to these two homes for a second visit already."

"Good." Ava memorized the location of both homes. She'd drive by on her way back to the Fairbanks house. Daily. She'd jog or drive by daily. Real slow.

"We're lucky this didn't happen in another part of Portland. In some neighborhoods, you'd see a dozen dots in a single block," he added.

She noticed Callahan's expression was carefully blank. No doubt he'd had his share of sex offender cases. Two agents strode into the command center and made a beeline for the grouping of computers next to Ava and Callahan. Tension radiated from the two men, and every head in the center turned to look as if they'd been expected. Uneasiness spread through the room. Ava scanned the curious faces watching the agents and decided to step away to give them some space. Already, other agents were moving toward the other men.

"Would you like a cup of coffee, Detective Callahan?" she offered. Now was as good a time as any to get some insight on the rest of the family. The blended Fairbanks family couldn't be as cheery as they projected, right? If she was going to spend time with them, she wanted every bit of information she could get. The investigation would look at the family first. Possibly, she'd see something in the house that wouldn't come across in a formal interview. She liked the parents; she hoped none of them were involved. But until the FBI cleared them . . .

Callahan held her gaze for two seconds. "I'll pass on the coffee, but I'll take a bottled water and maybe a donut."

She smiled and jerked her head at the table of preservatives. Callahan excused himself from the deputy, who simply nodded, not looking away from his screen of dots.

. . .

Mason followed Special Agent McLane in the direction of the food. He was starving. He hated to raid their food since he wasn't part of the official team, but he figured they wouldn't miss one donut. Besides, the pastries turned into rocks if they weren't eaten right away. Hopefully they had a maple donut topped with bacon from Voodoo Donuts. That would be as good as a real meal; it had protein.

He spotted his prey and took a bite of goodness, wiping his mouth with a napkin. "Hungry?" he asked Ava.

She shook her head. "I like donuts, but I don't know what they put in those. I'm not twenty anymore. My body gives me hell for two days if I load up on preservatives or unpronounceable ingredients."

He nodded as he chewed. He understood that. Wine gave him headaches, so he didn't drink it. That was an easy fix, since he didn't care for wine anyway, but avoiding donuts must have sucked.

Special Agent McLane was an attractive woman. He hadn't noticed it before and suspected she downplayed her looks. Her dark-brown hair was pulled back in a ponytail, and her makeup was minimal, but she had a freshness to her skin that spoke of good health and clean living. Her eyes were an intense dark blue that sparkled with intelligence. The longer he looked at her, the more surprised he was that her looks hadn't immediately jumped out at him. He was still taken in by the smooth voice. Maybe it had distracted him at their first meeting.

"What's your first name, Agent McLane?"

Blue eyes blinked. "Ava. I'm sorry. You're Mason, right?"

Mason nodded. *Ava. A movie-star name.* "And we're going to be housemates for a few days."

"Hopefully not for that long."

"Amen to that."

"What are your thoughts on this?"

It was a wide-open question. Mason took another bite of donut and thought carefully before answering. "I don't know. Her parents are good people. I'm leaning toward a stranger abduction—"

"Stranger abductions are very rare."

He took another bite of donut and slowly chewed. If she was going to interrupt him, then she could wait. "I know. But I don't think you'll find the answer in the immediate family. Now, people *outside* the family are a different matter. Maybe a client or coworker of Lucas Fairbanks's, or a past boyfriend of Lilian's."

The pocket of her navy blazer vibrated, and he popped the last of the donut in his mouth as she pulled out her phone and glanced at her screen. Annoyance flashed across her face, and she dropped the phone back in her pocket.

"Need to make a call?" he prodded. She hadn't been happy to see the name of whoever had contacted her. His gut told him it was personal, but he didn't want to keep her if it was her job.

"No. It's not work."

Score one for his gut.

He kept his mouth closed, giving her a chance to explain. People usually liked to talk about themselves if you gave them the chance.

Special Agent McLane didn't fall for his usual interviewing trick. She smiled politely at him, took a drink from her bottled water, and went back to their topic. "You don't think the girl ran away? How well did you know her?"

"I didn't know her well at all. I'm going by what Robin says. That woman, I do know. If she's convinced Henley's not a runner, then I'll take her word for it."

"But kids hide things from their parents all the time. I doubt Robin or Lilian knew everything Henley looked at online."

"That's why the FBI took the computers, right? I assume that's the first thing they'll be looking at. I don't know why you're asking me about it." He gave her a pointed look. "You're FBI, why don't you look into what they found?"

The reaction on her face was a miniscule flicker. If he hadn't been watching closely for her answer to his barb, he wouldn't have seen it.

Frustration.

She was on the outside of the case. Just like him.

"I understand you're filling in for the victim specialist. I'm gonna guess that means you don't have any active role in the investigation."

The flicker again. "Not really. My primary role is to be what the family needs. Shoulder to cry on, chauffeur, hand holder, media interference."

Her hands were about as tied as his.

"Dishwasher?"

"Maybe."

"So you shouldn't be in here, either."

She gave a half smile, and he was charmed. She had a subtle, dry humor that he suspected he could banter with for hours.

"I can't stay away completely, either," Mason acknowledged. "I'll push the envelope as far as they'll let me, but I understand my role."

"Sanford? You need to take a look at this," stated one of the agents who'd recently entered the command center. Ava and Mason exchanged a glance and moved toward the gathering group of agents.

Mason looked over the shoulders of a few agents and saw the black-and-white view from a camera on a school bus. Children moved away from the camera as they filed onto the bus, bulky coats and backpacks hiding their identities. As they turned to sit in the rows of bus seats, glimpses of faces revealed their sex.

"What do you have?" Special Agent Sanford pushed through the group to the men directly in front of the screen.

"We just finished interviewing the last child from Henley's bus stop," said the older agent. "There's a consensus that she wasn't on the bus."

Sanford nodded. "I've been making a lot of my decisions with the assumption that your interviews would back up what we heard from the two kids first thing this morning."

"There were five altogether," the agent continued. "Each kid stated that Henley wasn't at the stop and didn't get on the bus, but we also wanted to see for ourselves. The school district emailed this video a few minutes ago."

The other agent pointed at each kid on the screen as they sat down, reciting their names. "These are the kids getting on at Henley's stop. You have to wait until they turn around, but I recognize each child we talked to this morning. They're all correct. Henley didn't get on."

The group of agents was silent as the video froze, highlighting an image of a dozen children seated on the bus. Mason squinted at the screen, studying each face. No blonde girls with delicate features looked back at him.

"No chance she got on at a different stop?" Ava asked.

"We asked the kids that, too. All of them say she didn't get on." The first agent put a finger on the face of a dark-haired girl. "This girl said that she usually sits with Henley when she rides that bus and swears her friend wasn't on this morning. I've watched the whole video. When the kids get off at the school, I had a clear shot of each face. There wasn't even a question." The agent next to him nodded emphatically.

"I agree," the second agent said. "She's not there."

Sanford blew out a breath. "Okay. Pull all but two agents from the school. I want everyone back at the area between the Fairbanks house and the bus stop. Our current target area just narrowed for now."

Ava tipped her head at Mason, and they quietly moved away from the group a few feet.

"I don't know whether to be pleased about this turn of events or not," Ava whispered.

"I think it helps. It essentially eliminates investigating the entire school area. It really narrows down the time frame and location," Mason stated. He made a mental plan to do some of his own footwork in the neighborhood. There could never be too many eyes on a scene.

Ava nodded, her forehead creased in concentration, and he suspected she was making the same plan.

Sanford answered a phone call, listened for fifteen seconds, and said, "We'll be right there." He touched his screen to end the call and addressed Ava and Mason. "One of the BAU agents is ready to give me a preliminary profile. You two want to stick around for that?"

Mason nodded in unison with Ava.

BAU. The Behavioral Analysis Unit. The "mind hunters." They knew how to analyze information and come up with a profile of the kind of bastard who'd kidnap a kid. Mason admired the practice but didn't quite understand how it worked. There seemed to be a lot of hocus-pocus and generalizations involved. But if one of them had insight into Henley's kidnapper, he wanted to hear it. He'd take any help they could get.

They followed Sanford out of the command center and a short way down the hall to a small room with a circle of chairs and huge windows. An agent flipping through a file folder on a table in the corner turned as they entered. Sanford made introductions. Special Agent Bryan Euzent wore glasses, had a firm handshake, and looked young enough to be Mason's son. Mason reserved judgment. This was one of the bigger brains in the BAU unit, Ava had whispered to him. No one knew more about the workings of a kidnapper's mind.

Their group filled the circle of chairs and looked expectantly at Special Agent Euzent.

"I spent the flight analyzing the information that's been collected on the case," Euzent began. "I've been reviewing the interviews and the cast of people who interact with Henley. There's still a lot of information I need to examine, but there are some specific messages we need to get out to the public as soon as possible to bring in some more good tips. First of all, we want the public to look for behavior changes. This person might have missed work today. They might have been a no-show or offered a plausible excuse. Or they might have missed a scheduled appointment. Perhaps they suddenly left town."

"We can't ask the public to report on something so common. We'll be swamped with useless calls," Sanford stated.

Mason silently agreed.

"I know it seems very general," Euzent answered. "But it's just part of a list of behaviors. Of course we don't want reports of every guy who didn't show up for work today. I'll get to the rest." He glanced down at the papers in his hands. "They may have changed the vehicle they always drive, or have altered their vehicle in some way.

"Typically, abductors are white males between thirty and forty. They tend to have a history of problems with relationships in general, but especially with women."

Mason glanced at the circle of white men, wondering who in the room didn't have some sort of female relationship issue. Ava was the only woman in the room, and she was intently focused on Euzent.

"They tend to be somewhat socially isolated, but not always."

Mason felt like a spotlight was suddenly shining on his head.

"It's possible there is a history of sexual assault or being sexually inappropriate with women."

I'm in the clear on that one.

"How often is sex the motive for an abduction?" an agent asked. Out of the corner of his eye, Mason saw Ava flinch at the question.

Euzent cleared his throat. "Often. With a child, the motive may be a little different. But usually it boils down to domination and control. It's about the power. They are in charge, and they are doing exactly what they want to do."

"Bastards," Ava whispered.

"Usually, children are taken by strangers for one of three reasons. The first is for profit, and usually they contact the parents quickly because they want to keep the child for as short a period of time as possible. The second was the one I already mentioned . . . the person wants the child for sexual gratification or domination. Usually, they don't want any contact with the parent. The third reason is someone is truly sick and simply wants a child for their own. They don't make contact, either."

"Or it's the parents," Mason stated.

Special Agent Euzent met his gaze. "Exactly. That's why we clear them first. There's been no ransom requested yet, so right now the motivation seems domination oriented. Whether it was random or premeditated will be determined. I read the mothers' interviews. When they were asked if anyone had been hanging around Henley, or if she'd mentioned any odd encounters with adults, they both said no."

"We could still get a ransom note," Ava interjected.

Euzent paused and smiled. "I pray that is the case here." His smile vanished as he shifted back to business. "If it was premeditated, our guy has to have a place to keep her. Someplace that won't draw attention. A basement, a barn, an abandoned outbuilding. Even bathroom facilities have to be considered by the kidnapper. Trust me, he's thought about this. Henley may have simply been in the right place at the right time for him, or he picked her specifically."

"He's a predator is what you're saying," said Ava.

"I believe so," answered Euzent. "I know I haven't given you much to work with, but I'll add more to my profile as the facts come in." He nudged his glasses, suddenly looking ten years older as he lowered his gaze. "I'll be here nonstop until we find her," he said quietly as he closed the file.

The agents took that as a signal to leave. Mason followed Ava out of the room.

"I'm headed back to the house," she said as they moved down the hall. "Are you?"

"Yes."

She stopped midstride and turned to face him, her blue eyes serious. "If you know of any family dynamics I need to be aware of, I'd like to hear about them. So far I've seen a united front from all three parents, but my past experience tells me that appearances can be deceiving."

Mason fought back a smile. For someone not investigating, she definitely had some questions. "I think you'll find Robin and Lucas are what they appear to be. I don't know Lilian that well, but Robin has always said they have an understanding."

"An understanding?" Her nose crinkled, and Mason noticed she had freckles. Not a lot, but a few across the nose and cheeks.

"They get along. They really do. They have a mutual respect for each other and care about Henley. I don't know what else to tell you. There's no psychotic bitch hiding anywhere. I don't know Lilian's past, but I'm sure it's being pulled apart as we speak."

Ava glanced at her watch. "Lucas Fairbanks is being interviewed right now. They must be using a side room here somewhere. I warned the family they'd be doing a lot of talking to the police, and that most of it would be repetitive."

"I told them the same thing," answered Mason. He glanced out the doors, a movement catching his eye. "Holy crap. The media has found the command center." Two Clackamas County deputies were putting up crime scene tape to hold the camera crews back from the building and corral them into a tidy spot. Another deputy stood directly in front of the double doors, guarding it, his hands on his hips, shaking his head. Mason understood how he felt.

"Two satellite trucks already," muttered Ava. "I wonder how many are at the house."

Mason shoved his hat on his head. "Good point. Let's go see if they need any help."

A cell phone sounded, and Agent McLane reached into a jacket pocket, a different pocket than the one that held the previous vibrating cell phone.

Work pocket, personal pocket. Mason had given up the personal phone a few years ago. Jake was the only person outside of work that he communicated with, and that was limited to a few texts. He didn't feel it was any abuse of his work phone.

"Special Agent McLane."

Mason watched her face. Her eyebrow twitched once as she listened, and she kept her calm gaze on the growing media crowd.

"I'm on my way now. I'll be there in less than five." She ended the call and gave Mason a half smile. "Sounds like there's a bit of a to-do going on back at the house. The mothers are yelling at each other, and the deputy assigned to sit in front of the house says that the media outside can hear it."

Mason pressed his lips together. He'd just preached to Agent McLane about how in sync the two women were.

Sounded like their tempers were in sync, too.

7

9 HOURS MISSING

The deputy shooed the reporters away from the driveway entrance as Ava pulled up. The reporters stepped back, turned their eagle-eyed cameras her way, and bent over, peering to get a good look inside her vehicle. Ava wished for privacy glass. How long would it take for them to identify her as FBI? She watched the reporters pull the same routine on Callahan as his vehicle pulled in behind her.

The deputy had been correct. When Ava stepped out of her sedan at the top of the Fairbankses' long driveway, she heard yelling inside the home. When she'd left the home a few hours ago, the only car visible had been a patrol unit parked in front of the house. The Fairbankses' vehicles were parked inside their three-car garage, and Lilian had left her vehicle at her condo. Now there were the patrol unit, a television satellite truck, news vans, and other media vehicles all squeezed onto the formerly quiet street. The sun had set, and the streetlight in front of the home lit up the small crowd of reporters and cameras.

The more media coverage for Henley, the better. But when the media got bored or felt the need to outdo each other, Ava had seen them get pushy or overstep their boundaries. Focus on the missing child, she wanted to lecture them, don't sensationalize every factor.

Luckily, the house sat far back from the street, placing a wide stretch of manicured grass, shrubs, and bark dust between the reporters and the home. Would some of them venture onto the property? She'd make certain the doors and windows of the home were locked at all hours. And they'd keep the blinds closed. What a pain in the ass. Thank goodness Clackamas County had seen the need for a patrol unit in front of the home.

She and Callahan strode to the front door. She hit the doorbell then tried the handle. Locked. *Good.* "Robin? It's Agent McLane," she hollered close to the door. The yelling inside had stopped at the sound of the doorbell. She looked directly at the peephole, waiting, feeling like she was on stage with the reporters staring at her back.

"Damn vultures," muttered Callahan. "They're going to freaking multiply like randy rabbits."

The door opened, and Ava was surprised to see Jake's face.

"Get back," she and Callahan told him in unison. The kid didn't need to be on the news. Those camera lenses could get a close-up of his face from the street. She and Callahan stepped in, and he closed the door behind them.

"Use the peephole," he instructed Jake. "Open the door only for people with police or FBI ID. And stay behind the door when you do open it."

"How long will they stay out there?" the teen asked. "Won't they leave for the night?"

Ava exchanged a glance with Callahan. "No," they replied together.

"What is with your mom and Lilian?" Callahan asked. "I could hear them outside."

Jake dropped his gaze, his shoulders hunching slightly. "I don't know. I'm trying not to listen. Something about a guy Lilian dated."

Ava sucked in a breath. *Here we go.* The truth was leaking out.

Callahan's boots were loud on the wood floors as he headed toward the family's great room. Ava followed. He glanced back at her and pointed at himself. She nodded. She'd let Callahan ask the questions. The women knew him better. If she got the sense one of them was holding back, they'd separate the women and question them one-on-one.

In the great room, Lilian sat in an overstuffed chair, her shoulders slumped and her hands over her face. Robin stood in front of her, her arms folded across her chest, her face red and her eyes wet. Robin turned as the two entered the room, her chin lifting.

"What the hell is going on?" Callahan started, looking from one woman to the other. "We could hear the shouts outside. And all those damned reporters can hear you, too."

Robin didn't look at Lilian. "Tell them," Robin snapped. "Tell them what you told the agent in your interview today and what they discovered about the men you date."

Lilian lowered her hands and dug her fingers into her jeans, her jaw tightening. "One guy. This is about one guy, and I had no idea what his past was like."

"That's why you dig into their background before you bring them into your home!" Robin's lips were a white slash where her mouth had been.

Lilian looked at Callahan and then Ava. "It's a guy I went out with a few times this summer. The FBI just told me that he's a registered sex offender. I had no idea!"

"Why did you stop going out with him?" Callahan asked.

Lilian shrugged. "It didn't work out. We just didn't connect."

"Did he feel the same way?" Ava asked. "Would his version of the breakup be the same?"

Lilian flinched and looked away. "I don't know."

"What do you really think he'd say, Lilian?" Callahan prodded. "Was he angry? Was the breakup one-sided?"

Lilian rubbed her nose and shifted in her chair.

"He was pissed. We only went out a half-dozen times, but I wasn't feeling it. I guess he was hoping for more. He called me a few choice names on the phone when I said we shouldn't see each other anymore."

"Did he meet Henley?" Ava asked softly.

Lilian's face crumpled. "Yes, twice when he picked me up. Just for a minute or two."

"Stupid," stated Robin, rolling her eyes at the ceiling. "Why introduce him to your daughter? You shouldn't do that unless you think it's going to last."

"I go into every relationship hoping it's going to last!" Lilian shouted at Robin. "What type of person goes in with the mindset that it's doomed to fail?"

Ava mentally raised a hand.

"Calm down!" Mason stepped between the two women, showing a palm to each one in a "stop" gesture. "Lilian," he continued in a quieter voice, "what did they say his offense was?"

"Statutory rape. She was seventeen."

"Pervert," spat Robin.

Mason shot Robin a warning look but continued with his softer tone. "Did the agent say anything else about the case?"

Lilian sniffed. "He'd claimed she'd told him she was twenty."

"Of course that's what he'd say," Robin said. "Did he ask your age before you slept with him?"

"I didn't sleep with him," Lilian yelled, straightening in her chair.

"Knock it off!" Mason pointed at Robin. "You! Go in the kitchen and get something to drink." He shot a glance at Ava.

Robin glared at him but obeyed. Ava nodded at Callahan and followed Robin into the huge kitchen, leaning against the counter as she watched the woman open the fridge and stare inside. She didn't pick out anything. She simply stood and looked, blinking rapidly. "He's just trying to put some space between the two of you," Ava offered.

"I know. And I shouldn't have yelled at her." She turned red eyes toward Ava. "But why wasn't this the first thing she told the police this morning? Why did she let someone like that into Henley's life?"

"She obviously thought there was nothing to it," Ava stated. "Have you told the police about every single encounter you've had over the last few years?"

Robin slammed the fridge door, turning toward Ava. "I've never cheated on my husband. Ever!"

"That's not what I meant. I mean did you tell them about anyone in your life you've parted with on a sour note? Even the little things." She watched two lines appear between Robin's brows as she thought. "See? It's not so easy. An encounter that might seem trivial to you might have been devastating to another person, angering them— whether the slight was real or imagined. You never know how people think."

Ava saw a flash of movement behind Robin, in the hallway. Jake was listening. She hadn't said anything that should alarm the kid. In fact, he also needed to hear this.

"It's impossible to know everything, let alone pass it on to the FBI," Robin said. "You could mean someone I accidentally cut off with my car. But this was someone she *dated*. Why didn't she tell them before now?" Robin's eyes pleaded with Ava.

Ava infused her gaze with as much sympathy as possible. "It's still the first day. Be glad the information came out as early as it did."

"But what if there's more? What if she's not telling everything?"

"Her daughter is missing. Don't you think she's doing everything she can to help?"

Robin stared back for a long second. "I don't know," she whispered. "I'm starting to wonder if I know Lilian as well as I believed I did." She teared up. "Poor Henley. She must be terrified. I can't stop thinking about what she could be going through. I'm never going to sleep tonight." Her voice trailed off.

Jake stepped silently into the kitchen. He hesitated. With the instinct of a mother, Robin spun around, his name on her lips.

The teen looked miserable. His face was puffy and his hair was a disaster. Ava hadn't seen much of him all day. He seemed to prefer to stay in his room. She admired his bravery for stepping out into the center of the drama. She studied him carefully, knowing teens needed special attention in this sort of case. His sister was missing; his parents were distracted. He was lost in the background while everything was focused on his sister. But he ached, too. He needed to express his feelings out loud before he cracked.

Ava kicked herself for overlooking him.

"Jake," she said, pulling out a stool at the kitchen breakfast bar. "Sit," she ordered kindly. *Now was as good a time as any.* She wondered if his mother's presence would help him open up or make him censor his feelings. The teen slunk over to the stool and sat, his head down, one finger tracing a pattern in the granite counter. Ava looked at Robin and held her gaze, jerking her chin at the teen. *He needs to talk.*

"You heard me tell your mother that we need to know about any odd encounters, right?" Ava asked. The teen nodded, his gaze still on the countertop.

Ava licked her lips. Teens were foreign to her. She tried to remember how she'd handled her sister and her moodiness as a teen. Jayne had been all about the drama. Ava had been the peacekeeper and the one to draw her sister out of her black moods. Considering the constant ups and downs of her sister's personality, Ava should have an honorary doctorate in Teen Therapy.

"Has something come to mind? You talked with one of the agents this afternoon, right? Have you thought of something since then?" Ava wasn't certain who'd interviewed Jake.

"No."

Ava waited. There was a reason Jake had ventured into the kitchen. Was he trying to protect his mom from Ava's direct questions? She glanced at Robin and raised a brow.

The frown lines were still between Robin's brows. "Jake, honey," she started. "You've only been back in town a few days. Who've you talked to?"

He lifted his head, meeting his mom's gaze. "Just the guys. You know, Eric, Jack, Lincoln. The usual. And McKenzie."

"Are they all back from college for Christmas?" Robin asked. She glanced at Ava. "McKenzie and Jake dated a bit last summer, but it never was exclusive, right, Jake?"

Jake shrugged. "We're friends. She's really upset about Henley. They're all worried." His voice cracked.

"Have you seen any of them since you got into town?" Ava asked. She was certain an agent had already gone over this with Jake, but the investigator in her wouldn't be quiet.

"No. Not yet. I was going to see Eric and Lincoln this weekend. Hang out somewhere. But that's on hold."

"You got in Wednesday, correct?" Ava asked. "Where have you gone since you've been home? Tell me every stop, no matter how unimportant it seems. 7-Eleven or Barnes & Noble. Nothing is too small."

Jake's eyes widened. "You think someone I know did this?" Terror crossed his face. Robin rushed to comfort him, hugging his shoulders. She laid her cheek on his head.

"No honey, they're simply looking under every rock. Something one of them saw might be the key to bringing Henley home. Think hard. Don't hold anything back."

"Jeez." The teen blinked hard.

"It's only been two days." Ava gave an encouraging smile. "There can't be that much to remember, right? Don't college kids sleep twenty hours a day anyway?"

"Yes," Robin said under her breath. "I've hardly seen him since he's been home."

A heavy door behind Ava opened, and she turned to see Lucas Fairbanks step inside from the garage. Behind him like a silent shadow was the tall, slender form of Special Agent Zander Wells. Lucas looked like he'd been up for thirty-six hours. He had the same puffy eyes as Robin and the sad hunch to his shoulders that Ava was starting to associate with this traumatized family.

Robin stepped into his arms, and Lucas buried his face in her hair, closing his eyes.

"Anything?" Ava heard Robin whisper to him. Lucas shook his head. Robin's back trembled as fresh sobs filled the kitchen.

Ava met Wells's gaze. He gave a slight shake of his head.

Nothing earth shattering from the father's interview.

She watched Jake out of the corner of her eye. He'd turned as his stepfather came into the kitchen and silently watched Lucas embrace his mother. Jake looked like a boy who'd lost his new puppy.

Ava looked from Lucas to the teenager. How was the relationship between the two? Callahan had spoken highly of Fairbanks but hadn't expanded on his son's perspective of his stepfather.

Lilian rushed in from the other room with Callahan right on her heels. She slid to a stop as she saw Lucas and Robin's embrace.

"Henley?" Her voice slid up an octave.

"No news," Wells answered.

Lilian closed her eyes, and Callahan put a comforting hand on her shoulder.

Ava stared at the mother and swallowed hard. Behind the panic on Lilian's face, and for the briefest second, she'd exposed her heart.

Lilian was still in love with her ex-husband.

How many layers are there to this family?

"Just because he can't tell you that Henley's turned up doesn't mean there's no news," said Callahan. "McLane and I got some good insight into some of the work that's being done."

The three parents gave him hopeful looks.

"That command center is turning into a hive of worker bees," Callahan stated. "They've already pinpointed and talked to the sex offenders in the area. We reviewed video from the bus and verified with our own eyes that Henley wasn't on there. McLane found out the video from Lilian's apartment building shows no sign that Henley went to her place. They already had a preliminary profile drawn up by one of the experts at Quantico who flew in to brief us today."

One after the other, he held each parent's gaze. "We're making progress. We're going to chip away at every lead until we find her."

• • •

A few hours later, Mason sat in the big family room and stared at the gas fireplace. It was nearly 10 P.M. The mothers had each settled into the couch with a book, but Mason had noticed that Lilian rarely turned the pages, her eyes frequently focusing on the fire instead of her novel. No one spoke of going to bed. The guest room Mason was staying in had been attacked by Hello Kitty. It would be fine for sleeping but not for thinking or pacing. The only chair in the bedroom came up to his knees, and he felt bad every time he stepped on the huge kitty-face area rug.

So he shared the depressed family room. The TV stayed off. Mason didn't want to see any news reports and figured the family felt the same. Jake had stepped into the room and stared at everyone like he was lost. Mason quirked an eyebrow at him, but he'd gone back to his room and turned on his Xbox. If games kept Jake's mind off his sister, Mason was all for them.

Where was Mason's distraction? His mind kept spinning with what ifs.

After Lucas had arrived, Ava brought in a bag from her car. Robin gave her a grateful look and directed her to the purple butterfly room across from Mason's.

Currently Ava was having a long discussion with Special Agent Wells in the backyard. Mason had a good feeling about Zander Wells. The quiet agent seemed competent and focused, his sharp eyes missing nothing. The two agents came in through the French doors at the back patio, a rush of icy air blowing in with them.

Was Henley outside somewhere? Was she cold?

Lilian flinched as the cold air hit her, and Mason knew she was having the same thoughts.

He put an image of the freezing child out of his brain.

He moved to intercept the agents as Ava moved with Wells toward the front entrance. The two stopped, regarding Mason with wary eyes.

"Is there something else I can update the family with?" Mason asked.

The two exchanged a look.

"Our focus has shifted to the neighborhood as you know," Wells said. "We've had teams of agents knocking on doors and searching the green spaces. Three of the homes have turned over their home security cameras, but none of the recordings show Henley this morning." He took a deep breath. "I just heard that they found her lunchbox an hour ago."

"Where?" asked Mason.

"It was actually up in a tree a few houses down from the bus stop."

She'd been so close. "She almost made it," Mason stated. "But up in a tree? How?"

"It was pretty well hidden between the dense fir branches and a good eight feet off the ground, which explains why no one spotted it for a while." Wells made a face, acknowledging the bureau's frustration with missing the clue and the several hours of lag time. "My guess is someone threw it. I don't think it could have been planted after we searched that area. We've had people in the neighborhood nonstop."

"Could Henley have thrown it?" Mason asked.

Wells nodded. "We think so. Maybe she was trying to leave something behind as she was being snatched. It doesn't make a lot of sense for a kidnapper to try to leave something so obvious."

"Are you sure it's hers?" Mason asked.

"It matches the description the mothers gave us. They sent me a photo of it, but the actual box is on the way to the lab for printing." He showed Mason a picture on his phone of a pink lunchbox made from synthetic fabric, with a top that folded over and buckled closed. "I'll send it to you, and you can show the parents."

"What was inside? Does it match what Robin said was packed?" Mason's brain spun. *Who threw it? Henley or her kidnapper?*

"It practically pinpoints where she was grabbed. He wouldn't have left something like that behind on purpose," Ava muttered, shaking her head.

"It held what Robin had listed," Wells answered. "And I know what you mean, Ava. It makes no sense. My best guess says that she threw it as he grabbed her."

The three nodded in agreement.

"What about vehicles spotted on the home security cameras?" Mason asked.

Wells nodded. "We're working on enhancing some images they caught."

"Anything else I need to know?" Mason asked.

"Just reassure them we'll be working through the night. Three members of the CARD team landed already. You met the one from BAU. Three others will be here within a few hours."

"What do they bring to the case?"

"Experience. One is a hostage negotiator, another is evidence recovery, and there's a computer-forensics expert. A few more agents from BAU." Wells glanced at McLane, who nodded again.

"No indication yet that this will be a hostage situation?" Mason asked.

"Not yet," answered Ava.

"I almost wish it was," mumbled Mason. "Then maybe we'd know she's . . ."

Ava's gaze softened. "We'll deal with whatever arises." Her gaze went past Mason. "How're you holding up, Lucas?"

Mason turned. Lucas looked like hell.

"Fine. Is everything okay?" He looked from Wells to Ava.

"I'm just updating Special Agent McLane and Detective Callahan. I'll let them relay what I've said. I'll say good night now. I'm going back to the command center."

He shook hands with them and vanished out the heavy front door. A small rumble could be heard from the pack of reporters.

"What gives?" Lucas asked.

"They found Henley's lunch box not too far from the bus stop," Ava said gently. "It looks like it was hurled up into a tree. It could have been done by Henley or the kidnapper."

Lucas scowled. "I don't get it."

Mason nodded. "Join the club." He pulled up the image Wells had sent and handed Lucas his phone. "Does that look right?"

Lucas stared at the image. "I honestly don't know. I think so. I'll show it to Robin."

"Maybe when they check the prints we'll have a better lead," Ava said. "The best thing you can do is get some rest."

"But it's something, right? At least they found *something*." Lucas clutched the phone with white fingers, looking at Mason and Ava with hope in his eyes, and ran a hand through his mussed-up hair. He didn't seem interested in resting.

"It helps," Ava said noncommittally. "Why don't you go ask Robin and Lilian? And then try to convince them to get some sleep. I'll wake them if I hear anything else."

Lucas nodded and left.

Mason held Ava's gaze. "What else? What are you not saying?"

She sighed and smoothed her ponytail. "There's a heated email exchange on Lucas's work account from two weeks ago. They're interviewing the client tomorrow."

"Lucas mention that in his interview?"

"Wells had to bring it up. Lucas brushed it off. Said that's how that client always communicates. Sounds like he's a bit of an asshole, and Lucas took a strong stance to deal with him. Lucas claims that there's no bad blood there, but we're looking into it."

Mason waited.

Ava simply looked at him. She was finished. If she knew more, she was keeping it to herself. For now.

Mason glanced at his watch. "It's late. I'm going to bed. Good night, Special Agent McLane. I hope tomorrow's a better day."

"You and me both," she whispered.

8

23 HOURS MISSING

Mason woke to the vibration of his work phone. It echoed through the wood of the little white nightstand next to him, sounding like a jackhammer next to his head. He snatched it off the table and glanced at the digital princess clock. Six thirty. "Callahan."

"Mason. You up?" Ray Lusco's voice barreled through the line.

"I am now." Mason rubbed his eyes. "What's up?"

"Schefte call you this morning?"

"Not yet." Mason pulled the phone from his ear and touched the screen, blurrily checking for any missed calls or texts, knowing he couldn't have missed anything vibrating on that little table. He was tired, but not that tired.

"There's some weird evidence in Josie's case," Ray said.

The morning shifted into crystal-clear focus. "How weird?"

"There's another eyewitness placing a guy in cowboy boots and a hat at her place the day before the murder."

"So? Schefte mentioned other people had seen something similar. I'm not the only one who dresses like that." An odd buzz burned in his gut. *Another sighting?*

Silence.

"Well, yeah, not many guys dress that way in downtown Portland," Mason backtracked. "What of it?"

"Your fingerprints have turned up in three places in the apartment."

Ice encased Mason's spine, but he kept his tone neutral. "I've been there, remember? Hunsinger and Morales knew that. My prints shouldn't surprise anyone. What's the point here?"

"On the toilet handle?"

Mason sat up, alarms clanging in his head. "I didn't touch that when we were there yesterday."

"I know! But if you hadn't been there for months, why would your prints show up there? They should be totally blurred out."

"I never used Josie's bathroom." Mason thought hard, trying to remember what he'd done on his short visits to the woman's apartment. He'd looked in the fridge, sat on the couch, put money under the saltshaker. "They might find my prints on the fridge handle and the saltshaker. I probably touched the front door handle, but surely that's been touched several hundred times since I was there last."

"This isn't right," Ray said. "Something's up. You need to figure out when you were there last."

"Christ." Mason rubbed his eyes. "I'll have to look back at my log. I know it was relatively hot, because I remember her complaining about not having air conditioning. Probably at the end of September, during one of those freaky hot weeks we get before the fall weather fully kicks in. I'll have to look on my computer in the office."

"Do you remember what cases we were working on? Does that help with the time period?"

Mason thought for a long moment. "No, I don't remember. I only remember that it was really warm in her place and that I got a bottled water out of her fridge." His mind jumped through hoops, searching for an explanation. *Yes, he'd been there. But it'd been forever ago. There was no reason for his prints to show up. No reason at all.*

Bile rose in his throat. *What was happening?*

"I'm going into the office for a few hours this morning. Want me to look back at your calendar?" Ray offered.

"Sure. I don't know when I can get over there. Depends what's happening here today." Mason spoke through clenched teeth, fighting to project a nonchalant tone for Ray while his brain was flashing with red warning signs.

But why were his prints in Josie's apartment?

It had to be a mistake in the evidence.

He hadn't been there.

"No news?"

With a conscious effort, Mason shifted gears to Henley's kidnapping. "Henley never made it to the bus, so they think she was snatched between here and the bus stop. And they found her lunch box not far from the bus stop."

"That should help narrow things down. That's the type of neighborhood where security cameras are kinda standard, right?"

"Eh. They're looking through some footage. People don't usually have camera views of the street or sidewalk in front of their homes."

"How's everyone holding up?"

"Running on adrenaline, prayers, and coffee. Lilian and Robin had a blowup last night. As you can imagine, tempers are short and emotions are high around here." He set his thoughts about Josie's murder to one side and stretched his jaw. The muscles felt like he'd been chewing thick gum all night. His dentist had asked if he ground his teeth in his sleep. How would he know? He was asleep. Going by the pain in his jaw, though, he estimated he'd ground off a good millimeter of enamel last night. "I assume you're not watching the news broadcasts?" Ray asked.

"Hell, no."

"Henley was the featured story on the dinnertime and late-night broadcasts. Saw you, too. A brief shot of you at the front door of the Fairbanks home."

"Did the cameras zoom in on Jake? He's the one who answered the door."

"Not on the network I was watching."

"Good. Hopefully, no one caught a view of his face. I don't want him on the news."

"The news reports have mentioned she has two sisters and an older brother. I don't think they used his name. At least not yet. I haven't looked at the paper this morning. That might have more detail."

"Lucas doesn't get a paper here, thank God. I don't want to imagine what the papers might be speculating."

"A lot of people don't get papers anymore." Ray coughed away from his phone. "And I haven't caught any speculation yet. I'll ask Jill to keep an eye on the news broadcasts and see what sort of twists they're adding."

"Robin and Lilian will be under the media microscope. Lucas, too."

"Stranger abductions are rare," Ray stated, even though Mason knew that.

"I firmly believe that none of the parents had anything to do with Henley's disappearance. Someone that they know or someone angry at one of them could be a possibility, but it's not one of these adults."

"What about you? It could be someone striking out at you. You've pissed off enough people to fill a small town."

Mason snorted. "Then why target Henley? She's not my kid." *What if Jake had gone missing?* Guilty acid burned in Mason's gut over the relief that his son was safe.

"Yeah, good point."

The line was quiet as Mason's brain shot in a million different directions, weighing scenarios. He suspected Ray's mind was doing the same thing. He ran a hand through his short hair, making it stand on end and fighting an overwhelming urge to rush to the FBI command center and demand to hear what they'd discovered while he was sleeping.

He ended the call with a reminder for Ray to check Mason's log on his calendar at work. They knew each other's passwords. Seven years of working together had created a deep trust. He'd trust Ray with his son's life, and he knew Ray felt the same.

Ray will figure out what's wrong at Josie's house.

He pulled himself out of bed and headed for the door. First a shower, then coffee. If he'd been at home, he'd do the coffee first. But he didn't want to run into anyone while looking or smelling like he'd slept in a doorway in downtown Portland.

He turned the doorknob, noticing that he was taller than the entire Hello Kitty measuring chart on the back of the door. Someone's size had been proudly highlighted at the height of Mason's hip. He barely remembered when Jake had been that size.

Special Agent McLane stepped out of her room across the hall, fully dressed in jeans, boots, and a long-sleeved casual blouse. Blue eyes surveyed him in amusement.

"Morning, detective."

Mason wanted to go back to bed.

. . .

Ava reviewed her email at the kitchen nook table, sipping hot coffee as she scanned the latest update from ASAC Ben Duncan. Someone in the Fairbanks house hadn't slept last night. She'd found fresh homemade chocolate-chip scones, blueberry coffee cake, and cinnamon rolls on the kitchen counter. No one else was up, and the kitchen was as neat as a pin. Was Robin or Lilian the midnight baker?

She placed her money on Robin.

Taking a second piece of preservative-free coffee cake, she prayed Robin didn't keep up the custom bakery routine. Ava had a serious weakness for homemade sweets. She kept her daily food choices as simple as possible, avoiding processed foods with seventy-five ingredients on the label, and from what she'd seen in Robin's refrigerator and cupboards, the woman seemed to follow the same philosophy. No store-bought Twinkies, but bring on the home-baked goods.

If it calmed Robin to bake, maybe Ava could run what they didn't eat down to the command center. It would save the FBI money on their donut budget and get the temptation out of Ava's vision. Heck, she wouldn't mind getting some flour on her hands. Her job was to stick with the family, so maybe they could have a big cookie-making day. Churn out a few hundred Christmas cookies. That would keep some minds occupied.

Guilt flashed through her. What if cookie making was a tradition with Henley and her mom or stepmom? Would the process be more painful than helpful? Ava had good memories of her mom, herself, and Jayne spending countless hours in the kitchen during the weeks before Christmas making lemon bars, frosted sugar cookies, thick oatmeal-and-cranberry cookies, and chocolate haystacks.

In the kitchen, Jayne had never turned baking into a competition. Unlike every other aspect of her life: grades, boyfriends, clothes. Jayne had always fought to be one step ahead of Ava in everything. And Ava had let it roll off her back. It'd bugged the hell out of Jayne that Ava hadn't had the same urge to outdo her sister. Ava had always kept a cool head and ignored her sister's rants. Even now, Ava took pride in the fact that she was the calm and mellow sister, while Jayne was the fiery and emotional sister. Was Ava passive-aggressive in how she handled Jayne's competitive spirit? Absolutely. It was the one thing her sister couldn't take away from her.

And look what I have here. On her screen was an email from Jayne with a dozen exclamation marks in the subject line.

That described Jayne in a nutshell: excessive exclamation marks. Ava counted to three and exhaled before clicking on the email.

Why are you ignoring my texts??? Call me, please!!! I need to talk to you about next weekend. I just need a place to stay for a few nights until I round up some roommates. It wouldn't be more than a week. I've got a lead on a possible watercolor showing! This could be a big break for me!
XOXOXOX

Ava deleted the email. Jayne believed every word she wrote, but Ava knew they weren't true; she'd been burned twice before. If she let Jayne under her roof for one night, she'd end up like Charlie Harper on *Two and a Half Men*, with the sibling who never moved out. Jayne would break her microwave, eat all her food, and leave her wet laundry in the washing machine for a week. And those were the small issues.

Never again.

The big issues would be the variety of men Jayne invited to sleep over and the illegal drugs she'd hide from her sister. Ava closed her eyes and rubbed her forehead. Tough love. She wouldn't let Jayne drag her down. Jayne claimed she'd been clean for two months, but Ava didn't care. Jayne had a thirty-five-year history of lying to Ava, and it'd taken the last decade for Ava to break the bond her twin held over her.

Jayne and Ava might have been identical on the outside, but inside they seemed to have different genes. Somehow God had given Ava all the common sense, while Jayne got the judgment of a drunken flea.

Why? Why can't my sister see who she is?

Because Jayne didn't care. Something was missing inside of her. She operated as if the world revolved around her. She couldn't see the needs of others. She couldn't see the hurt and damaged people in her wake. As children, when Jayne was suffering, she pulled Ava down by whatever means possible to suffer along with her. She couldn't bear to be alone in her misery.

Ava wouldn't let Jayne's current misery affect her life. She'd learned that lesson several times. Too bad it'd taken so long to stick. And as for the art showing? Ava would believe it when she saw it. Every other month, Jayne was excited about a lead on an art show or someone interested in her watercolors, and she always swore she was days away from making a fortune. Jayne had never stuck out a real job. She'd been chasing the art dream forever, convinced she'd make it big and never have to worry about money again.

Until then, she believed Ava should financially support her.

"Everything okay?"

Ava started in her chair, jerking her head up to meet curious brown eyes. She hadn't heard Detective Callahan enter the kitchen. He had a cup of steaming coffee in his hand. She hadn't seen him pour it or heard the clank of the coffee pot.

Feeling distracted?

"It looked like you were about to rub through the skin on your forehead." The detective took a sip of his coffee, his gaze never leaving her.

Ava gave a weak smile. "Personal email. My sister knows how to get under my skin." The detective nodded and didn't probe further. She appreciated his manners. Anyone else would have launched into a hundred questions about her sister. He straddled a stool at the kitchen counter, hooking a boot on a rung, and eyed the bounty of baked goods. His salt-and-pepper hair was still damp from his shower. She'd clearly surprised him a half hour ago when he'd opened his bedroom door. He'd been groggy with sleep.

At least he'd slept. Ava figured she'd nabbed a total of two hours in fits and spurts.

He hadn't acted embarrassed that she'd caught him half-dressed. He'd politely greeted her and disappeared into the bathroom where she'd showered earlier. His sleepwear, loose athletic shorts and a T-shirt, had shown a man who took care of himself physically. He might grab an occasional donut with bacon, but he burned off any excess calories. He had the leanness of a runner and the lined face of someone who'd spent time squinting in the sun.

Overall, Callahan was a well-put-together package. Excessively polite, fit, smart. She studied his face. She wouldn't call the man attractive. Instead, he had a comforting weathered look. A trustworthiness to his features that tugged at her female side. Gorgeous men didn't impress her; she was impressed with character. Callahan had it in excess.

He chose a chocolate-chip scone. She'd pegged him as a cinnamon-roll type of guy. He took a bite and smiled, looking at her with happy eyes. "Somebody has been busy."

"I'll guess it was Robin."

Callahan nodded and took another bite. "Any updates?"

Ava looked at her email screen, hitting the refresh button. Nothing new popped up. "They're still reviewing video from the neighbors. Henley's photo is on every news network and paper. They plan to interview the guy that Lilian dated. Duncan says he agreed to come in today."

"I'd like to be a fly on the wall for that interview," Callahan muttered.

"They want to talk to Jake today, too." Ava watched the detective's face carefully go blank.

"I'm surprised they haven't dug deeper with him yet. He's eighteen, but I plan to be there."

"I started to talk to him yesterday," Ava remembered. "He seems like the type of kid who keeps all his feelings bottled up. I'm worried he's going to pop if he doesn't express himself."

"Yeah, he's always been pretty quiet. Feels things deeply, though. He's the kind of kid that brings home birds with broken wings and gets upset when someone is bullied at school."

"Perhaps he should be talking to someone, then. Someone professional."

The smallest touch of alarm went through Callahan's eyes. It was plain that he loved his kid, but he was out of his element when it came to talking to Jake about his inner feelings.

"I can put in a request for a child psychologist," Ava added.

"He's not a child."

"True. But he's not an adult. I want him to talk to someone who has experience listening to teens. I can only do so much. I'm here to meet the needs of the family, but I'm a bit lost with teens. I only have my own teen trauma to refer to."

"Trauma?" He cocked an eyebrow.

She waved a hand. "Typical teenage-girl stuff."

Serious eyes studied her. "I doubt you were anything but typical as a teenager. Is your sister older or younger than you?"

Ava braced herself for the usual rash of questions her next statement would bring. "We're twins."

"Huh. I bet that was interesting. My brother's a few years older than me."

Ava waited. Callahan focused on another bite of his scone.

That's it? She didn't know if she was relieved or disappointed the detective didn't want to know more.

"Morning." Lucas Fairbanks entered the kitchen. He was dressed in wrinkled sweats, but his hair was perfect. He grabbed the coffee pot and poured a giant mug of coffee. "Any news on Henley?" He turned toward Callahan and Ava, spotting the mass of baked goods. He froze. "Holy shit. That's what Robin was doing last night. I thought I smelled cinnamon in the middle of the night." He grabbed a cinnamon roll and took a place at the table. He looked at Ava expectantly, his bloodshot eyes hopeful.

She shook her head. "They're reviewing all the tape they got from your neighbors' cameras. Nothing yet."

Lucas slumped in his chair, his cinnamon roll ignored. "I'd hoped to wake up to good news." He rubbed his eyes. "Robin was in and out of bed all night. At one point I heard her bawling in the bathroom. She's out cold now. I don't know if she slept at all last night."

His sad brown eyes reminded Ava of a lost puppy.

"I don't know if I have any tears left," he muttered. He picked a chunk of frosting off his cinnamon roll, looked at it, and then set it back on the plate. "Henley loves cinnamon rolls. I'm surprised Robin made them. Usually, that's something they do together."

"Maybe it made her feel better," Ava offered. "An indicator that she knows Henley could come walking in at any minute to eat one."

Lucas met her gaze, all his emotions suddenly packed away and out of sight. "Yeah, maybe. What's the FBI going to do today to find my daughter?" His voice was flat.

Ava swallowed. *It's normal for him to be angry. It's not personally directed at you.* "More interviews, pavement pounding, door knocking, video review, computer forensics—"

"They took all the computers out of my business yesterday. Even my partner's computers. How the fuck am I supposed to run a business without our hardware?" Lucas ran a hand through his perfect hair.

"Don't you guys close down for the holidays?" Callahan asked. "Who expects their accountant to work Christmas week?"

Lucas gave him a sour look. "Clients don't give a rip that it's nearly Christmas. They care that they've exercised every possible tax break before December thirty-first."

"You have everything backed up to a remote location, right? So you just need to rent or buy some new hardware," Callahan said.

"We're trying to find out. Our IT guy is on vacation in Italy."

"Smart guy. Takes the holidays off," Callahan said with an even face. Lucas glared at him.

Footsteps distracted the men, and Jake shuffled into the kitchen. He stopped and stared blankly at the group. "Henley?" His voice cracked.

"Nothing yet, son," Callahan answered. "Get something to eat."

Jake moved to the counter full of baked sugar, his gaze widening. "Mom was up all night?"

"Yep. Hey, you sleep in your clothes?" Callahan asked.

He was right, Ava noticed. Jake was still wearing the jeans and shirt from yesterday. The shirt had picked up a few more dozen wrinkles.

"Don't have anything to wear," Jake said around a mouthful of coffee cake. "Airport lost my suitcase and still hasn't found it. Mom was going to take me shopping . . . and she hasn't done laundry. I already wore the only clothes I still have here."

"You know how to shove clothes in a washing machine, right?" Callahan asked at the same time Lucas stated, "You know how to drive to the mall."

Jake blinked at both men. "Mom said she'd go with me. And I was hoping someone would have found my suitcase by now."

Ava spoke up. "The airline lost your luggage? Where do you go to school?"

"Duke. North Carolina. I changed planes in Denver, but the airline's computer system says my suitcase made it to Portland with my flight."

"That's the worst." Ava had lost luggage three times. Once it'd never been recovered. The airline had said the same thing—that her suitcase had made it to its location. Something shifted on her computer screen, and she scanned the new email. "They want to talk with Jake in an hour." She looked at both dads. "One of you want to go with him? I'd like to be there if I'm not needed for anything for a while.

The two men looked at each other. "You go," Lucas stated. "I'll wait for Robin and Lilian to wake up."

Callahan nodded. "Go shower," he ordered Jake. "Steal a shirt out of my bag."

"But Dad, your clothes—"

"Do it. You only have to wear it for an hour."

The teen shuffled out of the kitchen, his cake in hand.

"I've got a Duke sweatshirt he can borrow," Lucas offered. "He can't complain about that."

Callahan nodded but didn't look at the stepdad. Ava studied the two men. What was it like trying to raise a teen and not step on the other parent's toes? She knew Jake spent most of his time with his mother and Lucas. What did that do to Callahan's sense of fatherhood? Had he felt that Lucas should accompany Jake to the interview? Had Lucas's offer to stay home felt like pity?

The four adults in the home had created one hell of a sociology experiment.

9

25 HOURS MISSING

Mason noticed that the number of cars outside the church command center had tripled. Fewer police vehicles, but more plain-looking American-made sedans and SUVs. More federal help. Mason turned his vehicle into the parking lot. The media had set up another camp in the far corner of the church lot, a mass of tents, RVs, and cameras. He drove in the opposite direction, looking for a parking spot that wasn't too far from the doors.

The FBI had picked a good location for their command center. The lot and church building were huge. There was room for everyone. But what about church services tomorrow?

"The church announced it was cancelling all services tomorrow," Ava announced beside him, as if reading Mason's thoughts. "That's a bit of a hard thing, considering Christmas is next week. It asked its members to stay home and pray for Henley or attend the candlelight vigil downtown at the water tomorrow night."

"What?" Jake shifted forward from the backseat, sticking his head between the front seats. "What vigil?"

"I don't know who organized it," Ava answered. "Possibly the church. Waterfront Park tomorrow at seven." Her words sped up, her voice rising a bit. Mason understood the hint of emotion in her speech. It hurt to think of Henley missing another thirty-six hours. The longer the girl was gone, the less likely she was to be found alive.

"Maybe they won't need it," Jake mumbled.

"We're all praying for that," Ava said.

Mason parked and the three of them exited the vehicle and headed toward the church doors. He fought an urge to tell Jake to hold his head up and not slouch. The kid looked like he'd suffered a beating. Emotionally, he had. Mason's coat pocket vibrated. He glanced at the screen and told Jake and Ava to go ahead. Ava gave him a careful look but nodded and guided Jake inside with her hand at his elbow. Mason watched them walk away, Jake slumping and Ava with her chin up, walking with the purpose and confidence expected from a federal agent. Mason shook his head. Why did he even notice the sloppy and insecure impression Jake was making? That was the last of his priorities.

Mason glared at Schefte's name on his screen, Ray's warning from that morning going through his mind.

"Callahan."

"Mason, it's Denny. Got a minute?"

"Yep. I heard you found my prints in Josie's place." No point in bullshitting around.

"Yeah, there's no doubt. I went to the lab and made them show me in person. They're clear as day from the toilet handle and fridge. There's one from a doorframe that's not very good."

"I didn't touch anything, Denny. You can ask Ray, Morales, and Hunsinger. One of them was with me the entire time."

"I did talk to them. They said the same. Ray says you were in the kitchen for a moment by yourself, but I assume you didn't help yourself to any soda from the fridge?"

"Fuck, no. And there was a uniformed officer in there. I was in the fridge on a previous visit, but that was months ago. There shouldn't be prints there or on the toilet handle. I don't know how they can be finding my prints."

"Let's get you printed again. Maybe the comparison prints are crap."

Mason wiped his forehead. It was forty-five degrees outside, but he was sweating.

New prints would definitely clear this up.

"What about the cowboy hat sightings? What's with that? I haven't been anywhere near that building in months. Inside or out."

"You know the type of people who hang around that building. I wouldn't put a lot of weight on their observations."

Mason frowned. Why was Schefte so quick to downplay the evidence? If he were in Schefte's shoes, he'd be yelling at him on the phone. "Ray was going to check my calendar for my last visit with Josie. I think it was in September."

"Yeah, I saw Ray a few minutes ago." Schefte cleared his throat. "We'd already pulled your hard drive."

"What?" Mason's vision tunneled.

"We're checking your calendar, too."

"You don't take my whole computer to look at a calendar. What the hell is going on there?"

Schefte was quiet.

"Do I need a lawyer?" Mason asked. His brain spun like he was drunk. *What was happening?*

"It wouldn't hurt to talk to your union rep," Schefte answered. "I don't know about a lawyer. I don't think that will be necessary."

A sharp pain shot through Mason's temple.

"Denny, I don't have time for this! I'm trying to help my family stay sane while their daughter is missing! My son is so stressed he's about to cave in on himself." *And so am I.*

"I know you've got a lot going on. This was a good time to take some time off. Come down and get your prints done again. Then we'll talk." Schefte sounded distant. His usual good-buddy tone gone from his voice.

Did they think he killed Josie? Impossible.

Something was screwed up somewhere. Evidence lines were getting crossed.

"Fine," answered Mason in the same even tone. "I'll have my rep with me." He ended the call and slipped the phone in his pocket, feeling as though his support system was being chiseled away. His family was dealing with the worst imaginable horror. Now his job was in jeopardy? He felt like he was being ripped in half. As slowly as possible.

How did his prints show up in that apartment?

Josie. What did you get into?

• • •

Ava signed in and led Jake through the command center, appreciating the heat. Outside was crisp and cold. No rain or snow was predicted this week, just near-freezing temperatures.

Was Henley warm?

She put the thought firmly out of her mind. Someone had taken the girl for a purpose. She didn't like to think what purpose, but whatever it was, she prayed they'd kept her indoors. An image of a small, motionless body hidden deep in the woods flashed through her head.

Stop it!

They would find that girl. This case would end happy. She glanced at Jake, seeing the first sign of life in his eyes as he took in the hustle and bustle of the command center. It was good for him to see. Sitting at home, he probably felt like no one was doing anything. The FBI could tell him over and over that they were searching high and low, but seeing it in action made it believable. Every seat in the space was manned. Various conversations filled the room. People were busy; people were focused.

Jake wiped his eyes.

Ava spotted Special Agent Sanford in a conversation with two other agents at a computer screen and raised a hand at him. He held up one finger. She and Jake stayed put. The boards on the walls were filling up with notes and photos. She spotted a board with about ten large photos of homes, recognizing them instantly. All the homes Henley would have walked past on her way to the bus. Ava had stared at the homes in person, wondering about the people who lived inside.

Was their kidnapper a passerby? Was it intentional or spur-of-the-moment?

At nearly eight in the morning?

Her experience told her it was intentional. Premeditated. A complex plan.

How else did a child vanish from between her house and the bus stop?

Sanford hurried over. "Morning. Ready to talk for a bit?" He directed the question at Jake, who silently nodded. Sanford forced a tired smile. He looked like shit, and Ava wondered when he'd slept last.

"You bring a guardian?" Sanford looked from Jake to Ava with a frown. Even though Jake was eighteen, it would make everyone feel better to know he had an adult with him for an interview. The look on Sanford's face plainly said he didn't consider Ava to be that person.

"His dad is outside on a phone call. He'll be a minute."

The three stood silently for a moment, eyeing each other.

"Do you have any leads?" Jake asked, and Ava's heart broke at the teen's whisper. She'd told him all she knew on the drive over. Her gaze pleaded with Sanford to be gentle with Jake.

"Ah . . . we have a lot we're following up on. Tips are coming in from the public. We're looking into each one."

Jake shifted his weight from one foot to the other, hope on his face.

"And all the specialists made it in last night. We pulled them from a half-dozen states. We've got senior special agents in evidence recovery, hostage negotiation, computer forensics, and even some guys from BAU working with us."

"BAU?" Jake asked. "Like from *Silence of the Lambs*?"

Annoyance flickered for the fleetest second on Sanford's face. Ava had no issue with the public's view of the movie. So what if an agent-in-training was pulled in on a huge serial-killer case? The movie still showed the talent of that department. But other agents didn't feel the way she did.

"Yes, but without the Hollywood gloss," Ava answered. "We met one of them yesterday. He was very helpful with some of his insights."

"How long will all these people be here?" Jake asked.

"As long as we need them," replied Sanford.

Callahan joined them, nodding at Sanford. "Sorry I'm late." He rubbed Jake's shoulder.

Ava picked up a highly annoyed vibe coming off the detective. He seemed distracted. What had happened on his phone call? It couldn't have to do with the case. He would have immediately brought up anything they needed to know. She had a hunch it was about his time off from his department. Perhaps they were struggling with his abrupt departure.

"Where are we doing this?" Callahan asked.

Sanford pointed at a door leading back to the hallway. "Wells is waiting two doors down on your left."

The three found the room. Wells was typing on a laptop at a large, round table and motioned for them to take seats. The room appeared to be a small library. Books lined the shelves, and several comfortable chairs were available for reading. Spiritual posters with scripture and clever quotes lined the walls.

DOWN IN THE MOUTH? TIME FOR A FAITH LIFT.

7 DAYS WITHOUT PRAYER MAKES 1 WEAK.

The peace and quiet was a welcome relief from the buzz of the command center. Ava breathed a sigh of relief that Wells was doing Jake's interview. She knew he'd be thorough and thoughtful of the boy's feelings.

"Okay, Jake. Why don't you tell me about Duke," Wells began with a small smile. "What are you studying, when are your classes, who do you like to hang out with, and how's the college food?"

Jake glanced at his father, who nodded. Jake launched into a description of his school life, and Ava let her mind wander for a few seconds. College seemed forever ago. She'd gone to UCLA, wanting to live the Southern California experience that she'd seen on TV. It hadn't been like TV. It'd been packed with people, and her apartment had been a near-slum, but that's all she could afford. She and Jayne had grown up in a quiet Northern California community. Almost a rural experience.

Jake seemed to like his college. As a freshman, he lived in the dorms and ate mostly at one of the campus cafeterias or restaurants that took college dining credits. He hadn't joined a frat, his closest friends were his roommate and two other guys in his hall, and he had a hard time getting to his 8 A.M. classes. He shot a look at his father with his comment about the early classes. Callahan shrugged. "You were never a morning person."

Wells led him through some casual conversation about his major—engineering—and Ava saw the boy gradually relax and stop analyzing every answer in his head before he spoke.

"When did you get to Portland?" Wells asked.

"I landed around 4 P.M. on Wednesday. Mom met me at the airport. But we didn't leave for another two hours because they couldn't find my bag."

"Were you at baggage claim when the bags started coming out on the carousel?"

"Nah, I hit the bathroom and then stopped at the coffee place to get something to eat, but there was a big line. They didn't serve us anything but snacks on the plane, and I was starving. Mom met me at the waiting area past security. By the time I got down to baggage, the suitcases were already going around."

"So someone could have grabbed your bag."

Jake nodded. "The airline thinks that's what happened. They scanned it when it arrived, so they knew it should have been on the carousel. We waited a while to see if someone would bring it back if they'd grabbed it accidentally. It's a black roller bag. Looks like every other bag except for the luggage tag with the Duke logo."

Wells tapped on his computer. Ava would have been requesting camera views from the airport. She suspected he was doing just that. But was a suitcase related to Henley's disappearance? Any unusual activity surrounding the immediate family had to be investigated. No matter how trivial it seemed.

"Give me a rundown of what you've done since you've been in town. People you've seen, places you've gone, who you've talked to online or via text."

Jake surprised them all by pulling a piece of paper out of his pocket. He glanced at Ava. "Special Agent McLane asked me about that yesterday. I spent some time writing down everything I could think of."

Ava mentally patted herself on the back. She met Wells's gaze and smiled. *You're welcome.*

Wells scanned the sheet. "Looks like the only time you've left the house was a grocery store run Thursday midmorning. And a stop at your friend McKenzie's after the store. You were only there fifteen minutes?"

"Yeah, her parents were taking her somewhere. I went out because mom needed creamer for her coffee. I went to the little neighborhood store, not the bigger grocery store. Got one of those Hostess pie things, too. Chocolate. Ate it in the car on the way back. Mom doesn't like to see me eating processed junk."

Ava thought of all the fresh-baked items on Robin's counter and agreed with his mom. Homemade junk was much better.

"Anyone else in the store besides the clerk?"

Jake shrugged. "I have no idea. Maybe. I want to say there was someone else by the cooler doors in the back of the store when I grabbed the creamer. I didn't talk to anyone but the clerk."

Wells made another note that probably asked about cameras at the store.

"Think about the conversations you've had with your friends since you've been back. Anyone ask about your sister? Talk about her school?"

"I've thought about this," Jake offered. "I didn't talk about Henley with anyone before she went missing. I let some people know I'd made it to town. Two of my friends aren't getting in until tonight, so I don't have anything to do until then. Yesterday I slept in until almost noon. I didn't even know Henley was missing." He blinked rapidly.

"Did you talk to Henley when you got home from the airport Wednesday?"

He nodded. "Yeah, she hugged me when I got home." The teen gave a sheepish smile. "She's cool for a little kid. Not a pest like some of my friends' younger siblings. We watched *The Princess Bride* Wednesday night. Mom watched, too. I think Lucas was working late. Henley talks a lot, and she talked through the movie. She always wants to discuss what she's seeing, you know? Keeps up an ongoing commentary about everything in front of her. I tune her out quite a bit. I mean, she doesn't *stop*." He looked at the three adults with wide eyes, asking for forgiveness for not listening to his little sister.

"Small kids can have a lot to say," Ava said.

"Thursday, I didn't see her until dinnertime. She had school, and I was in my room all afternoon. She sat by me at dinner and talked. As usual. She was excited for the last day of school, and there was going to be a used-gift exchange. She'd picked out a stuffed animal to give and was worried that the other kids would think it was a baby gift. Mom had told her it was fine and to add some candy to the present if she was concerned. No kid gets upset about getting candy."

For someone who usually tuned out his sister, Ava noted, he'd listened to her concerns that night.

"I played games after dinner. I don't remember seeing her any-more that evening," the teen said quietly.

"Games online?" Wells asked.

"No. I signed out. Some games are better played alone."

"What do you mean signed out?" Ava asked.

"Microsoft's Xbox community. When I don't want to be inter-rupted, I hide myself so no one pops in to talk or message me."

"Your room overlooks the street. You see anything unusual since you've been home? I know you can't recognize every car on your street."

"It's a quiet neighborhood," Jake answered. "Cars drive by. I don't look. The house sits pretty far back from the street."

"How about UPS or FedEx? See or hear any of those trucks? It's the week before Christmas; I'd imagine people are getting deliveries."

Ava knew Wells was trying to prompt Jake's memory. The roar of a delivery truck was a recognizable sound.

"Yeah, I remember hearing a truck. I don't know if it was Thursday or Friday morning. The house next door got a delivery, and their dog went nuts. It could have been the house next to them getting a package, I guess. I was awake but still in bed. That dog next door always barks at strange vehicles in the driveway." Jake looked surprised that he'd recalled the incident.

"Hear that dog any other times?" Wells prodded.

Jake stared in his direction, his eyes blinking rapidly as he thought. "Yesterday afternoon," he said after a long pause. "Once all the media started showing up. They must have moved the dog in the house because I didn't hear it last night. With all those strangers and vehicles out there, it should have been barking its head off."

Wells nodded. "Nice job. Let's talk a bit more about your neighborhood. Who typically leaves their cars parked on the street?"

"Two houses down," he replied promptly. "A red Taurus is always in front of their house. It's more of a magenta, actually. And there's always a big Chevy pickup on the street farther down on the opposite side. It's black.

"Most people don't park on the street. Mom told me the neighborhood discourages it. When I was learning to drive, she always made me park in the driveway. That's how I noticed who parks on the street. It's a bit narrow. You always have to veer around the same vehicles."

Wells looked through his notes and stopped at an aerial photo of the Fairbanks home and surrounding houses. "Your house does sit back pretty far. I'd imagine you can't see very far up the street." He set the photo in front of Jake.

Jake nodded and tapped his street on the photo. "From my window, I can only see the street directly in front of the house. I can't see to the neighbors' houses on either side of us because there are too many trees. I can hear the neighbor's dog, though, and I can see part of the house directly across the street, but it sits back a ways, too." He dragged a finger along the picture, indicating his lines of sight.

"Notice any walkers or joggers since you've been back?"

The teen shook his head.

Wells silently studied his notes. Ava glanced at Callahan. The man was watching his son carefully but seemed distracted. He kept glancing at the clock on the wall and shifting in his seat. He'd brought a pencil and notepad but hadn't written a word. He just kept spinning the sharp pencil between his fingers. He caught her watching him and set the pencil down but didn't make eye contact.

Something's up.

She looked to Wells, but he was engrossed in his notes. If Callahan's pencil spinning had bothered him, he didn't show it. She suspected Wells was taking careful mental notes of every movement Callahan made. He was a born observer.

"I saw one of the news station reporters say Lucas's business is being investigated," Jake said slowly. "They also said Lucas wouldn't talk to them."

All the attention in the room went to Jake. His lips were pale, and his gaze bounced between the three of them, seeking reassurance.

"Don't listen to what the media says," started Ava. She leaned forward and touched the boy's hand. "They're looking for ratings, and Lucas is smart to not talk to them. We advised him not to." She didn't know that fact for certain but figured it was a safe bet. "Yes, they're looking at his business. They need to know if there are any issues with clients that could drive someone to harm Henley. It's common sense to look."

"I'll be doing all the talking to the media for the family," Callahan added. "That was my agreement with Lucas and your mother."

"They said he has a lawyer. Why did he get a lawyer if he didn't do anything? They make it sound like he's hiding something." Jake's voice wavered.

"It does make it sound bad, which is why the media makes a big deal of it. The business has a lawyer to protect its rights. Hiring a lawyer is not a sign of guilt," Callahan reassured the teen. "It's the right thing to do. Innocent people need lawyers, too."

Jake didn't look convinced, and Ava suspected that was a hard line for Callahan to sell. Lawyers slowed down police investigations, and there was no doubt Callahan had vented his frustrations in the past within Jake's hearing.

"Online, too. People are saying horrible things about Lucas in the comments under the stories on the news websites. They all think he did something to Henley."

Ava's heart cracked. "Don't read that stuff, Jake. They are uninformed people wanting to share in the public speculation. Making a stupid comment makes them sound smart in their heads. Anyone with half a brain knows they're full of shit."

He blinked at her choice of words. Ava didn't care. Online speculation would be the family's worst enemy. Nothing good ever came from it—just a lot of hurt feelings and anger.

"You need to keep your chin up. Some idiots will try their hardest to make the family look bad in this case, and they will do it where everyone can see it, read about it, and add fuel to the fire. You know the truth. Not them. Ignore it. There's a chance it could get out of hand. I pray it won't, but you need to realize that if it happens, it's up to you to stay out of it. Don't give them reason to focus on you. Your first reaction will be to defend your family. You have to stay strong and ignore what people say."

"Stay offline," Callahan ordered. "Keep the TV off, too."

"They took my laptop last night," Jake said.

"Don't use the browser on your phone, either," his father stated.

"Will I get my computer back before I go back to school?" Jake looked at Wells.

The agent nodded. "I'll make certain we get it back as soon as possible." He scratched a note.

"Will we know what happened before I leave for Duke? Before Christmas?" Jake whispered. He looked down at his clenched hands on the table, his knuckles white.

Ava bit the inside of her lip. Jake hadn't asked if Henley would be back.

Had her brother given up already?

10

26 HOURS MISSING

Jake rubbed his eyes and stared out the window. After his interview, he'd excused himself to use the restroom and then wandered to the far end of the church. The building felt more like a school. Lots of small rooms and hallways. He peeked in the windows of the doors, passing an obvious nursery and toddler playroom. He kept going. God was somewhere in this building. Or at least there was a good place to talk to him.

His family didn't go to church. Some of his friends did. He'd gone with a few of them on Wednesday evenings, when a big group of kids would get together and go bowling or hit the batting cages. No one had pushed God down his throat during these times. He'd waited for it, expecting them to all pull out bibles and pray at some point in the evening. Instead, he'd seen simple, clean fun. He figured they saved the preaching for Sunday morning.

He turned a corner and spotted three sets of huge double doors across the end of the hallway, indicating the sanctuary.

That had to be it.

The hall was silent; the noise of the FBI had dissipated as he walked through the big building. He stopped and peeked through a window in one of the doors. Rows and rows of chairs filled the room. A traditional-looking pulpit stood alone on a low stage, two huge screens hung in the front corners of the room, and . . . was that a drum set on the stage? He pulled open a door, and it snapped loudly as it swung out. He stepped inside and quietly shut the door behind him.

The room was silent.

He waited.

Nothing happened.

Wasn't he supposed to feel God in church? Shouldn't he feel at peace and comforted? Maybe it only worked on members. The lights were dim in the sanctuary; only the stage was lit. He moved forward, scanning the stage. Drum set, microphones, piano, electronic keyboards. Weren't churches supposed to have giant organs?

He sat down in a seat in the front row and waited again.

He didn't know what he was waiting for but figured he'd know it when it happened.

"Is she safe?" he whispered.

His voice was swallowed up in the silence of the gigantic room.

He leaned forward, his elbows on his thighs, listening hard.

"Did he kill her?"

Silence.

He blew out a deep breath and closed his eyes, letting his hearing explore the room. A very quiet buzz came from the lights above the stage. He breathed deep and relaxed. At least here it was quiet. No parent or cop watching him with eagle eyes to make certain he wasn't about to have a nervous breakdown. No escapist video games to turn off the horrible images in his brain. It was just him.

Please bring her home. She's just a little kid.

Henley was a sparkly child. Her laugh infectious, her smile wide, and her eyes engaging. From the very beginning, he'd been fascinated with making her smile. Nothing made him happier than his power to transform his baby sister's face. Although she lived with her mom a lot of the time, when she came to stay at his house, it was like she'd never left. They always picked up right where they'd left off. He was her source of information about the world, and she always had questions. Questions about weather, dirt, school, boys, and music.

Last summer they'd done a family trip to Disneyland. He could still see her spinning in the teacups with his mom while he and Lucas watched. As he looked back, he realized the trip had centered around Henley and his little sisters, Kindy and Kylie. But he hadn't cared. Half his fun had been watching them squeal and scream and dance when they spotted a princess or Pooh. He and Lucas had snuck away to do the scarier rides, but what stuck in his mind was watching Henley enjoy her kiddie rides. When they'd discovered A Small World was closed, Henley had burst into tears, and Jake had been overwhelmed with the need to fix the situation. He'd surprised her with a souvenir from the Small World gift shop, bought with his own money. Her tears stopped and her eyes had worshiped him. He'd felt like a real superhero.

At what age had his sister's happiness become more important than his own?

Jake opened his eyes.

God hadn't appeared or spoken in his head. He still missed his sister and had no answers. At least he didn't want to punch the wall anymore. He'd considered it in the bathroom a few minutes before, when anger and rage had been swirling beneath his urge to bawl like a baby. He hadn't given in to either need.

He was helpless, useless. How could he find his sister?

He'd lost his superhero cape.

• • •

Ava slowly washed her hands. The church bathroom was immaculate and smelled like citrus air freshener. She soaked in the peace and quiet, stalling to avoid the hustle and noise of the command center. It felt good to let down her guard for two minutes without an agent or family member watching her. She counted slowly to ten, taking deep breaths and letting her mind wander, avoiding any thoughts of a kidnapper or the sad family. She shook the water off her hands and stared in the mirror, trying to ignore the signs of her twin in her features.

She knew they were there. The same eyes, the same lips, the same facial shape. That's where the similarities ended. Or at least that's where they'd ended last time she'd seen Jayne. Was Jayne in a cycle where she wanted the two of them to look alike again? The obsession seemed to crop up every few years. Ava, however, kept her look consistent. Her hair was always its natural dark brown, shoulder length, and her makeup was usually minimal. Jayne, on the other hand, changed with the seasons, often going through a platinum-blonde phase as she tried to imitate her namesake.

Their mother had named them after classic movie stars, Ava Gardner and Jayne Mansfield. Her sister rotated through stages, wanting to live up to her namesake's glamour, while Ava had always been happy to be herself. She rarely explained the source of her name, preferring not to draw comparisons between herself and the movie star. It was easier now than it had been as a child. The movie stars had faded into obscurity in most people's minds, and Ava was rarely in a position where her sister was with her to announce the story of their names to strangers. Too often as youngsters, her mother had introduced them and then immediately set into a lengthy explanation of their names. Ava would squirm in embarrassment as a stranger suddenly scrutinized the twins. Jayne had loved the extra attention and never stopped sharing the stories of their names, seeking fresh attention.

In middle school, Jayne had wanted to embrace the movie-star lifestyle, wearing only dresses to school and sneaking into their mother's makeup. She'd been twelve when she'd decided she needed to be blonde for the first time. Their mother had cried at the sight of Jayne's horrible orange dye job. Later attempts at becoming blonde were more successful, but Jayne never seem satisfied with who she was. She was always searching for her true self and involving people in her immediate circle in her quest.

Ava had been dragged into Jayne's drama for years. If Jayne was unsatisfied, then she seemed to think that Ava should be, too. If Jayne hated their algebra teacher, then Ava should, too. If Jayne thought a boy was hot, then Ava had to be in love with him, too.

Ava had fought it. On principle she'd take the opposite stance. It didn't matter if Chris Stemple was the hottest boy in the seventh grade. If Jayne was interested in him, then Ava found him lacking. If Jayne wanted to know who Ava liked, she kept it to herself. She'd learned that any interest she had in a boy or a dress or a bike resulted in that object being consumed by Jayne. She had to hide her likes, her emotional reactions, everything.

Jayne couldn't enjoy her own life; she always wanted Ava's.

Her sister's morning email flashed through Ava's mind. There was no way she was letting Jayne get a toehold in her current existence. She'd been in the Portland office for several years and liked it. Part of her reason for requesting a transfer to Portland had been to be closer to her sister, to help keep an eye on her. But she'd quickly learned she had to keep a wall between them. She loved her sister. She worried horribly for her sister, but she couldn't let Jayne's poison seep into her own world. Jayne was a human tornado, uprooting emotions, tossing them carelessly, and then leaving behind a disaster as she moved on to the next victim.

Ava used too many paper towels to dry her hands, delaying reentering the real world. It was time for Special Agent McLane to be strong for a teenage boy who was missing his sister. She threw the towels in the trash bin, risking one last glance in the mirror. No Jayne.

I'm not like her.

She found Detective Callahan in a discussion with Agent Sanford and two other agents at one of the workstations in the big room. She swore the timeline on the wall had lengthened by three feet during Jake's interview, and another wall had vanished behind more charts and photos. The bureau in motion. She didn't see Jake as she moved to join Callahan, who stepped aside to let her in their group.

"They've got a partial image from the neighborhood of a black or dark-gray Toyota Sienna minivan at seven fifty. Within the time frame that Henley vanished. No one on that street owns one of that color or model," Callahan announced.

Excitement rushed through Ava's chest as she focused on a blurred picture on the computer monitor. "Excellent." The image showed the rear third of a minivan. She squinted. The license plate was partially cut off.

"Can they get the rest of the plate?"

"We're working on it," said the agent seated in front of the monitor.

She stared harder at the image, willing the blur to focus, hoping to see a child's face through the dark privacy glass on the rear windows. "Where was the image taken?"

"Two houses past the bus stop. As you can see, the family's camera was set to cover the driveway. Their son's car was broken into one night, so they keep the camera trained on the driveway, and we got lucky that it covers part of the street. We didn't see any other vehicles."

"Did you catch the bus going by?"

"Yes, the bus goes by eight minutes after this minivan."

Ava fought to keep her excitement down. "That has to be it," she whispered.

The agent in the chair raised and dropped one shoulder. "It's a good lead," he said. "Best we've got going at the moment."

"Where's Jake?" she asked Callahan. "Has he seen this?"

"Bathroom."

She nodded. Was he seeking the same quiet she'd needed?

She always needed alone time to refuel after intense situations. Jake's interview hadn't been too intense, but her concern for the boy's feelings and Callahan's apparent distraction had yanked her emotions in too many directions. The three agents moved into another discussion, and she stepped back, touching Callahan's sleeve.

"What happened before the interview, detective? You were totally distracted in there."

Surprise flashed in his eyes. "That obvious?"

She shrugged. "Probably not to anyone else. I notice things."

He broke eye contact, looking toward the screen with the minivan. "Crap at work. It's nothing."

The tension in his jaw shouted that it was more than nothing. She waited. She wouldn't push. He looked at her again, and she kept her gaze neutral. "Does this affect the family?" she finally asked.

"No, definitely not."

"We've got a press conference scheduled in two hours," Sanford interrupted. "I assume the parents don't want to make a statement?"

"No," Callahan replied. "I'll talk to them and find out what they want said."

"It might be good to see the moms on camera. It could personalize his captive," Sanford added.

Ava knew the mentality Sanford was referring to. Sometimes kidnappers compartmentalized their victims as "things." It was easier to destroy or hurt a thing instead of the daughter of a crying mother on television.

Callahan nodded. "I considered that, but my main goal had been to maintain the family's privacy and to keep them out of the media circus while they struggle."

"Think some more about it," Sanford said. "They don't all have to come. I think at least one person might be helpful."

"I'll run it by them. What if I read a statement from them? Would that work?"

"It's better than nothing. It might be beneficial for the public to see the family."

Callahan's shoulders straightened as he looked hard at Sanford. If he'd had his cowboy hat on, Ava could imagine him tugging down the brim to intensify his stare. "You want the public to see the family, or you hope the kidnapper will? Their pictures are already all over the news. Do you really need them?"

Sanford blinked. "It's up to them. I'm trying to utilize every tool we have to keep that girl safe. If a kidnapper gets a twinge of guilt because he sees her mom crying on camera, I'm going to use it."

"He's got no guilt," Callahan snapped. "He grabbed a little girl off the street. We aren't dealing with a normal human being. This is a screwed-up sicko."

"Dad?"

The trio turned to see Jake. His eyes were wide, and his lashes trembled.

"You know who took Henley?" he blurted.

Ava squeezed Jake's upper arm and turned his attention to her. "No, Jake. We're discussing what kind of twisted human would do this."

Jake looked at Callahan and Sanford. "Have you found anything?" he asked Sanford.

The special agent took a deep breath. "We caught an image of a vehicle on your street in the time frame Henley went missing. We'll find it."

"Could you see Henley in the vehicle?" he asked, his voice shooting up an octave.

"No, son." Callahan put a hand on his shoulder and pointed at the computer monitor. "That's what they've got. Look familiar to you at all?"

Jake studied the screen, and Ava watched his reaction. His eagerness rapidly faded to disappointment. "No. I can't even tell what kind of minivan it is."

"Toyota Sienna," Ava told him.

The teen shook his head. "I don't think I've seen it before. Can you find it off that partial plate view?" His nose wrinkled as he leaned closer. "What are the last two numbers?"

"A two and a four. We cross-referenced those numbers with that model and got a list," stated the agent seated at the monitor. "We've narrowed the list to the Portland metro area, and we're sending out teams to knock on doors as we speak." He glanced at his watch.

"Nice," commented Callahan. "We need to get back to the house. I want to talk to Lucas about the press conference. I think I know what his reply will be, but I'll ask."

"Oh shit," swore the agent at the monitor.

"What?" asked Sanford, Ava, and Callahan at the same time.

"I've got a report of a stolen Toyota Sienna, dark gray, with a two and a four at the end of the plate number. It was stolen two weeks ago in Salem."

"Two weeks ago?" muttered Ava. She looked at Sanford. "Someone's been planning this for quite a while."

• • •

Mason's brain throbbed. His day was continuing on a downward shitty spiral. Not only did his fellow officers wonder if he was involved in Josie's death, now Henley's kidnapping looked like it'd been carefully planned. They probably weren't dealing with a spur-of-the-moment kidnapper who'd grabbed her from the street on a whim. Those slobs were the easy-to-find perps. They acted fast without thinking, were sloppy, and made mistakes, practically begging the police to find them. Now, it was possible that someone had meticulously planned the abduction for weeks.

He'd ridden back to the house in silence with Jake and Special Agent McLane. *Ava.* She'd asked him to call her Ava, but he kept forgetting. Probably because she kept calling him *detective.* They were living in the same house; it was time for first names. She'd been great with Jake today. For someone who didn't have kids, she seemed to have an instinctive knack for knowing what the teen needed to hear. There was still some power play going on between her and Sanford, but she didn't let it interfere with her work. The fact was, Sanford's responsibility was to manage the command center, and Ava's job was to keep the family in hand. Two very different positions. And it looked like they were both doing their part.

The announcement of the stolen van had elevated the energy in the room. Though the thought that someone had possibly mapped out Henley's kidnapping for weeks was upsetting, the bureau looked at the theft as a possibility for leads. Two teams had immediately been sent to Salem to interview the theft victim and dig up what information they could on the crime. That didn't mean the first list of minivans with those plate numbers had been abandoned. Agents continued to pursue those leads.

Mason's mind boggled at the sheer manpower needed to rapidly process every lead. Thank God the FBI made child abductions a priority. An immediate AMBER Alert had gone out. The full plate number of the stolen minivan was announced on electronic highway signs, TV, and radio, and also sent to every cell tower in the Portland area. It'd been eerie to hear the pings and vibrations in the big room as his and every agent's phone received the alert within a few seconds of one another.

Fuck those people who objected to getting AMBER Alerts on their phones and took steps to deactivate the public service. If their kid had been missing, they'd be screaming at the police to send an alert to every phone in the nation. What type of asshole got upset when a missing-kid announcement landed on their phone?

He and Ava had sat down with Lucas, Lilian, and Robin and asked them if they wished to participate in the press conference. Lilian had immediately flinched and drawn back. "I don't want to go on camera," she'd begged. Lucas and Robin had looked curious and asked why the sudden change in plans. Mason had already agreed to handle all media appearances. Why was he suggesting something else now?

Ava had gently explained the FBI's reasoning of putting a face on Henley's family. Robin blanched at the description of Henley as an "object," and Lilian immediately burst into tears.

"So this could help? This could be a little trick to help protect her?" Lucas asked.

Ava had taken a big breath. "It might. It might not. Your family pictures have already made the rounds. The media has shown plenty of happy photos that demonstrate Henley was part of a loving family. But this might add a degree of realness that the photos do not."

The three adults had looked at one another, scanning for reactions and searching for a common ground. Lucas finally spoke. "I'll talk. I'll say something." Robin and Lilian had nodded, relief on their faces.

"I'll prepare a more formal statement," Mason told him. "I think seeing a united front from the three of you is a good idea. My first instinct was to protect all of you and keep you totally out of the public eye, but maybe I overreacted. It doesn't hurt for the public to see that you guys really exist and are hurting, but I don't want Jake up there." He paused, eyeing Robin, who nodded in agreement.

Now Mason stared at the blank notepad in front of him. Why had he offered to be the spokesman? He hated speaking to reporters. He usually passed on that duty to the public information officer at work. It was his own dread of interacting with the media that'd made him want to protect the family from the experience. Now they were all going to be part of it.

Thirty minutes to go.

Crap. His mind spun, trying to form a coherent minispeech.

He was failing.

Ava crossed his line of vision as she paced in the backyard. She was on her phone, gesturing as she spoke. Her hand moved abruptly and sharply in a cutting motion in front of her. He couldn't see her face, but the angle of her head was stiff.

She was not pleased with the person on the other end of the line. *Personal? Work? Argument with Sanford? Something wrong with the press conference?*

She ended the call and rubbed a temple, shaking her head, her breath showing in the chilly air. His gut told him it was personal. She'd made a similar motion that morning after an email as he'd walked into the kitchen. *Her sister.* She looked at her phone screen and tapped it, then lifted the phone to her ear for another call.

Ray had said he'd ask around about Ava McLane. Mason tapped his perfectly sharpened pencil on his notepad and wondered what he'd found out. He hadn't heard from Ray since the crack of dawn, and he hesitated to call his partner. What was being said behind his back at the office? Why hadn't Ray called or texted him since that morning? Paranoia swept through him. Was Ray busy or giving Mason space to deal with Henley's family?

Or was Ray being questioned about Mason's actions in the days leading up to Josie's murder? Had he been ordered to not talk to Mason?

Fuck me.

No wonder he couldn't get anything on paper. He stared at the blank yellow pad. *Just thank the public for their concern. Say the family—*

Ava swept in from outdoors, bringing a rush of icy air. Mason jumped in his seat, his focus shot again. He started to glare at her but froze at the expression on her face. Her eyes were bright, and she clutched her phone to her chest. His pulse skyrocketed. In the split second before he spoke, Mason's brain shot to two opposite assumptions.

Henley is dead.

Henley is alive.

"What happened?"

"They've found a ransom note."

11

28 HOURS MISSING

Ava sat motionless at the dining-room table, her mind spinning through the possibilities a ransom note could indicate. Yesterday when she'd sat in the exact same spot, meeting the Fairbanks for the first time, she'd known next to nothing about these people. Now they almost felt like family. She lived and breathed for the safety of their daughter. And she'd fight to keep their son from beating himself up with guilt.

How had her perspective changed so fast?

Henley had been a girl in a photo; now she was the daughter of friends. She'd known this would happen. Ava couldn't work a case like this without getting emotionally caught up in it. Yes, it was painful, but it also made her more effective.

Robin clanked dishes in the kitchen, preparing coffee and putting together a plate of her midnight pastries as they waited for Wells to arrive. Ava admired the woman. She'd channeled her grief into keeping busy. The bathroom floors had received a scrubbing like Ava suspected they'd never experienced, and then Robin had moved on to the windows. The woman was levelheaded and practical, and knew how to calm and comfort her husband. Ava wondered if Callahan saw what he'd lost when they divorced.

Wells had called her, passing on the ransom news within twenty minutes of finding the note. He'd been brief with details, offering to stop by and talk with the family. "Don't get them too excited about this, Ava. Let's find out what we've got here. Don't let them jump to conclusions."

Translation: It could be fake. Don't assume Henley is alive.

She'd blurted the news to Callahan, who'd immediately assembled the three parents.

Wells arrived and laid a photocopy of the note on the table in front of Lilian. Robin set the pastry plate on the table. "Coffee is brewing," she stated, her gaze on the note.

"This was found at about eleven this morning on her elementary school playground," Wells started.

"What?" Callahan asked. "That area has been covered a hundred times."

Wells nodded. "Correct. Covered yesterday. Once it was determined Henley wasn't on school grounds, and once we saw the video that showed she never even made it on the bus, everyone's attention was focused elsewhere. The school was considered clear."

"So someone left it last night," said Robin.

"Or this morning," added Wells. "We haven't had any eyes on the area since yesterday."

Ava stared at the note. "Is that crayon? Seriously? Someone wrote it in crayon?" Red print covered the page. It was too neat for a child to have written, but someone had deliberately chosen a child's writing instrument.

"It's not Henley's writing," Lilian stated. The blonde woman looked thinner to Ava. How had she lost weight in one day? She felt a bit guilty that she hadn't spent any one-on-one time with Henley's mother since their ride back from her apartment yesterday. She'd been focused on Jake and had let Lilian's needs slide because she'd been quiet.

"It's not a child's writing according to our handwriting experts," Wells said. "A full analysis is in process, but that was one thing we wanted clarified right away. We had to determine if this was worth following up."

Lilian's gaze flew up. "Of course it's worth following up! It's a goddamned ransom note! I'd hope the FBI would take something like that seriously!"

Sitting beside her, Lucas took her hand and rubbed it. "They're taking it seriously. If it'd appeared to have been written by a ten-year-old, they would have handled it differently is all he meant." He nodded at Wells, encouraging him to go on. Ava eyed Robin, wondering if she'd react to her husband holding his ex-wife's hand. Robin had watched the action and then ignored it. Either she was extremely secure in her marriage or skilled at hiding her feelings.

"It was found on one of the play structures, folded up inside a plastic bag so that Henley's name showed through the bag." Wells flipped the note over, showing *Henley Fairbanks* printed in one-inch letters. "A mother found it. She took her two children to the school to play on the equipment this morning and discovered the plastic bag. Henley's name caught her attention immediately, and she opened it, thinking it'd been left behind by Henley. After reading it, she called 911."

"Why in the hell did she open it?" Lucas asked. "Why didn't she call the police first?"

Wells shrugged. "She didn't think it was anything. She was pretty upset when she realized she might have compromised some evidence. She said she hadn't wanted to call the police simply because she found Henley's name written in crayon on something."

Ava nodded. As much as she hated that the woman had opened the note, she understood her reasoning. "It was left to be found," she said. "I doubt she ruined any evidence. Whoever left it knew it'd be analyzed by the FBI, so they'd have taken steps to eliminate anything that could give them away."

"No cameras on the area?" Callahan asked.

"None," answered Wells.

"So what happens now? Will you do as the note asks?" Lucas's voice trembled. "I don't have that kind of money. Just because I own a business doesn't mean I have a ton of money sitting around. I don't know what we're supposed to do."

If you wish Henley returned, leave two million dollars in a black backpack at the west side river walk in downtown Portland at 7 P.M. Saturday night. Place the backpack behind the second bench from the south end in front of the seafood restaurant. The child will be left somewhere safely Sunday morning before 8 A.M.

"Don't worry about money," Wells stated. "No one expects you to come up with two million dollars. That's not what we're focused on. We're trying to figure out if this is a legitimate ransom note or someone taking advantage of the situation."

"It's not logical to ask for that kind of sum on a weekend," said Ava. "Or expect us to wait until the next day for the child to be returned. And why did they wait so long to leave a note? This lacks credibility to me."

"But we can't just let it slide by!" exclaimed Robin. "What if they hurt her because we didn't act?"

"We have negotiators here," Wells reassured her. "And there is a negotiation specialist among the CARD team that we flew in."

"But there's no one to negotiate with. It's a note! There's no phone number or person to talk to. It's simply 'do this!'" Robin argued.

Ava sympathized. The note writer hadn't left an avenue for communication, so the parents felt they needed to follow the directions of the note. Would it evolve into a hostage negotiation? She'd done the FBI's specialized training for hostage negotiation and participated in three incidents while in LA. There was no bigger stress than realizing that your voice on the phone and the words you chose were the only things keeping a hostage alive.

She knew the negotiator from the CARD team; he'd been her instructor. There was no one better at talking down an angry person who wanted to strike out.

"We're moving on it," Wells said. "We've got agents headed to that area, and the actual note is being analyzed for any trace evidence the writer might have left. You'd be surprised what we can find on a piece of paper. Or on a plastic bag."

"It's not real, is it?" Lilian whispered. "It's just someone trying to get some money out of us. There's no proof here that this person has Henley. Wouldn't a real kidnapper have known that's the first thing we'd question? He would have put in some of her hair, or taken a picture to show he really has her." Tears streamed down her face.

Ava leaned closer and put a hand on her shoulder. "There are going to be jerks out there who try to take advantage. They don't care who they hurt along the way. Do you not want us to bring this sort of thing to you until we know for certain if it's real?" She included Lucas and Robin in her question.

"Yes, we want to see this sort of thing," Lucas stated after exchanging glances with Robin and Lilian. "We don't need to know every trivial thing, but something like this is big. We need to see that things are being done." He looked at the note again. "They're very specific about how to leave the money. Black backpack. Which bench it should be set by. Someone seems to know the area very well."

Wells nodded. "It's typical for them to pick a site they're familiar with. It gives them a sense of control over the event."

"Do you think they work or live near the area?" Robin asked.

"It's very possible. And we'll look into that."

"What did you find out on the stolen minivan?" Callahan asked.

"It was taken from a park in Salem," Wells replied. "It belongs to a family with three young kids. Mom had the kids at the park and swears she locked the van, but she couldn't find her keys when it was time to leave. She doesn't know if she left the keys in the van, or if they were stolen out of her purse while the kids played.

"They were pretty shook up to hear it might have been involved in Henley's abduction. The mother was rattled to find out that her kids might have been near a kidnapper," Wells finished.

"Nothing on the AMBER Alert?" Ava questioned.

"All sorts of stuff." Wells lifted both brows. "We're getting calls about every minivan in the area. Our people manning the phones are trying to weed through the responses. You'd be surprised what people will call in. We posted the plate and color, but people are calling in with different-colored vans and completely unrelated plates."

"Everyone wants to help," Ava said with a sad smile at the parents. "Henley's turning into the city's child." She turned to Wells. "Will the ransom be discussed at the press conference?"

Wells dropped his gaze and shuffled his papers around. "We're gonna cancel the press conference. When this came in, it took priority and all available hands to process it as quickly as possible. I don't think we should be using that manpower on a press conference."

Ava saw Callahan's shoulders relax. The man had been dreading the conference. Not everyone enjoyed pubic speaking, but Ava didn't mind it. She'd welcome the chance to get up there and inform the public about the search for Henley. Should it really be cancelled? She bit her lip, not wanting to question Wells in front of the family. Judging by his behavior, Wells hadn't wanted to break the news to them . . . Were there other reasons to cancel the press conference, reasons he was holding back? Callahan, his razor-sharp gaze on Wells, appeared to be having the same thoughts.

What wasn't being said?

Wells pushed back his chair. "I guess that's it for now. I'm going to find out where they're at on the note."

"Are they sending it back east to their lab?" Callahan asked.

"They will. They're using the state police lab to run some tests first."

"That lab is notoriously backed up," Callahan pointed out.

"OSP is making this a priority. We've got a deadline of seven tonight."

• • •

Mason munched the last of his Big Mac and washed it down with a Diet Coke. He crumpled up his napkin and shoved it in the white bag, then smashed the bag into a ball. He tossed the garbage into the can outside the door of the Oregon State Police building.

He didn't feel right raiding Robin and Lucas's refrigerator for food, even though they expected him to eat there. There was plenty of food because neighbors had dropped off casseroles left and right. When people didn't know what to say, they made food and brought it over. He probably could have found something healthier in one of the casseroles. One of these days, his fast-food diet was going to kill him. Preservatives. Shouldn't those make him live longer?

The hamburger churned in his stomach as he made his way to the building's fingerprint lab, feeling like a common crook. A walk of shame. Why in the hell did he feel guilty when he hadn't done shit?

Something was foul in this investigation.

His fingerprints weren't in Josie's apartment. At least not where the investigators claimed they were. Making new prints today should clear up the confusion. He swiped his ID card through the security pad outside the fingerprint lab and pulled on the door handle. A red light flashed on the keypad. He swiped his card again. Still red.

The acid in his stomach increased.

He peeked through the narrow window in the door and knocked. Relieved that he recognized the tech on duty, Mason relaxed as Tom Hannah strode to let him in. A tall, gangly guy, Hannah always had a big smile. Seriously yellow teeth, but you forgave him because his smile was so infectious.

"Hey, Callahan. Schefte said you'd be stopping by. Need new prints?"

"I guess. Looks like I'm turning up in places I haven't been." Mason hung his hat on Tom's coat tree inside the door.

"We can't have that happening. Let's get you scanned again."

"Say, Tom. My card didn't work on the keypad."

Tom Hannah frowned. "That's weird. You get demagnetized somehow?"

"Beats me."

"Maybe they're fooling with the system."

"Yeah, maybe." *Like fooling with the system to lock me out?*

Tom led him over to what looked like a photocopier with a computer monitor on top. He typed for a minute. "Date of birth?" he asked.

Mason told him.

"This info look accurate?"

Mason scanned the screen. Name, address, DOB, birth city, and state. "Yeah."

Tom rattled the keyboard a bit more. "Okay, let's get the slaps first." He took Mason's hand and laid all four fingers on the lighted pad while he watched the fingers appear on the screen.

How many times had Mason watched this done? Usually he and Ray stood back and silently smirked. There was a bit of vulnerability to getting prints taken, no matter what the reason. It was psychological. And he'd tried to make people feel as guilty as possible while they were scanned. Now it was his turn.

Next Tom took one of Mason's hands and carefully rolled each finger across the pad, watching for the computer to give him a thumbs-up on the quality of each scan. He took Mason's other hand and started to roll. The first finger slipped. Tom repositioned the finger, and it slipped again. "Your hand is too sweaty. Try wiping it on your pants."

Sheesh.

Mason brushed his hand on his jeans. Sweaty was right. Christ. You'd think he was a terrified perp.

"Happens to everyone," Tom muttered. He rapidly rolled the rest of Mason's fingers and nodded at the screen in satisfaction. "Looks good."

"You gonna run them against the prints found at the Josie Mueller scene now?"

"Uh . . . not at the moment." Tom sprayed the lighted pad and wiped it with a soft cloth. "I'll wait until that request comes down the chain." He avoided Mason's gaze.

Mason watched him for a split second longer. Clearly, Tom didn't want to run a comparison while Mason was standing beside him. No problem. His prints weren't going to match anyway. He didn't need to be here to see it. He'd head upstairs, tell Schefte that he was done with prints, and ask to look at the calendar on his computer to see for himself when he'd last visited Josie Mueller.

"Thanks, Tom. See you around." Mason grabbed his hat and strode out of the lab. He skipped the elevator and took the stairs. His usual move when he needed to be alone to think. He jogged up the metallic-sounding steps.

His card hadn't worked in the security slider.

Tom wouldn't run the print comparison in front of him.

Schefte had pulled his computer.

He had a few questions for Schefte. When he reached his floor, he hit the stairwell door and sped down the hall to the big room where he and Ray had a corner for their desks. Several other pairs of Major Crimes detectives shared the room. For a brief second, heartburn stung his upper gut as he thought about facing his peers. *I've got nothing to hide.*

Maybe they were pulling a practical joke on him.

Mason stopped, sheer relief flowing over him like a cool breeze. Why hadn't he thought that before? A smile fought to cross his face. It made perfect sense. What better way to get him riled up than to make him think—

No. They wouldn't do that to him when there was a kid missing in his family.

Possible answers to the questions surrounding Josie's murder were slowly being crossed off his mental checklist. His buddies weren't playing a gag on him. That left human error in the evidence collection and . . .

Mason couldn't fathom the last possibility on his list. This wasn't a movie; he wasn't being framed for a murder. That didn't happen in real life.

Impossible. Or was it?

Feet suddenly heavy, he pushed open the door to what he'd always thought of as the corral. Six Major Crimes detective teams worked in adjoining cubicles along the edges of the big room. In the center of the room was a stack of cabinets with a coffee pot, crappy sink, and a fridge.

No one was at their desk in the corral. That wasn't unusual, especially for a Saturday afternoon. He glanced over at Morales and Hunsinger's corner of the room. Their desks were relatively neat. Where were they at on Josie's murder? Were they out pursuing leads or watching their kids play soccer?

Mason walked over to his desk. His monitor was present, but the tower under his desk was gone. He closed his eyes for a second. So much for hoping it wasn't true. Somebody was after his ass. But who? And why?

He walked around and stood in front of Ray's monitor. Ray still had a tower. His heart pounded in his ears as he touched Ray's mouse and his screen sprang to life. Mason stared at the log-in page to get into the Oregon State Police's system.

Will my log-in work? Or has that been deactivated, too?

Mason sat heavily in Ray's chair and tapped on the keyboard. Sweat dripped down his back as he typed in Ray's user name and password. He eyed Ray's email program. What could he find there? Had Ray passed on everything he'd been told regarding the suspicions around Josie's case? Or had everyone kept their mouths shut around Ray, knowing his friendship with Mason ran deep?

Was he violating that friendship?

Simply typing in Ray's information created a record he had no ability to erase.

Shit.

Mason logged out and immediately felt better.

What about Hunsinger's email? That's where he could find out what was going on with Josie's case. He'd learned Hunsinger's log-in during a case last year. Maybe he still had it somewhere.

Mason heard the door open behind him and popped up out of Ray's chair, moving to the far end of the cabinets to get a view of who'd come in the door.

"Hey, Callahan. Tom told me you'd been in here."

His immediate supervisor Denny Schefte was a silver-haired long-distance runner with a black mustache that belonged in a porn flick. Mason liked the man. He'd always found him to be a straight shooter and brutally honest and fair. All high marks in Mason's book.

"Prints are done. That should clear up anything from Josie's murder," Mason stated. He studied Denny's gaze, searching for a sign that this misunderstanding was about to vanish. "I'd like to look at my calendar. My computer available somewhere?"

Schefte shifted his weight. "No, it's still being looked at."

"Did you look to see when I last went by Josie's? I put every meeting with my CIs on my calendar."

"I did. You logged a visit on September fifteenth."

He'd been right. September. "It was a scorcher that day. She didn't have air. I knew that was the last time I was there."

"How come you actually went to her place? That's not SOP."

Sweat sprouted in Mason's armpits. "Usually, I didn't. We typically met down the street at a Starbucks. That time she had forgotten something, so I walked back to her place with her."

Schefte looked him straight in the eye. "Were you fucking her?"

"Jesus Christ, Denny! God, no. I don't do that shit. And wouldn't ever even consider it! Especially with a . . ." He dropped the sentence. He'd been about to say hooker. But Josie deserved better than that. She'd been a good kid. She'd just had hard times and made bad decisions.

"I wasn't fucking her. Never even crossed my mind." He held Schefte's gaze.

He was on trial.

"It's okay if you did, Callahan. It wouldn't be the first time someone fooled around with a CI. It's not against the law to have sex."

Disgust filled his chest. Not only was Schefte playing mind games, he was trying to cheapen Mason's character. "Fuck you, Denny. I didn't sleep with Josie. I've never slept with an informant or a witness or even fucking considered it. *You* know me better than that. Don't play games with my head." His vision tunneled until Schefte's face was the only visible thing in the room. "If you've got something to tell me, say it. Don't try to manipulate me to confess to something I never did."

Schefte was silent.

Mason's anger burned away, ice-cold fear taking its place. "What's going on?" he whispered to his boss. The silence in the room was almost painful in its enormity. Something had happened. "What did they find now?"

Schefte took a deep breath. "You're a good cop. You always have been, and I consider you a friend. I've known you a long time, and I like to believe I know your depth of character. You're a bit old-fashioned, Mason. But that's you. You get pissed at the things that are wrong in this world, and you work hard to fix them. Most things are black and white to you."

"Damn right." The room seemed to spin. Mason blinked, keeping his focus on Schefte.

His supervisor looked away, sorrow flashing across his face. When he looked back, determination had hardened his gaze. "After your new scans today, your prints still match. And they're also on the bat used to murder Josie. I'm gonna ask for your weapon and badge. You're on administrative leave."

Mason couldn't breathe.

It wasn't erroneous evidence collection.

Someone was deliberately framing him.

Who?

12

34 HOURS MISSING

Mason sat on the steps to his porch. His ass was one degree from freezing on the cold concrete, but the chill felt good. He needed to feel something. Since he'd turned over his gun and badge to Schefte and walked out of the police building, he'd been numb. The icy air was welcome. Right now he wanted to go inside and sleep for ten days. As long as he sat in the crispy-cool weather, he wouldn't succumb to the part of his brain that screamed for him to hit something.

His prints were on the bat that killed Josie.

Impossible.

His brain couldn't move beyond those two thoughts. They warred inside his head. Even though he'd been sitting motionless, the exhaustion sweeping his body made him feel like he'd run a marathon. Or two.

He ached to get drunk. Or run. Or drive for several hours. He could be at the coast in ninety minutes and run on the beach. The ocean always calmed him. Now that he was on administrative leave, no one cared what he did or where he went.

No one.

A wet nose touched his hand.

"Hey, boy." Mason rubbed the dog's head, and its tongue flopped out the side of its mouth in joy. He'd noticed the food bowl was empty when he'd arrived. He'd promptly filled it and peered inside the solid-sided crate he'd borrowed from a neighbor. The old outdoor furniture cushion he'd placed inside showed a thin coating of black hair. The dog must have approved of the sleeping space. Mason pulled out the cushion and whacked it on the porch rail to loosen the hair, then placed it neatly back in the crate.

The dog seemed chipper despite sleeping outside in such cold weather, Mason thought. He could hear his father's voice when a very young Mason worried about the cows and sheep sleeping outside: "That's why God gave them fur coats."

He ran his fingers through the dog's fur. It was awfully thick. And that crate was probably the warmest place the dog had slept in weeks. He should have rigged up a bed for the dog sooner.

But he'd wanted the dog to return to its home. The argument for it being a stray was growing stronger and stronger. Maybe he should take it in to a vet and get it scanned for a chip.

Maybe a young boy was missing his dog.

Jake had begged for a dog for years, but neither Mason nor Robin had seen themselves as dog people.

Mason frowned, a memory of Jake hovering just at the edge of his consciousness. Had Jake tried to bring home a dog? *No.* It was a memory of Jake playing baseball and a dog running around the infield. One of the dads had caught the dog, and it didn't have a collar. Jake had begged Mason to bring the dog home with them. He must have been about ten. The batter's helmet was big and loose on his head, and the bat looked like a caveman's club next to his bony arms.

Mason had refused, and Jake hadn't spoken to him for the rest of the day.

Mason scratched the dog's ears, and the dog rested its chin on his knee, staring at him in adoration. He felt his antidog stance slowly crumbling to pieces. So far, this mutt hadn't been any extra work. He seemed self-reliant. Just needed some food and shelter. And definitely a checkup.

Maybe he'd let the vet decide. If there was no implanted chip, then Mason would keep him.

His phone vibrated. Ray.

Mason stared at the screen. *You've got to talk to him.*

The last thing he wanted to do was talk to a human. Right now, the dog was ideal company.

"Hey." Mason's manners wouldn't let him ignore the call.

"Mason. Where are you?"

The dog huffed at the sound of Ray's voice.

"Was that a dog? Are you at home?" Ray asked.

"Yeah, I'm outside."

"Why? It's freezing."

"I'm just checking on the dog. Then I'm headed back to Jake's." Real life was slapping him in the face. As much as he wanted to run away to the coast, he had a responsibility to his son and his extended family to see them through their tragedy. Henley missing made his personal problems the equivalent of chewed gum on the bottom of his boot.

"Schefte said he talked to you," Ray started.

"Say what you mean. He didn't talk to me. He took my fucking gun and badge."

"I was getting to that."

Mason bit his tongue. Ray didn't deserve his anger. "Fuck, sorry."

"Yeah, I know." Ray was silent for a moment. "Jill wants to know if you'll come over for dinner."

"Hell, no. You think I want Jill's sad eyes staring at me all evening? Besides, I need to be at Jake's. That's what I'm supposed to be doing."

"They'll get it straightened out, Mason."

"I know I didn't beat Josie's head in with a bat. But for some reason, I'm feeling as guilty as I would if I had done it. Schefte talks to me like I let down every person in blue, when the fact is, I didn't do it!"

"I know you didn't do it," Ray stated.

"Shit. Hearing you say that makes me feel guilty, too. What the hell is wrong with me?" Mason scratched the dog's chest, wanting to toss the animal in the back of his vehicle and take him to the beach. What kind of pansy was he that he wanted to run away with a dog?

"Someone is messing with things. Schefte told me you had new prints done and they still matched. That means someone planted your prints in Josie's apartment. And I suspect that will be the person who killed Josie. Who would have your prints?"

"Any OSP employee," Mason stated. "Any server at any restaurant I've ever eaten at. Take your pick. With some simple supplies, it's pretty easy to pick up and transfer prints."

"Okay. Let's look at this a different way. Who did you piss off that wants some payback?"

"Over twenty years of perps. Robin's divorce attorney. The jerk who cut me off on the interstate today, who I honked my horn at."

"Shit. So half the state. What'd you do to Robin's attorney?"

Mason snorted. "I don't remember. I may have called him a money-hungry asswipe for dragging out the process. For an amicable divorce, it cost a hell of a lot and went on forever."

"You're being targeted for something."

Mason thought on that for a long second. "But why? What's the gain? I'm not going to go to prison for something I didn't do."

"No, but you're gonna look really bad until it's all sorted out. Wait until the press gets a hold of this."

Mason groaned. "I don't need this right now."

"I'm going to start looking over Morales's shoulder on Josie's case and asking some questions. Something is very wrong there."

"What've Morales and Hunsinger been saying in the office?"

"Not a word. But I've been swamped, so I haven't seen them for more than thirty seconds. I'm kinda enjoying working with Makitalo on his cases. He's quiet and mellow."

"Fuck you."

"And Makitalo doesn't swear at me. Go see your son. Tell him to stay strong for his sister. How are the rest of them handling it?"

"Shitty."

"As to be expected. Any developments?"

Mason gave him a brief rundown on the minivan and ransom note.

"A note? So there's going to be some action downtown tonight?"

"We'll see. I don't think anything will come of it. I firmly believe it's some sick person trying to make a buck."

"What's the FBI think?" Ray asked.

"They're looking at everything. These are the two biggest leads we've had, and they're throwing everything they've got at them. If they think the ransom note is a joke, I'm not hearing that from them. They know better than to blow it off. You can bet there will be some heavily armed agents surrounding that bench tonight. I pity the guy who tries to take on the FBI when they're hunting a child abductor."

"I asked around about Special Agent McLane. She's got a good rep. I found one guy who'd dealt with her on an earlier case. He sang her praises. Said she got him everything he needed before he even knew he needed it. She's smart as a whip and down-to-earth."

"Yeah, she seems okay," Mason admitted.

"Just okay?"

"She appears very sharp. She communicates well with the women and Jake. They're all relieved to have her in the house, and she seems to genuinely care about everyone involved." Mason remembered the look on Ava's face as she'd rushed in with the news of the ransom note. She'd been flushed from the cold, her eyes sparkling from the excitement of the new lead. For a split second, he'd been simultaneously terrified that she had horrendous news and electrified by her female appeal. The adrenaline had lit her up in a way that'd struck him deep in his chest.

Mason felt peculiar about the attraction at such an inappropriate time. Work and relationships were kept far apart in Mason's life. He'd watched too many pairs of cops heat it up and then explode in the aftermath. The job and one's personal life were best kept worlds apart.

He missed a question from Ray, caught up in his Ava distraction. "What?"

"I asked what they found out about Lilian's ex with the sexual-predator history?"

"I'll find out the results of their interview today. I'll let you know."

Mason signed off the call. It'd felt good to hear Ray's vote of confidence. He'd never been in a position where a bunch of red arrows pointed directly at him. He knew he was innocent, so why was everything going to hell in his life?

Who had it in for him?

. . .

He'd watched Mason leave the police building, and through his binoculars from his hidden perch a hundred yards away, he'd seen how deflated the man was.

Glee swept through him. *Suffer. You deserve every moment.*

Mason Callahan was going to lose his job and every ounce of credibility. Wait until the newspapers picked up the story of the dirty cop. A man who brutalized and then murdered his confidential informant.

It'd been incredibly easy to hook the whore on meth. He'd supplied it for free for several weeks until she'd started seeking him out to get more. It'd been fascinating to watch her spiral into addiction.

He'd worked so hard to place the dominos, and now they were tipping over in perfect unison. At the end was Callahan's sanity.

Served him right.

• • •

Three hours to go.

Ava had run to the grocery store with Robin. The woman had wanted to get out of the house, but didn't know what to do. The last thing they needed was groceries. The house had been swamped with food from neighbors and friends. But Robin needed to bake. It gave her something to do and kept her from going crazy, so Ava supported her.

They'd taken Ava's vehicle after sneaking Robin into the car and hiding her in the backseat. The media and cameras had watched them pass and ignored them as she drove off. She'd blown out a deep breath.

At the store, Robin loaded up on flour, sugar, butter, and chocolate. Ava grabbed yogurt and bottled water. Robin was distracted in the store, unable to focus on her short list.

"Don't look at people. Just get what you need, and we'll get out of here," Ava instructed.

"It doesn't feel normal," Robin said, steering the cart down the wide aisle. "Everything feels off-balance and too bright. Why is this one little trip exhausting me?"

Ava knew she didn't mean the brightness of the fluorescent lights in the store. "It's the waiting. The waiting is getting to you. Every nerve in your body is on high alert and braced for a phone call or word from the police. It's sapping your energy. And your calm."

Robin nodded. "Exactly. I just want it to be over. I miss my little girls. I want Kindy and Kylie to come home," she said softly. "It's so hard that I can't hug them when I need to."

"You've talked with them, right?"

"Yes, they're having a wonderful time at my parents'. It's like a vacation for them."

"And they haven't asked any questions about the agents keeping an eye on the home?" Ava asked.

"No. They haven't said anything to me. I doubt they'd notice. They're simply too young. My parents are grateful the agents are there. I miss my mom, too."

"They don't have to stay away. It's good to have family around you right now."

"I know, but I don't want the girls to be affected. They're keeping them away from the news. They'd immediately pick up on the stress at our house." She paused. "We'll tell them when we need to." Her expression closed off as she mentioned breaking bad news to her daughters.

Hopefully soon, Ava thought. *And it will be good news.*

Ava didn't put much weight on the ransom note. It didn't ring true. Was it simply meant to mess with their heads? Or was someone hoping to challenge the FBI's skills and win?

Good luck with that.

Back at the house, she left Robin to work out her frustrations in the kitchen. Lucas and Jake were watching an Indiana Jones movie in the spacious family room.

"Where's Lilian?" she asked.

"Reading in her room," Jake answered, without taking his gaze from the screen. "We're doing a marathon. She said she'd rather read."

In Ava's opinion, a marathon of Harrison Ford was good medicine. She went upstairs and tapped on Lilian's closed guest-room door. The woman answered, tissues in hand, her eyes bloodshot.

"Hey," said Ava. "Up for some company?" She'd planned to simply ask if Lilian needed anything, but the puffy eyes made her heart hurt and moved her to offer a shoulder.

"No, I'm good actually," Lilian said, dabbing her nose. "I was in a funk for a while, but I think I cried myself out of it."

"Sometimes crying is what you need." That statement was lame, but Ava had no idea what to say to the woman. She was acting on her gut instincts. Duncan had said she was the right person for this job, so he must have seen something in her that he believed would work well with the family. *Just be here to listen.*

"Jake and Lucas are watching movies. Do you want to come down? Maybe simply getting out of this room would help. A change of scenery." Lilian had spent a lot of time in the spare bedroom. Too much time alone.

"No, I think I'm going to nap. Crying wore me out," she said with a forced smile. Ava studied the woman, wondering if she should do more for her. Was she failing Lilian?

"Okay. Come down if you can't sleep."

"I suspect I'll be asleep in sixty seconds." Lilian closed the door.

Did she have sleeping meds? Ava stood in the hallway. Should she ask if Lilian was self-medicating? Was it any of her business?

She'd done her part. She'd offered and been refused. She wasn't a psychologist.

She was an investigator, and every cell in her body was itching to get to the command center and see what was going on. She'd checked in with her charges. All were stable. She should be allowed to leave, right?

She strode through the kitchen. Butter and sugar were being creamed together in Robin's stand mixer. More desserts. Robin looked satisfied and calm in her kitchen. Ava couldn't improve anything there. "Have you heard from Mason?" Robin asked.

"No. He told me he had to address some things at work and didn't know how long he'd be."

"I'm here." Mason stepped into the kitchen from the utility room next to the garage entrance.

Ava started to smile at him and froze.

What'd happened?

He looked . . . fake. As if he were trying to hide an uproar behind a calm face. She glanced at Robin, who didn't indicate she noticed anything unusual. She'd greeted Mason and gone back to her mixer. Ava looked at him again. His eyes were expressionless and his smile was forced. He'd removed his cowboy hat, his knuckles white as he gripped the brim.

She raised a brow at him. He wasn't on her list of family members to babysit, but something was clearly up. Why wasn't his ex-wife picking up on it?

Because she had enough on her mind.

She jerked her head toward the family room and he nodded. She led the way behind the sofa where Lucas and Jake were sitting and outside to the covered deck area. He closed the door behind them.

"What happened?" She folded her arms across her chest. Her thick sweater would be fine for a while in the chilly air, but not for a lengthy discussion.

Mason worked the brim of his hat, his gaze going past her to the landscaped yard. His lips pressed into a pale line. She wondered what he thought when he looked at the luxury home and grounds. Mason was a police detective. His salary couldn't buy a home like this. Ava knew few people whose salary could. Did he feel like he'd failed Robin and Jake? Or was he happy for them?

She suspected it was both. From what she'd seen, he wanted his ex and Jake to be happy. He treated Lucas with a respect that seemed rare among divorced couples. Mason worked hard so the people around him could have better lives. Possibly to the point of ignoring his own well-being. Some people had it in their DNA.

"There's some issues at work."

"And?" She wasn't going to let him off easy.

"Some stuff I need to deal with. But it won't affect what's going on here."

Did he expect her to leave it at that? His shoulders were stiff, and he was still avoiding her gaze. He looked like he'd rather be anywhere but talking to her. Her gaze narrowed.

"Hold still." She stepped closer, slowly holding out a hand. His gaze shot to hers, his eyes wide in alarm. "I'm just touching your coat," she stated. She moved in slow motion, not wanting to startle him, and patted his jacket under his arm. An empty shoulder holster.

"They took your gun. Now tell me what the hell really happened."

His story was crazy.

"How well did you know the victim?" Ava asked. Her mind sped through his tale, and she agreed with him. Someone was out to get him.

"She'd been a CI for two years. I probably met up with her a dozen times. I'd like to think she trusted me."

"Prostitutes don't trust anybody. A druggie probably trusts everyone. You think she was hooked on something the last time you saw her?"

"Something changed. She might have been a casual user to start with, but the dead woman I saw had the physical appearance of a die-hard addict—the weight loss, the facial sores, the teeth. I didn't know things could change so fast."

Pity for the dead woman was plain on his face. Ava could also see some self-blame going on for not recognizing Josie's problem. "Nothing you could do."

His gaze met hers; he didn't believe her.

"Don't tell me you think you can save the world. Haven't you been on the job a little too long to believe that? I thought that mentality disappears within six months of being hired," she joked.

He gave a small smile. "Gotta keep some faith. Otherwise, it gets to you."

An optimist. He acted like a pessimist, but at heart he wanted to see the good in everything. Something she ached for, too.

Ava nodded. *Damn it. Why'd he have to be a cop?*

She didn't get involved with cops. She'd played that game before. It might take someone on the job to truly understand what she went through every day, but dating cops was a no-no. They thought with their dicks. Women loved the uniform and threw themselves at it. Talk about an ego booster. She'd dated one for eighteen months in LA. She'd heeded the warning not to get involved with a man in blue, but she thought she'd found the exception. She hadn't. He'd cheated, twice.

First time, shame on him; second time, shame on her.

She put in for a transfer.

This guy is different. She fought an urge to laugh.

"What? You find my attitude amusing?" Mason asked.

She snorted. "No. Thinking of something else. It's good to know you're still optimistic when your department thinks you kill prostitutes."

"Ouch." He thumped his hand on his chest, but his eyes wrinkled in a faint smile.

"I don't think you're a killer."

"Good to know. And I return the sentiment."

13

Ava gazed at her date in the romantic restaurant. The lighting was dim, the crowd was festive, and they had a sweeping nighttime view of the sparkling Willamette River from their table near the window. On the river walk outside, the second bench was in their line of sight, where an agent sat waiting with a black backpack.

Ava glanced at her watch. Nearly seven. The agent would walk away at seven, leaving the backpack tucked under the bench next to the legs. ASAC Ben Duncan sat across from her, his gaze glued to the agent, his phone at his ear. She tried to look calm, but felt hyper-aware, as if she needed to memorize the movements of every diner in the restaurant and every passerby outside. Two other agents sat in the restaurant, taking up another prime table. The restaurant must have hated to lose it this last weekend before Christmas.

Tonight the Christmas Ships were out. Private yachts and sail-boats paraded up and down the river, decked out in Christmas lights. Fans made reservations at restaurants with river views months in advance, the beautiful sight a Portland tradition. The ships paraded in December and sailed a few different routes, but tonight was a prime viewing evening for this seafood restaurant.

Walkers and shoppers strolled the twenty-foot-wide walkway in front of the restaurant. The concrete path continued north along the river and deeper into the city. On the west side of the walk stood the shops and restaurants; on the east side, the landscaped bank sloped gently down to the river and marina. Tiny white lights covered the trees that lined the walk. Die-hard diners sat at outdoor tables along the east side of the walk as waiters dashed between the outdoor tables and the restaurant. Huge propane heaters kept the diners warm. Supposedly. Ava saw a lot of scarves, bulky coats, and steaming drinks. She was thankful to be assigned indoors.

She knew teams were located at both ends of the walkway, and another team was down at the edge of the river in case their suspect had a water escape planned. Would their note writer come? Or were they sitting around waiting for nothing? She fought the urge to jump up and physically check the status of each team of agents. She could hear light chatter in her earpiece, but she felt blind. This was the hard part: waiting and trusting each person to do their job.

She was surprised the ransom note specified such a public drop. Granted, the writer may have believed the masses of people gave good cover. She took a sip of water and tried to slow her heart rate as she felt the minutes crawl by. Agents had been staking out the area since they'd received the note. The rest of the teams had arrived an hour ago. Ben hadn't planned to include her, but she'd put her foot down. She was the eyes for the family, and the FBI needed every available set of hands. Or feet. Depending what the suspect decided to try.

The suspect could grab the cash and go north or south, assuming he didn't head straight for the water. North offered a solid wall of shops and restaurants along one side of the walk. He'd have to go at least a hundred yards before he could leave the walkway. Heading south on the walk would offer him better options. Open streets, parking lots, and other freestanding buildings. Lots of nooks and crannies to lose someone in. Somewhere in that area were two cars with agents with a good sight line on the bench.

The bag held a small amount of money. Anyone who looked quickly would see stacks of hundreds. Anyone who took the time to dig through the money would find stacks of ones.

Ben reached across the table and took her hand, his gaze telling her to loosen up. She blinked and then relaxed. They were supposed to look like any other married couple out for a special dinner before Christmas, but she was probably putting out the vibes of someone who was ready to run a marathon. She'd layered a slinky top with a gold jacket and even worn flashy earrings and bracelets. The holiday look was compliments of Robin, who'd seemed to enjoy dressing her up. The bottom half of her outfit was her own. Sensible black slacks and black flats that worked for sprinting. She knew that because she'd put them to the test. Ben looked his usual business self in a jacket and button-down shirt.

He needed to put down his phone. Anyone watching them must feel sorry for her because her husband had been on his phone for their entire dinner. They both wore earpieces, but Ben had also made a half-dozen calls.

The agent at the bench gave the backpack a shove with his foot, tucking it farther under the bench. He stood, glanced around, straightened his jacket, and walked south. A young couple had sat on the bench with him for a solid ten minutes, cuddling and pointing at the water. Ava had breathed a sigh of relief when they'd left moments ago. The backpack seemed totally obvious to Ava, when in reality it probably went unobserved by most. The lighting in the area wasn't the best; a casual passerby shouldn't notice the bag. She squeezed Ben's hand, and he gave a slow nod, ending his call.

Go time.

Minutes ticked by. Shoppers continued to stroll, people at the tables outdoors continued to eat and drink, and Ava sat straighter and straighter in her seat.

"Relax," muttered Ben. "You look like you're about to jump out of your chair."

She forced her shoulders to slouch. A bit.

A busboy with a water pitcher filling glasses at an outdoor table did a double take at the backpack.

No. Leave it alone.

He glanced around the area and back to the pack. He filled glasses at the next table and then headed for the bench.

Damn it. A do-gooder.

He bent over and pulled out the pack, paused, and looked around again for the owner. He headed for the front door of the restaurant.

"Shit," said Ben.

"An employee has picked up the backpack and is headed into the restaurant," came through her earpiece.

Ava lost her view of the employee.

"Wait! He's running for it!"

Ava and Ben leaped out of their chairs in unison with the other two agents in the restaurant and dashed for the front doors. Other diners looked up in surprise and jerked in their chairs as the agents thundered past.

They must think we're dining and dashing.

She followed Ben, and out of the corner of her eye, she saw a ruckus outside the restaurant. They pushed through the heavy front doors in time to see a black figure running down to the river.

Yes!

He was going to run straight into the arms of their agents at the water. Shouts filled the air, and Ava felt adrenaline pump through her system. She followed Ben past the bench and down the rough slope. Ahead, she could tell two agents already had their man on the ground, an agent's knee in the center of his back.

She slid to a stop, trying to get a look at the face of their kidnapper. He struggled on his stomach, fighting the two men who held him down. Both agents yelled at him to hold still, and she heard one ask where Henley was.

The man stilled, his head slumping to the ground.

Ben shoved at him with his toe. "Where's Henley Fairbanks? If you've hurt that little girl, you're a dead man."

The man strained his neck to look up at Ben. His youthful appearance startled Ava.

"I don't have her," the teenager said.

. . .

Mason couldn't believe it as he stared through the glass. A teenager sat slumped at the interview table.

He's about the same age as Jake.

The FBI had taken the boy to the closest holding facility, the downtown Portland Police Department's building. The teen had been processed and then handcuffed in an interview room, where he'd had a pleasant conversation with Special Agent Wells.

Ava had called Mason immediately. "A nineteen-year-old grabbed the backpack and ran. He says he's not a kidnapper and that he was just trying to make a buck."

"Did he leave the note?" Mason had asked.

"Yes. He claims he didn't think anything would come of it, but he decided to give it a try."

Mason had relayed this information to the family. The other three adults had just stared at him.

"He's not the kidnapper? He doesn't know anything about Henley?" Lilian had whispered. Lucas made her sit down. She appeared dizzy and unstable on her feet and seemed to crumple in on herself when she heard the news.

"We're right back where we were," Lucas said slowly. "All this time focusing on the ransom note, and it wasn't even real." The man looked numb.

"The FBI has been pursuing leads other than this one," Mason answered. "They said from the beginning there was something fishy about it. Even Ava questioned why the note was left in such a public place, where it was bound to fall into the FBI's scientific hands."

"A stupid kid," muttered Robin. "Yanking us around. Like we haven't been through enough."

Mason had left them to lick their fresh wounds and driven downtown, thankful the kid hadn't been taken to OSP, where Mason might cross paths with some of his coworkers.

He wasn't ready to face anyone yet.

Ava joined him at the window. "He's just a kid, but I still want to slap him silly."

"Slap him silly is too kind."

"He has no idea the stress he's put us and the family through," replied Ava. Her hands were shoved in her slacks like she didn't trust herself to be near the teen without popping him. Mason studied her out of the corner of his eye. The agent had fiercely aligned herself with the family. It was bound to happen, considering the close quarters they were living in and the turmoil she was witnessing. No one could be around Henley's parents without their own heart breaking at the sight of their pain.

"You've adopted them," Mason commented.

She turned to him, her eyebrows raised. "You're surprised? What did you expect from me? I'm human."

"I don't know. More removed, I guess," he answered lamely. Her blue eyes seemed to bore through him, and he realized she was wearing heavy eye makeup instead of her usual light look. And her hair was down and curled softly around her face.

"You look nice," he said.

She dropped her gaze and picked at her gold jacket, staring at the fabric like she didn't recognize it. "Robin dressed me up to look like I was out on a holiday date." He immediately felt awkward for commenting on her appearance.

"I didn't mean that you don't usually look nice." Mason fumbled for words. "Your hair looks different . . . in a good way . . . Not that it doesn't usually look good . . . I guess you just look different. But a good different."

Her eyes crinkled. "Wow, detective. You've got some smooth lines there. I bet Jake could give you some pointers."

He wanted the floor to swallow him up. "I didn't mean it . . . I mean, I shouldn't have said you looked nice. Oh, fuck it."

She laughed.

He watched her, abruptly blown away at the beauty of her face as she let go of her stress for a few seconds. "You should laugh more."

"I could say the same to you."

"I haven't felt like laughing for a few days."

"Amen," she said. Her eyes were serious again, but there was a relaxed air about her that hadn't been there before. He felt it flow over him, soothing him. "This has been a horrible few days, but that doesn't mean we can't still enjoy bits and pieces of life when the funny times strike. We don't need to walk around in total despair. That'll kill a person after a while."

"You're like the cop whisperer or something," he said. "You see the good in the shittiest situations. They should put you on *Oprah*. Or *Dr. Phil*."

She smiled at him, holding his gaze. "Now that was a real compliment. Thank you, detective."

"I can see why Duncan picked you to stay with the family."

"Well, that's good, because most of the time I don't have the foggiest idea what I'm doing. I don't have the psychology background that our victim specialist does, but I guess the people I work with see something in me that I don't."

"You seem to know what to say."

"That comes from years of trying to calm my sister. I told you she was a little off. She liked nothing better than to stir up drama. I spent a lot of time counterbalancing that. I strove to be rational while she went off the deep end. I guess I have a knack for calming people around me and seeing the good side in everything."

Something flashed in her eyes.

"You still balancing her out?" Mason asked.

"Now I try to simply avoid her. Makes my life easier. You know how sometimes being in the same room with certain people exhausts you? She is my kryptonite. She tears away my strength. To survive, I stay away."

"Where does she live?"

"She lives in Portland."

"That doesn't sound like you're staying away."

"After five years in LA, I thought I was strong enough to deal with her. Part of me misses her like I'd miss my right arm. She's my twin. When I'm not with her, something doesn't feel right in my soul. But when I'm with her, she destroys me. I had to choose what I could live with. I really thought she'd changed enough to let us coexist in the same city. Instead, I found that nothing had changed; if anything she is worse. So now we communicate by text or email. The city is big enough that our paths don't cross."

The earlier light had gone out of her eyes. Her flat tone told him volumes about her relationship with her sister. Mason felt a bit guilty for bringing up something so deeply personal, but he was touched that she'd confided in him. Ava McLane had many layers. Sharp investigator, empathetic agent, and wounded sister.

He wanted to know more.

He looked back at the teen, who was now being interviewed by a pair of agents. "So where does this leave us? How certain are they that he had nothing to do with Henley's disappearance?"

Ava swallowed hard, and he watched her shift her concentration back into work mode.

"They're 99 percent certain. He spilled his story on the way over. He'd heard about the kidnapping in the news, and his family has taken a bit of a financial hit. Sounds like he's a daydreamer. Spends too much time in his head, dreaming up ways to get his hands on money. Said he often had wondered what it would be like to stumble across a stash of cash, and the kidnapping sparked a fantasy of him making a fast buck. He acted on it."

"He didn't think the FBI would catch him?" Didn't the kid watch TV? Or maybe that was the problem. He'd watched too many movies where the guys get away with the cash. Something like *Ocean's Eleven*, where the thieves were glamorous.

"I guess his first plan had been to pretend to turn in the money at the restaurant and then try to claim it later. When he saw the rush of agents, he panicked and ran."

"Dumb. Where are the smart crooks these days?" Mason muttered.

"I know where one was yesterday morning," Ava said softly.

"Not smart. Lucky," stated Mason. "And his luck will run out soon."

· · ·

"What an idiot," the man told his television. Had the child really thought he could steal two million dollars out from under the FBI's nose? He kept his respect for the abilities of the police at the forefront of his mind. He might have hated the police, but he knew they had skills. Maybe not every member of the police force, but most of them. Police had a set purpose in the world. They caught the bad guys and offered them up for justice. Without a police force, the country would fall out of balance.

Balance was vital.

If only everyone could see what he'd seen; they would understand that they needed to work to restore the balance in their personal lives. It'd taken him years to see the truth. He'd made a lot of wrong turns and horrible decisions in his life that had hurt the people around him. But he'd finally understood how life worked. Give and take. Rest and work. Black and white.

By thinking before he acted, he was able to make the right decisions. Every action a person made had a decision behind it. He chose what to eat for breakfast. He chose what to watch on TV. These decisions might have seemed like nothing, but they were everything.

He chose not to eat a donut for breakfast. From that simple decision, he avoided the chemicals and saturated fat. The ability to choose gave him power. Power over his health and weight. Thinking about every bite he put in his mouth made him strong. And kept his health and weight in balance.

He rarely turned on his TV except to watch the news. Sex, advertising, gluttony, noise. By hitting one button, he removed those aspects from his everyday life, uncluttering his brain. He didn't need the excess crap pitched to him on television; he had important things to think about. It kept his mind calm and balanced. Why were so many people unable to push that button? Their lives would have been better for it.

A Christmas commercial danced across the television screen, and he changed the channel. It was impossible to avoid every cheap celebration of the season, but he tried. Christmas didn't mean what it used to.

Most people looked away when a mother was dealing with a screaming child. He would always look right at her and smile. He remembered those days. It was a rite of passage for a parent to deal with a public situation. It was his way of acknowledging her pain and being thankful that he'd survived his son's childhood. If you chose parenthood, you should experience the painful moments *and* the happy ones. You didn't pick and choose what moments you wanted; you embraced it all.

And you had the right to be a parent. If someone took that right away, they should lose their right, too.

Balance.

It was so simple, so clear. Why couldn't more people see the truth?

That boy who tried to steal two million dollars didn't deserve it. It wasn't his money. The police were right to stop it, and now the boy would be punished for fighting the natural balance.

His own personal gifts were the ability to see the natural balance and the brain to figure out the steps to restore it. He closed his eyes, studying the colors on the back of his eyelids. He would experience a green aura when things were good in his life. He didn't actually see the colors; it was more like he felt them, breathed them. Right now things weren't quite right; his aura seemed more of a muddled yellow. He knew what big step he needed to take to restore his life's harmony, but he hadn't found the right opportunity. But tonight there was a small step he could take. It would help get him through until he could take the final leap.

An eye for an eye.

He wasn't a religious person, but there was truth and strength in those words. The phrase vibrated with power and precision.

They were words to live by.

14

48 HOURS MISSING

Ava closed one eye and focused on the figure in front of her. She slowly exhaled, then held her breath as she smoothly pulled her trigger over and over. She emptied her magazine and smiled at the paper figure full of holes in his chest.

Nothing was more relaxing than seeing those holes. With one swift movement, she swapped out her magazine for a second one on the table in front of her and filled the paper man with holes again, ignoring the hot shell that bounced off her neck and burned for a brief second. She welcomed the prick of physical pain. She laid down her weapon and listened to other weapons firing in the sheriff's facility, her earplugs and hearing protection muffling the shots into soft thumps.

She'd had enough.

She'd felt the need to hit or shoot something this morning. She pulled off her eye protection, gathered her gear, and headed through the double sets of doors of the firing range and into its lobby. Her brain was clear and her energy renewed as she stepped outside and unlocked her bureau vehicle. She loved to shoot. She'd never had to pull her weapon on the job, but she relished her trips to the firing range. Some of the agents she worked with hated the mandatory qualifications with their service weapons. She'd seen both men and women sweat as their test day drew near. Not her. She loved it. And she was damn accurate.

She'd never touched a gun before she entered Quantico. The academy had taught her to shoot. Some agents never became comfortable with their weapon, but since the first day she'd touched hers, she'd known it was a skill she wanted. So she'd worked her ass off until her instructors were impressed.

Now she used it for stress relief. After the anxiety of waiting all day for last night's ransom drop, she needed to blow off some steam. She was surprised she'd managed to sleep. She'd been wired enough to consider a run at two in the morning. The utter disappointment of the ransom drop had shaken the whole team. The late briefing last night had been overcast with anger. The agents were angry at the young man and the time and effort they'd put into the situation, only to have it go nowhere.

They felt like they'd been hurled back to square one.

She drove to the church, parked, and went in for the morning briefing. The blown-up ransom note was still on the whiteboard. No one had taken it down. Ava scowled at the note, a symbol of someone who had jerked the FBI around and pulled vital resources from the real investigation. Maybe the note should stay up; it would remind everyone to take every lead seriously and not get distracted. No one knew which tiny lead would find Henley.

But today was another day. Henley had been missing two full days, and it was time to find her and bring her home. Renewal and fresh determination swept through Ava.

She stood in the back of the small conference room, listening to ASAC Ben Duncan and Special Agent Sanford discuss the digital recording of the Portland Airport's luggage pickup area. Sanford touched his laptop, and a grainy video appeared on the big screen at the front of the room. "Here's what we got from the airport security cameras. If you watch this man, you'll see him grab a black wheeled suitcase." A yellow circle appeared in the video, highlighting a man in a baseball cap. He stood close to the baggage carousel, carefully watching each bag, occasionally checking the tag on a black bag. Every few seconds he scanned the growing crowd. He finally grabbed a suitcase after taking a hard look at the tag. He immediately extended the handle and headed out of the frame, the bag rolling behind him. A second video clip appeared, showing the man walking across the traffic lanes outside of baggage claim, heading for the parking garage directly on the other side. Ava squinted at the figure. Light baseball cap, simple black jacket, jeans, dark shoes. Was his hair gray or blond?

The video vanished. She waited for the next clip.

"That's all we've got so far," Sanford stated.

"What?" Ava was shocked. "What about inside the parking garage? Every inch of that place must have cameras."

"We've gone through every angle twice. We can't pick him up after that shot of him walking across to the garage."

"What about at the pay station?" Another agent asked from the group. He was familiar, but Ava didn't know his name. There were probably forty agents and local police squeezed into the small conference room.

"We've reviewed all the images from the pay station up to an hour after the incident. We haven't spotted him. I've still got agents combing through video from the garage and pay station. We're going through everything a third time and expanding the time frame."

"How do you know that was Jake Callahan's bag?" asked a local cop. "That guy looked at three other bags before grabbing one."

"We don't for certain," started Duncan. A groan went up from the room. "Hang on a minute." Duncan gestured in a "settle down" motion. "I'm not done. What we do have is Jake's agreement that this looks like his bag, and another video of this guy coming in the doors from outside to grab a bag. He didn't come from upstairs, where the passengers disembark, and no one else on that flight reported their bag missing."

"Can we see that clip?" asked the local cop.

Sanford fiddled with his laptop on the table at the front of the room, and Ava watched their man with the cap stroll through the automatic spinning door from outside and take a position at the carousel.

"He knew exactly which carousel to go to and what time to stroll in," said Sanford. "We put him at about six foot one and two hundred pounds. We tried to get a better shot of his face, but the cap is too low and the cameras are positioned too high."

Convenient.

"His hair is gray, his shoes are black Nikes, and he's wearing jeans."

"No brand name on the jeans?" someone muttered, and laughter scattered through the group.

"Age?" asked Ava.

Duncan met her gaze and shook his head. "The hair suggests forty and up, but that's not very precise."

"He moves like he's older," she said. She scowled, not knowing why she thought that. There was nothing she could put her finger on to explain it.

Duncan nodded. "I agree. There's a bit of a stiffness to his stride that suggests age. But it could easily be a past injury that slows his walk."

"And the way he pulled the suitcase off the carousel makes him look older," offered a Clackamas County deputy. "He pulled with his whole body, not just using his arm strength like a younger guy would, you know?" Several of the other agents nodded in agreement. Sanford ran the clip again, and Ava saw what the cop meant. The man didn't simply lift the bag off the carousel, he lunged with it, using his body to lift and pull its weight.

"Also, there's no video of him before he entered the luggage area, and nothing on the parking garage tapes," stated Sanford.

"So he probably didn't park in the garage. What about one of the shuttles? Did he park in the economy lot and take a shuttle? They're located in the same direction he's walking," said Ava.

Duncan shook his head. "We checked the video feed there, too. Our theory is that someone must have given him a ride and picked him up, which we've searched for and can't find a visual record of."

Mutters of disappointment rumbled in the room.

Their suspect vanished into thin air?

"We're still looking. We'll figure out where he went," promised Duncan. "It could be a fast thief that's totally unrelated to this case. Just like the ransom note. Or it could be something more."

"But why did he take the bag?" Ava asked. "What was in the bag that he wanted? He kidnapped a young girl. How does that connect with her stepbrother's bag?"

"Good questions," answered Duncan. He scanned the group. "Any theories?"

The investigators looked at one another.

"Maybe this is focused more on the family, not just on Henley. Perhaps Henley is just part of what he's doing. Are any other family members missing things?" an agent tossed out.

Ava noticed several agents nodding along with the theory. Were the other family members in danger? She swallowed and fought an urge to dash back to the house. Clackamas County had deputies outside the Fairbanks house and at Robin's parents' home, where her two younger daughters were staying.

A number of agents shifted uncomfortably in their chairs, feeling the same unease about danger to the children.

"Nothing like that has turned up in their interviews. No oddities reported," answered Wells from the front row. Ava leaned to the left to see Wells. She hadn't noticed the agent in the room.

"Let's ask them specifically if they've noticed anything is missing," suggested Duncan. "Anything at all."

Ava raised her hand. "What about Detective Callahan? He's had some weird things happen at work."

Duncan nodded at her. "I've been following that." His gaze covered the room. "One of Detective Callahan's confidential informants was murdered the night before Henley vanished. I'm keeping in touch with his supervisor."

Ava's personal phone started vibrating, and a few cops glanced her way. She pulled it out of her pocket and turned it off after seeing Jayne's name on the screen.

"Another focus is Lilian Fairbanks's ex-boyfriend," Sanford stated. "He doesn't have an alibi for Friday morning. Basically, he was alone in his apartment, asleep after a late night out watching college football at a sports bar in Tigard."

Wells picked up the narrative. "He interviewed well. He was shocked about the child's disappearance and seemed genuinely concerned about her welfare and Lilian's. He wanted to contact Lilian and join one of the volunteer groups searching the parks, but we discouraged it for now. He understood why we were talking to him, and he wasn't defensive at all."

Duncan was nodding in agreement. "He's not too high on our list. He allowed us to search his home and talk to his friends and family. He'll be talking later today with one of the BAU agents who is a child-exploitation expert. We'll see what kind of read he gets from him."

"Did the mother have any other past boyfriends?" asked a deputy.

"She gave us two other names, but the relationships were pretty old," Duncan stated. "One has been married for two years, and the other lives in Florida. We've talked with both and consider them low on our list.

"We've got the National Center for Missing and Exploited Children involved. They'll be handling a big media push to get Henley's face out there and expanding the coverage to neighboring states. Local media has been helpful, but they're wanting an in-depth press conference. We gave them a statement last night about what happened at the waterfront, and we've told them we support the candlelight vigil at the park tonight. In my opinion, the more people who know, the better."

"Who's in charge of the security coverage at the vigil?" asked a Lake Oswego officer.

"We're coordinating with the Portland Police Department since it's on their turf." Duncan made a face. "It's a few hundred yards from where the ransom drop took place last night."

Ava's brain rapidly processed those two facts. Was there any connection between the two locations? "Who organized the vigil?" she asked.

"The Parent Student Organization at Henley's elementary school," answered Sanford.

Ava deflated a bit. It was doubtful that there was a relationship between the parents who made up the PSO and a busboy who failed to trick the FBI. Sanford nodded at her. "Yes, we found the location odd, too. But I think it's a coincidence. The busboy is from Troutdale, miles away from Lake Oswego. He doesn't know anyone in Henley's neighborhood or school. He's not the sharpest tool in the shed. I'm surprised he managed to find the school to drop off the ransom note."

Duncan wrapped up the meeting, and Ava waited until she'd reached her car before checking her phone. She listened to Jayne's lengthy voice mail and tried not to roll her eyes. Jayne's car wouldn't start and she needed a ride this morning. To a job interview? Who had a job interview on a Sunday?

Her phone vibrated in her hand, and she tried to decline the call but hit "Answer."

Shit.

"Ava?" asked Jayne.

Ava closed her eyes. "Yes, I was just listening to your voice mail. I was in a meeting when you called earlier."

"A meeting? On Sunday? Are you going to church now?" Her sister laughed.

"No. It was work."

"Can you come pick me up? I need to get there before eleven. You don't have to give me a ride home."

"Who has job interviews on a Sunday?" Ava asked. She'd learned the hard way not to believe a word her sister said. Where did she so badly need to be on a Sunday?

"It's a restaurant. They want me to come in before the lunch rush. They need a bartender."

"Is that a smart job to consider?" Jayne's history was littered with drug and alcohol addiction. Every time she told Ava she was clean and never getting high again, she'd lose a job because she was too stoned or hungover to show for her shifts.

"Jesus Christ. Don't get all bossy. I need a job, and they're hiring. You don't know what it's like not to have any income. You managed to find a great job."

Jayne had special skills; nothing was ever her fault, and she could make Ava feel guilty about her own success with one sentence—and imply that Ava only had a good job because of luck. Not because she worked her butt off and made personal sacrifices.

While Ava was running obstacle courses and studying her brain out at the FBI Academy, Jayne was flitting from boyfriend to boyfriend and trying every drug they laid in front of her.

"Where is your interview?" Ava looked at the clock in her vehicle. She'd told the Fairbankses she'd be back by noon. She still had a few hours.

Jayne gave a squeal of joy and gushed with love for Ava.

Ava gritted her teeth.

Fifteen minutes later, she pulled up in front of Jayne's apartment building and sent a text that she'd arrived.

She waited, tapping her steering wheel as she debated the wisdom of doing her sister a favor. Every encounter with her sister seemed to cause some havoc in her own life. Ava would drop her off at the restaurant and leave. End of event. That couldn't cause any repercussions, right?

Jayne dashed from the building, and Ava caught her breath. She hadn't seen Jayne in several months. She was blonde again. And extremely thin.

Ava reached to move her purse from the passenger seat, but Jayne grabbed it. "I'll hold it. It's not in my way. Good to see you, sis!" She leaned over the console between the seats and gave Ava a hug and kissed her cheek. She prattled on about the job while Ava took stock of her sister's appearance. Jayne's hair was long and curled, parted on the side and dyed a bright blonde that made Ava's eyes hurt. Her brows were shaped into strong dark wings, and her top was cut way too low. Especially for a job interview. She had to be wearing the best push-up bra in the United States. Her sister was deep in a Jayne Mansfield phase.

Ava wanted to cry.

When Jayne embraced the image of the actress, it meant she had lost touch with herself. She became someone else, an actress who'd died violently in the prime of her life.

The phases terrified Ava on a visceral level. Jayne demonstrated what Ava could be capable of. She hated her sister for displaying how low Ava's genetics could take her. Only sheer willpower and determination kept Ava on a different path than Jayne.

She focused on the road, holding the steering wheel in a death grip as Jayne continued to talk. She couldn't look at her sister anymore; she saw herself with platinum hair and boobs that screamed for attention.

I'd never be like that. I'll never be like that.

Or would she? What if her life suddenly went to shit? What if that bottle of wine became all she could think about? What would she do to find a job?

"Hey, did you get a new car? What happened to the Honda?" Jayne's question penetrated her fog.

"I still have the Honda. This is a company car." She tried not to talk about her job with Jayne. It would lead to more questions and trigger Jayne's habit of giving backhanded compliments.

"That's right, you said you had a work meeting today. That's crazy that they make you work on weekends. You'd think that a prestigious job like that would be nine to five."

See?

"Crime doesn't take the weekends off."

"What are you working on today? You don't look like you're dressed for the office. You look like you're going to the county fair."

Ava bit the inside of her cheek. She was wearing jeans and boots. Her standard weekend wear. She swallowed a comment about Jayne's skintight jeggings. Teenagers could get away with wearing those, not women her age.

"I'm not in the office today. We're working on site."

"Ohh. Did someone get killed? Where are you working?"

Ava strangled her steering wheel. "No one has been killed. There's a child missing."

"The little blonde girl on the news? I saw that. That's so sad. You're searching somewhere for her today?"

"No, I'm staying at the family's home, keeping them informed of the investigation."

"Like sleeping in their house? Living there? That's got to be weird. I don't know if I could do something like that. It's a good thing you got that job and not me." Jayne went into an in-depth description of an art show she'd attended recently.

Ava sighed. Whenever Jayne heard about Ava's job, she changed the topic to art to demonstrate that her life was just as important as her sister's. Jayne always talked about Ava's position like Jayne had been an inch a way from working for the bureau but simply chose not to. Familiar territory. And Ava let Jayne think that way; it seemed to make her feel better.

Plus, it wasn't worth starting an argument. Jayne would never agree that Ava had her career because she'd worked damned hard.

She pulled up in front of the restaurant. It was a dive bar. Ava wanted to drive away and take her sister with her. This place looked exactly like the type of place Jayne shouldn't be working. It screamed easy access to drugs and losers.

The type of place that always drew Jayne.

Ava suddenly knew there was no job interview. Her sister had simply needed a ride to a bar. What type of person was she meeting? The excitement and shine in Jayne's eyes told Ava it was a man. No doubt one she was eager to sleep with. Ava wanted to bang her own head on the steering wheel.

"What the fuck are you doing, Jayne?" she said in a low voice under her sister's monologue.

Her sister stopped midsentence and turned wide eyes to Ava. "What? Why did you say that?"

"You don't have a job interview here. You just needed a ride."

Jayne's eyes narrowed, and thin lines framed her mouth.

Ava shuddered. She'd triggered the bitch. When would she learn?

"You don't know what's going on in my life. How dare you make assumptions," her sister spat.

"Do you have a job interview?" Ava slowly and loudly stated the words, holding her sister's gaze.

Please don't lie to me again.

Jayne stared back; her mouth opened and closed a few times. "No," she finally said.

Ava closed her eyes. *Thank you.*

"Why didn't you just say you needed a ride?"

"Because you wouldn't come get me!"

Jayne was right. If she'd told Ava she needed to meet a friend, Ava would have told her to find someone else.

"You're right. But it pisses me off when you lie to me to get what you want. I'm not your bus service. What's wrong with your car?"

"I don't know. It just makes clicking sounds when I try to turn it on. David says he'll look at it."

Ava didn't ask who David was. She didn't care and definitely didn't want to start a discussion about his role in her sister's life.

"Could I borrow your car until I get it fixed? You can't drive two at a time."

"No."

Jayne pouted. "You're so selfish."

Ava wanted to pull her hair out. Of course she couldn't drive two cars at once. The point was that Jayne had no respect for anything. She'd loaned Jayne a vehicle before. It'd come back with spilled coffee on the dash and an empty gas tank. Ava had considered herself lucky. Her sister didn't associate value with any item. Because she'd never worked for anything.

She saw Ava's home and car and assumed Ava should share.

"You never answered if I could stay with you for a few days."

"You know you can't."

Jayne turned in her seat, pointing her chest at Ava and giving her sister her best dumbfounded look. "It's almost Christmas! You won't even open your home for me at Christmas? Mom would be horrified at how you treat me."

Their mother had died of ovarian cancer five years ago. Their father had left before they were born.

"Don't you dare bring mom into this, Jayne."

"You've become an absolute bitch."

"Get out." Ava kept her gaze forward. "Don't call me anymore. You only call when you want something."

"Well," Jayne sputtered. "You never call. I at least call you when it's an emergency."

Ava looked her sister directly in the eye. "This is your definition of an emergency? I've got an eleven-year-old who was snatched from the street. Her parents are sick with worry that their girl will never come home. *That is an emergency!*"

Jayne threw her door open and leaped out, spilling Ava's purse in the street. She glared at Ava as if the spill was her fault, but she bent over to shove the items back in the bag. Ava's jaw dropped as her sister's low neckline gave her a view down her shirt.

"Did you get a boob job?" Ava squeaked.

Jayne glanced up from shoving Ava's wallet back in her purse. "That's none of your business."

"You did! You can't afford to get your car fixed or find a new place to live, but you can shove money into your chest?" Ava's mind spun. Disbelief and horror swept over her simultaneously. Jayne had always moaned about their lack of assets, but Ava had accepted that they would both always be small chested and moved on.

Now they were physically different.

Hair could be dyed. Weight could be gained and lost. But Jayne had gone under the knife to change herself permanently.

"You're jealous."

Ava wanted to slap the smirk off Jayne's face. "Give me my purse and go get yourself sloshed."

Jayne tossed the purse on the passenger seat and slammed the car door. She spun on a heel and marched into the bar. Ava watched her leave and fought to control her shakes.

It was a twin thing. In the past, they'd fight like wolves and then love each other the next day. It wasn't unusual for them to be cruel to each other, because it was assumed that their bond couldn't be broken.

I could never be like her.

Ava had a sickening feeling that their bond was beyond repair.

15

50 HOURS MISSING

According to Mason's neighbor, she'd seen the dog around eight when she'd put some food in its bowl. Mason stared at the bowl of food. It'd been filled the night before and was still full? He squatted down and peered in the kennel. The cushion was free of fur. Yesterday he'd brushed off quite a bit of dog fur from one night's sleep. The dog hadn't slept on his porch last night.

Had he finally gone home?

The dog had to have several sleeping places. Perhaps he'd chosen one of those last night. It might be warmer than the spot Mason made for him. But his porch had to be a good spot for the dog to sleep. It was partially enclosed and always at least ten degrees warmer than the surrounding cool air.

Mason straightened and scanned the neighborhood. The morning was quiet and still. No dog. But what about the food? Why was there so much left? The dog always attacked the food when Mason filled his bowl. What if he was sick?

He kicked himself for not taking the dog directly to the vet. Then he would know if there was a chip under its fur and whether or not it was healthy. He'd put off the task.

You didn't want to know if he belonged to someone else.

Fuck that. He wasn't a dog person. He didn't have time to take care of one. They needed walks and shit. He was too busy with work.

Mason pushed his hat back with one finger. He and the dog had established a frail pattern of food and company. Now the animal had broken the pattern, and Mason was acting like a pansy. Dogs were tough. It would be back when it felt like it.

He sighed and shoved his key in his front door. He hadn't even stepped inside his house when he first arrived. He'd gone straight to the neighbor's when he spotted the full food bowl. He closed the door and didn't look at the blanket on the floor. He moved to the window beside the door to check once more in case someone had appeared to eat his doggy breakfast.

Nothing.

A spot of white under the dog-food dish caught his eye. Mason hadn't seen it from his position on the porch a minute ago. He stepped back outside, lifted the food bowl, and read the piece of paper under the bowl.

I don't leave ransom notes.

His heart tried to pound out of his chest.

He's been at my house. Henley's kidnapper. He knows where I live.

A sour taste gathered at the back of his throat, and a flood of thoughts crashed through his brain.

He's reaching out. He wants to be heard, and he just slipped up.

Mistake number one.

We'll catch you, you bastard.

Fury narrowed his vision. He read the note again, snapped a picture with his phone, and carefully picked it up by one corner to check the back. Blank. He laid it back in the exact position he'd found it and called Ava.

• • •

"I think he took the dog," Mason stated to the small group of agents. He shoved his hands in his pockets and rocked back on his heels.

Ava had shown up within fifteen minutes of his call. She'd taken his address and called Wells, who said he'd stop by with a forensics team. Mason hadn't expected Ava to show up; he'd called her because it was the quickest way to get his message up the chain of command. When her vehicle stopped in front of his house, something inside him calmed. It wasn't that she signaled the arrival of the FBI, it was simply her presence. She had a rational way of treating people and problems that made them feel better. Anxiety had percolated under Mason's skin as he waited for the team of agents, but it vanished as she stepped out of her vehicle and frowned, causing two lines to form between her eyebrows. "Anything else missing?" she'd asked.

"I haven't looked," Mason answered. "I was waiting for you guys before I snooped inside."

She moved up the stairs to the porch and looked at the dog bowl and kennel. "What kind of dog do you have?"

"A black kind. It must have a half-dozen breeds in its genes. It's not really my dog. It sorta started hanging around a couple of weeks ago, and I started feeding it."

Ava looked at him and smiled. "No collar?"

He shook his head. "And no, I haven't taken it to the vet to be scanned for a chip."

She continued to smile at him, her blue eyes sparkling.

"What?" he asked.

"Nothing. You seem like a dog type of guy. I'm surprised you didn't already have one."

A dog type of guy? Is that good?

"I haven't had a dog since I was a kid. Did the command center briefing go okay this morning?" Mason changed the subject.

"Yes, you saw the airport footage already, right?"

"Yes, I saw it when they showed it to Jake to ask if he thought it was his bag."

"They haven't been able to trace the guy outside of baggage claim. And they've checked out that ex-boyfriend of Lilian's who has the sexual-offender record. He doesn't have an alibi, but he let agents search his home, and his interviews went well. They've given him a lower priority. The big question is why someone who'd kidnap Henley would also take Jake's bag."

"That's been bothering me, too," Mason admitted. "It makes me want to believe Jake's bag was simply stolen by some scum."

"But now you've had something taken," Ava pointed out. "And at the briefing I brought up that you'd had a CI murdered the night before Henley disappeared."

Mason stared at her, pieces of a puzzle clicking together in his mind, and he didn't like it. *He was not connected to Henley's kidnapper.* "It's just his way of letting us know he wouldn't do a ransom. It was convenient."

"You're not looking at the big picture. One of the things we talked about was if anything unusual had happened to any other family members. I'd call this and your CI's murder unusual," Ava said. "He's possibly taken Jake's bag and now your dog. You're connected here somehow."

"The dog probably wandered off. It doesn't stay here all the time."

"Then why did you say you thought he'd taken the dog? Those were the first words out of your mouth." Ava's gaze was frank and direct. "You are in serious denial. Why won't you consider these as possible links to Henley?"

Mason stared back. *Was he avoiding something?* "I don't know. I'm hoping that the dog just wandered on." He paused. "And in my mind, I'm not really family. I'm just Jake's dad."

Silence filled the porch.

Ava shook her head at him. "You're family," she said firmly. "You were married to Robin, and you're Jake's dad. You're as tied to them as Henley is. Face it." She turned to look at the dog's dish. "The note was under his dish," Ava said. "I think someone is being clever. He's using the note to state that he didn't have a connection to the ransom last night, but he's also flaunting that he can walk up to your home and take something."

"Cocky."

"Yes, which is usually what will trip them up."

"But why me?"

"Why Henley?" Ava pointed out. "When we figure that out, it will all fall into place and we'll find her."

Two vehicles joined Ava's on the street, and Special Agent Wells's lean figure got out from behind the wheel. Two forensic specialists climbed out of the SUV behind him.

The interruption unbalanced Mason. His conversation with Ava had already thrown him for a loop. He'd always felt like an outsider in the Fairbanks home. He held himself apart from any family activities. He rarely had the time to spare, and he'd come to rely on Robin and Lucas to supply the family-oriented life for Jake. Was that mindset keeping him from looking at the odd happenings surrounding Josie's case and now the dog dish? Could there be a connection to Henley?

Wells jogged up Mason's stairs, and Ava moved to greet the man and gestured at the dog dish. The two agents and specialists talked while Mason stood useless, like a drunkard trying to get his equilibrium back.

One investigator placed the note in a bag, and the other snapped pictures. "Any security cameras on the property?" the female investigator asked.

"No," said Mason. He saw Ava raise a brow at him. Some cops felt the need for a heavy security system in their homes. He'd never been one. He had a damn good dead bolt, locks on his windows, and a weapon in his nightstand. That was good enough for him.

"One of the points discussed at the meeting this morning was whether or not any other family members have had something go missing," Wells said to him.

"We don't know if the dog was taken. It may have just wandered off somewhere else to sleep and eat last night." Mason argued. "I think it was just a good place to leave a note."

"Someone is watching your movements," Wells pointed out. "Someone knows you're involved with the family. The same person must have known about the fake ransom note."

"They couldn't have learned about the note until the late evening news," said Ava. "At least the general public didn't know what was going on until then. We tried to keep the operation quiet beforehand, but the restaurant management and the Portland Police Department knew a ransom demand had been made. Leaks happen."

"And the woman who found the ransom note at the grade school. I'm sure she told someone. We asked her not to, but people talk," added Wells.

"So there's a slim possibility that the person who left this note on my porch may have found out before the eleven o'clock news. Or not. We can't use that as a guide for a possible time when he could have been here," stated Mason. "But my neighbor said she filled the food dish around eight. Usually the dog finishes the food within minutes. There's a good chance that someone was here close to that time."

"We're going to go knock on doors," said the male forensic specialist. "See if anyone else has camera views of the street." The duo headed down the stairs.

"Ready to go inside?" Wells asked Mason.

"I went in but didn't go farther than inside the door. I spotted the note when I looked back out the window." Mason opened the door with Wells right behind him. Ava stooped to pick up the Sunday newspaper that had been tossed on the porch. She handed it to Mason.

"The door was locked?" asked Ava.

"Yes." Mason scanned his living room. Everything looked normal. He glanced at Ava as her gaze took in his bachelor existence. What did his home look like to a woman?

. . .

Ava could tell Mason had been thrown for a loop. He'd stared at the dog dish for several minutes, shaking his head as they theorized that Henley's kidnapping was linked to his dog. His feelings were getting in the way of his objectivity. He didn't want to be connected to Henley's disappearance. Wells seemed to feel there was a strong link, and she did, too.

Mason appeared to be in some serious denial. Maybe he was too close to the situation to look at it objectively. If he'd been an outsider on the case, he would have pointed it out right away as something to consider.

Mason's phone call about the note couldn't have come at a better time. She'd been struggling to drive straight after leaving Jayne. Her twin had managed to put Ava's thoughts into a tailspin. Mason's issue had yanked her out of it and given her something to focus on. There was truth in the statement that we hurt the ones we loved the most. A simple car ride had resulted in Jayne shredding Ava's psyche, and she'd lashed back. Would she never learn?

She firmly put Jayne out of her mind.

Ava took a deep breath and surveyed the inside of Mason's home. It was a bachelor pad, but a clean and neat one. The house was a small ranch-style home with a partially enclosed front porch. The grass in the front yard was neatly trimmed, and the landscaping spoke of someone who sought low maintenance, not flash. Inside, his living room had a couch, an easy chair, and a huge flat-screen TV. His kitchen didn't have a single knickknack on the counter. Just a block of knives and a toaster.

She and Wells stood back as Mason tossed the newspaper on the kitchen table, opened a few drawers, and shook his head. "I don't think anyone has been in here." He strode down the hall to the back of the house, peeking in rooms. He vanished into a bedroom at the end of the hall, and she heard him open a closet. Wells moved through the kitchen and checked the back door to a deck. It didn't budge. Mason reappeared. "I don't see anything missing or disturbed. All the windows are still locked. If he came in, I can't see it." His brown eyes looked stressed as he mashed his lips into a tight line.

No one liked the thought of someone in their home.

Mason's gaze went to the newspaper, and he shook it out of the thin plastic bag. He bypassed the front page and went to the Metro section, where the top story was the ransom attempt. Ava stepped closer and read about their wannabe ransomer. The teen's mug shot accompanied the story. She scanned the article, finding it mostly accurate.

"Sounds like I missed quite the party last night," Mason stated.

"You didn't miss anything," replied Ava.

Mason sucked in his breath, and Ava spotted the smaller headline a split second after he had.

OSP Detective on Leave in Prostitute Murder Case

"Damn it," Mason whispered. The paper quivered in his hands.

"Oh no," Ava said. She placed a hand on his upper arm in sympathy.

"What's going on?" Wells asked.

She and Mason didn't answer. They were both speed-reading the article. He flipped the pages to see the end of the story, and Ava mentally exhaled. The reporter hadn't stated Mason's name in the paper.

"'We believe there was some inappropriate behavior,'" Mason read dryly. "Nothing like seeing your boss talk smack about you in the press."

Ava winced. That had to hurt. "They don't say your name. And the reporter does say the quote was given with the understanding that it was anonymous. Anyone could have said that. Or the reporter could have made it up."

"Want to place bets that my name is in the paper tomorrow? This is going to drive the reporters to dig a little deeper. Nothing cranks up the public interest more than a report that a cop has crossed the line. And this was a big fat line."

"But you didn't do anything. No matter what they say now, they'll have to publish the truth eventually," Ava pointed out.

"Yeah, they'll bury it on page twelve. An innocent cop doesn't sell papers. Speculating that a cop murdered a prostitute puts dollar signs in their eyes. I'm surprised they didn't put it on the front page." He closed the paper and tossed it back on the table. Wells picked it up and scanned the article. He looked hard at Mason.

"What's going on?" His gaze took in Ava. "You didn't mention that he was on leave this morning. You just said he had a CI murdered. Does Duncan know?"

"He does," said Ava. She gestured at Mason. "He obviously isn't a killer. Someone has tried to make it look like he killed this poor woman. She was his informant."

Wells looked at the paper again. "This happened Thursday evening?"

Ava could almost see the wheels spinning in Wells's brain as he made the same conclusions that she'd pointed out to Mason minutes ago.

"No," stated Mason, shaking his head. "It's not all tied together. That little girl has nothing to do with a murdered prostitute. Don't let this distract you."

"Mason, you're not considering—," Ava began.

"Look. My dog, who isn't my dog, has wandered off. That shouldn't merit the attention of the FBI."

Was he trying to convince them or himself?

"Christ. What am I saying?" Mason muttered. He stepped away from Ava and leaned over the kitchen sink, staring down the drain. The color had left his face.

It was finally sinking in.

Ava felt for the man. Not only were his coworkers speculating about what had happened with the prostitute, now the public was, too. She had a friend in LA who'd fallen under public scrutiny when his spouse had gone to a reporter with a story about how her FBI agent husband would beat her. The truth had finally come out, but not until he'd been crucified in the newspapers. He'd divorced his lying wife and been granted an immediate transfer to Texas.

He'd never been the same. The utter stress from the public exposure had been like nothing he'd ever experienced. He'd told Ava he'd rather go through months of academy training all over again than spend a single hour being tried in the public eye.

"We won't jump to conclusions. But even you see now that we have to consider this might be related to Henley and your CI," said Wells. "Will you be available to say a few words at a press conference? We're going to hold one near the candlelight vigil tonight. Most of the news stations will already be there."

A glance told Ava that Wells was struggling to hide his sympathy for Mason. It was easy to picture herself in Mason's shoes. People with their jobs were held to a higher standard, and once the papers offered a whiff of scandal, any truth was often buried under speculation. It easily could have been any one of the investigators.

Mason blew out a breath. "Tonight? You've moved it to tonight?" He shook his head. "I don't know. What if they've discovered my name by then? Is that who you want speaking for the family tonight?"

"That's up to you and the Fairbanks family," stated Wells.

Mason thought hard for several seconds and then nodded. "I told them I'd do it. The women are convinced they can't do it without bursting into tears. This isn't the time to worry about my own problems."

"Do they know what's going on with you?" Wells asked.

"No. They have enough to think about."

Ava felt as if an invisible shield had just covered the man. The person they'd seen leaning over the kitchen sink, stressed out of his mind, had vanished and been replaced by a cop focused on his case. She silently applauded his shift but worried for his mental health. Her old coworker had nearly broken under the stress. Mason seemed to be able to compartmentalize his personal issues. He was the type of man who put his family before his job.

Or was he? Something had ended his marriage. Robin had hinted that he was a workaholic.

He wasn't putting his family before his job, Ava realized. He was placing them before his own mental well-being. His job had been snatched away from him.

"What about your garage? Have you checked in there since you've been home?" asked Ava. She'd noticed the detached garage that sat behind the home. Mason shook his head and led them through the door to the deck. He didn't say a word, and she could tell his mind was still processing the story and its potential to blow up to front-page news.

Who could he talk to? He must feel isolated from his peers.

He unlocked the side door to the single-car garage. His vehicle sat parked on the driveway in front of the building. They stepped inside the dark space, and he yanked on a light's string over a workbench. There wasn't room for his vehicle in the garage. He had three different workbenches full of woodworking saws and tools, and a row of cabinets overflowing with sports equipment. Looking closer, Ava noticed the sporting equipment was more suited to a child or teenager.

Jake's stuff. He's kept everything.

She wondered how long it'd been since Jake had used any of it. What appeared to be a four-wheeled ATV was covered by a tarp, taking up a large portion of the space. The area smelled of fresh-cut wood and old motor oil. Exactly how a garage should smell.

Wells pointed at a large metal locker. A gun safe, Ava realized. A huge one. She couldn't imagine what it must have weighed. "You must have used a forklift to get that in here," Wells commented.

Mason nodded. "Just about." He spun the combination on the front and opened the door to a wealth of weapons.

"I know where I'm going during the zombie apocalypse," Ava muttered.

Mason smiled at her over his shoulder then turned his focus back to the weapons. "Nothing missing here." He slammed the door and spun the dial. Ava thought of her tiny safety gun case by her bed. She owned one weapon. It was enough for her.

He opened a few cabinets, scanning each one and then moving to the next. Ava glimpsed paint cans and gardening supplies mixed in with Jake's sporting equipment.

"Looks like Jake played every sport there is," Wells commented. He was watching Mason with sharp eyes. He hadn't asked to look closer at Mason's arsenal. Most men would have asked to spend a few minutes gazing at the weapons. Wells was private, and he respected other people's privacy. It was one of the reasons Ava liked him. He wasn't pushy or nosy.

Except when he needed to be for his job.

"Jake tried every sport at least once," said Mason. "Some stuck, some didn't." He opened the last cabinet, scanned it, and started to close the door. He stopped and opened the door wider. And froze. Ava and Wells both stepped forward after exchanging a glance.

Ava saw baseball mitts, batting helmets, a catcher's mask, a dozen baseballs, and three wooden bats.

It looked harmless.

"What's wrong?" Wells asked.

Mason was quiet for a long moment. "There's a bat missing."

16

50 HOURS MISSING

When would the FBI finish asking questions?

Jake glanced at his mom. She sat stiff in her chair in the dining room next to Lucas with his hand clasped in hers. Lilian sat next to Jake and opposite his parents as they listened to Special Agent Sanford ask his million questions. Jake noticed Lilian couldn't hold still. Her hands moved from the tabletop to her lap and to her cup of coffee and back again. Over and over. She shifted in her seat like she wanted to run away.

He understood that.

He was sick of being trapped inside the house. Trips to the command center didn't count. He wanted to go see his friends or go to a movie. But that didn't feel right. He shouldn't have fun while Henley was still missing.

He brushed at his eyes with the back of his hand, fighting off the images that flooded his mind when he thought of his little sister. Henley tied up in a cellar. Henley outside and cold. Henley not breathing with her eyes closed in death. If he was struggling, then her mom and Lucas had to be suffering a hundred times worse. He shuddered and concentrated on Sanford's questions.

"Have you looked closely at your personal things? Sometimes you don't notice that something is missing until you go to use it." Sanford looked at the women. "What about jewelry? I'd like you to take an inventory and pay close attention."

"What?" asked Jake's mom. "For something to be missing, you're suggesting that he's been in our homes!"

Lilian froze, her hands in midcycle on her coffee cup. "In my house?" she whispered.

Sanford lifted his hands in a "calm down" motion. "There's been no evidence that he's been in anyone's home. Someone was on the porch of Detective Callahan's home, but we haven't had any police there watching over the house. You've had protection every hour since Henley was reported missing, and we don't plan to end that any time soon."

Lilian pushed back her chair. "I need to go look at my place. When I was there Friday, I didn't look for that sort of thing." Her voice shook, and Jake noticed that she hadn't applied makeup that morning. Lilian always wore makeup. Without it, her eyes looked swollen and dark.

Or that could simply be from crying her eyes out over Henley. Jake knew he looked like hell. They all did. He'd heard that stress had physical effects on the body; today he was seeing it. Even Lucas looked older than usual.

His easygoing stepdad had become a hermit. Lucas would watch a movie with Jake if he asked, but Lucas didn't talk and joke with him the way he had before Henley went missing. He was on the phone with people at work, in his home office alone, or sitting quietly with Robin. The two of them sat in easy chairs that looked out the big window over the backyard. Or else they went and sat outside in the cold. Their conversations low and private.

His mom had baked enough to start a large bakery. Jake noticed Robin didn't eat her desserts, but she offered them to every person who came in the door. Every time an agent or cop walked out the door, they took a big bag of cakes or pastries with them. Right now Special Agent Sanford had a thick piece of lemon pound cake on a plate in front of him. Robin hadn't asked him if he wanted it; she'd simply served it along with his coffee. That was typical of his mom. She liked to take care of people and feed them. Her stress about Henley was causing her need to nurture to expand exponentially.

"What about you, Jake?"

Jake blinked at Sanford. He'd clearly missed something important.

"I'm sorry. Can you repeat that?" Jake cringed inside. He'd been caught daydreaming when he should have been listening.

Sanford gave a strained smile. "Have you noticed anything missing since you've been home? It must be a little hard to spot since you've been gone for a few months; things are bound to be out of place. But have you looked closely at the stuff that's important to you? I noticed you have a ton of sports trophies in your room. Are they all there?"

"Uh, I think so. I'll look, but I think it would stand out if one was missing. There'd be a hole." Jake thought hard. Had he even looked at his shelves since he'd been home?

"What about out in the garage? Do you have sports equipment? I assume you haven't used anything since summer. Would you notice if things were disturbed?" Sanford asked. His eyes had brightened, and he watched Jake closely.

Was this a trick question? The agent seemed highly interested in his answer.

"You're right. I haven't looked at that stuff since summer," Jake answered, watching the agent for his reaction.

"It's not exactly baseball season, right?" Sanford smiled.

No shit. "It's been too cold," said Jake. "And it hasn't crossed my mind since I've been home. I pretty much just slept until Henley went missing."

Sanford smiled and nodded as if Jake had confirmed what he was thinking.

What was going on? "Do you want me to go look?" Jake asked.

"Soon as we're done." Sanford smiled again.

Jake didn't like his smile. It was fake. Judging by the frowns on his parents' faces, they didn't care for the agent's smile, either.

"The woman who had her minivan stolen remembers chatting for a moment with an older man who'd sat on her bench at the park," Sanford stated, abruptly changing the topic.

The adults at the table straightened in their seats, their focus rising ten notches. Jake felt the tension inflate the room.

"Could she give a good description of him?" Lucas asked. "What did he say to her?"

Sanford shuffled his papers, annoying Jake. The man had dropped a bomb in the room, then paused to make everyone wait to hear more. A jerk of a move in Jake's book. Sanford studied a sheet from his pile.

"She says a man sat next to her for a few minutes reading a novel. He made some polite comments about the kids, asking if they were excited about Christmas, that sort of thing. It was a breezy, cold day, so he was bundled up. She said he wore jeans and a heavy wool black coat that reminded her of a sailor's coat."

"A peacoat," Lilian offered. "Like with a wide collar and lapels and buttons down the front?"

Sanford nodded. "Exactly. He also wore a black knit cap and glasses. Our witness says she didn't really look at him in the eye because he was beside her and her focus was on the kids. But she noticed what he was wearing. He was gray haired and he needed to shave. She mentioned thinking that he seemed like 'an old sailor' with the cap, coat, and day-old beard growth. He left before she did.

She'd felt bad that the noise from the kids might have made it difficult for him to read."

Something slid into place in Jake's brain.

"Did he have an opportunity to get into her purse and get her
keys?" Robin asked.

Sanford nodded. "She thinks so. She said she had to help the kids
with the playground slide a few times."

Jake struggled with a faint memory. "A sailor?" he asked.

Sanford nodded. "She didn't say he was a sailor. She said his coat
and hat made her think of one."

Jake's mind sped backward. He scratched the top of his head.

"What is it, Jake?" Sanford's sharp gaze was on him.

Jake scratched again. "I don't know. That sounds familiar . . ."
Where had he seen someone like that?

"You've seen a man wearing that type of coat or hat? Was it in the
grocery store the other day?"

He shook his head. That wasn't it. "I can't remember. Maybe I'm
thinking of something I saw on TV." The four adults watched him,
and his mind went blank. "I don't know. I could be mistaken."

"You've only been home a few days," Sanford said in a calm voice.
"You said you'd only been to the store and your friend McKenzie's
house, right? Did you see someone like that at the airport?"

Jake looked at the ceiling and then the chandelier. Then his mom.
He couldn't place the memory. "Not the airport," he mumbled. "And
the man you have on video wasn't dressed like that."

"Exactly. He had a black coat and cap, but not like what the
woman at the park described."

Everything clicked into place, the image suddenly clear in his
head.

A rush of excitement flowed through him and he leaned toward
Sanford. "I've got it. It was a few weeks before I came home. I was
walking toward the dorm when a car pulled up beside me, and a man
offered me a ride."

Sanford's pen scratched his paper. "What'd he look like?"

"Exactly like you said. The knit hat and . . . peacoat?" Jake looked at Lilian, who nodded.

"Do you remember the kind of vehicle?" Sanford asked.

Jake searched his memory. It'd been dark, late at night. "Sedan. Four door. Not fancy. I don't remember the make, but it wasn't anything flashy. I notice nice cars, and I would have remembered if it'd been a Beemer or something."

"Beat up? New?"

"Neither?" Jake rubbed at his chin. The car was a blur in his mind. He really hadn't paid it any attention.

"What day was it?"

Jake took a deep breath. "I'm thinking . . . I was coming back from . . ." His brain raced. *What had he been doing? Josh had been with him at first . . .*

"Pizza. We'd gone out to pizza on a Monday night. Josh and I. He stayed later because another group of guys came in, but I had an early class the next morning, so I left."

"You walked home alone? In the dark?" his mom asked.

Jake shrugged. "It's safe. Everyone does it there. It's not that far." He looked away from the fear in his mom's eyes. Would she have asked the question if Henley hadn't been taken?

Everything was different now.

"What did he say?" Sanford grabbed his attention.

Jake thought. "He pulled alongside the curb, the car still running, rolled down the power window, and asked if I needed a lift."

"Did that seem odd to you since you weren't that far from your dorm?" Sanford asked.

Jake nodded. "A bit. Most people walking that stretch are headed to the dorms. They don't need a lift for that short of a distance. I don't know why he thought I might be going farther. I told him no thanks and that I was almost home."

"And then?"

"He said something like, 'Oh, do you live in the dorms?' And I told him I did."

Lucas shook his head as Robin gasped.

"I guess I shouldn't be saying that sort of thing to people I don't know. I see that now," Jake said. *Shit. How stupid was he?*

"Things look different now," stated Sanford, and Lilian nodded. "Did he say more?"

"Something like, 'Have a good night' and drove off," said Jake.

"Do you remember looking at the plate? Was it North Carolina or maybe out of state?"

"I don't remember looking," said Jake. He had a mental image of taillights in his head but didn't see the plate between them. "It creeped me out a bit. I just wanted to get back to my dorm room. I started jogging home after he left. Felt like a dork for running."

Sanford nodded and made some more notes. "You said a Monday. How far back? Not this past Monday, right?"

"No, it's been a few weeks."

"More than a month?" Sanford asked.

"Noooo . . . I don't think it's been that long. Maybe three weeks? Two sounds too short."

"Were you watching TV or sports at the pizza place? Do you remember if there was a game on?"

"No TV in there. That would have been a good way to figure it out, though."

"How about tests or school projects? Were you eating out because you'd finished—"

"That's it!" Jake leaned forward. "We'd both turned in a history paper that day. That had sucked big time. It was due on the fifth." He smiled as he sat back in his chair, memories of the pizza night clear in his head.

"Good job," Sanford said. "Any chance the man was in the pizza parlor before you left?"

Jake slowly shook his head. "I don't know. It was packed, and I wasn't looking at the people. You'd think an older guy would stand out, though. Most people in there are college kids." Jake froze. "Holy cow. Do you think that guy tried to get me in the car to kidnap me? On the other side of the United States? That can't be right!" Shock rocked through him. *Had* he *been the kidnapper's target?*

"How many police are at Robin's parents' with the little girls?" Lucas asked. Robin paled.

"We've got two Clackamas County deputies at their home. One outside and one inside at all times."

"Are they safe?" Robin asked. She rubbed her eyes in frustration. "I want to bring them home, but I don't think they should be around this stress and agents and police coming in and out of the house constantly."

"They're just fine," Lucas reassured her. "When I talked to them on the phone last night, they barely slowed down to say hi. They wanted to get back to baking cookies with your mom. They're in the right place for now."

"I know." Robin wiped a tear. "They didn't even blink when I got up to leave after visiting them this morning, but I miss them."

"I think you made the right decision," added Sanford. "Kids are perceptive. They'd know something was up. What are your thoughts on going to the vigil tonight?"

"I want to go," said Robin, looking at Lucas and Lilian, who both nodded in agreement. "But maybe Jake should stay home."

"Aww, Mom!" Jake wanted to be there for Henley. He looked at Sanford. "There will be police everywhere, right? I'm sure it'll be safe. Who would try anything in plain view of the cops? And we don't know that someone tried to get me, right? It could be a coincidence."

The adults looked at Sanford, who shrugged. "He's right. He'll be protected whether he goes or stays. I'm sure Special Agent McLane would stay at his side the whole time. I'll talk to her about it."

Jake nodded and sat back in his chair. He knew McLane would support his decision. He wasn't going to hide in his bedroom while the community prayed for his sister.

• • •

Mason stood in the center of his garage and waited for Detective Duff Morales to answer his phone.

Don't think about it. Just say it.

Ava was in deep discussion with Wells. They'd immediately contacted Sanford to inform him of the missing bat and called the forensics team back to process the garage. Mason watched them carefully examining his cabinets.

Shit. The garage was going to take forever. And he needed to see if anything else was missing. In his gut, he knew the only missing item would be the metal bat.

"Morales," he answered his phone.

"It's Callahan. You got a minute?"

"Yep. What's up?"

Mason heard the instant cooling in Morales's tone and closed his eyes. *I'm not the enemy.*

"I know why my prints are on the bat that was used in Josie's murder."

"Why is that?" Morales's voice perked up.

"Because it's mine. The FBI and I discovered it missing from my garage twenty minutes ago. It'll probably have my son's prints on it, too. He handled it more than I ever did."

"I've got the report on the bat right here," Morales answered. "There're no other prints except yours."

"That's impossible." Mason was stunned. He remembered picking up the bat and putting it in the garage last spring. Jake had left all the bats, several mitts, and a number of balls in the backyard after he'd had some friends over. "It has to have more. Possibly even some of his friends' prints."

"Just yours."

Someone wiped it down and placed my prints. Why?

. . .

Mason closed his eyes, mentally crossing his fingers that Ray would answer his phone. The two FBI agents were in his home with the forensics team. He'd escaped to the front yard, needing some air after reporting the missing bat.

Who? Who would do this?

"Mase? What's up?" Ray finally answered just as Mason was about to give up.

Mason couldn't speak. His mind was blank.

"Mason?" Loud background cheers came through the line.

"Ray," Mason forced out. "I was about to hang up."

"Sorry. We're at my son's soccer game. I didn't hear my phone."

"Shit, sorry. I'll let you go."

"No. It's good. What's going on?" Ray's voice intensified, and the background noise faded a bit.

Mason paused. *What did he want to say? Help me, Ray. My life is going down the shitter?*

"Are you at the Fairbankses'?" Ray asked. His voice grew sharper, pressing for information.

This was why he'd called Ray. He needed someone who knew him. Someone who knew the right questions to ask, because he was lousy when it came to expressing how he felt. Ray knew him better than any wife ever could.

"No. I'm at home. Someone was here. Looks like Henley's kidnapper may have left a note under my dog's dish."

"What?"

"And someone was in my garage. One of Jake's bats is missing. And it's the bat that was used on Josie. The one with my fingerprints." It all spilled out. He took a deep breath, his emotional load suddenly lighter.

"Holy fuck." Ray paused. "That was your silver bat? Are you sure?"

Mason knew Ray was recalling the sight of Josie's abused corpse. Just as he had a few thousand times.

"Mine is missing and my prints are on the one at the scene. But Jake's prints aren't on it. That's what's weird. He should at least have some partials on it. I just talked to Morales. Told him what I'd discovered."

"Shit. What was the note? You said it was under the dog dish? That's fucked up."

"Yeah, it said he doesn't leave ransom notes."

Ray snorted.

"And I can't find the dog. He didn't eat his dinner last night."

"You think he took the dog?" Ray was incredulous. "It's a stray, right? Maybe it went home."

"I've got a bad feeling about it." Mason had a gut-wrenching pain at the thought of the innocent animal being abused simply because it had been coming around his house.

"I doubt he took your dog. But the bat . . . that's crazy. Does that mean . . ." Ray trailed off, and Mason could almost hear the gears grinding in his head. "He implies with the dog note that he took Henley? And before that, he took your bat and murdered Josie? There can't be two different people who decided to pay your house a visit."

"I know," said Mason. "It's linking Josie's murder and me to Henley's case."

"That doesn't make sense. There's no common element between Josie and Henley."

"Not yet."

"What's the FBI think?" Ray asked.

"They're wondering what the connection is. Same as we are." Mason swallowed hard. "What are they saying about me downtown, Ray?" He shouldn't care. It shouldn't matter what a bunch of cops were whispering behind his back.

But it did.

He'd spent nearly twenty-five years as a cop. He had the soul of a cop. He'd lost his wife and most of his relationship with his son because he'd put the job first. His integrity as a person and a detective was all he had left. If that was ripped away . . .

"Christ, I don't know."

"Yes, you do. What's going around?"

Ray was silent for five seconds. "Everyone is stunned, but no one is believing it. Sure, there's evidence that you were there, but it doesn't prove that you did anything to hurt Josie. The guys are behind you, Mason."

Mason exhaled, feeling mildly dizzy from holding his breath.

"I'm doing what I can, Mason. I'm pushing for every scrap of evidence to be reexamined. I've talked to the techs, making certain things were handled correctly. So far, everything seems on the up and up, but I'm fighting for you."

"Thanks. That really means something." It did.

"You talk to the union?" Ray asked.

"Someone has called twice and left a message for me to call them back."

"Call them back!"

"I don't have time. I don't want to deal with that right now. I'm trying to stay focused on Henley," Mason argued. He didn't want to talk to the union rep. He had no patience for bureaucracy.

"They'll keep an eye on the investigation. You need to let them know you were placed on administrative leave."

"I think they know," Mason said dryly. The first voice mail from a union rep had come an hour after Schefte had taken his gun. He figured Schefte had informed them.

"This is your job, Mason."

It's my life. Without my job, I've got nothing. "Yeah, tell me something I don't know."

"They'll be knocking on your door if you don't call them back."

"I'll talk with them then. You see the newspaper this morning?"

"Yes, Jill showed it to me. At least your name isn't in it."

"But for how long? That article just screams for some deeper questions," Mason said.

"No one downtown will give a reporter your name."

Mason snorted. "Sure they will. I can think of at least three guys who'd love to see me miserable."

"You need to learn to be nicer to people. No more burning your bridges when someone pisses you off."

"I'm not very good at turning the other cheek," Mason admitted.

"No shit. Don't worry about it. If it happens, it happens. You'll be cleared eventually."

"After they call for my head to be mounted on a pole." Mason rubbed his forehead. Maybe it was time to retire. A quiet little cabin at the coast or up on Mt. Hood. Somewhere there weren't any people.

He'd be bored out of his brain in a month.

"What's Schefte's position?" Mason asked, not certain that he wanted to hear the answer.

"He's walking the line. Doing everything by the book."

"I know that. But what's he saying?"

"Nothing."

"Shit."

"I know. I'd expect him to at least tell people not to jump to conclusions. He's been strangely silent on the whole thing. I tried to ask him about it, and he told me it wasn't any of my business and to get back to work." Ray was angry. "If my partner isn't my business, then what is?"

"Thanks, man." Mason didn't know what to think of Schefte's reaction. Was there someone higher up that was pressuring him? Telling him to keep his mouth shut? "What about IA?" Internal Affairs hadn't approached him yet, but it was inevitable.

"If they're poking around, I haven't heard or seen anything yet."

"They will."

"All they'll find is that you didn't kill anyone. We all know it, Mason."

"Yeah, but why do I have to prove that I didn't do it? That's not how it's supposed to work." He exhaled. "This is sucking the life out of me. I don't know what I'll do if . . ."

"I know."

Ray did know. Ray understood that Mason's life was simple. Work and . . . not much else. And he knew that Mason's integrity meant everything to him. If it was ripped away by the loss of his job, he'd be decimated.

"You need to stay strong for the Fairbankses," Ray said. "I can't imagine the hell they're going through right now."

"It's horrible. They walk around like zombies. The waiting is the worst. The not knowing what's happened to her." Ray was right. His problems didn't compare to losing a child. What would he do if it'd been Jake? And from the sound of the call from Sanford a few minutes ago, Jake may have just missed abduction himself. He told Ray Jake's story of his encounter back at college.

"They think it was the same guy?" Ray asked. "On the other side of the country?"

"They have to consider it. The descriptions are really similar."

"But why Jake? Henley's age indicates that she might have been taken by a pedophile with a taste for young girls. Usually full-grown males aren't compatible with their taste."

"Damn it, Ray." Mason gagged a little. He'd tried to avoid the thought of a pedophile involved in Henley's case. Yes, there was a good chance she'd been snatched by someone like that, and the FBI was still looking hard at known pedophiles in the area.

"Sorry. It's true, though. I don't see how someone asking Jake a question relates to the abduction of an eleven-year-old girl on the opposite coast."

"I know how unlikely it sounds. But you have to take into account that someone stole his suitcase, too. Something seems to be circling around him. The FBI isn't going to ignore it," said Mason. "Someone knows where Jake goes to school and when he was flying home. And this same person may have stolen a minivan and then kidnapped Henley? Someone knows a lot about my family."

"The FBI profilers are going to go nuts with this information," Ray added.

Mason needed Special Agent Euzent to update the profile on their kidnapper. What did it say about their kidnapper if he wanted a college-aged boy *and* a young girl? What kind of person spent time researching the minutia of someone's daily movements?

"This is going to create a bunch of different angles on their opinion of Henley's kidnapper," said Ray. "But what are you going to do? Are you going to fight for your job, or are you going to sit back and let Josie's investigation run its course?"

"There's not a hell of a lot I can do. I maintain my innocence. I give them any evidence they want. And I try not to slit my wrists. I don't know what you mean by fighting back. No, I'm not going to roll over and let them screw me like a drunken whore, but what steps can I take?"

"Get a lawyer," Ray said firmly.

"I don't like lawyers."

"I don't, either. But you need one. If your name turns up in the paper, you need someone to protect your interests."

"What the hell does that mean?" Mason started to steam. "People say that all the time. I don't have interests. I have a life. And it can't be taken away from me. If they charge me with a crime, I'll get a lawyer. But you and I know it won't come to that. It can't, because I never committed the crime."

"We've never arrested innocent people?" Ray asked.

"I haven't. Not on purpose, anyway."

Ray sighed. "I think you're being completely naive about the situation. All I ask is that you look out for yourself, okay?"

"I always do. But frankly, right now, I'm more interested in finding Henley Fairbanks."

"Everybody wants to find Henley. I've had three people ask me about the case during the game I'm watching right now. She's turned into everyone's child. Everybody gives a damn. This may be sad, but it seems to matter more because Christmas is this week."

Mason had forgotten Christmas was in a few days. How could that happen when he'd walked by Robin's tree each morning? Had his mind blanked it out? He looked at his neighbor's home across the street. Lights, deer, and a sleigh. They always went all out with decor for the holidays. He hadn't hung lights since Jake was tiny.

"I gotta get ready for the vigil tonight," Mason said. "I'm going to say a few words for the family. You know, the 'stay strong and please bring her back' type of thing."

"All I want for Christmas," said Ray quietly.

"Yep. That's all everyone wants this year."

17

60 HOURS MISSING

Ava pulled her coat collar up over her nose and mouth to guard against the cold. Next to her, Jake did the same thing and seemed to shrink inside of his bulky coat. For the past thirty minutes, they'd watched the crowd grow in the green space at the riverfront, while organizers handed out candles with small plastic trays to catch the wax drips. Both she and Jake had taken a candle, but Mason had shaken his head. He seemed tense.

Why wouldn't he be? He was about to speak to the press and had discovered a murder weapon had come from his garage. He'd held his cool as he'd told her and Wells the significance of the missing bat. He'd seen the bat at the crime scene but hadn't thought much of it. Thousands of people owned the same type of bat.

"Detached" was a good way to describe him. At his home, he'd pulled out his cell and immediately informed the detective in charge. Listening, Ava had realized he could have been talking about any other case, he seemed so monotone. But this was his life, and he was being sucked deeper and deeper into the murdered prostitute's case.

Ava knew how simple it was to place fingerprints. With the right sticky substance and a clear print to lift, they were easily transferable. And it appeared that someone had done it with Mason's. She hoped the detectives would find something to pull Mason out from under the microscope. He didn't deserve to be falsely accused in the woman's death. Although no one had formally accused him yet. They'd placed him on administrative leave pending further investigation. It didn't mean they thought he'd done it; they were simply following procedure.

Mason knew that and expected no less of his employer. That didn't mean he had to enjoy the process.

ASAC Ben Duncan gestured for Mason to join him and three other agents closer to the platform, which held a single microphone on a stand for the press conference. Jake slapped his dad on his back, and Ava realized she'd never seen a physical sign of affection between them. Mason glanced back at his son and nodded, and Ava figured that the slap and nod had a deep meaning between the two of them. She gave Jake a smile and looked past him to Robin, Lucas, and Lilian. Lilian had brought a close girlfriend for support, and the two women stood with their arms linked, speaking in hushed voices.

The vigil organizers had put up a small table with coffee and a second table was draped with a huge banner. COME HOME, HENLEY, it read in large letters. Attendees took turns signing the banner with short messages of hope. Moms from Henley's school hugged parents and other kids. Tears shone on most of the faces. A small stream of people stopped to talk to the three parents, and Ava and two other agents carefully watched the strangers. They'd given the three parents a hand signal to flash if they were approached by someone they didn't recognize. So far, they'd known every adult who'd stopped by and wished for Henley's safe return.

It was a tight community.

The contact with the public was good for Robin. Her chin was up, and she engaged each adult who stopped to speak to her or offer a hug. She seemed to absorb strength from the well-wishers. Lilian was the opposite. She shrunk back and relied on her friend to greet the attendees. She looked like she wanted to vanish. Ava noticed Lilian would shift her position to keep Lucas in her sight, and she frequently glanced his way. Ava's suspicions about the woman's feelings for her ex-husband grew stronger.

Don't bother, Lilian. Anyone can see his commitment to Robin.

Maybe Lilian was simply missing what they'd once had. Robin and Lucas were lovely together. They frequently touched and exchanged glances. Ava would kill for a relationship like that.

ASAC Ben Duncan stepped up to the microphone. The platform stood across the grassy clearing from the banner and coffee. The local press had set up their cameras to get a good view of the platform and the crowd. CNN and Fox News had joined the local stations. Ava sighed at all the cameras, but any publicity about Henley could be helpful. It was national press that'd speedily spread the word when a sixteen-year-old was kidnapped in California, and it'd led to her being recognized in Idaho by strangers. The FBI's hostage-rescue team had tracked down the kidnapper and rescued the girl.

Ava prayed for the same successful ending for Henley.

"Excuse me, folks," came Duncan's voice over the microphone. The crowd immediately quieted and turned his way, their candles glimmering in the dim light. "We're going to take a few minutes to update you on Henley's case. Then we'll take a *few* questions." He emphasized the word "few," eyeballing the reporters. Duncan was a natural in front of the press. He commanded their respect, and they gave it to him.

"Last night we arrested someone unrelated to Henley's disappearance. This person staged a fake ransom note for his own gains, and it took vital resources away from the search for Henley." Duncan glared at the crowd. "Henley doesn't have time for us to be distracted by fools. We want solid leads, not someone's made-up story. We've regrouped and moved on, following up on every lead that's come into our command center. I ask you to be vigilant and keep an eye out for this little girl. We just need the right tip from an alert member of the community to find her.

"This is Mason Callahan, the spokesman for the Fairbanks family." Duncan stepped back and gestured Mason forward. Mason removed his hat and made eye contact with several people in the audience. Ava tensed, aching for him to do well for the family.

"I'm here because tragedy has struck some good people," Mason began. His voice was clear and low, his folksy way of speaking instantly capturing the audience. "An evil has touched our community and ripped holes in the hearts of everyone here. Henley Fairbanks is everyone's child. Your sons and daughters may be safe at your side, but until we bring Henley home, no one will be at peace. Her special light is missing."

He paused and looked down at his boots. Ava heard sniffling around her and realized she also had tears. Mason looked up and met her gaze. His face blurred behind her tears.

"Lilian, Lucas, and Robin appreciate your presence and your prayers for their daughter's safe return. No parent deserves to go through what they've experienced over the last few days. And no child should ever be yanked from the safety of their parents' arms." Anger infused his tone, and the crowd hung on every word.

He's a natural.

"I'll repeat what Ben Duncan said. Be vigilant. Study the faces of the children you come in contact with. Henley's face should be burned in your memory. One of you will see something that will lead the authorities to her. And we can't ask for a better force to be searching for Henley. The rapid response of the Clackamas County Sheriff's Office, the City of Lake Oswego Police Department, and the FBI has been unparalleled. These heroes were on the scene immediately and have been working night and day to find Henley. When a cop hears a child is missing, it doesn't matter who he works for—he responds with 110 percent. And that is what the Fairbanks family has experienced. We'll be forever grateful."

Mason took one last, sweeping look at the crowd and stepped back, putting his hat back on. Duncan gestured at Sanford, who stepped up to the microphone. Mason stepped off the platform and maneuvered his way through the crowd toward Ava and the family.

"I'm Special Agent Sanford with the FBI, and I'll be answering a few questions," Sanford stated in a clear voice. The emotional words were over, and Sanford changed the tone of the crowd back to the business at hand. Ava tuned him out as Mason approached.

He gave her a questioning look, and she nodded at him, barely able to form words. "You did good," she whispered.

"Nice job, Dad," said Jake. He gave his dad a long hug, and Ava's eyes watered at the love on Mason's face. He clung to his son. "You had the whole crowd in tears."

"Thank you, Mason," said Robin. She stepped forward and gave him a quick kiss on the cheek. Mason watched her move back to her husband, who threw an arm around her and Jake in a family hug. Ava felt a pang in her stomach at the hungry look in Mason's eye as he gazed at the threesome.

He misses having a family.

At first she'd thought he was watching his ex-wife, but he was focused on Jake and Lucas and their closeness. He looked away at the few boats that dotted the Willamette River behind them. Without thinking, Ava touched his arm. He looked her way with eyes that belonged to a battered animal. He was ripped up inside. His job, his kid, Henley. What else was life going to pound him with?

Ava tried to smile but faltered. For a brief second, he'd hung it all out, showing a deeply suffering side of himself that no one ever saw. He patted her hand on his arm, and his emotions vanished. He was back in cop mode. Protective mode.

For a moment, she'd seen his true self.

Her heart cracked at his pain.

Under that by-the-book, tough cowboy was a gentleman with a big heart.

Sanford's voice penetrated her focus, and Ava glanced back at him. The agent was droning on, responding to the press questions with answers that said a lot of nothing new. They'd agreed not to share Jake's encounter with the man at his college's campus. Sanford held up a big photo of the type of minivan they were still searching for, along with its license-plate number.

It was still their best lead.

Ava's personal phone buzzed. *Legacy Emanuel Hospital* flashed on her screen. Curious, she stepped away from the family and answered.

"Is this Ava McLane?" came an unfamiliar woman's voice.

"Yes, it is."

"I'm calling from Emanuel Hospital's ER. Your sister Jayne McLane is here and has been involved in a car accident. She requested you be contacted and informed of her condition."

"What? Is she okay? What happened?" Ava's heart stopped.

"She's been in a car accident, ma'am," the woman repeated. "She's conscious and on her way to Radiology. She's banged up. Some possible broken bones and a concussion. We'll know more soon."

"How did it happen? Who was driving?" If Jayne had been riding with some drunk boyfriend, Ava would strangle her.

"I don't know, ma'am. Let me see if the officer who came in with her is still here."

The police accompanied her?

Ava waited and paced in a small circle. Mason looked at her questioningly, but Ava forced a smile and shook her head at him. A male voice spoke. "This is Officer Suarez. Is this Jayne McLane's sister, Ava McLane?"

"Yes. What happened?"

"Your sister plowed through a red light on Tenth Avenue downtown and hit another car. She's lucky the other people weren't injured."

"She was driving?" Ava squeaked.

"Yes, ma'am."

"Was anyone else in her car?"

"There was a male passenger. He seems fine. He's getting checked out, too."

Ava sighed. This was why she didn't loan Jayne her car. Hopefully, the man had good insurance.

"I'm sorry, but your sister will be arrested for driving with a suspended license once the hospital releases her."

"Are you kidding me? Her license was suspended? I had no idea." Could Jayne mess things up any worse?

"Yes, for a previous DUI."

Ava closed her eyes. Alcohol. Of course. "Was she drunk this time, too?"

"We've requested a blood alcohol test. She was in no condition to do a Breathalyzer at the scene."

"Do you think she was drunk?" Ava pushed.

Suarez paused. "I could smell alcohol on her breath, which was why I ordered the test. We won't know until we get the lab results back."

Definitely drunk. Jayne, what have you gotten into? Ava wanted to scream at her sister. And shake her. Shake some sense into her.

"The vehicle will be at the police lot. You can call to find out when it will be released," Suarez stated.

Ava blinked. A sense of dread creeping up her spine. "I don't want to deal with the car. Doesn't the car belong to the passenger?"

"Uh . . . no. The car's registration says Ava McLane. That's you, right? Do you own a black Honda Accord?"

Yes, she did.

· · ·

At the vigil, Mason had watched Ava get a phone call and nearly blow her stack at the caller. She'd been polite, but Mason was glad the person on the other end couldn't see her body language and facial expressions. It'd been enough to make him blink and listen closely. A minute later, she asked him to drive her to the hospital, because she was concerned she'd cause an accident.

Mason followed her as she stopped to check in with ASAC Ben Duncan. "My sister's been in a car wreck and is in the hospital. I need to be there," she told him with no preface.

Duncan nodded. "I'll have extra men at the Fairbankses' all night in case the press conference stirred some things up. Take as long as you need, and check in with me later."

Once they were in Mason's car, Ava explained that her twin had stolen her car and wrecked it.

"How'd she get the car?" Mason asked as he maneuvered his vehicle through the quiet downtown Portland streets.

"I have a hunch." Ava dug through her purse. "My Honda keys are missing. Damn her! She spilled my purse when I dropped her off earlier today, and she must have grabbed them then."

Mason was stunned. "She stole your keys?" *Her twin stole from her? What kind of relationship did they have?*

Ava leaned her head against her window and covered her face with one hand. "I'm going to kill her. I don't care how injured she is. This is the last time I let her do this to me."

"The last time? She's done it before?"

"Not exactly." Ava sighed. "Last time she broke my television and the microwave when I let her stay with me. I had to make a personal rule that I wouldn't let her sleep under my roof ever again. Or even come for a visit. I go out of my way to meet her somewhere else if she wants to get together."

"I don't understand," Mason said slowly. "What's wrong with her?"

Ava was quiet. "It's complicated," she finally said.

"I can see that." *Should he press the issue?* He wasn't one to pry, but twice he'd seen Ava rattled by her sister's actions. He bit his lip, overwhelmed by his desire to know what was going on in the FBI agent's life. She'd been exposed to the nastiness that'd enveloped him in the last few days. Now it was his turn for a peek at what was upsetting the usually calm and cool agent.

Ava turned to him. "Have you ever loved someone, and the existence of that emotion was completely out of your control? Someone who knows you inside and out? Someone who is closer to you than anyone else in the world? That deep-down soul connection where you physically feel them moving about in the world?"

She paused, and he felt her staring at his profile. He was scared to look directly at her. It might make her stop talking.

But had he? "No. Not even in my marriage," he answered honestly. "The person who knows me best is my partner, Ray. But even he doesn't know everything."

She nodded and slumped back in her seat. "You can't understand unless you have a twin. There's no other bond like it. We shared everything. Growing up, she took what was mine just like I helped myself to what was hers. There was no division of anything between us. But as an adult, there have to be boundaries. I learned about those boundaries when I went to college. Jayne never did. She operates as if we're still twelve."

"So your car is her car, and she believes there is nothing wrong with that," Mason guessed.

"Exactly. In her eyes, I'm being selfish by keeping my car from her when she believes that half of it is hers."

"Even though you paid for it. She doesn't understand that?"

"No," said Ava. "She can't assign a value to something that she never paid for. She's horrible with money. She's never saved a dime in her life and flits from job to job and man to man. She operates like the world owes her everything."

"And you owe her whatever you've worked your butt off for," Mason said. A picture of her twin had started to form in his mind. A narcissist. A woman who believed the world should rotate around her. He'd met women like that, maybe even dated a few. How would it be to grow up with one of those women as your sister? Your *twin* sister?

"Then there are the addictions. She's been arrested for meth use and selling oxy. I can't count the number of times she's been picked up for drunk and disorderly. Not only is she drunk a lot, she's a mean drunk. She's been in and out of every rehab program there is. I paid for two of them and then said no more. But every six months she approaches me with a new one. 'I know it will work this time,' she claims. But how can they work when she puts no effort into them? As soon as she walks out the door, she's back to her old ways."

"That has to be hard on you," Mason answered.

"It rips me to pieces," she said in a soft voice. "She's part of me. She *is* me. When I see her like that, it shows who I'd be if I'd made different decisions in my life. It's only by the grace of God that I'm not the one in the hospital this minute."

"That's not true," asserted Mason. "You don't have a narcissistic bone in your body. You two might share identical DNA, but somehow it operates differently in you. You are nowhere near the person your sister sounds like."

"But I am!" Ava cried. "I want it all! I want my life to be a fucking piece of cake. I wish I could curl up in bed all day feeling high as a kite and let the world go on around me. Do you know how great that sounds? I wish I had a Mercedes like my neighbor. I feel a stab of envy every time he drives by. I understand how she feels!"

"So do you walk into his house and steal his keys?" Mason snapped. "Hell, no! That's what's different about you. That's what separates you from your twin. You have morals and standards. Everybody wishes they could escape from their shitty life sometimes, but they don't do it. They get up and go to work and act like decent human beings."

"But some days I feel so close to that line," Ava said. "What happens on the day I finally trip and take the plunge?"

"You're being too hard on yourself. Think about a little kid. What kid doesn't want to grab that candy bar from the grocery shelf when their mom isn't looking? Some of them actually do it. But you know what? They learn it's wrong. They learn to control their impulses. But a few people never learn. They're the reason we have a job. It sounds like your twin is still a little kid who can't control her impulses."

Ava was quiet for a moment. "Jayne used to steal from stores. She'd make me feel guilty because I wouldn't do the same. I even lied to cover for her."

"Hell, I stole some shit when I was a kid. My dad beat me over the head, and I never did it again. A lot of kids are tempted. It's a normal life lesson to learn. The problem happens when someone doesn't learn. Something in their brain keeps them from understanding right from wrong."

"I enabled her," Ava said. "I should have let her get punished. I covered for her all the time. When she didn't do her homework or when she snuck out with boys. I shouldn't have done all that. Maybe she'd be a different person."

"You can't tell me your sister is in the hospital because you covered for her behavior in high school." Mason stopped at a traffic light and looked at Ava. "She stole and wrecked your car. There's no excuse, and I'm not going to let you make one for her. None of what happened today or anytime in her life is your fault. She's done this to herself." He stepped on the accelerator, watching Ava out of the corner of his eye. "You have every right to be pissed as hell."

"Oh, I am. That's why you're driving. I didn't want to hurt anyone. I can barely see straight."

"Good. Hang on to that feeling when you confront her."

"I don't know what to say to her. I don't know how badly hurt she is."

"It doesn't matter how hurt she is. Get mad at her for hurting herself! She could have killed someone. Her injuries shouldn't affect what you have to tell her."

"Argh!" Ava thumped a fist on the car door. "She's so infuriating. It's always been like this, and that's why I stay away from her."

"So why did you move to Portland? You said she was here first."

"I thought it would be different. I thought she'd finally grown up. We'd been in different states for several years and our mother had passed, so I thought it was time to be sisters again. I wasn't here for a week before I realized I was wrong. I've tried to talk to her about how she acts. She says I'm full of it."

"Truth always sounds like lies to a sinner."

"That's exactly how she responds. Like I'm lying to her and making things up. I can't believe I've allowed her to do this to me again."

Mason snorted. "Agent McLane, you'll be lucky if this is the worst thing you ever have happen to you." He pulled into a parking space at Emanuel Hospital. Ava leaped out of the vehicle and strode toward the Emergency Room entrance. Mason jogged to catch up with her, and then hung back as she checked in with the desk.

His phone rang. Jake.

"Hey, son. What's up?"

"Is it okay if I go over to McKenzie's for a little bit? She couldn't make it to the vigil and wants to hear about it."

Mason scowled. "Did you ask your mom?"

"Yeah."

He waited. "And?"

"She said no."

"So why are you asking me?" Mason shook his head. Had Jake already forgotten that he might have been face-to-face with Henley's abductor?

"I haven't gotten to see her hardly at all. And it's almost Christmas."

"Jake. Do you remember your conversation with the FBI today? *No one* is going anywhere without an agent or a cop with them. Agent McLane is busy this evening, and I don't think it's wise to ask one of the Clackamas County deputies to go with you so you can visit with some girl. Got it?"

"She's not just *some girl*. I like her—a lot—and this is totally unfair."

Mason was speechless. But only for two seconds. "What the hell is unfair? That you're not allowed to wander the streets while there's a kidnapper possibly targeting your family? That part is unfair?" Anger infused his voice. *What was the kid thinking?*

Jake wasn't thinking. His hormones were.

"Whatever."

"Listen. I get that you like this girl. But that needs to be put on hold. Go play your Xbox or watch a movie. You are not to leave that house tonight. Your mom told you not to, and I'm standing with her. Get over it."

Jake mumbled something that sounded like good-bye and clicked off.

Mason blew out a breath, sliding his phone back into his pocket. *Boys.* Jake was thinking with another part of his anatomy, and his parents' refusals were making him grumpy. And stupid.

Mason glanced around at the waiting room and was surprised at the size of the crowd for eight o'clock at night. It was packed. A TV droned on, set to CNN. A second TV showed kids' cartoons, but the sound was off. The four kids watching didn't seem to mind that they couldn't hear the show.

Ava gestured for him to follow her and a woman in scrubs. They moved down a hall that widened into a larger room with a dozen curtained-off beds. Feet were visible under the curtains around the beds. Some in scrubs and hospital clogs or white sneakers. Visitors obvious in their jeans and street shoes.

"They're waiting for a bed in the hospital," Ava said to him in a low voice. "The cops left because they're keeping her overnight for observation for a bad concussion. Tomorrow, she has to report downtown to be processed for her arrest." Her voice shook as she ended her sentence.

The nurse stopped at a curtained bed. "Jayne? You've got some visitors." She smiled brightly at Ava and Mason as she whipped back the curtain.

So that's Jayne McLane. The woman with closed eyes lying in the bed didn't look anything like Ava. Her hair was a bright blonde, and she seemed paler and bonier. She had a dozen lacerations down the left side of her face and a large bandage on her forehead. Her left wrist and hand were bandaged. Her eyes opened, and the resemblance punched Mason in the stomach. Ava's eyes stared out of the other woman's face.

"Ava!" Jayne sniffed and rubbed her nose with her forearm, avoiding her bandages. "I was so scared. I can't believe this happened!"

Ava stood at the foot of the bed, staring at her sister, her face unreadable.

Jayne held out her good hand for her sister to take. Ava didn't move. Jayne glanced at Mason and back to her stiff sister, her gaze confused. She let her arm drop.

"How badly are you hurt?" Ava asked.

"Well," Jayne gestured at her head. "I think you can see most of it. I sprained my hand on the steering wheel, and they say I have a bad concussion. I don't hurt too bad right now."

Her glassy eyes told Mason she was enjoying some potent painkillers.

"Were you drunk?" Ava asked.

Jayne looked away. "Not really. I'm sure my test will come back—"

"How much did you drink?" Ava's words sliced through the air.

"I don't know!" Jayne yelled back. "I can't remember." She gritted her teeth as she stared at her twin.

Mason took a half step backward. The tension around the bed was stifling. If Jayne was expecting some sympathy from her twin, it wasn't coming.

"You stole my keys out of my purse this morning."

Jayne jerked her head like she'd been slapped. "No, I didn't."

"Then how did you *wreck my car*?"

Jayne burst into tears. "Jesus Christ, Ava! You don't have to yell at me. I'm hurt! I have a concussion and have to stay in the hospital."

"You. Stole. My. Car."

Jayne sniffed. "You have no sympathy for me at all. How can you be such a bitch at a time like this? I mean, the car is insured, right?"

Mason blinked. *Ava hadn't been exaggerating.*

"You stole my car. You drove it drunk. You wrecked it, and you hit another car. You're lucky you didn't kill someone! You're probably going to jail for drunk driving. And if I feel like it, you'll be charged with stealing my Honda, too!" Ava clenched her hands into fists, and Mason rocked onto his toes in case he had to stop her from taking a swing at her sister.

"You're so mean to me! You've always hated me!"

Jayne is nuts. How does Ava put up with it?

Ava closed her eyes, and Mason imagined he could hear her counting to ten.

"You're going to survive," said Ava calmly. "But you've interfered in my life enough this decade. Don't call me." She turned around and walked away.

Jayne sat upright in her bed. "Ava! Wait! I need someone to give me a ride home tomorrow."

"Ask your boyfriend," Ava tossed over her shoulder as she departed.

Jayne gasped and turned to stare at Mason. "Who are you?"

"A friend of your twin."

"Are you dating her? She only pretends to be nice at first. Deep down she has a lot of issues, especially when it comes to men. You should be careful around her," Jayne said with a straight face, blue eyes full of innocence.

"Thanks for the advice," said Mason, touching the brim of his hat. "Good luck to you, ma'am. I hope your cellmate doesn't have irritable bowel syndrome."

He followed Ava's footsteps.

18

62 HOURS MISSING

Ava strode blindly out of the hospital, brushing the tears on her face. Her twin had looked like a battered doll, and Ava had been cruel to her. Jayne was being kept overnight in the hospital, and all Ava cared about was that she'd wrecked her car, and then told her to never call again.

Which twin was the selfish one?

She yanked on the door handle of Mason's vehicle. Locked. As she'd known it would be. He was the predictable type who always locked his doors. She laid her forehead on the cool metal of the car and blinked away her tears. Predictability was something she could use a big dose of right now. She was exhausted from having the rug ripped out from under her.

It left her silently bleeding inside, where no one could see.

The car doors clicked as Mason hit his remote. Ava didn't move.

"Hey." He cleared his throat. "Your twin is a real piece of work."

Ava lifted her head, wiped her nose, and nodded. "You saw a good example tonight. Did you notice how she didn't admit she stole my car? And never apologized for wrecking it? In her mind, it was her right. She believes she doesn't need to apologize to me for anything." She leaned against the car, shaking her head.

"Would an apology have helped?" His voice was low and gentle as he leaned an arm on the car's roof, by her shoulder.

Ava thought about it. "I don't know. I guess I wouldn't believe she meant it, so it wouldn't have helped at all. I simply want to hear her say the words, because I don't believe she's capable of it." She looked at him; his brown eyes weren't visible under the brim of his hat in the dim hospital parking lot. "Did she say something to you after I left?"

His mouth twitched into a half smile. "Yeah, she was concerned for my well-being if I continued to hang around with you."

Ava wished she was surprised. "She tries to destroy any friendships I have."

Mason nodded. "She told me you have issues. Especially with men."

"Oh Lord." She cringed.

"She asked if we were dating."

Ava felt her cheeks darken and was thankful for the poor light. "In the past, she'd get my boyfriends alone and tell them horrible lies about me. Then she'd hit on them. It's pretty surprising how many fell for it. I know of three who cheated on me with her."

"That's sick."

"If you'd stayed any longer, I'm sure she would have flirted with you. Even when she's drunk and high on pain meds, she can come on pretty strong."

Mason leaned closer, and his eyes became visible. Ava's pulse pounded in her ears as she met his gaze. *He's not thinking of my twin.* His concentration was on her. Every bit of focus and determination she'd seen in the man over the last three days was laser beamed directly at her. She caught her breath.

"What would you do if I kissed you right now, Special Agent McLane?" he drawled.

Playing up his cowboy side did odd things to Ava's stomach.

"Why would you want—"

His mouth cut her off.

All anguish and emotion about Jayne evaporated. The only thought in her head was that Mason Callahan knew damn well how to kiss a woman. Warm lips pressed hers, urging her mouth open, and she complied. He caged her against the car. One hand slid up her neck into her hair and took a firm hold of the back of her skull, holding her where he wanted her. He didn't keep anything back, pressing his chest against hers.

His kiss was demanding; he wasn't asking permission for the intrusion. Ava welcomed the distraction and mentally sank into the pleasure that he offered. Sensations of silk and heavenly friction danced through her mouth. A headiness enveloped her, rushing from the touch of his lips and shooting through every nerve fiber until she was dizzy.

He was cowboy through and through, from his hat to his boots to his manners to his ethics.

She'd never kissed a cowboy before.

And this wouldn't be her last time.

Mason pulled back a fraction. "I'm not interested in your twin, Special Agent McLane. I've been interested in you from the first moment I saw you."

Ava couldn't think.

Inches away, he held her gaze and his eyes crinkled. "I take it you don't have an objection."

"We work together, detective," she forced out. She didn't know where the thought came from, but if he wanted an objection, she'd come up with one.

"That's the best you can do?"

She sputtered.

"I thought so." He kissed her again and ran a slow finger down her cheek, lighting her up like a fire. His touch rocketed pathways through her limbs, and she felt like she'd taken a megadose of speed.

How'd he do that?

She wanted to get lost in him, forget that her sister had turned her life upside down, and that a family she cared about was missing their little girl. She'd been going nonstop for three days, worrying about Henley and her family. Ava needed to catch her breath and recharge. Mason Callahan fit the bill.

"Can I take you home, Ava?"

"Yes," she breathed.

She didn't ask whose home. They were both on the same page.

• • •

The crowd had nearly melted away. He stepped out from his hiding spot across the street. He'd hung back during the vigil, afraid of cameras and police recordings. All the police cars and news cameras were gone. A few people scurried about and picked up the garbage that'd been left behind. It had to be pretty safe by now. He took a hard look at each person in sight.

The FBI agents were so easy to spot. They were constantly looking every which way, scanning every person around them. They didn't listen to the people on the small stage; they were too busy looking for a criminal.

They should have been looking straight ahead.

He strolled across the street and into the grass, feeling a need to interact with the people who'd come to support Henley. "Do you need a hand?" he asked the three women folding up the banner.

They smiled at him but turned him down. "This is the last of it, and we've got it. Thank you for showing your support for the family tonight," one woman said. Her two helpers nodded in agreement.

False words.

The women acted out of fear. They'd thrown the vigil together in the desperate hope that their own children wouldn't be touched. Karma said that if they helped others in their darkest times, then evil wouldn't cross their own doorstep.

He believed firmly in Karma. But he'd been waiting two decades for it to take its course. Now he'd waited long enough, and it was time to give it a hand. Small steps. Careful steps. His plan was coming together. He'd seen the pain on the faces of the family tonight, and it'd felt like cool ice on a burn. It'd eased the hole in his heart. The hole could never be repaired; he'd accepted that fact after years of alcohol and the loss of his family, job, and self-worth.

He'd had to fall to the bottom before he could pick himself up. In his misery, he'd torn down the innocent people around him. Twice. Thankfully, they'd rebounded. He cared about the people in his life and hadn't meant to hurt them. His first wife had moved on after trying to pull him out of his soul-deep depression for three years. His second wife had caught the brunt of his anger from his losses in life. She'd stuck it out for two years, believing she could heal him. But she'd eventually left, too.

It'd taken his wife and son abandoning him to open his eyes. The boy wasn't his. When he'd met his second wife, part of her appeal had been her son. He'd believed that having a child to nurture would be good for him, but it'd been the opposite. He'd resented the boy and resented the mother for their close relationship. He'd never bonded with the child.

After they'd left, he began his search for healing. He'd examined his life and his past and had clearly seen where he'd lost the balance. He'd made the corrections.

Now he walked along the Willamette River, leaving the sounds of the vigil cleanup behind him. The musty, wet scent of the river filled his nose. The river had a beautiful park on its west side, lit by the tall buildings of the city, and people strolled the long walk in spite of the cold night air.

Christmas was coming. People flocked to the city to get in the holiday mood. Stores put up decor and lights. Even the Morrison Bridge was lit up with green and red. If he hadn't spied on the vigil for the missing girl, he would have sworn all was in balance with the world.

But it wasn't. He'd waited a long time to set things to rights. His pain and loss had to be atoned for; the person who'd created his pain had to suffer the same. Then he could be at ease. He'd be able to breathe again. His life wouldn't have the gray shadow that had consistently hung over him, reminding him that the guilty one hadn't paid. His nightmares would ease.

He'd been the one who'd done all the paying. *He'd* been the one to have his life ripped away.

Soon.

He breathed faster. He was so close to that blessed peace he'd sought for so many years.

He hadn't been driving the minivan. He'd used it only that once, and it'd been hidden away since Friday morning. He'd been surprised to see the AMBER Alert on the news. That had happened a bit faster than he'd expected.

Where had they gotten the license-plate number? How had they connected the stolen van with Henley Fairbanks? He smiled to think of all the minivans that'd been pulled over with the hopes of finding a small blonde child in the back. Let the police waste their resources. The van had served its purpose. By the time they found it, they'd realize their focus had been misdirected from day one.

His plan hadn't gone completely as expected, but he'd managed nicely when curveballs had been thrown his way. It was important to keep his options open. He hadn't given up on his primary goal; it was still possible.

He'd kept a careful eye on the girl's family tonight. They'd stuck together in a small group, never letting one another out of their sight. It was heartwarming to see their pain. It'd been worth every step so far. They were an odd blend of a family. Two fathers, two mothers. The other child. Everyone seemed to get along; they hadn't turned on one another like he'd hoped.

They had to have their suspicions. When would they start to act out against one another? When would the inner dismantling begin?

He thought about the paper bag sitting in the trunk of his car.

It was time for the next phase.

19

Mason drove straight to his house. Ava was silent in the car. She didn't comment as he took the freeway exit for his home instead of the Fairbankses'. When was the last time he'd taken a woman back to his place?

It didn't matter. What mattered was how he handled this woman. Standing by his car, he'd been overwhelmed with the need to touch her. Not to comfort her, but to connect physically and emotionally. It'd been brewing under his surface since he'd first seen her. Perhaps the frankness of the emotions at the vigil had made it erupt. He'd known he'd never sleep tonight unless he acted on the small but intense fire that'd slowly built in his chest.

He'd done the right thing.

Ava had melted into his touch and fanned that fire.

Ava McLane was different.

She had the brains and dedication needed to succeed in her job. And she had the heart and compassion to do it well. An investigator who gave a damn about people.

He understood her. And wanted to know everything about her.

This wasn't about a physical desire that just needed to be scratched. This was more.

What kind of burden was her twin? He'd known people who'd have strangled a family member like that, twin or not. Ava had looked pretty close to giving him permission to shoot her sister.

Jayne was mentally ill. Addiction had enhanced her problems. He'd arrested dozens of people just like her, and it made him want to protect Ava from the pain her sister created. A part of him would always be a protector; it was what had driven him to become a cop. Ava wasn't the type to need protection, but damn it, she brought it out of him.

He stopped at his house, they got out of the car, and he followed her up to the front porch. Unlocking the front door, he glanced at the still-full dish of dog food. The sight of it stung.

Ava moved the dish with her foot, checking to see if anything else had been placed underneath. Nothing. She gave him a sad smile. "I'm sorry," she whispered in that low, utterly sexy voice of hers, meeting his gaze.

Her voice had snagged him from the start. It was like a warm bath. He'd dipped a foot in and discovered the ideal temperature. Now he wanted to sink his entire body into it. He pushed open the door and stepped back. She moved past him, her shoulder brushing his chest. She smelled of candle smoke and outdoors from their time at the vigil. Cold breezes and fresh river.

His kind of scents. Natural, not bottled and sold in a store.

Special Agent McLane ticked a lot of his boxes. Boxes he'd never known existed. And right now, he wanted to see what kind of flames they could create together.

He closed the door behind them and grabbed her hand, leading her to his bedroom. She followed.

• • •

Her brain was in the off position.

She liked it that way. It kept her from thinking about Jayne and Henley and let her focus on the man in front of her. Detective Callahan fascinated her. He'd won her respect and slowly worked his way under her skin until she'd wondered what would happen if they touched. It'd been the right move on his part. His hand on her face and his mouth on hers had set her brain ablaze.

She wanted more. She wanted to get lost in this man's touch and forget every responsibility.

Tomorrow would be here too soon, and she'd return to her badge and standing strong for everyone around her. Tonight, she didn't want to be strong.

Without a pause, Mason tossed his hat on a table in the hall. His strong grip on her hand spoke of what was to come. He was in charge. His home, his rules.

She was good with that.

They stepped into his bedroom, and he pulled her to him before she could study her surroundings. His hands clasped the sides of her face as his mouth took control of hers. Ava slid her hands under his coat, feeling the heat of his chest through his shirt. He was solid. He had the body of a man who moved, not one who sat behind a desk. His mouth told her he needed a heavy amount of physical touch. Their second kiss was as deep and commanding as their first had been, outside the hospital.

She leaned into his palms, needing the pressure to relieve the ache that had slowly built since his lips first touched hers. Pleasant lights danced on the backs of her eyelids, and she melted at the feel of the heat that curled in her belly. His mouth still on her, Mason pushed her coat off and let it drop to the floor as she copied the movement with his jacket. He kicked them to the side and started unbuttoning her blouse.

Ava came up for air and took over the task as his fingers fumbled on the miniscule buttons. He stepped back and sat on the bed, his gaze holding hers. He kicked off his boots and sat frozen, watching the movement of her fingers. She paused on a lower button, and his gaze flew back to her eyes. Anticipation enlarged his pupils. The light in the room was dim, but she could see his face.

Hungry. Eager. Ready.

"Hurry up," he whispered.

"In a hurry?" she asked, taking her time with the last button.

"Only for the first round. Then I plan to take my time."

Fire flashed up her spine. His voice was throaty and full of want. She threw her blouse and bra on top of her coat on the floor and added her pants to the pile two seconds later. He reached for her and pulled her onto his lap facing him so that her legs straddled his thighs. Her inner heat pressed against the bulge in his jeans. She wrapped her arms around his neck and stared into his dark eyes. He smelled good. The hints of fresh air and coffee and male skin drifted into her brain and sparked her happy neurons. He smiled, and she felt the thoughts of the last twenty-four hours melt away.

She and the detective had some energy burning to do together.

• • •

Mason couldn't stop touching the skin of her back as she sat on his lap, her face inches from his. Ava was smooth and silky, her breath warm on his cheeks and lips. She looked ready to meet him all the way. This was no one-sided encounter. This was full-steam-ahead, how-hard-can-we-shake-the-bed sex coming up.

He kissed her again, wondering how he'd held back for the last twenty seconds, and he heard her moan softly in the back of her throat. The sound sent a blast to his groin. *What would she sound like later?* She scooted closer and ground against him, her lace panties against his denim.

There was too much fabric between them.

She started working on his shirt, apparently having the same thought. She bared his chest, shoving the shirt over his shoulders, and ran the backs of her nails over his skin, softly scratching until he thought he'd die from the sensation.

His groin ached, needing release. Deft fingers worked his belt, snap, and zipper. Her gentle fingers found him, and her touch made him want to explode. Immediately. He traced down her skin until he found her lace panties. He couldn't remove them with her legs straddling him, but he didn't want to lose the touch of her heat so close to his need.

He ran two fingers over her lace-covered crotch and she sighed into his mouth.

He pushed the lace aside and explored.

Wet.

Silky.

Needing.

He was still in her hand. She worked her fingers up and down his shaft and around the ridge of his head. Drips of wet made her fingers slide and the sensation quadruple. He still wore his jeans and shirt while her body was nearly bare, covered only with thin wisps of lace. Her thighs tensed and she lifted herself up and closer to his groin. Abruptly, she stopped and pulled back from his mouth.

"Do you have a condom?" she whispered, fear in her voice.

Mason tensed. *How had he not considered protection?*

"Yes, don't move." He fell backward and stretched to reach his nightstand drawer, pulling the two of them further onto the bed. Blindly, he dug around in the drawer until he touched a packet. He ripped it open and covered himself within seconds.

Ava pressed her mouth against him. "Thank you," she whispered against his lips, running her hands over his hard member.

Mason kissed her back, exploring her mouth, tasting her, and keeping his desire in check for the moment. He wanted to feel her hands on him forever. She lifted herself up with her legs, guiding him to her entrance that he'd exposed moments before.

Her heat surrounded his head, and lights shimmered in his brain. She lowered herself onto him the slightest bit. Teasing? Taking her time? He didn't care. She was prolonging his release, and the pain of it was the best pain in the world. She lifted slightly and lowered a little further, easing him into her. Mason sank his hands in her hair and kissed her lips, her cheeks, her ears, and her neck. He wanted to devour all of her. Now.

Her thighs tensed, she lifted, and she sank again.

He was buried. She shuddered, and he felt her gently quiver inside.

Mason lifted his head from her neck, looking up at the face in front of him. Ava's lips were open, her breath short, and her eyes closed.

She was gorgeous.

He grabbed her thighs and pressed her down as he ground up and into her. Her eyes flew open, and she gasped. He did it again, loving the hoarse sounds she made.

He needed deeper.

He pulled her to him and spun her over on her back.

Her sounds made explosions dance up his spinal cord. Her gaze met his, and she wrapped her arms around his neck, pulling his face close to her.

She whispered in his ear. "Don't hold back."

Mason didn't.

• • •

Ava relaxed, enjoying the heat of a solid man at her back. She felt sore, well used, and giddy. The usual effects of sex. Mason hadn't surprised her. She'd had a hunch there was a lot of hidden passion and emotion under that calm exterior. And she'd been right. He saved it for special occasions, and this had been one of those occasions.

What a night. The vigil. Jayne's accident. And now this. At least her night had ended on a good note. After her fight with Jayne, she could have easily gone home and cried herself to sleep.

Mason's hand slid up her arm. "You're thinking really loud."

Ava laughed. "I was. Sorry about that."

"Jayne?"

She sighed. "Yes. I think tonight was a new low for both of us."

"I don't think I've ever met anyone like her. And I've seen a lot."

"I don't know how to help her anymore."

"You've done more than any sister should. Until she sees that she needs to change, all of your help goes to waste."

Ava rolled onto her back and stared straight up. A neighbor's light at the back of the house cast shadows across the ceiling. "I always feel like I've failed her and myself. Sometimes . . ." She couldn't finish her thought.

"Sometimes what?" Mason asked, his voice soft as if he knew what she wanted to say.

"Sometimes I've wished she was dead."

Mason lay silently beside her. His hand found hers, and she wanted to cry.

"Everyone wishes that at some point in their life. Especially when the other person has created nothing but heartache. And I don't think you wish she was dead. You wish she would simply vanish. No pain. No loss. Just gone."

"Yes." That was her feeling. Exactly.

"You want the sorrow she creates to disappear. Not necessarily the person."

"Yes," Ava repeated. She loved her sister, but she hated what her sister did.

"I've caused death before. It's not something I'd wish on anyone," Mason said quietly. "Have you ever shot anyone?"

Ava drew herself up on an elbow and tried to meet his gaze in the dark, but his face was in the shadows. "No. I've never pulled my weapon on a person."

"You're lucky."

"I know. I pray all the time that I'll never have to do it." She wished she could see his eyes. "What happened?"

A long silence ticked by, and she wondered if he'd open up to her.

"Three people. I've taken three lives. Two were in the same incident."

Her heart cracked at his quiet tone. "A long time ago?"

"Decades. But both times are as fresh as yesterday. It never goes away."

"No, I don't think it ever will. It's part of the curse of our profession. We do it to solve crimes, to help the people who can't help themselves, but sometimes we're forced into horrible situations."

Mason exhaled loudly. "Amen. Both times I know I had no choice. But my mind still reexamines whether or not I could have done something slightly different. I drag myself down into a well of depression and then slowly climb back out, arriving at the same conclusion each time.

"The first time a guy leaped out of his car at a traffic stop. He took one step and fired at my partner, who was approaching his vehicle. I'd just stepped out of our car. I shot. He died instantly."

"And your partner?" Ava breathed.

"Saved by his vest. The bullet hit directly on his sternum. It would have killed him."

"You would have been next."

"Yes. He was already aiming at me when I fired."

Mason shuddered, and Ava ran a soothing hand down his cheek to his shoulder. "What else happened?" She could feel his need to tell her. He wouldn't have brought it up if he hadn't wanted to get it off his chest. She wondered how long it'd been since he talked to someone about it.

"The second time one of them was a child."

"Oh no!" Ava froze.

"A homeless man had the child in front of him as a hostage and was slicing his throat open."

"What?"

Mason nodded in the dark. "It was awful. I fired at the man at the same time the child jumped. The bullet hit both of them. If the boy hadn't moved . . ."

"Oh, Mason. How horrible." Tears dripped down her face.

"The boy would have died if I hadn't fired. It was a no-win situation," he said flatly.

Ava scooted closer, seeking his heat and offering her own as solace. She kissed his forehead, trailing her lips down the side of his face to his mouth. "You did the right thing."

"I know," he whispered. "But it doesn't make it any easier."

Wanting to heal his emotional wounds, she gave him the comfort of her body.

· · ·

From a dead sleep, Ava grabbed her buzzing phone and answered without opening her eyes. "McLane," she said without an ounce of sleep in her voice.

"Ava, can you leave your sister? We could use you," came ASAC Ben Duncan's voice.

Ava opened her eyes and looked at Mason's digital clock on the bedside table—3 A.M. Mason sat up and swung his legs out of bed. She instantly missed his heat. He sat silently, his back to her, listening.

"Yes, no problem. What's happened?"

"We've found some bloody children's clothing at the Woodburn rest stop on I-5."

Ava knew that rest stop. Partially wooded, partially grassy. At least a few acres in size. Along a mostly isolated stretch of freeway. "You're searching the area?"

"Yes, we've got a big crew going over every inch."

"What clothing did you find?"

"A pink Justice zip-up sweatshirt. Rhinestone hearts. Size ten. There's blood inside the hood. Not a lot."

Ava's heart sank. Henley's sweatshirt.

• • •

Mason followed Ava through the crowded parking lot. The freeway rest stop had been closed to the public and now overflowed with police cars and FBI sedans.

A woman's dog had discovered Henley's jacket at the rest stop. The traveler from southern Oregon had taken her dog to the far border of the grassy area, stretching her legs and letting her dog roam, when the dog had returned with the pink coat.

The woman reported pulling it out of her dog's mouth and feeling bad that a child had lost her coat, but hadn't thought much of it until she'd noticed the dried blood. The entire state knew that Henley had vanished. She'd quickly Googled some news articles until she found one describing Henley's clothing and then immediately called 911.

Mason felt sick to his stomach. The rest stop could indicate that the kidnapper had immediately jumped on the freeway and headed out of town with Henley. All those man-hours spent combing the neighborhoods and areas near where she'd vanished could have been for nothing.

After Ava's phone call, she'd jumped out of bed, kissed him, and disappeared into his shower for five minutes. Mason had used his guest shower and been dressed by the time she stepped out.

"I'll drive since your car is still downtown," he'd said.

On the way down, she'd told him no one had informed the family yet. He'd argued a case for at least calling Lucas, but Ava had overruled him. The FBI wanted to wait until morning before calling the family. Mason saw their point, but that didn't mean he agreed with it. If Jake had been missing, he'd want to know the second any huge leads came up.

The family was sleeping. Hopefully. And Ava had a point about waiting to see if anything else turned up at this scene before notifying them.

They signed in at the scene log and headed toward a small group of agents. Mason could see Ben Duncan and Sanford in the group. The rest stop was crawling with police and FBI. The trash had already been pulled and transferred to a location where lucky forensic investigators would examine every scrap of garbage that travelers had left behind. Diapers, chip bags, pee bottles. Good stuff. Huge portable lights illuminated the woods and grassy areas.

The group of five agents opened as Mason and Ava approached, welcoming them in.

"Anything new?" Ava immediately asked.

Sanford shook his head. "We're still looking. The blood is human. We've found that out so far. Next test is to compare it to what we have on file for Henley Fairbanks."

"How long ago was it found?" Mason asked.

"About 10 P.M." Sanford turned to point toward the line of fir trees at the far edge of the stop. "A dog found it right over there. The dog's owner was talking to one of us within thirty minutes. One of the first agents on the scene took the sweatshirt directly to a lab."

"At nearly midnight on a Sunday?" asked Mason.

"We do what needs to be done," answered Sanford simply.

Standing at a freeway rest stop at four in the morning fell under what needed to be done when a child was missing. No one looked sleepy. Everyone was wide-awake and on high alert. It comforted Mason to see the response. In a way, he was fortunate. Henley's parents had to wait for him or an agent to update them on the investigation. Mason, however, got to see it hands-on. He'd go crazy if he were sitting at home wondering if anyone was searching for his child.

"If this is fake, heads are going to roll," stated Ava. "Robin mentioned that those pink jackets like Henley wore are still in the stores. If someone bloodied one and dumped it as a prank, I'm not going to forgive this time."

A murmur of agreement went through the group. They were still smarting from the fake ransom note.

"Are there cameras here?" Mason asked.

"No," said Sanford.

Too bad.

Sanford was studying him intently. Mason raised a brow at him.

"You surviving away from the job?" Sanford asked.

Mason froze. *Was that an insult or a genuine question?* "Not an issue."

"There are a lot of rumors out there," Sanford probed a bit more. The other agents looked at Mason with interest. Beside him, Ava stiffened, and Mason felt her annoyance zero in on Sanford.

ASAC Duncan had stepped out of the group to talk to the local police. Duncan knew everything that was going on with Mason's work situation. Apparently Sanford had heard some side talk, or Duncan had brought him up to date. Either way, he was being a deliberate dick.

"There's always rumors," Mason said. *Don't let him know that he's irritating you.*

"Any idiot could see that the fingerprint evidence is pretty strong," pushed Sanford.

"An idiot did," answered Mason with a touch to the brim of his hat. Ava quivered as she swallowed a laugh.

Sanford had the grace to smile.

A chorus of shouts from the edge of the field grabbed the group's attention. As one, the agents and Mason moved in the direction of the noise. As they drew closer, Mason saw a field investigator with two small white objects in her hands.

Mason squinted. Socks. Someone had found a pair of small white socks. Exactly what Robin had written on Henley's clothing list from the day she vanished. Drawing closer, he could see the brown splotches on the white. Dirt or blood?

"Oh no," Ava breathed.

20

72 HOURS MISSING

"What happened? How long have we been gone?" Ava asked as she eased down the street in front of the Fairbanks home. The media presence had tripled. Vans, people, cameras. It was nearly eight in the morning, and Ava was feeling the lack of sleep and the exhausting effects of standing at a crime scene for four hours and then riding downtown to retrieve her car.

Beside her Mason stared out the windshield. "Holy cow. Did they find out about the rest stop?" By some miracle, no media had turned up at the rest stop. For once, everyone who was supposed to keep their mouth shut did.

Ava honked her horn at the cameramen blocking the drive. They parted but turned their lenses their way. Some of the reporters started to shout and moved their microphones closer to her car. But they weren't looking at her. They were looking at Mason.

"Detective Callahan!" Ava heard the shouts through the window. *Oh no. They found out he's been put on administrative leave.*

She stole a look at Mason. His lips were pressed together, and he tugged his hat down an eighth of an inch closer to his eyes. He said nothing. She saw his Adam's apple move in his throat as he swallowed hard, and her stomach tied in knots. Nothing was worse than hungry reporters wanting a bite of you.

She pressed on the gas and the car surged, scattering the reporters. She drove to the far side of the home and parked out of sight of the vultures. She turned off the car and sat quietly.

"Looks like the cat's out of the bag," Mason stated.

"It doesn't change anything," said Ava.

"Yes, it does. It applies pressure to my department to take some action. They may have placed me on administrative leave, but the public will want something bigger. Like my beheading."

"You haven't been charged with anything. And you won't be."

Mason nodded. "I know. I didn't kill anyone this time."

His words stung, and she wanted to ease his pain. He'd offered her an intimate look at his soul last night in a way she suspected hadn't happened in a decade or two. He was human. He'd buried his mistakes and moved on, but current events had ripped them out of the dirt and brought them up to the surface, their pain as fresh as the day they'd happened.

His ex-wife, his son, his career.

"We need to go in," she said. Henley had been missing for just over seventy-two hours. Her window of survivability was shrinking exponentially. "Are you ready to talk to them?"

Mason had called and warned the family a half hour ago, letting them know new evidence had been found at the rest stop, but that nothing had led them to Henley. Yet.

"Yes, this is what's important."

She took his hand. "You're important. You're a good man and a good cop. You give a crap about what happens to people. It's a tragedy that your hands are tied when you could be helping more people. I'm glad you're here to help me."

Brown eyes studied her. "We make a pretty good team. Too bad you're a fed."

She smiled. "Does that affect anything?" she asked lightly, holding her breath for his answer. Sometimes men couldn't deal with her title and position. Especially cops. They felt like they had to prove their jobs were as important as hers.

"Not at all."

She believed him. "Good."

He got out of the car, and she followed him into the home. Lilian, Robin, Lucas, and Jake were in the breakfast nook of the kitchen. The house was warm and smelled of spices. Robin pulled a tray of cinnamon rolls out of the oven as Ava and Mason joined them. The only people who looked interested in the food were the two cops hovering in the background. The family was tired of sweets.

Ava pulled the eight-by-ten photos out of a folder and set them on the table. Lucas spread them out. Images of the front and back of the pink sweatshirt and the socks. To Ava, the bloodstains glowed. Lilian caught her breath. "Yes, that's the same sweatshirt as Henley's."

"But can you tell for certain that it's hers?" Ava pressed.

Lilian slid the photos closer and studied each one. "I don't know. It was new. It didn't have any tears or stains, and I didn't write her name in it. So I guess I can't say for certain. But it's the right style with the rhinestone peace emblem."

"And the socks?" Ava asked.

"Plain white socks. They look like what she has."

"Is that blood on the socks, too?" Jake asked.

So the boy *could* speak this morning. "Yes," said Ava.

"Did they find anything else?" Robin asked. She'd stayed back from the table, behind the island in the center of the kitchen, as if she didn't want to get too close to the photos. She cut two cinnamon rolls out of the pan, plated them, and gave the breakfast to the cops, who graciously accepted. No one else asked for a roll, and Robin didn't seem to expect any other takers. Ava hadn't eaten since before the vigil last night, but she wasn't hungry. The thought of biting into a gooey cinnamon roll didn't appeal at the moment.

"Nothing else turned up at that scene," answered Mason. "They searched the whole place before we left, although they still had the garbage to finish sorting. But the early lab results say the blood is the same type as Henley's."

Lucas looked ready to vomit. Silent tears streamed down Lilian's cheeks.

"But that's hardly any blood," Lilian said. "That's not enough to show that someone has been . . . hurt." She whispered the word "hurt," and Ava mentally substituted "killed."

"We agree," she said to Lilian.

"I can't think of her out there in the cold," cried Lilian. "Did they really look everywhere? She'll be so cold without her sweatshirt and socks." She dissolved in her seat, breaking into sobs, and laid her arms and head on the table. Lucas wrapped an arm around her shoulders, his face carefully blank. Robin came forward, took the chair next to Lilian, put her arms around the woman, and rested her head on her shoulder.

Jake shoved back his chair and left, his shoulders sagging and his face hidden. Mason followed him out of the room.

The cops stopped eating.

Ava wanted to run away. Instead, she moved closer to the table. "We went over the area with a fine-toothed comb. We still have people searching the fields outside the rest stop. If she's there, we'll find her. But frankly, I think the items were left for us to find. Like a distraction or something to put us off the real trail. Who loses both socks in the same place?" she asked.

"That doesn't make sense," agreed Lucas, his face hopeful. "They were probably placed there. Do you think it's a fake, like the ransom note?"

Ava shook her head. "We don't know. There was a general description of Henley's clothing in the paper and on the news the first day, but from what I've seen, that clothing store has put out dozens of pink sweatshirts with different rhinestone patterns, right?"

Robin nodded, still embracing Lilian.

"So someone got lucky and picked exactly the right one? I don't think so. I think it's Henley's clothing, but I think it was purposefully left for us to find. The big questions are why, and what does it mean? That's where we're at now," Ava said gently.

Lucas reached for the seat beside him and picked up a newspaper. "Before we heard about Henley's clothing, we were already concerned about what's going on with Mason." He tossed the paper on the table. "We wanted to ask Mason about this article. Jake saw it, too. We've all read it."

Ava picked up the paper. Mason's name was there in clear print. She scanned the article. It was a rehash of yesterday's article but with his name added.

Who leaked?

"What do you need to know? Obviously, he didn't do this."

"Has he really been placed on leave? Why hasn't he said anything?" Lucas asked.

Ava glared at him. "Because he's worried out of his mind about your daughter. He's putting every ounce of his strength into finding Henley and keeping his personal problems locked away. He didn't want you to worry about anything else."

"He could have said something." Lucas toyed with the paper that Ava had tossed back on the table, his gaze averted.

"That's how Mason operates," said Robin slowly. "He sees it as his problem and no one else's. He shoulders stuff like this alone. I'm not surprised one bit."

"But he's family," argued Lucas.

Robin shook her head. "You don't understand. That's not how he thinks. In his brain, it's none of our business." She looked at Ava with experienced eyes. "He'll keep it in until it eats him alive. I've watched it happen before. He needs someone to talk to about it, draw it out of him."

Ava blinked. *Did Robin suspect something between her and Mason?*

. . .

Jake's door slammed shut two seconds before Mason reached it. He pounded on the door. Jake knew he was right behind him. His boots weren't exactly quiet. Mason counted silently to three.

Jake opened the door. The boy's eyes were red and swollen. He turned away and walked over to the window and stared outside. "She's dead, isn't she?"

Mason took a deep breath. "We don't know that."

"But the police think she is, right?"

"No one is saying that. Not at all. They're still balls to the wall trying to find her."

"It's been too long, Dad. If she was left outside somewhere, she wouldn't survive in this cold."

Mason moved to stand next to his son, fighting the urge to pull him into his arms as if he were a child and hug him until the pain was gone. Jake angrily rubbed his eyes.

"Don't assume anything, Jake."

"What's the deal with that article in the paper this morning? They're saying you've been placed on leave? Is that true?"

Mason's heart sank. "Yes, that's happened."

"How can they do that? They really think you killed that woman?" His son was stunned.

"No, they don't think I killed her," Mason started. "There's some evidence at the scene that makes me look really bad. They have to react to that. They can't simply ignore it."

"Why? How bad is it?" Jake looked like his favorite superhero had been shot.

"At first look, it's bad." *How much should he tell the boy?*

"You're not telling me something. What do you mean *first* look?"

Mason looked hard at the boy. "My fingerprints are on the murder weapon."

"What? There has to be a mistake. That can't be right."

"I agree. Especially since I know I didn't do it," Mason said wryly. "We both know fingerprints can be planted. I'm just waiting for them to figure out what really happened. Someone set this up to make me look bad."

"They did a good job," Jake said. "I thought I was going to get sick when I read that. Mom tried to hide it from me, but I found it."

"The truth will come out," Mason said. He wasn't about to tell Jake that the weapon had been one of his practice bats.

"I fucking hate this."

"Don't swear. Everybody—"

"Stop telling me not to swear! You swear all the time!" Jake looked him right in the eye, anger burning on his face.

He's reacting about Henley, not you.

"Swearing doesn't sound weird when it comes out of my old redneck mouth. You're a fresh-faced kid. It sounds like you're trying to be older than you are." As soon as the words spilled out of his mouth, he knew he'd made a mistake.

Jake turned another shade of red.

Damn.

"I'm not a kid. I'm in college! I can drive, I can vote, and I can go to war. Don't treat me like I'm a child!"

McKenzie again.

"Look Jake, this isn't about last night. I'm sure McKenzie's a nice girl, and I get that it sucks that you can't go over there. But these are special circumstances, you know? There's a reason the FBI wants you where they can keep an eye on you."

Jake slumped. "She makes me feel better. It's been miserable here for the last few days."

A thought chilled Mason's brain. "Uh . . . are you using a condom?"

Horror crossed his son's face. "Jeez, Dad! No! I mean we haven't . . . Christ!" Jake spun away and strode in a small circle, shaking his hands like they were wet and making an *ugh* noise.

Mason blinked. *Ugh? Is that for me or the girl?* "Uh . . . well if you do, use a condom," he asserted. There. His parental advice for the decade.

"I don't want to talk about that," Jake put his hands over his ears and kept walking in circles.

Mason reached out and grabbed an arm, halting Jake's trek. "Look at me. I know you're upset about Henley. We all are. I understand that seeing McKenzie makes you feel better. It's great when you have that special someone that you can spill your guts to and they don't judge you. Maybe McKenzie is that person for you right now, but you can talk to her on the phone or text her or video chat. I'm glad you've got someone to talk with, because keeping it all in will make you explode."

Frozen in place, Jake stared at him with wide eyes.

Is he listening?

"You're not to leave the house without an agent or cop with you. Got it? If Ava's not available, someone will be," Mason said.

"I can't take a cop with me to McKenzie's house," his son said. "That's embarrassing."

"Then video chat."

"It's called Skype, Dad."

"Whatever," said Mason, employing one of Jake's favorite terms. "I'm not letting you fall into the same situation as Henley."

"But Dad, I can't walk around with a guard all my life!"

"It's not for all your life. It's just for a little while."

"Until when?" the boy pleaded.

Mason understood. Jake felt he was being treated like a prisoner and a child.

Tough shit.

"Hopefully, not much longer. If this kidnapper is cocky enough to purposefully leave some of Henley's clothes for us to find, then he's going to trip himself up soon. The FBI is made up of a lot of really smart people. They'll find him."

Jake held his gaze, searching Mason's eyes for the truth behind his statements. Mason projected as much confidence as he could toward his son.

"Are you sure, Dad?" Jake asked softly, his gaze still begging for assurance.

"I'm positive."

Mason's phone buzzed in his pocket, and Jake looked away, the intimacy of their moment destroyed. Mason glanced at his phone and didn't recognize the number, but noticed it was similar to the numbers at his office.

"Callahan."

"Detective Callahan? This is Derek Alward with Internal Affairs."

Mason bit his tongue so he wouldn't swear out loud. "I thought I might hear from you guys." Jake went and sat on his bed. He watched Mason on the phone, not trying to hide that he was listening. His son's eyes looked like they belonged to someone much older.

Am I treating him like a child?

"I'd like to set up an appointment for us to chat, Detective Callahan."

Chat? Like on Oprah?

"Tomorrow is Christmas. It's the one day I really don't like to report downtown."

Alward laughed like he'd never heard anything so amusing. "Neither do I. How about the day after?"

"Now, that's not giving me much of a holiday," Mason drawled, and Jake narrowed his eyes at him. "How about next Monday?"

Alward coughed. "We'd really like to chat with you sooner than that, Detective Callahan."

Mason suddenly developed a strong dislike for the word "chat."
"Well, tell you what. I've been helping my family out because we've
got a little girl missing. I'm sure you've heard about it. When we find
the asshole who kidnapped her, then I'll be available to *chat*. But
right now, I'm a bit tied up. Merry Christmas." He ended the call and
turned his phone off.

"Who was that? A reporter?" Jake asked. "You only talk like that
when you're really pissed or think someone's being an idiot."

"Talk like what?"

"Real slow, as if you're a hick."

Mason thought about it. "I guess you're right. He *was* being an
idiot, and I was talking slower so he'd understand me." He turned his
focus back to his son and put Internal Affairs out of his head. "Why
don't you come back downstairs and have one of your mom's cinnamon rolls? It'll make her feel better."

Jake made a face. "She's turned the kitchen into a bakery. I'm
sugared out."

"Yeah, she does that."

"Dad, tomorrow's Christmas."

"I know, son."

"Henley's present was in my suitcase. That pillow pet thing." Jake
looked about to cry. "I haven't been able to go shopping and replace
it. I don't want her to think I didn't get her anything."

Mason pulled his son up off his bed and enveloped him in a deep
hug.

He didn't know what to say.

•   •   •

He had the wrong dream again. Wyatt hadn't visited him in his
dreams for a few nights, and usually his visits were calm and happy. He dreamed of his son at the playground near their first house
or jumping the waves during a trip to the ocean. He enjoyed his

nighttime visits from his boy. Except when they went back to the grocery store where his son had been viciously ripped from his life.

He abruptly sat up in bed, sweating, his heart trying to escape from his chest. He stood and paced the room, trying to slow his breathing, recognizing the panic attack. He'd learned to deal with them over the years, but some nights he wanted to climb out the window to find enough air to breathe. The bedroom walls seemed too close, and he strode to the bathroom for a drink of water. Under the harsh light of the bathroom, he leaned on his hands on the counter and stared into his bloodshot eyes, softly counting backward from fifty.

When he had the upper hand, he faced the dream and let it flow through him. This time the memories were under his control, and he could safely explore the familiar territory.

The lights of the grocery store had been ultrabright. He and Wyatt had made a late-afternoon trip for last-minute items for Christmas Eve. His wife wanted more whipping cream and a particular dessert wine.

He grabbed the whipping cream and stopped in the wine aisle.

"Dad, can I go look at the magazines?" Wyatt asked, bouncing from foot to foot. Kent nodded and let him go, not taking his gaze from the labels of wine bottles.

"I'll come find you when I'm ready to go," he tossed after his twelve-year-old, not looking to see if the boy heard him. He scanned the labels, looking for the brand his wife wanted. Spotting it, he grabbed two bottles and wished they were cold. Perhaps he could find a cold one in the refrigerated area. He tucked the bottles under his arm and continued to browse, smiling at the wines that had humorous labels.

Christmas music played over the loudspeakers, and wine-bottle-shaped stockings hung along the wine aisle, tempting buyers to dress up their bottles before giving them as gifts. He touched one, wondering if he should grab it to gift a bottle to his boss.

A woman screamed, and Kent froze.

Jesus Christ. She sounded like she'd been murdered.

"Wyatt?" Kent said. Ice shot up his spine as he glanced around for his son.

Magazines.

He spun on a foot and headed out of the wine aisle. Male shouts made his feet move faster. Another woman screamed, and he started to jog. "Wyatt?" he shouted. He ran across the back end of the aisles, glancing down each one to find the books and magazines. More shouting sent his heart rate escalating. "Wyatt!" he shouted again.

He slid to a stop at the end of an aisle. Magazines.

No Wyatt.

He swallowed hard. Maybe he was looking at the magazines by the check stands.

He ran down the magazine aisle to the front of the store and scanned the check stands. Employees and shoppers were gathered at the front of one aisle. A male employee ran past him, his face alarmed.

"What's going on?" Kent asked. The man didn't stop or answer. He shoved a key in an office door and vanished inside.

People had abandoned their shopping carts, blocking the wide front aisle between the check stands and store aisles. In the crowd, women pressed their hands over their mouths. A few men stood at the front of the group, talking to whoever was down the aisle, their hands making calming gestures. Kent pushed through the crowd and looked down the freezer aisle.

A homeless-looking man had his arm wrapped around Wyatt's shoulders, clasping him to the front of his body.

His knife's blade dug into Wyatt's throat.

Kent saw blood.

Wyatt's wide gaze met Kent's. "Dad!" he shrieked. The man tightened his arm and pressed harder with his knife. Kent watched blood flow from under his son's jaw and run down the man's arm. The man's hair was long and greasy, his clothes dirty and his shoes torn and ragged. The stink of his body odor and fear filled the aisle. The man's crazy eyes sought out Kent's.

Kent stepped forward out of the group, and a man grabbed his arm. "Careful, look." The shopper pointed past Wyatt at a male shopper propped up against a freezer case fifteen feet behind the knife-man. A smeared trail of blood led from the shopper back to the knife-man and Wyatt. The shopper had a hand clasped over his shoulder, blood oozing heavily between his fingers.

"He tried to pull the boy away," the man said in a low voice to Kent. "The crazy guy slashed at his chest and was going for his face when he ducked out of the way and fell." The injured shopper was very pale, and Kent estimated him to be in his seventies. Probably someone who shouldn't be losing blood so quickly.

Kent stared at his son. Wyatt's eyes were wide and terrified, pleading with Kent to get him away. His captor scanned the crowd of shoppers, yelling at them to keep back. Kent had no doubt that the man would slash Wyatt's neck if he wished to.

"I saw the demon!" the knife-man screamed at the people staring at him. Every few seconds he glanced back at the shopper on the floor. Knife-man's feet wouldn't hold still, and his arm slid up to trap Wyatt by the throat. "The demon is in his eyes! He lives in his soul!"

Kent pulled his arm out of the other shopper's grip and took a half step closer.

"Don't move!" the knife-man shrieked at him. He pulled the knife from Wyatt's neck and pointed it at Kent. "He has to die!"

Kent's heart almost stopped. "He's just a boy. He's not a demon."

"He is evil!" the knife-man shouted. "I've seen it!" He brought the knife back to Wyatt's jawline.

"Someone went to call the police," the man next to him said in a low voice. "We need to keep him distracted until they get here."

Sweat pooled under Kent's armpits. What could he do?

Wyatt's lips moved, but Kent couldn't make out the words. His boy was terrified.

"That's not how you kill a demon," Kent stated. "You need a priest to do it."

"I am a priest!" the knife-man yelled. "God has commanded me to find and destroy his demons." The homeless man's eyes were wide with several levels of insanity.

Kent couldn't reason with crazy.

Notes of "Silent Night" filled the grocery store, the utter wrongness of it sweeping through Kent. "You can't kill a demon the night before Christmas," he pleaded. "It doesn't work."

The knife-man blinked at him.

He'd gotten through to him.

"Put down the knife. The boy isn't a demon. He's a child." Kent took another half step closer and held his hand out to the homeless man. A good twenty feet separated him from the two.

"Get back," the knife-man shrieked. His limbs tensed as he gripped Wyatt tighter.

Kent stopped moving and slowly lowered his arm.

"Shoppers, for your safety, please leave the store," came a voice over the loudspeaker.

The knife-man cowered behind Wyatt and scanned the ceiling of the grocery store. "Go away! Get back! Don't speak to me!"

"Attention shoppers, please leave the building."

"Shut up!" the knife-man screamed at the ceiling. "You can't see me!"

"Oh my God," breathed the man next to Kent. "He's on drugs."

Kent didn't care if the man was on drugs or simply nuts. He had to get Wyatt away before he cut him deeper. So far, Wyatt's cut didn't seem to be too bad. The knife-man had smeared the blood on Wyatt's face with his jerky movements, covering his cheek with red.

A murmur of voices behind him made him glance over his shoulder. The crowd of shoppers had diminished to himself and three other men. Two Oregon State patrol officers had stepped inside the store and were talking to an employee. The employee pointed toward Kent and the group, speaking frantically as the officers nodded, assessing the situation.

"Tell them not to use the loudspeaker anymore," the man next to him said to one of the others, who nodded and darted away.

Good idea.

"I need you guys to leave the store," said a cop behind them.

Kent shook his head without looking back. "That's my son. I'm not leaving."

"Stay away!" Knife-man pointed his knife at the new arrivals. "I hate cops!"

"Hey, Jerry," said one of the cops in a soothing voice. "I thought you weren't supposed to come in this store anymore."

Kent breathed easier. The cops had dealt with the knife-man before.

"Get the fuck out of here!" Jerry yelled at the group. He jerked Wyatt's head, causing the boy to cry out and Kent to gasp.

"Now Jerry," continued the cop in the same voice. "That's a good kid you've got there. You don't want to hurt him. He's got Christmas presents to open tomorrow."

"He's a demon!" shrieked Jerry. His wild gaze went from the still-bleeding shopper on the floor to the cops, then to Kent. His eyes darted madly, no rhythm to their movements.

"Holy shit," murmured the other cop. "I've never seen him this bad."

Kent glanced at the two cops, noticing that the other male shoppers had backed off. "He on something or just crazy?" The cops looked too young.

The one who'd been speaking shook his head. "Definitely mental issues, but something's different tonight. We've taken him in several times, but usually he's pretty harmless."

"He ever hurt anyone?" Kent said quietly, looking back to his son. *Besides my son and the old man on the floor?*

"I don't think so," said the first cop. "He turned up around here about eighteen months ago. We've been dealing with him ever since."

"He's never pulled anything like this," said the second cop. Both cops had one hand close to their weapons, but they hadn't drawn them. "We've got backup coming with a mental-health counselor. Just keep him talking. See if he'll put down the knife."

"Hey, Jerry," said the first cop. "Can I get that guy on the floor out of your way? You don't care if we move him, do you?"

"Don't touch him!" screeched Jerry. He moved closer to the old man, dragging Wyatt by the neck.

"He's bleeding pretty bad, Jerry. I'd like to bandage his cut. He's not a demon, right?"

"He interfered! He will die for interfering!"

The old man's eyes widened, and he scooted a few inches away from Jerry.

"Holy fuck," muttered the second cop.

"I think the shopper will be okay for a little bit longer," murmured the first cop. "He's holding his head up pretty good." He raised his voice and looked at the older man. "You holding on all right?"

The bleeding man nodded. "Don't worry about me." He moved his gaze to Jerry and Wyatt.

"He's a tough one," said the first cop. "Okay, Jerry. We'll leave the guy there for a while. But how about putting down that knife. You're a lot bigger than that little boy. Do you really need a knife?"

"He has to die!" Spit flew from Jerry's mouth.

"What do we do?" breathed Kent. He couldn't take his gaze from his son. Wyatt was brave. There were a few tears on his face, but he'd been staying strong since Kent had appeared. If he didn't break eye contact with the boy, he'd be all right.

Don't look away.

"We keep him talking until our backup gets here," said the first cop.

"Three minutes out," said the second.

"Hey, Jerry. What did you ask Santa for this year?" asked the first cop.

Jerry's expression blanked and then immediately morphed into rage. "There is no Santa, you lying sack of shit. Santa is Satan. I saw it on TV." He waved his knife at the cop.

Bad question. But at least the knife was away from Wyatt.

"You're all pawns of Satan," Jerry shrieked at the cops. "You turn children into demons and try to fool the innocent. They must die!" He moved his left arm from Wyatt's chest and grabbed his hair, yanking his head back and exposing his neck. He brought the knife back to Wyatt's throat.

"Noooo," screamed Kent as he leaped forward. Dimly, he heard the cops shout at the man to put down his knife.

Time slowed.

Jerry's gaze was locked on his blade. Wyatt held eye contact with his father, his eyes widening to expose an alarming amount of white. In one smooth motion, Jerry reached across Wyatt's neck and dug the blade under the left side of Wyatt's jaw.

Wyatt knew. He pushed up on his toes, throwing his head backward into Jerry's nose.

Noise exploded on Kent's right side, and Wyatt's head jerked.

Blood sprayed the glass doors behind Jerry's head.

Jerry collapsed to the floor, pulling Wyatt down with him.

Kent scrambled to his son and fell to his knees, yanking him away from the dead man.

Wyatt's hair was a bloody mess. Kent pressed his hand on the top of the boy's head to stop the bleeding.

It was soft.

Kent's ears buzzed. He couldn't hear, but he knew the cops were shouting at him.

Part of his son's head was missing.

• • •

In the bright bathroom, Kent breathed hard, still staring into his own eyes. Wyatt had been rushed to the hospital but didn't survive the night. He'd been declared dead on Christmas Day. When Wyatt visited him in his dreams, he was whole. But Kent could still feel the softness of his brain under his fingertips. A sensation no father should feel.

The dream never went further than that. He had no memory of how he got to the hospital or of notifying Wyatt's mother.

His life had stopped on that day. Twenty years later, this Christmas would be different.

Now, he had a plan to bring the world back into balance.

21

76 HOURS MISSING

Jake sank further into the couch and stared at the TV screen. The movie wasn't registering with his brain. It was *Star Trek*, but he had no idea which one because he couldn't focus on it for more than five seconds before his mind galloped off in a different direction. Lucas was sprawled in one of the big easy chairs. He snored.

Jake was jealous. He would have loved a good sleep. It was bad enough that he thought about Henley during the day, but she also invaded his dreams and kept him up at night. Horrible dreams. Nightmares.

Talking with his dad had been good. Except for the part about condoms. He'd wanted to sink through the floor when his dad had told him to use a condom. *No shit.* He'd been pissed last night when he was told he couldn't go see McKenzie. They weren't sleeping together. How could they when they never were alone together? Fate had been screwing with him when it brought them together at a party a week before he left to go to college. Since then they'd talked, texted, and Skyped daily. He'd been counting down the days to winter break because he'd finally have the chance to see her in person again.

So far he'd seen her for all of fifteen minutes last Thursday after he'd run to the market for his mom. Her parents had dragged her off to some family event. Last night, he'd needed to get away. For days this house had offered nothing but depression. After the vigil, he'd craved some fresh air and peace. A chance to hang with people who weren't crying every hour. It'd felt good to get out of the house and go to the vigil, but it'd made him want to escape afterward. He could have just left. No one would have even noticed. But he'd done the right thing and asked permission and been shot down.

It'd made him angry.

McKenzie's parents had been at a party last night, and Jake and McKenzie would have been alone. Finally. If he didn't get some alone time with the girl, she was going to start looking for someone else to hang out with. Someone who lived in town. Like that asshole Scott Sinclair she kept talking about. She had him in one of her classes at Portland State, while Jake was a continent away at Duke. Why shouldn't she see someone closer to home?

He sank deeper into the couch. There were cool girls at Duke, but he was being faithful to McKenzie. They'd had such a short time together before he'd left for school in August, but it was enough to tell him this was a girl he wanted to hang on to. Bright blue eyes, shiny black hair. Gorgeous. And nice. She was funny, too.

He'd had two texts from her so far that day. She thought her parents would be leaving to go to another party that afternoon, and did he think he could come over? He'd replied that he'd try. He could jog to her place in less than five minutes if he cut through the green space areas. But after his conversation with his dad a few hours ago, he didn't think he'd be going anywhere today.

He'd even approached Ava that morning, asking if she thought it would be okay if he went to McKenzie's for an hour or two. She'd offered to accompany him, and his face had turned red. Then Ava had laughed. "That wouldn't be very cool, would it? An escort on a date. It'd be like old-fashioned dating, where the girls had to take an older female companion with them everywhere."

Jake had no idea what she was talking about. He was pretty certain his mom had never taken an older woman with her when she dated in high school. He'd politely laughed and slunk away. But instead of going with him, Ava had gone to the grocery store with his mom and Lilian. The two women had decided to prepare a big Christmas Eve feast. He and Lucas had looked at each other when the women announced their plans and said they didn't think they'd be very hungry.

Lilian had replied that they'd feed it to the reporters outside, and that the point was to give the women something to do so they didn't go stir crazy. He and Lucas had nodded like they understood and proceeded to line up a bunch of movies for the day. The theme was *Star Trek*. All the generations. They wouldn't be able to watch all of them today, but they'd make a good dent. They could always continue tomorrow.

Jake glanced at the huge Christmas tree in the corner. Its branches seemed to droop a bit, and he wondered if his mom had forgotten to water it. He could do it. But Christmas was tomorrow, so what would be the point? The amount of presents hadn't changed since Henley had vanished. During a normal year they would have tripled over the last few days. No one wanted to go shopping, let alone wrap presents.

Now Ava, Lilian, and his mom were in the kitchen making food for an army. Lilian had complained about visiting three stores before they'd found a turkey that wasn't frozen. He'd asked why they couldn't just thaw it in the microwave, which had led to peals of laughter from all three women. Once again, he'd slunk out of the kitchen. The turkey was probably too big to fit in the microwave. At least it'd felt good to hear them laugh.

His phone vibrated, and he opened the text. McKenzie had sent a picture of her family's Christmas tree. He smiled and tapped out a response.

PRETTY TREE

Her reply popped up. CAN U COME OVER? THEY'RE LEAVING AT 2

Jake sighed and looked at the holiday picture again. I'LL TRY

She sent three hearts and a pair of lips.

He swallowed hard and desperately wanted out of the house. Ava passed through the family room on her phone, heading to the back patio for a private conversation. That was becoming the norm. Whenever Dad or Ava got a work call, they took it to the backyard. His dad was still outside on his phone. He'd been on his phone for several hours. Work stuff, he'd said.

No doubt there was all sorts of fallout from that newspaper article. What were they saying on the newscasts? The family had agreed on a no-news-coverage blackout. Movies were the only thing they'd been watching. Jake hadn't even been watching his regular shows in case there was some "breaking news." Ava had promised to keep them informed of anything important, and she'd kept that promise.

He watched Ava outside on the phone. His dad had ended his phone call and now was intently listening to Ava's side of her conversation. Dad stood stiffly, his posture perfect. Even without his cowboy hat, his dad always looked like he was ready to gun someone down. He had that look of tension and preparedness that spoke of razor reflexes. Jake sat up straighter on the couch.

What had happened?

Ava ended her call, and she and Jake's dad talked heatedly for a moment. Ava used her hands when she talked, reminding him of a stereotypical Italian woman in a movie. Jake studied her face. She looked worried. She glanced his way, and he knew she couldn't see him through the lightly tinted windows. She looked back at his dad and shook her head. Dad stepped forward and pulled her into a deep hug.

Jake's jaw dropped.

Ava embraced him back. Her eyes closed. His dad rubbed her back with one hand, but Jake couldn't see the expression on his face. *Dad and Ava?* He looked over at Lucas, who continued to snore. No one else had seen the hug. Jake studied the pair again. *Dad could do worse. But maybe he's just comforting her about something.*

A big part of him wished McKenzie was there to comfort him in the same way. There was something about being next to her that made him relax. She always smelled so good and was interested in what he had to say. He was tired of Skyping when he knew she was so close. They should be spending time together. He felt like a piece of him was missing because she wasn't sitting beside him. He had to get over there today. Just for a few minutes. It'd fill that hole he had in his chest.

His dad and Ava separated. Both were nodding as they talked, and they turned to head back into the house. Jake whipped around and stared at the screen, pretending he hadn't seen the embrace outside. Patrick Stewart was giving orders for an away mission to rescue a crew member. Jake recalled from somewhere in the back of his brain that the mission would be a success.

Why couldn't his family's nightmare be resolved within ninety minutes?

"Hey, everyone. Could you all come in here for a moment?" Ava called out as she and his dad came in from outside. Lilian and Robin stepped into the family room from the kitchen, both wiping their hands on towels. Lucas jerked awake and blinked.

"I've just had a phone call from the command center," Ava said. "Someone called in to 911, claiming that Henley has been released. They gave GPS coordinates for us to find her."

"What?" Lilian grabbed Robin's shoulder for support. "She's safe? She's okay?" Tears started.

Jake held his breath as every muscle in his body froze. *Could it be true?*

"Hold on." Ava held up her hands. "We don't know. We're sending several teams to the spot. It's remote and wooded. *And* there is a chance that this is another fake, like the ransom note. Please keep that in mind. The caller also refused to answer when the operator asked him if the girl was alive." She looked earnestly at Lilian. "Mason and I were just talking about whether or not we should even tell you before we know if it's real."

Jake's dad nodded.

"Dad didn't want to get our hopes up," Jake guessed, excitement making his voice crack. *Would Henley come home today?*

"No, it was the opposite." Ava glanced at his dad. "He thought you should know. He'd said he'd want to know as a parent."

"Thank you for telling us," Robin said. "We understand you're just trying to protect us."

"You've been through a lot of ups and downs. So have I. I wasn't sure this was a roller coaster you'd want to ride again," said Ava.

"We'll be fine. Where is the location?" asked Lucas. He looked ready to grab a jacket, hop in his car, and race to find Henley.

"Up the Sandy River. The spot is part of the National Forest, and it's a really rugged area. If this is real, someone put some effort into getting Henley to that location," answered Mason. "The FBI is sending teams, and they've called the search and rescue organization that handles that area."

"Can we go?" Lucas asked.

Ava shook her head. "Mason and I are going to the location. Clackamas County has a few deputies outside, so you can contact them if you need something. We'll let you know as soon as possible if it's legitimate. It's going to take us at least an hour to get up the river to that location. Maybe more."

Lucas turned to look at Robin, and Jake's heart cracked a little bit at the look of longing on his stepdad's face. Robin left Lilian's side and came around Lucas's chair to sit on his lap. Lucas wrapped his arms around her and buried his face in her hair. Jake glanced back at Lilian. She stood still, both arms wrapped around herself as she watched the couple.

She's got no one but Henley.

And Henley might never return. For a brief second, he thought about giving Lilian a hug, but her expression signaled that she didn't want to be touched. She was sinking deep inside herself again, where she seemed to have spent so much of the past few days. This morning in the kitchen was the first time Jake had seen her nearly back to normal.

This has to be for real.

He glanced at his dad and saw that he and Ava were watching Lilian closely, too.

"Could they trace the call?" Jake asked.

Ava shook her head. "A disposable cell. Triangulation of the cell towers indicates the call originated from downtown Portland. He picked the most densely populated area to place the call from." She glanced at Mason. "I'm going to change into jeans and boots and we can go."

"Is it bad terrain?" Robin asked.

Ava nodded. "Some of the worst. Riverbeds and cliffs. We'll see exactly what it's like when we get there." She strode out of the room.

Jake watched her leave. *Please God, let this be true.* He glanced at the clock over the fireplace. *An hour before we hear any news? I'll go crazy waiting. What am I going to do?*

McKenzie.

No. Not now. Not when we're so close to finding Henley.

He studied the adults in the room. Lilian abruptly spun on her heel and went down the hall. Jake heard the guest bedroom door close and knew she wouldn't be out until they got some news. His mom got up from Lucas's lap and started loading dishes in the dishwasher. Lucas stared into space for a few moments and then grabbed his tablet and started tapping on the screen.

There was nothing to do but wait. And he could do it alone, or somewhere else, with someone to talk to.

I'll just be gone for a little while. I'll be back before Dad calls us about Henley.

No one noticed as he left the family room.

22

77 HOURS MISSING

Mason floored his SUV up the twisting highway. Ava had spent the majority of the ride on her cell, talking to both Sanford and ASAC Duncan. Sanford was on his way to the same location with a dozen agents. He'd contacted the Forest Service and Search and Rescue. Both were going to have teams at the site. Mason had watched the temperature gauge on his dashboard slowly drop as they'd left the city limits. It had been hovering at forty degrees for the last few minutes.

"Not much farther," Ava commented, studying a map on her phone. She'd changed into hiking boots, jeans, and a heavy jacket. Mason had swapped out his cowboy boots for the hiking boots he always kept in the back of his vehicle. Ava had grabbed a duffle from her trunk. He figured it held the same basics as the one he kept in his vehicle: extra clothing, blanket, ammo, water, protein bars. Whatever a cop thought they might need for a sudden twenty-four-hour mission with no time to stock up. He'd offered to drive, suspecting Ava had phone calls to make, and he'd been right.

They'd soon left the city behind. The highway followed the twisting path of the Sandy River up toward its source in the Cascades. Fir trees towered on both sides of the road, sometimes leaving breaks that gave breathless views down a steep slope to the riverbed. As they rose in elevation, the temperature went lower. Mason hadn't seen any snow along the road, but he expected it any minute.

Please let her be safe.

Was this a real call? Would it direct them to a little girl or a corpse?

"Take the next right," Ava directed.

Mason saw a small clearing on the right side of the road a hundred yards ahead. He slowed and pulled into the opening of a Forest Service road. The metal gate was open. Had the Forest Service opened it or had their caller? He had a hunch those roads were all closed this time of year. The Forest Service typically closed the dirt roads during the winter to keep drivers from getting stranded.

He spotted fresh tracks in the thick mud at the gate. He knew from Ava's last call that Sanford had just arrived with his men and they were getting ready to trek into the woods.

"Your car wouldn't have handled this," Mason stated as he shifted into four-wheel drive to move through the mud. Some of the ruts looked a foot deep.

"Definitely not," Ava said. "Thank you for driving." Stress showed in her tight jaw.

He understood her tension. What would they find down this road?

They bounced through the ruts, and Ava grabbed her door to stay still in her seat. A half mile in, they spotted a group of other trucks. The familiar odd green of the Forest Service vehicles stood out from the drab colors of the FBI's SUVs. People stood in small groups, and Mason let out a breath. It appeared no one had set out yet. He parked behind the closest vehicle and grabbed his personal weapon out of the console. Ava watched him check the weapon but said nothing. He was licensed to carry his own concealed weapon. His boss couldn't take that away from him. He slid the nine millimeter into his shoulder holster under his coat.

They strode to the group, and Mason nodded at the faces he knew from the FBI. A short guy seemed to be giving commands. Not FBI. Sanford introduced Mason and Ava to the group. The short guy was Jim Wolf from the Madison County Search and Rescue, and he was also a deputy in their sheriff's department. He sized up Mason and Ava in a single glance, seemed to find them acceptable, and continued his explanation of what was about to happen.

Former military.

It showed in Wolf's stance and delivery.

"The GPS coordinates indicate a location to our south," said Wolf. "We're going to divide up into three groups of six, and one of my guys will lead each group. We'll all be headed in the same direction. It's downhill and steep. Watch your step. Use your ropes and your brains before doing anything that doesn't seem right. Hopefully, we won't have to go very far."

Mason raised a hand, and Wolf nodded at him. "Was the Forest Service gate locked?"

An older man in a Forest Service coat spoke up. "Someone cut the chain. It was open when we got here, and there were fresh tracks in the mud."

Mason could feel Ava's excitement at his statement. Someone had come through recently. "What made you stop right here?"

"Tracks showed a vehicle turned around here," answered Wolf. "It makes sense for the coordinates that were given. Any other questions?" He scanned the group, and several people shook their heads. "Let's go."

Mason and Ava were assigned to the same group as Sanford. Their leader, Brynn, was a woman with blond hair and sparkling brown eyes. She set a steady pace in the same direction as Wolf's group, but fifty feet to their left. A third group was to the far right of Wolf, making a wide path through the woods. Shouts of "Henley!" and shrill whistles went off every sixty seconds.

Mason watched where he put his feet. The steep slope was packed dirt with scattered ferns and fir debris from the tall trees overhead. "Were there any tracks leading into the woods?" he asked Brynn.

She shook her head. "That was the first thing we looked for. The tire tracks were apparent, but we couldn't see that someone had actually gotten out of a vehicle."

"Shit," Ava muttered.

Brynn smiled Ava's way. "As you saw, there was a lot of rock, too. Someone could have moved all the way down to the river without leaving a track."

Mason heard the quiet roar of the river. He couldn't see it, but he knew they'd eventually meet it at the bottom of the slope. He continued to pick his way down the hill, frustrated that he couldn't survey and scan his surroundings unless he stopped moving. He risked a bad fall if he looked up from his foot placement. He reached out a hand and balanced against a tree, walking carefully through the brush at its roots.

"Henley!"

After each call, searchers paused briefly and listened. As they drew closer to the river, it was harder to hear. It took thirty minutes to move down the slope to the water's edge, where he swore the temperature had dropped another five degrees.

The three groups convened and looked to Jim Wolf for instructions. The man consulted his GPS and scanned the area. "Okay, we are right on top of where we're supposed to be. Half of us will go upriver and half down. Report in twenty minutes," he told his leaders.

Mason and Ava moved downstream with Brynn and several men. "What if she's on the other side of the water?" Ava asked.

Brynn paused and looked over the river. The water was fast, pounding over huge boulders as it worked its way down and out of the mountain range. The far bank was twenty yards away, but with no bridge, it might as well have been a mile.

"Let's pray she's not," Brynn said. "We'd have to bring in a chopper to access the other side." The woman studied the rushing water with an apprehensive look and shuddered. Mason didn't blame her. The water was deadly to anyone who considered crossing. One of the Forest Service workers blew his whistle, and they all paused to listen. Then moved on.

A few minutes later Brynn halted, looking around. "Do you hear a dog?" she asked.

Mason listened hard and shook his head. He glanced at the rest of their group, who did the same thing. Brynn continued to listen. "I didn't bring my dog. Usually she's with me on searches, and I swear I heard her for a second." She gave a laugh. "I'm hearing things."

Thirty seconds later, Mason heard a bark. Judging by the heads jerking up around him, he wasn't the only one. "I heard it!" said one of the agents. Brynn nodded and scanned the area.

"Here, boy," she called and gave an impressive whistle with two fingers.

More barks.

"It's up the slope," said Ava. "Not near the river."

Brynn changed direction, taking them back up the slope. The barking grew louder and more insistent. Brynn gave a few more whistles, which seemed to set off a flurry of barks each time.

Huffing from the uphill climb, the group moved into a clearing in time to see a dog dash away. The dog stopped, looked back at them, and ran off again.

Mason blinked. *That looked like . . . It couldn't be.*

The group followed the dog, who dashed ahead again, then stopped to look back and check their progress. A black dog and a white chest. Mason was too far away, but damned if that didn't look like his missing dog.

· · ·

Jake knocked on McKenzie's door, excitement making him almost dance. Finally. Some time alone with his girl. He'd texted her that he was on his way, but he couldn't stay for long. He'd told his mom he was going to take a nap and to wake him if she heard anything about Henley. She and Lilian were hard at work in the kitchen, and Lucas had vanished into his home office and closed the door. Jake had walked right out the back door without anyone noticing.

He'd dressed for jogging so no one would question the sight of a teen running in jeans through the neighborhood. He had one fear—that his mom would knock on his door and find him missing. He'd have to answer for that if it happened. At least he'd left a note on his bed saying where he'd gone, so she wouldn't panic that he'd been grabbed like Henley. She'd be pissed but not frightened. And he didn't plan to stay for very long. He hoped he'd be back before anyone noticed.

Jake knocked on the door again and rang the doorbell. He knew she was home; he'd received a text before he'd left the house verifying that her parents were gone for a few hours. He waited a few seconds then tried the door handle. Unlocked. He pushed open the door a few inches. "McKenzie?" he yelled through the space.

"Come in, Jake," she yelled from far back in the house. "In the kitchen."

Relief swept through him, and he confidently pushed the door open the rest of the way. He stepped into the entryway and headed toward the kitchen. He stepped into the cheery room—

Jake froze.

"Hello Jake," said a man to his right.

Jake's hands turned to ice and his heart skipped several beats. The silver-haired man had McKenzie tied to a kitchen chair in front of him and was holding a knife at her neck. McKenzie had a gag in her mouth, and her eyes pleaded with him as her chest heaved up and down. The man held McKenzie's cell phone in his other hand.

"I have a deal to offer you, Jake," the man said pleasantly. "You do what I say, and I won't slice your girlfriend's neck open. How's that sound?"

Jake stared at the man, unable to speak. The man looked like anyone's grandfather.

"Are you wondering if I'd really kill her?" The man arched a brow at him. "Do you want to try me and see? Maybe you should consider what I did to your little sister."

Jake clenched his hands into fists.

• • •

Ava pushed through the brush, trying to keep up with Brynn's long stride. The dog galloped ahead of them, constantly stopping and then starting, trying to get them to follow. She'd heard Mason gasp as he'd gotten a good look at the dog. They'd all been shocked to see the domestic animal in the woods. Especially a dog who'd tried so hard to get their attention.

But what was it leading them to?

Please let Henley be alive!

Surely the dog was taking them to the little girl and not to some friendly campers.

"Over there!" Brynn shouted and broke into a jog. Ava could see the little girl at the base of a fir tree. A dark hat covered her bright hair. She didn't get up or move as they approached.

Please.

The rest of the group started to run toward the girl. Brynn knelt by her, lifted her head, and felt for a pulse. "She's alive!" The child was tied to the tree with several lengths of rope around her chest. Brynn pulled a knife out of her pocket and thrust it at an agent. "Cut the ropes," she ordered. He fell to his knees and started sawing at the rope. Two others produced knives and did the same.

"Henley," Mason said over Ava's shoulder as she kneeled beside Brynn. "Can you hear me, honey?" The girl moved her head and made a feeble attempt to open her eyes.

"She's freezing," Brynn stated. She pulled off her daypack and started rummaging through it. She pulled out several small hand warmers and a microthin blanket. "Let's get some warm liquids in her." The ropes broke away from the tree, and the girl fell forward into Ava's arms. Brynn reached under the oversized brown jacket the girl was wearing and tucked the hand warmers into her armpits. Henley's eyelashes fluttered as she tried to open her eyes.

"Good girl," Brynn said. "Open your eyes. We're going to get you warmed up."

Ava brushed something black on the girl's coat. Dog fur. She looked at the dog, who sat nearby, watching their every movement with careful eyes. *Had the dog stayed close to share its body heat?* Dog fur covered Henley's mittened hands as if she'd been clutching the dog.

Ava's eyes watered. "Good dog," she whispered.

Mason stepped over to the dog and patted its head. "Good boy." The dog rubbed its shoulder against Mason's leg, and Ava sat up straighter.

"Mason, is that your dog?" Ava asked.

Brynn stopped her ministrations on Henley to glance back at the dog and Mason.

"Damn right, it's my dog," he whispered. He thumped the dog's sides with both hands, and Ava could have sworn the dog smiled.

· · ·

The dog pranced between Mason and Henley on the hike out of the forest. The men took turns carrying Henley, using their body heat and Brynn's thermos of hot water to get the girl warmed up. Mason had tried to call Robin but couldn't get cell reception in the ravine.

"That's why we use radios," said Brynn. She'd notified the other teams that Henley had been found. Mason noticed she kept a careful eye on Henley, monitoring her breathing and doing everything possible to get warm fluids into the girl.

"Are you a nurse?" Mason asked after watching her peer under Henley's eyelids.

"Yes," Brynn answered. "But I volunteer for the SAR team."

"She gonna be okay?" he asked in a low voice, and the woman gave him a warm smile.

"I think so. She's got good circulation going to her fingers and toes, and her pupils are responding to the light. She's not dehydrated, just cold. She was bundled up pretty warmly, and that made all the difference. And it looks like the dog stuck close, sharing his body heat."

"Thank you, Lord," Mason said.

"How did your dog get out here?" Brynn asked. She gave the dog a pat as he darted by to get closer to Henley.

"Looks like the same guy who took Henley took my dog. I'd suspected as much."

Brynn screwed up her brows, trying to make his statement add up. "But why?"

"Good question. But I want to know why he made us haul ass all the way out here to find Henley. Why'd he go to all that trouble?" Mason asked.

Ava spoke up from behind him. "I don't like this. He clearly didn't hurt Henley, but she could have easily died out here. He left her warmly dressed, but what if we couldn't get to her in time? Why orchestrate this search?"

Henley stirred in the Forest Service worker's arms. "Mommy?"

Mason caught up to the pair. "We're gonna take you to your mom, Henley." Blue-veined lids fluttered again, and brown eyes peered at him for a split second. "Hey, do you know who I am?" Mason asked.

The child blinked, her head resting on the shoulder of the man carrying her.

"Henley," Mason said. "I'm Jake's dad, Mason."

Her eyes flew open, and she stared at him. She started to squirm in the man's arms. "Hey!" he said, nearly dropping his suddenly active load. She stopped, exhausted, and her eyes fell shut, her head flopping back on his shoulder.

"What was that?" Ava asked.

Mason was stunned. "I don't know. She looked scared to see me."

"Maybe it's because you're a man. I wonder if Brynn or I should be carrying her," Ava worried.

"She looks fine now," Mason muttered. "That was freaky."

"Does she know you?" Ava pressed.

Mason shrugged. "I've only met her a few times. I barely remember it. I figured she'd have a clearer idea of who I am if I told her I was Jake's dad."

They hiked on in silence for a few more moments. Mason kept stealing looks at the sleeping child ahead of him. Her blond hair was messy and greasy under the hat. He'd noticed earlier that she'd been wearing a man's socks, not little-girl socks. They were baggy above her shoes like they were ten sizes too big. No pink sweatshirt, but she was wearing an old brown coat that also appeared to belong to a man. Her hands had disappeared inside the long sleeves. The Forest Service worker handed her off to one of the FBI agents for a turn. Mason thought Henley seemed small for an eleven-year-old, but carrying her up the rough slope was still a hard job.

He stepped carefully around some rocks and looked up to see wide eyes staring at him over the agent's shoulder.

"You know who I am now, Henley?" Mason asked. A small nod answered him. Relief flowed through him. She squirmed in the agent's arms, trying to find her hands in the too-big coat she was wearing.

"Hold on there," the startled agent said as he stopped and adjusted his grip. Henley found one hand and dug at the neck of her jacket.

Mason stepped closer, not wanting to scare her again. "You okay, honey? What's the matter?"

She pawed at the zipper, but her fingers wouldn't function right.

"Your coat bugging you?" Mason reached over the agent's shoulder and tugged Henley's zipper a few inches. "I don't want you to get cold."

Henley plunged her hand under her coat and felt around. Mason heard the crinkle of paper as she pulled a folded note from a pocket inside the jacket. She thrust it at Mason. He took it, his heart racing. Had she gotten away from her kidnapper with something that would identify him? Mason unfolded the paper.

Hello, Mason. Now it's my turn to destroy something precious of yours.

Mason's hands shook, making the paper quiver.

"What does that mean?" Ava asked, reading beside him. She looked at Henley. "Did someone tell you to give that to Mason?" The girl nodded and laid her head back on the agent's shoulder. Her eyes closed in exhaustion. "That's why she was thrashing around when you said your name. She'd been instructed to deliver the note." Ava's voice cracked. "Poor little thing. She took her duty very seriously. I wonder if he threatened her?"

"Ava. I need to call Jake." Panic ricocheted through his nerves. Nothing else was precious to Mason. They could burn his house, wreck his vehicle, and destroy his health. His son was everything, and someone knew it.

He pulled out his cell. No reception. "Anyone else have cell reception yet?" he yelled.

Everyone in their party checked their phones. No luck.

"We're not far from the vehicles," Brynn said.

Mason wanted to run up the hill. He didn't care if he left his team behind. Sweat dripped down his back, and Ava put a hand on his arm. "Hey," she said. "A few more minutes."

"Something's wrong. I can feel it."

"We left Jake safe at home."

"And a big chunk of the FBI is up here to rescue Henley," Mason pointed out. "There were just a few Clackamas County deputies outside the house when we left. Something could have happened."

"No one has Jake," Ava said, but her gaze faltered.

23

His team reached the top of the road, and Mason jogged ahead. The other teams had beat them back and were waiting at the vehicles. Mason checked his phone. No service.

Jake.

"Anyone have service?" he shouted at the other group as he ran to join them. The agents dutifully checked their phones and shook their heads.

"I've radioed the ranger station and asked them to call the number you gave Brynn. I haven't heard back yet," Wolf told him. "The little girl okay?"

"Brynn says she looks good. Just cold," Mason replied. "I need to head back to town."

Sanford caught up with him. Ava had shown him the note Henley had been carrying. "We're heading there, too. We may have Henley back, but it sounds like this isn't over."

"I'll drive," Ava said, holding her palm out for Mason's keys. He handed them over. It was his turn to be on his cell as they drove. He was about to climb in his passenger seat, but turned and dashed over to where Brynn was buckling Henley into the back seat of an Explorer.

"Where are you taking Henley?" he asked. The little girl looked calmly at him as she let Brynn fuss over her. Her eyes were tired and glassy, but she was awake and sitting up on her own. Brynn slid into the seat next to her.

"Emanuel Hospital. We'll get her checked out." She met Mason's gaze, and Mason realized she was concerned about a sexual assault. His heart dropped. "I'll keep trying to reach her parents," Brynn continued. "If you get ahold of them first, tell them to meet us there."

"Right." Mason took one of Henley's mittened hands. "You ready to see your mom?"

She nodded, and her eyes lit up.

"Good. She's missed you something terrible. We all have. Jake's gonna be happy to know you're okay."

She leaned over to look past him. "Dog," she whispered and held out her hands. Mason's dog jumped past him into the SUV and sat on the floor at Henley's feet, his tongue hanging out as he gazed at Mason. The dog was taking his sentry duty very seriously. Mason rubbed his ears. "Good boy."

"What's his name?" Henley asked in a soft voice.

"He doesn't have a name," Mason answered. "Do you want to give him one?"

The girl nodded and screwed up her face in thought. "Bingo."

"That's a good name. Bingo." The dog tilted its head at the name and held Mason's gaze. "I think he likes it."

He nodded at Brynn and slammed the door.

He went back to his truck and climbed in. Ava gave him a questioning glance.

"They're taking her to the hospital to get checked out. Let's go," he stated.

Ava guided them down the service road while Mason kept an eye on his phone, waiting for the service indicator to grow some bars.

It flickered, and he hit Robin's cell number.

"Mason?" Robin answered.

"You heard?" he asked.

"Yes, we got a call from the Forest Service station. They said your group radioed in that Henley is fine. Is that true? Is she really okay?"

"Yes, she's sitting up and talking. She seems good."

Robin burst into tears, and Lucas came on the line. "They're taking her to Emanuel? Is that right? Was she hurt?"

"She seems okay, Lucas. She really does. I talked to her for a bit. I think it's just a precaution. Is Lilian all right?"

Mason heard Lucas relaying his information and female voices answering.

"Yes, Lilian knows and is ecstatic. We're leaving for the hospital in a minute."

"Can I talk to Jake?" Mason's heart sped up.

"Hold on."

Mason heard Lucas giving instructions and then he returned to the call. "Robin's getting him. We'd almost forgotten about him since the Forest Service called a minute ago." His voice cracked. "I still can't believe Henley's okay. Dear God, Mason. There are so many different ways this could have ended."

"I know, Lucas. I know. Believe me, I've thought through every one of them."

"Me too." Lucas sucked in a deep breath. "I can't believe it," he repeated.

Mason heard Robin's voice in the background.

"What do you mean he's not there?" Lucas asked, his mouth away from the receiver. "He went *where*?"

Mason closed his eyes. *Jake.*

"Robin says he left a note on his bed saying he was going to McKenzie's house for a while. He didn't tell us he was leaving. I'm gonna strangle that kid!"

"I've got to call him." Mason could barely speak. He looked away from the road, the blacktop they were speeding over making him dizzy. *What was Jake thinking?*

"Robin's already calling," said Lucas. "Hang on."

Ava shot Mason a worried glance from the driver's seat. "What's going on?"

"Jake left a note that he went to his girlfriend's house."

"What?" said Ava. "I told him this morning that he had to take someone with him."

"You aren't the only one," answered Mason. Nerves twisted in his stomach.

"Robin left him a message on his phone," said Lucas. "He didn't pick up."

"Shit. Those two Clackamas County deputies still there?" Mason asked. "Tell them to haul ass to McKenzie's house."

"What's going on?" Lucas's voice dropped. "Henley's safe. Why—"

"He's going after Jake now," Mason spit out. Hysteria sank its fingers into his brain. "He left a note for me with Henley, saying that what's precious to me is next. That'd be Jake."

"Holy shit," Lucas breathed.

Mason heard him shouting at someone in the background as he laid the phone on the seat. The curves of the road and the stress of the morning caught up with him. "Pull over," he muttered to Ava. "I'm going to be sick."

She yanked the steering wheel to the right, and Mason had the door open before the SUV had even come to a halt.

• • •

Minutes later, Mason and Ava were speeding down the twisting highway. Mason's brain spun as he tried not to think about Jake at the mercy of the same person who'd held Henley captive for three days.

"He didn't harm Henley," Ava stated, her focus on the road.

"Not that we know of yet," Mason mumbled. "I'm thinking this wasn't about Henley, or someone from Lucas's business trying to strike back at him. This is about me."

"What are you talking about?"

"That note. He's focused on me. No note was left for Lilian or Lucas. What I don't understand is why he even took Henley if his goal was to get to me."

"We don't know that was his goal. You're jumping ahead."

Ava drove toward Lake Oswego and McKenzie's home. Over the phone, they learned that Clackamas County had immediately gone to the girl's home and found the front door unlocked. Jake's girlfriend McKenzie was found inside, gagged and tied to a chair. She said that an older man had broken in earlier that day, hit her across the face, tied her up, and used her phone to text Jake.

He'd blindfolded and tied up Jake, then taken him, leaving Jake's cell phone behind.

The teen girl was helping police the best she could.

"How'd he know she was Jake's girlfriend?" Mason asked Ava as they pulled off the freeway toward McKenzie's home. Ten more minutes. He wanted to talk to the girl himself.

"Good question. Probably the same way he knew Jake went to Duke and that he was out for pizza the night when he was approached."

"You think that was him?" Mason asked.

"McKenzie's description sounds close enough. I'd say someone has been stalking Jake for a while. How much does he put out about himself on social media?"

"I don't know," Mason admitted. "I've told him to be careful."

"But have you looked?" Ava asked. "Is his Facebook page private? Do his other accounts list Duke in his bio for the world to see? Instagram, Twitter, ask.fm, Snapchat. All that crap. Kids post stuff all the time that they shouldn't and assume no one will ever see it but their friends."

"Shit." Mason rubbed his forehead. He had never asked Jake to show him what he posted about his life. "I can't keep up with that stuff."

"You don't try," corrected Ava. "You're like 99 percent of parents—you choose to not educate yourself about it. I hear it every day."

Mason wanted to deny it, but she was right. He knew there were sites out there where kids communicated. He'd never asked Jake to show him. And he'd never tried to look for his son's info other than a halfhearted peek at Facebook.

She pulled in front of McKenzie's house, mere blocks from the Fairbanks home. Cars from Clackamas County and the FBI filled the street. Mason wondered how long it would take the media to put two and two together about the activity so close to the hub of Henley's disappearance. He spotted a few neighbors watching from their windows and figured not long.

Inside, they found McKenzie sitting with a female deputy and ASAC Ben Duncan. Other officers and agents littered the scene. Mason had never met the girl. Heck, he hadn't even known she existed in his son's life until a few days ago. She turned swollen but beautiful blue eyes his way, and he understood why his son had fallen so hard. A welt was reddening on her cheekbone.

"Are you Jake's dad?" McKenzie asked before he'd said a word.

Mason nodded.

"The hat," she said. "He always said you were a cowboy."

Mason twisted the brim of the hat in his hands. "Who was it?" he asked, his gaze taking in Duncan and the female deputy.

McKenzie shook her head. "I don't think Jake knew him. He seemed completely surprised to see him and didn't say anything that indicated he knew him."

"I told you that you can wait to talk until your parents are here." The female deputy touched McKenzie's arm.

McKenzie shook her head, pulling her arm from the woman's touch. "I'm eighteen. I can talk to the police if I want. And they need to know *now* what I saw to help get Jake back. Not when my parents get home."

"You're doing just fine, McKenzie," Ben Duncan said. "You've been a big help already. Let's talk about what he looked like again."

"I told you what he looks like," McKenzie said, holding up her hands. "There isn't any more."

"Say it again for Mason to hear," Duncan suggested. "Maybe something will ring a bell with him."

McKenzie straightened and met Mason's gaze. "He looked like anyone's grandfather. Silver hair, tall, maybe six foot two, good build. It looked like he hadn't shaved in a few days. His shoulders were wide, not hunched at all."

"Age?" Mason asked.

The girl lifted one shoulder. "Sixties? I don't know. He was still strong. He hauled Jake out of here with no problem."

"He carried him?" Duncan frowned.

"No, he pulled on Jake's arms. They were tied behind him, but he was so fast, he had Jake nearly tripping over his feet."

"What did you talk about while you waited for Jake?" Mason asked.

McKenzie's eyes looked down and to her right as she remembered. "He wanted to know about us. How long we'd been dating, where we went on dates. I told him we mostly just texted and Skyped since we lived in different states. We hadn't really gone on a date since he left for school."

"He knew Jake went to school at Duke?" Mason's stomach was in a vise. His son was missing, yet part of him felt like he was analyzing the case of a stranger. His heart was being ripped in half, but his brain was on autopilot; his rational cop side was kicking in to protect his emotions and discover the fastest way to find his son.

"Yes, he seemed to know that already."

Mason exchanged a glance with Ava and Duncan, who both nodded. It looked more and more like the same man who had approached Jake near campus. His arms ached to wrap around his son and never let go again.

"Did he talk about Henley?" Ava asked.

"He asked Jake if he wanted to know what he'd done to his sister, but then he wouldn't say if she was alive or not. He kept taunting Jake about her fate. He told Jake he'd slit my throat if he didn't do what he said." She shuddered. "I thought it meant he'd done that to Henley. I think Jake thought the same thing."

A Clackamas County deputy stepped in the room. "None of the neighbors noticed a strange vehicle here today. One neighbor noticed when the parents left, but no one else spotted a car or truck nearby."

"He parked it in our garage while we waited for Jake," McKenzie told Mason.

"How'd he know your parents would be gone for that long of a time period?" Mason asked.

She blinked. "He asked me. I told him they were going to a party for a few hours. But he couldn't have known that before he came in."

"How were they dressed?" Duncan asked McKenzie.

"Nice. Dad had on a tie and mom a dress. They were clearly going to something."

"He was willing to take a chance they'd be gone," Mason mused, focusing on McKenzie's words instead of racing out the door to blindly search for Jake. "Did he seem stressed over the fact that they might walk in any second?"

McKenzie thought for a moment. "He seemed stressed the entire time. He was more focused on getting Jake over here. Over and over, he asked if I thought he'd come. I think he only asked about my parents once or twice."

"Did he have anything besides a knife?" Ava asked.

McKenzie nodded. "He had a gun."

Mason's heart stopped.

"She's described a revolver to us," Duncan added. "Kept it in a coat pocket most of the time."

"He kept touching it through his pocket," she added. "Like to make certain it was still there. He seemed more comfortable with the knife." She gestured at her neck, and Mason realized she had a thick bandage under her ear, hidden by her hair.

The man who did that has Jake.

Mason gritted his teeth. "I'm sorry you had to go through this."

"This? This was nothing," McKenzie's eyes sparked with anger. "He had Henley for days, and now he's got Jake. Who knows what he's got planned? I was tied up for a few hours. Big deal. We need to find out where he's taking Jake."

Mason admired her spunk but knew she'd feel the shock of her experience later. He glanced at the female deputy, who nodded back at him. She knew it, too. McKenzie would suffer emotional consequences for the rest of her life.

His cell vibrated in his pocket. *Jake?* His heart sank when he saw it wasn't his son's number. Of course it wasn't. Jake's phone was in an evidence bag on the coffee table in front of Ben Duncan.

He moved a few steps away from the small group and turned his back for some privacy. "Callahan."

"Hello, Mason. It's been a very long time."

Mason froze. He slowly turned back to the group and met Ava's curious gaze. He stared at her and saw understanding click in her blue eyes. She gestured at Duncan, who stood up, watching Mason carefully.

Mason didn't know the voice. "Who is this?"

"Someone who's made your life miserable. Just as you made mine."

His mind raced and a roaring rang in his ears. "Who are you? Where's Jake?"

The man laughed. "You don't remember me yet? You will soon. Very soon."

"What have you done with Jake?"

"I haven't done anything yet. I'm waiting for you."

"What? Waiting for me for what?" Mason watched Duncan have a hurried discussion with another agent, gesturing at Mason's phone. The other agent was shaking his head. They hadn't set up his phone to be tapped. The most they could do now was contact his carrier and triangulate the location of the call's origin. Not a quick process.

"I've been waiting for you for a long time, Mason. You ripped up my life and tore it apart."

"I did? You better remind me how I did that."

Ava moved closer, and Mason tipped the phone slightly for her to hear. His heart pounded, making his rib cage hurt.

"You'll remember soon enough."

Mason heard faint Christmas music on the other end of the call. *Was he in a public place? Or in a vehicle with the radio on?* "You didn't hurt Henley," he stated. "We found her. She's fine."

"Oh good. I don't have the heart to injure small, innocent girls. Naughty big ones are another story. They usually get what's coming to them."

Mason couldn't breathe. "Josie?" He forced the name out.

The man snorted. "She was worthless. But she served my purpose."

"What purpose was that?" *Keep him talking.*

"You haven't figured that out yet?" The man sounded surprised. "You're probably too focused on the small things. You haven't looked at the bigger picture."

What the hell is he talking about? Mason couldn't think straight. Next to him, Ava frowned as she listened to the call, leaning against Mason's arm with her hand on his shoulder.

She smelled like the icy air from their earlier search.

"I don't understand," he said to the caller as he stared into Ava's blue eyes. His pulse slowed down as he inhaled her calm. "You need to let Jake go. You haven't done anything to him yet. It's not too late." He purposefully didn't mention Josie's death.

"Oh, it's much too late," the man whispered. "It's been too late for decades. I just couldn't see it until recently."

The hair on Mason's arms stood up. *Decades? Who?*

"Tell me where I can find Jake. You didn't hurt Henley; you need to do the same with Jake."

"No, no, I'm afraid I can't do that."

The depressed tone set off alarms in Mason's brain. Ava dug her fingers into his shoulder as she listened.

A man's voice on a scratchy speaker announced something in the background of the call. Mason couldn't make out the words. *A radio station?*

"It's time, Mason," he said slowly. "It's time to bring everything back into balance. I'll meet you in the freezer aisle."

The phone call clicked off, and Mason's vision tunneled.

He knew where to find Jake.

"Dear Lord," he said.

24

"Get back!" Kent screamed at the woman in the freezer aisle.

"You don't want to hurt him," she said, stepping closer. "He's just a boy!"

He tightened his arm around Jake's neck, his hand clasping the knife close to his ear. The boy was tall, and Kent liked that Jake's body blocked most of his own. With the boy's hands still tied, there was little chance of him fighting back.

"Don't make me shoot you!" he shouted, holding a gun in his other hand. The woman kept moving closer. The rest of the shoppers had scattered when he'd fired the first shot into the ceiling to clear out the grocery store. This one seemed to think her age made her safe. She looked to be in her late sixties. Her shoes were sensible, and her hair was pulled back in a long gray braid. She'd been in the freezer aisle when he'd fired the first shot and hadn't even jumped. She'd slowly turned around and stared at him as the other shoppers screamed and ran, drowning out the peaceful Christmas music that had filled the store moments before.

Was she stoned? Who doesn't flinch at a gunshot?

She smiled at him as if she could disarm him with her kindness. "He's a good boy. You don't want to make any mistakes that will haunt you forever."

He pointed the gun at her and silently swore as he saw his hand shake. "Get the fuck away."

She took another step, her hands out as if he were about to hand her a baby. "Give me the boy. You can just leave. No one will stop you."

"Lady, if you don't back away, I will shoot *you*."

She shook her head at him. "You don't want to harm anyone."

Anger exploded in his brain.

His hand steadied and he fired. Her shoulder jerked, and she collapsed to her knees, clasping one hand over her shoulder. Shock filled her face, and her mouth opened in a large *O*, but she didn't make any noise.

Screams came from the far end of the aisle. In his peripheral vision, he saw people running past the aisle entrance at the back of the store. Jake's body shook, sending reverberations through his back and into Kent's chest.

A female spoke over the loudspeaker. "Everyone needs to get out of the store. Now!"

"You shot me." The woman blinked in shock.

"I warned you," he shouted at her. *Damn her. Why had she forced his hand?*

She scooted back until she was leaning against a freezer door. Blood slowly seeped between her fingers over her gunshot. "Why did you do it?" she asked.

"Because I told you to back off and you didn't!" His gun hand shook again. "Why didn't you listen?"

He glanced toward both ends of the aisle. A face peered around the corner at him from the front, but the back of the store seemed empty. He'd spent hours in this grocery store and had spotted all the cameras. One by the pharmacy, one near the alcohol, a few near the check stands, and one at each front door. The freezer aisle didn't have any camera angles and was only visible to someone standing at either end of the aisle or from the top of the freezer case. But he could feel people watching him.

His skin crawled.

This was it.

After today, all would be right in the world. He'd see Wyatt again and leave the world back in balance.

"Sir, I can see you're upset. What do you need?" A female voice spoke again over the loudspeaker in the store. Kent turned his head and saw a female employee peering at him from behind a check stand. Her body was well hidden, her head barely showing, and she lifted a tentative hand when he looked her way.

She had a lot more brains than the woman on the freezer-aisle floor.

"Tell the police I'm waiting for Mason Callahan of the Oregon State Police! I want to see his face in here," he shouted at her. Jake jolted at his father's name.

"Dad?" he whispered.

"Mason Callahan?" she repeated over the speaker.

Kent nodded at her.

"I'll pass that on. Will you let the woman get medical attention?"

Kent glanced at the older woman on the floor. "She has to leave on her own power."

The injured woman looked at Jake and back to Kent. "Let the boy help me out."

Annoyance shot through Kent, and he aimed the gun at her head. "Shut your mouth and start moving."

Anger flowed through her gaze at Kent. "You proud you shot an old woman? A strong man like you picks a boy as a victim? Hell holds a special place for people like you."

"Lady, I've been living in hell for twenty years."

She looked at Jake. "Hold on, son. God will watch over you."

"Get out!" Kent screamed. An inner hot flash heated his brain, and he fought the urge to shoot her in the face. His finger touched the trigger. She swallowed hard, sent an apologetic look to Jake, and started to slowly scoot on her rear toward the front of the store.

Relief flowed through Kent. He rubbed his forehead with the back of the hand holding the gun. He wouldn't have to shoot her again.

"Thank you for letting her go, sir. The police are on their way," said the employee through the speaker.

Good. I want this over with.

Faint sirens sounded from outside the store, barely noticeable over David Bowie and Bing Crosby's "Little Drummer Boy."

"What do you want my dad for?" Jake asked.

"Shut up, kid."

Time to wait. *Pa-rum-pum-pum-pum.*

. . .

Ava sat with Mason in the back of ASAC Ben Duncan's SUV as it sped toward the grocery store. She clutched Mason's hand as he stared out the window. More details of the story he'd first told her in bed had spilled out of him when they'd first gotten in the vehicle, but now he was oddly silent.

Mason had slowly lowered his cell phone after the kidnapper's call at McKenzie's home and stated, "I know where he is."

She and the other law enforcement had held their breath.

"It's Kent Jopek. I killed his son." He'd turned dead eyes toward Ava. "He's the father of the boy I told you about."

"That wasn't your fault!" Ava had shouted. She'd wanted to shake him. All life seemed to have drained from Mason as he stood stunned in McKenzie's home.

"It doesn't matter. Kent blames me. And now he wants me to suffer as he did. He's going to kill Jake." Mason had blinked a few times, shaking his head. "He's at the Safeway on Fifteenth in Portland," he'd stated to Duncan. "In the freezer aisle."

Duncan had immediately thrown the machine into action, calling the Portland FBI office for that branch's SWAT team. He discovered that Portland Police and their Special Emergency Response Team (SERT) had already received a call about a hostage situation in the grocery store.

And someone in the grocery store had already been shot.

"He's crazy," Ava muttered in the back seat. "Why? Why does he think this is the right thing to do?"

"I don't know," answered Mason. "He said something about bringing it back into balance. I guess that means I'm going to lose my son the way he did." He stared out the window.

"No you're not," Ava stated. Anger fumed through her. Jopek might be playing some mind games with Mason and everyone else, but he was going to lose. "The FBI will get Jake out of there."

"They don't have time," said Mason. "They aren't even going to be in position in time. SERT will get there first. They're good, but not as good as you guys."

"We'll do whatever we can when we get there. We need to talk to him, see what he wants." Jake's sad face filled her brain. The poor kid had been through so much in the last few days. His family had turned into zombies with Henley's kidnapping, and he'd been left to float in the breeze the best he could. She'd tried. She'd reached out and voiced her concerns to the other adults. Had she not done enough?

"I'm going to kick his ass for leaving the house," swore Mason. "We told him *not* to go anywhere."

"This guy was obviously paying attention to everything going on with Jake. He wouldn't have stopped until he had Jake. I wish we'd known Jake was his true focus."

"Police say the person who got shot was an older female." Duncan turned around from the front passenger seat. "She's on her way to the hospital. Don't know how bad it is. He shot her at close range when she tried to get the boy away from him."

"Jesus Christ," breathed Ava.

"He's holed up in an aisle with Jake. Looks like the only weapons are a knife and a gun."

"There wasn't a gun the first time," said Mason. "Except for mine and my partner's. The homeless guy only had a knife."

"I guess he's evening up the odds this time," replied Duncan. He looked at Ava. "Our SWAT team won't be there yet. The local SERT team has a negotiator on the scene. You've got the most negotiator experience in the office. You up to giving him a hand until the team gets there?"

"Absolutely." Adrenaline spiked through her. This could be the most important negotiation of her life.

"We're gonna get your boy back," Duncan said to Mason. "Jopek has got to have a vulnerable side if he's camped out in the middle of an aisle."

Ava glanced at Mason, who didn't seem encouraged by Duncan's words, but he nodded at the man. "Snipers?" he asked.

"Yep. We're bringing in ours, and I know SERT will have some. Someone will have a shot," Duncan said.

Mason's face paled, and Ava remembered that he'd believed he had a clear shot.

"You weren't a trained sniper," she said, squeezing his hand. "And if you'd done nothing, his son would still be dead."

"We don't know that for certain," Mason stated.

Ava wondered how often he thought about that day. Mason sat up straighter in his seat and looked out the window, tension growing on his face.

They pulled into a grocery-store parking lot, and acid pumped into her stomach.

Go time.

• • •

Mason stepped out of the FBI vehicle and put on his hat. The parking lot was crowded. Portland Police had already taped off the area and were interviewing witnesses in a cold huddle at the far end of the lot. *Were all the customers out of the store?* A SERT vehicle parked directly in front of one of the sets of doors. Men in military-looking gear grouped on the safe side of the vehicle, getting a briefing. Two police cars blocked the other doors. Portland Police and Multnomah County vehicles continued to stream into the lot. ASAC Duncan stopped beside Mason and scanned the lot. "Who's our guy?" he muttered.

Mason pointed at a group of Portland police officers, spotting a captain in the group who seemed to be giving orders. "Right there." He and Ava followed Duncan and two other agents over to the group, who eyed them with suspicion.

Duncan made introductions.

"You're the one who gave the ID?" Captain Hale asked Duncan.

Duncan pointed at Mason. "He got the call from the kidnapper. He's the father of your hostage."

Hale's eyes narrowed. "You're Mason Callahan? And you're with OSP?"

"Major Crimes," answered Mason. "This suspect lost his son in a shooting inside this store twenty years ago. I was there that day."

The captain nodded. "The store manager said there'd been a shooting a long time ago in the exact same spot. I haven't had time to verify it."

"Freezer aisle?" Mason asked.

"Yep. He's got a teen boy with him, and he keeps asking for you. He's making it clear he won't deal with anyone else."

"Who's talking to him?" Duncan asked.

"One of our hostage negotiators is in there now."

"Our SWAT team is on the way, but I've got a negotiator with me." Duncan gestured at Ava. "You mind if she gives your guy a hand?"

"We'll take all the help we can. I don't want this ending ugly," said Hale. He eyed Ava. "But if he starts reacting just because you're a female, you're out of there. Some assholes don't take kindly to being handled by a woman."

Ava's shoulders stiffened. "I know. And if I make him nervous, I'll back away."

"The store manager talked to him a bit over the intercom at first. She's a levelheaded one, and he didn't seem to mind her," said Hale. "She got the store emptied of customers and even got him to release the woman he shot. The guy—you say his name is Kent?"

"Kent Jopek," Mason stated. "How is the woman he shot?"

Captain Hale looked grim. "He shot her in the shoulder. She was able to get out of the aisle under her own power. The EMTs seemed to think she'd be okay. It didn't look like she lost too much blood. She's a tough bird. All the other shoppers scattered at the sight of his gun, but she kept moving closer, asking him to let the boy go."

"Brave," said Mason. "Stupid, but brave. You have snipers in position?"

"Not yet. SERT is working on a briefing and plan." Hale gestured at the group by the SERT armored vehicle.

"The snipers good?" Mason couldn't help asking.

Hale frowned. "Of course. That's what they train for."

"I know. I know. I just had to ask. I was the one who had to shoot that day. It didn't end well." Seeing the specialized rifles made him jittery. He needed to trust the men holding those weapons.

"Anything else you can tell us about this guy?" Hale asked.

"Not really," Mason answered. "My shooting was ruled good, but it's hung over my head for two decades. I can't imagine what it's done to him."

"Obviously it's been festering a long time," Ava said. "It's caused him to grab Mason's son and re-create how his own son died. It's possible he believes he's got nothing to lose."

"But I've got everything to lose," Mason stated. "And he wants to make that happen. He's been chipping away at me and I didn't realize it. He killed Josie—"

"What?" Duncan and Ava spoke at the same time.

"He told me on the phone. He set me up. I'm not sure why he did it other than to make my life miserable."

"Wait. What are you talking about?" asked Captain Hale.

Mason looked the captain in the eye. "I'm on leave for the murder of one of my CIs."

"Yeah, I heard something about that. An OSP detective. That was you?" Hale's brows came together.

"Yes. Jopek set me up. Now this."

One of the Portland Police officers in heavy SERT gear jogged over to their small group and addressed Hale. "Corello says the guy inside keeps asking for Mason Callahan. Corello's not getting anywhere in negotiations with this guy until Callahan arrives."

"That'd be me." Mason lifted a hand at the helmeted officer. "Got two extra vests?" He looked at Ava. "I guess we're going in together on this one."

"No, we're not," Ava stated. She looked at Duncan. "If he's waiting for Mason to show up so he can shoot Jake in front of him, then we're not going to march Mason in there first thing. We need to get an assurance from him that he won't immediately shoot when he sees Mason."

"Wait a—," Mason started.

"She's right," Duncan said. "One of the primary negotiation rules. He's got to do something for us before we give him what he wants. You're here. We can start with that." He looked at Hale. "Tell your negotiator we're sending in one of ours to help."

Hale eyed Ava. "We'll send an escort in with you."

She shook her head. "No. He knows you guys are here. A visible show of force outside is good, but we don't need to intimidate him any further. Me walking in alone is a lot less threatening, and this will buy you some time to streamline your plan." She took the vest Hale handed to her.

Mason felt the ground tilt under his feet. "No. This isn't right. You can't go in there. He's crazy. He wants to see me. That's what we should be doing."

Ava didn't look up from strapping on her vest.

"She's following the book," Duncan said. "We know how to do this."

Mason didn't care. He'd attended the FBI's hostage-negotiation seminars and knew their book was a damn good one. But that didn't change that Ava was walking into the lion's den. Alone. Every caveman instinct he had wanted to order her back into Duncan's vehicle and tell her to stay put.

She looked up and held his gaze, her expression all business. Special Agent Ava McLane was a highly trained professional. And he needed to get over it and let her do her job.

"Fuck me." Mason glared at every member in the group.

Ava raised a brow at him. "Can you handle this?"

"Yes."

"When I call for you to come in, you will follow my lead. I'll tell you what to say and what to do. No cowboy stuff."

"Yes ma'am," he drawled.

Her eyes softened. "We'll get him out. Have faith."

Mason nodded. He'd never felt more helpless in his life.

25

Sweat trickled down Ava's back, and the glass doors whooshed open as she approached. Her borrowed vest felt heavier than the one she kept in the trunk of her vehicle. She hadn't worked a negotiation in years. The Portland FBI office's head negotiator was lecturing at Quantico, and the CARD team negotiator had hopped on a plane to an active incident in Texas the moment they'd found Henley. Right this minute, Ava was the agent with the most experience. The negotiation rules spun in her head.

Calm him down. Find out his goals, motivation, and emotional needs.

Be sincere.

She sucked in a deep breath as she moved toward the SERT police negotiator standing at a center check stand. She'd warned the Portland Police outside that she was going to play up the FBI's role to Jopek and make it seem like they'd swept in to take over the incident and now were keeping the Portland Police SERT team at bay. Let Jopek feel he was important enough to warrant the FBI taking an active role.

"Kent, an agent from the FBI is joining me. She's going to stay behind the check stand with me," Corello spoke over the speaker as she moved closer.

Don't startle him.

She nodded at Corello and held out her hand. "Ava McLane."

"Ready for this?" Corello was a compact man in his fifties with kind eyes, but she could see the absolute focus behind the calm.

"As I'll ever be. What do you have so far?"

"Not much. He won't talk until Mason Callahan gets here. He arrived with you?"

"Yes, but I'm not letting him in until Jopek agrees to not hurt the boy the minute he sees Mason."

"Of course," agreed Corello.

Ava finally looked down the aisle and met Jake's gaze. His eyes were wide, and she nodded at him with reassurance. Kent Jopek stared at her, and she calmly looked back. Kent did not look like a killer. He looked like the nice older guy who lived next door and let you borrow his Weedwacker. Smeared blood on the floor told her where the woman had been shot. And reminded her that Kent was perfectly capable of shooting someone. Corello handed her the handset from the phone-like intercom system.

"Mr. Jopek," she spoke into the handset. "I'm Special Agent Ava McLane. I know you're waiting for Mason Callahan, and I want you to know that he is outside with the Portland Police Department." Her voice echoed through the empty store, sounding smooth and peaceful even to her critical ears.

"Get him in here!" Kent yelled back at her. He leaned against one of the freezer doors, his gun pointed her way and his other arm keeping Jake tight to his chest, his blade in hand.

"Mr. Jopek," Ava started. "I have one concern that I need your word on first. Detective Callahan is here for you to talk to, but the FBI needs to know that you're not going to hurt Jake the moment you see him."

Kent didn't say anything.

"I'm here to help you get out of this situation without injuring anyone else. That's my main goal. If speaking with Mason Callahan is going to help you do that, we'll bring him in. But if all it's going to do is make you shoot him or Jake, then I have a problem.

"You let Henley go free. You left her in a safe spot and let us know where to find her. That tells me that you didn't want to hurt a child. So far all that's happened is that you're holding Jake. That's not a huge offense. He's not that much older than Henley, so I can't imagine that hurting him is something you want to do. That would only make this situation worse."

Always make the consequences for the perpetrator sound minimal.

"Oh yeah? What about that woman I just shot?"

"She's going to be fine," Ava stated, hoping it was true. "You could have really hurt her, but you chose not to. And my understanding is that she was advancing on you, is that correct?"

"Yeah. She wouldn't back off. I warned her!"

"I'm sure you did, Mr. Jopek. And that works in your favor. So right now, this situation is manageable. Let's not give the police outside something to get angry about."

"Don't tell me what to do!" he snapped.

"Then please tell me what you want," Ava said. "Mason is here. Like I said, if you want to talk to him, I need a promise that you won't start shooting. Do you wish to tell him something specific?"

Do not empower by giving concessions without getting something in return.

"Damn right, I want to talk to him. I've only said it ten times!"

"So if I bring him in for you to speak with, you'll just talk to him? I can make him stay and listen to what you have to say. You don't need to hold Jake to make Mason listen."

"Get him in here!"

"I will. And I'll keep that Portland SERT team at bay as long as you agree not to shoot at him or Jake," Ava stated, pushing for an agreement from the man.

Emphasize that harming someone will make the situation worse.

Kent was quiet, but Ava could tell he was thinking hard. He wanted Mason in front of him, but he was realizing that wouldn't happen unless he made some concessions.

"Mr. Jopek, can you stop pointing the gun at the two of us? That simply puts the SERT team on edge," Ava requested.

"Good one," Corello mumbled as Kent moved the gun.

"Thank you," she said into the speaker. "Trust me when I say that reduced everyone's stress level outside. Let's keep them relaxed, okay?" Most of the front of the store was glass. Ava didn't know how good the SERT team's view was, but she was pretty sure at least one sniper had Kent Jopek in his sights.

Kent looked away, and Ava lowered the handset. "We'll let him stew on that for a while," she said to Corello. "He needs to know that his actions affect how he's viewed outside. And I want him to start seeing that there can be a different outcome from whatever he's got planned in his head." She firmly believed in a show of force. It was something to remind the hostage taker that dire consequences could happen if he reacted poorly. There was a time for forceful tactical maneuvers, but they hadn't reached that yet. The SERT team could wait. It was still time to talk, feel him out.

"You're good," Corello stated. "Your voice makes me want to crawl into bed and take a nap."

Ava snorted. "Thanks. I'm glad he's accepted me."

"This is the most relaxed I've seen him," Corello said. "His jitters have settled down. You've got him thinking."

"Do you think he's suicidal?" she whispered.

"I don't know," said Corello. "That's been going through my mind over and over. He's not acting like everything is hopeless. He seems very determined. The suicides I've worked with have always acted like it's the end of the world and they simply don't know how to go on. I don't see that here."

In her eyes, Kent Jopek still looked like a man ready to kill. But would he do it? She hadn't brought up the murder of Mason's informant, Josie. And she wouldn't address it unless Kent mentioned it first. As far as Kent knew, she wasn't aware of it. She brushed at the sweat on her temples. "He still needs to vent about his son's death. And he needs to tell it to Callahan. My concern is what he has planned after he vents. Is his goal to shoot Jake to make Callahan suffer as he did? And then what? Suicide by cop?"

"Tell the SWAT team to stay away!" Kent yelled.

"They will stay out of the store as long as you aren't hurting anyone. You have my word on that. The FBI isn't interested in initiating a shooting," Ava said.

"They're going to want to end this as soon as possible!" Kent shouted back.

Never set a deadline. Time allows anger to dissipate.

"No, they're not," Ava said calmly. "This is where the FBI has the authority, and I'm not going to rush you. The Portland Police guys are going to stay back until I say so."

"Sorry," she mumbled to Corello, acknowledging the inflated agency position she'd played up for Kent.

"I don't give a shit," said Corello. "Say whatever you need to say to end this peacefully."

"Okay," yelled Kent. "I won't shoot anyone. Send in Callahan."

Ava studied the man. "Thank you, Kent. I'm going to take your word on that and have Corello tell them to send him in." She nodded at Corello, who put his cell phone to his ear. "Since you're not going to shoot anyone, are you willing to put the gun down?"

"No," he shouted at her, his arm tightening on Jake.

"That's fine. You realize I have to at least ask, right?" Ava asked. "You can keep the gun. How about the knife? Why do you need the knife if you have the gun?"

"Shut up." Kent didn't yell this time. Not like he had about the gun.

She took it as a good sign. Perhaps he wasn't as attached to the knife as the gun.

"Okay. But I'm not going to let Mason close to you as long as you have a knife. He's going to stay back here by us. I'll make sure he hears everything you have to say to him."

"Hurry up."

She glanced at Corello, who nodded. Mason wouldn't hesitate. He'd been ready to rush the store the minute they'd arrived. "He's coming," she said to Kent. "You'll get your chance to talk to him." She repeated the fact, wanting Kent to realize that he was only talking to Mason because she'd allowed it.

She heard the swishing sound of the doors and turned to see Mason stride in, a determined look on his face as he came to save his son.

. . .

The energetic sounds of Mannheim Steamroller's "Carol of the Bells" filled the store, and Mason knew he'd hate the song for the rest of his life. He'd avoided this grocery story for two decades. He never drove by this particular store, taking time to detour around it. He couldn't stand to see that damned sign. He even avoided shopping in other Safeways.

Ava stood at a center check stand with Corello. She seemed small in the huge store, and he mentally repeated that she was perfectly capable of taking care of herself. Probably more than he was.

He'd been listening through Corello's open cell-phone line. Ava was going by the book, and she was getting Kent to listen. He held her gaze as he strode toward her. Thank God, Kent hadn't shot at her. Mason had wanted to hurt the man every time he'd yelled at Ava. She looked calm and in control; she was in work mode with her emotions tucked away. Something he understood very well. The flutter of the pulse in her neck told him she was on high alert. Just like him.

"I'm Corello." The other negotiator held out his hand to Mason. He looked like he should be teaching college-level economics instead of negotiating with kidnappers. Mason shook his hand and looked past the check stand and down the aisle.

Jake's calm gaze met him. His lips moved: "Dad."

Thank God, Jake is okay. Jake's hands were tied behind him, and he stood with his feet wide and firmly planted for balance. The only sign of a problem was the arm of a killer around Jake's neck, a knife gripped in one hand, a gun in his other hand pointed at Mason's head.

Hate flowed through Mason, and his hands started to sweat. His palms itched to draw his weapon to punish the man.

You killed his son. No doubt the feeling is mutual.

Mason looked into Kent Jopek's eyes and felt the hatred. It blew over him like a suffocating mass. The man had been fostering his hate for two decades, and right now Mason was the recipient of every ounce of it.

"Kent, would you not aim the gun our way?" Ava asked. "Let's not give SERT a reason to get trigger happy."

Kent Jopek slowly lowered the gun, holding Mason's gaze.

He'd seen Kent a few times after his son's death. There'd been an official inquiry into the shooting, and an attempt at a civil case, which had gone nowhere. Going on his lawyer's advice, Mason had never reached out to the Jopek family. He'd known the family had tried to inflate the incident in the media, but there'd been too many eyewitnesses who'd come down firmly in Mason's favor. The consensus both public and official had been that Mason acted correctly.

That didn't help a family mourn their son.

Nor did it take away Mason's own nightmares, in which he shot an innocent boy in the head.

Kent Jopek had changed little. He was still a big man with a firm gaze, but now his hair was gray. Deep lines framed his mouth—the look of a man in constant emotional pain.

Holiday music rang in Mason's ears.

"What's your side of the story?" Corello asked Mason.

"Twenty years ago, I was called to a scene right here where a homeless guy had Kent's son with a knife at his neck. He started to slice open the boy's throat and I shot, hitting both of them. The boy didn't make it. Jopek blames me. Now he's got my son." Mason didn't look away from Jake.

"Jesus Christ," murmured Corello.

"Mr. Jopek," Ava said over the intercom. "Mason is here to listen to what you have to say. What do you want to tell him?"

Mason braced himself for the avalanche of vitriol. Instead, Kent Jopek stared at him.

He waited. Jake turned his head the slightest bit, trying to look back at his captor as if to see if there was a reason the man wasn't speaking. Kent jerked his arm, and Jake froze.

Mason took the intercom out of Ava's hand. Her eyes cautioned him, and he gave her a faint smile. He held the handset to his mouth and lost all train of thought.

What did he want to say to the man?

Every night I relive the day your son died.

I can't imagine your pain.

I'd do the exact same thing again.

Every sentence was wrong. They were shallow next to this man's experience. How could he ask Kent to let his son go?

"Please let Jake go." Mason's plea echoed through the speakers. There was nothing he could say to fix the past or ease this man's pain. He had to say what was in his heart.

Kent finally broke eye contact and looked at the floor.

"I've visited Wyatt's grave every year," Mason admitted.

His gaze flew back to Mason's, disbelief flooding his eyes. "Bullshit."

Mason swallowed hard. "It's the truth." He gave a detailed description of the boy's headstone and location. "I've even taken Jake with me a few times. He knows I caused the death of a boy."

Kent said something to Jake that Mason couldn't hear. Jake nodded in response.

"I relive that day every night. Sometimes several times a night," said Mason.

Kent leaned forward a bit, his eyes hungry for Mason's words.

"Sometimes in my dreams, my shot misses."

The man nodded slightly. No doubt he'd had the same dream.

"But it never matters. The outcome never changes," Mason said, watching the man's eyes narrow. No doubt Kent had multiple dreams where Wyatt walked away unscathed.

"When Wyatt jumped up at the same moment I fired, I knew what would happen. I've wished a million times that I could have pulled back that bullet."

Kent blew out a shaky breath.

"My life has never been the same," Mason said.

"Don't you dare try to compare your pain to mine," Kent hissed. "You don't have the slightest idea of what I've gone through. I watched my son die, murdered by someone who was supposed to protect him."

Out of the corner of his eye, Mason saw Ava stiffen. A misstep. He'd triggered Jopek's defenses.

"I can't even begin—," Mason started.

"I cradled him and felt the destruction your bullet did to his head." Kent's gun crept back up to point at Mason. "I could feel the sharp edges of his broken skull. Inside it was soft." His voice got louder. "I tried to put him back together!"

Ava grabbed the handset. "Kent, please don't point the gun at us. Remember, there are eyes watching from outside."

Kent lowered his gun and his gaze, but his body shook with the effort.

"We're losing him," Corello muttered. "Get him focused."

"This is your chance to tell Mason what you wanted to say, remember?" Ava continued. "So far he's done most of the talking. What do you want him to hear?"

Mason watched the man try to get a handle on his emotions. And empathized. The man was searching for answers and trying to right a situation where he believed he'd been wronged.

"I've had two failed marriages," Kent stated, staring at the floor. "I can't stay with a woman because they don't understand what this has done to me. I'm an alcoholic. I haven't touched a drink in three years, but there was a time when all I'd do was drink. I lost jobs. I lost my home." He looked up at Mason. "I used to make a circuit of the liquor stores. I didn't want the employees judging how much alcohol I bought, so I'd drive an extra twenty miles so I'd never have to go to the same store more than once a month."

Mason listened.

"That's when I realized I needed to take control. I wasn't going to let externals dictate my life," Kent continued. "I stopped drinking. Every time I didn't stop at the liquor store was a success to be celebrated. I proved I had the power to make a change in my life. I decided to change other things. I needed to regain my health, so I made it happen. Sheer willpower. Mental toughness is what saved me."

Mason understood. That was how he'd survived his divorce. He'd moved into autopilot and set the program to run at optimum. From the outside, he looked pretty good.

Just don't look too deep.

Mason had cracks in his shell.

And Kent Jopek did, too.

"But I couldn't make the nightmares go away. I had control over every waking minute, but as soon as I went to sleep, Wyatt would talk to me, begging me to save him. So like everything else, I made a plan that would make things change." Kent looked directly at Mason.

Something inside him just changed. His eyes are wrong.

A warning went off in Mason's brain, his body hardening. Corello and Ava both took deep breaths. They saw it, too. Kent had disengaged his emotions from his actions.

"I needed to destroy you just as I had been destroyed. Bit by bit. Piece by piece. What was important to you? What could I take away? I watched you, Callahan. I spent weeks watching, seeing how you lived your life." Kent gave a short laugh. "You know what? Your life stinks. You work. That's it. Your home is a bare, empty box. You don't date. You don't hang out with friends. So I had to strike where I could. Phase one was your job, because it seemed to be all you had."

Kent had succeeded. Having the respect of his peers and position yanked out from under Mason had nearly toppled him emotionally. He'd been lucky he had Henley's case to focus on, and Ava to open his eyes.

"I'd tried to get a hold of this kid." Kent squeezed his arm around Jake's neck, and the boy's face turned pink.

Mason shifted his weight to the balls of his feet, ready to strike.

"Easy," Ava whispered.

He held his breath.

"I couldn't nab him. Three times I tried. I settled for the girl because she was easy. I thought she might be enough, but it didn't satisfy me. She wasn't close enough to your life. Her death wouldn't cause the level of pain I wanted."

Three times? Mason's gut twisted. Jake was never leaving the house again.

"And then I was surprised as hell to discover that you'd gotten a dog. Wyatt had a dog. I gave it away after he died. Dogs and boys belong together. I had no place in my life for it after that."

Ava slowly lifted the handset to speak. "You let Henley and the dog go. Why?" she asked softly.

Mason felt her voice flow through him like creamy hot chocolate, and his spine relaxed. She had a special gift that worked on Kent as well as himself.

Kent shrugged and looked away. "Killing them wasn't going to hurt you like I needed it to."

He turned an eagle-sharp gaze back to Mason. "I wanted to pierce you in the heart. The loss of the dog and the girl would give you anxiety, but nothing like the pain of losing your son. I knew I had to return to my original plan to fully destroy you." He twisted his hand with the knife near Jake's ear, laying the blade against the source of life flowing through Jake's neck. Exactly where the homeless man had held his knife on Wyatt.

"I know how to aim for your heart," he said to Mason as he slowly raised his gun.

Blood appeared on Jake's neck as Mason shouted, his vision narrowed on the movement of Kent's blade.

Time slowed.

Kent fired and Ava gasped. Mason drew his gun and heard the windows crack behind him with the retort of rifle fire. Kent jerked to his right, knocking Jake to the floor as he spun away. Kent raced to the back of the store, zigzagging to avoid more sniper fire.

Beside Mason, Ava gasped again and bent over the check stand, her hand clasped to her shoulder. Blood flowed from under her hand. Kent's bullet had caught her. Mason froze, torn between Ava and Jake and Kent.

Who first?

Corello grabbed Ava's arm and shoved her to the floor, putting pressure on her shoulder.

"Go!" she yelled at Mason. "Go to Jake." Her blue eyes pleaded. "I'll be okay."

Corello looked up and nodded, his face grim.

Mason raced around the check stand, dropped to his knees next to Jake on the floor in the freezer aisle, and ran his hands all over his son, checking for gunshot wounds. "Jake!"

"Dad! I'm okay." Jake squirmed in his grasp. "I'm not hit."

He wrapped his arms around Jake as they sprawled on the floor. Mason squeezed tight, trying to slow his skyrocketing heart. *Jake is safe.* Mason tilted his son's jaw away to get a look at his neck. The slice in Jake's neck was shallow. Nothing life threatening. He stood and hauled Jake up with him. "Get down behind the check stand with Ava. And stay there until they take you out of the store!" he ordered, giving the boy a shove in the right direction. Jake stumbled, his arms still tied behind him. He caught his balance and turned around to look at Mason.

"What about you?" Jake's eyes were wide.

"I have to stop that son of a bitch."

Mason heard shouts of "Everybody down!" as the SERT team rushed into the store. He didn't obey. He was going to find Kent Jopek first.

He ran down the aisle, following the drops of blood.

Jopek had been hit.

26

The drops led to the double swinging doors at the back of the store. Mason took a deep breath, stole a peek through the hazy plastic window in one of the doors, and then pushed through with his gun leading the way.

The back room of the grocery store was silent, the cheery holiday music confined to the aisles of the store. The floor changed from highly polished tile to concrete, and the lighting dimmed. The back of the store was like a garage. High ceilings, unfinished walls, and crap stacked everywhere: boxes; mops; brooms; damaged, unsalable goods. Pallets of groceries in cardboard boxes wrapped in clear plastic waited to be opened and unpacked. Mason scanned the room. The blood trail led to his left, around the corner of a huge walk-in cooler.

He followed.

Shouts came from the front of the store, where the SERT team was methodically clearing the aisles. Any moment they would find the blood trail.

Let them handle Kent.

Go check on Ava.

He couldn't do it. He pushed on. He had to find the man whose life he'd destroyed two decades ago. He couldn't let Kent Jopek walk away. Part of him felt he owed the man something. But what? He'd nearly killed Jake, Henley, and Ava. He *had* killed Josie Mueller.

You owe him nothing.

Mason had spent twenty years agonizing over the pain he'd caused Kent; it was hard to change his way of thinking. Over four days, the man had uprooted the lives of Mason's family. He didn't deserve to be handled with kid gloves. Kent Jopek was now a destroyer, not a victim, and Mason needed to wrap his brain around it.

He killed Josie in cold blood.

Mason slowed his steps. No doubt Kent would shoot the moment he saw him. He ducked his head around the corner of the cooler to catch a quick glance at the pathway behind it.

All clear.

He stepped quickly around the corner, weapon in front, eyes scanning for movement. The blood drops followed the back wall of the cooler. Mason moved forward, listening hard for Kent. Tall pallets of groceries and a cardboard-baling machine created a narrow aisle behind the cooler. He kept going, peeking between the pallets of dry goods as he passed.

Faint sounds of an ambulance siren sounded outside, making Mason nearly gave up his hunt. *Ava?* The gunshot wound to her upper arm hadn't looked bad. But what if the bullet had hit more than her arm? *Damn it.* Wouldn't she have mentioned that?

A rustle sounded ahead on his left.

"Kent?" he asked quietly.

"Stay away, Callahan."

Mason continued his progress. The blood turned the corner around the far side of the cooler. He stopped at the corner, imagining Kent on the other side with his gun trained at the point he believed Mason's head would first appear.

"You're shot." Mason stated the obvious.

"No shit," came the voice around the corner. There was no strength behind the words.

"SERT will be here in a moment. They'll get you to the hospital." Mason wondered how badly he was hurt. The drops of blood had increased to a trickle as he moved along the cooler.

"I'm not going to the hospital."

"Where do you want to go?"

Kent didn't answer.

"I'm going to come around this corner. You going to shoot?" Mason asked.

A long moment of silence made Mason wonder if the man had passed out.

"No, I won't shoot." Kent's voice was soft.

Should he go? Mason paused. He wanted to be the man to bring Kent down for the crimes he'd committed against the people close to him. But the smart thing would be to wait for the SERT team.

"I'm going to be with my son again," Kent said.

Mason spun around the corner, his gun trained on Kent. The man sat on the floor in the corner, propped up against the wall with his feet spread in front of him. The sniper's shot had caused more damage than Mason had realized. Blood soaked the front of Kent's jacket and pooled on the floor to his left. His eyes were slow to look up at Mason. He clutched his gun against his bloody chest; his other hand lay useless beside him. He looked at Mason's gun and then into Mason's eyes.

"I can hear him calling me," he stated. His eyes struggled to focus.

Mason heard commands being shouted out on the floor of the store. "I think you hear the SERT team," Mason said. Kent looked like a man who'd given up, and Mason felt a pang of sympathy.

"No, it's Wyatt. He's telling me to hurry up."

Shouts of "*Go, go, go!*" echoed into the back room.

Mason squatted at the feet of the defeated man, his gun ready. "I never meant to hurt your son. I did what I thought was right. And I know I wouldn't have done anything different."

Kent nodded and winced in pain, shifting on the floor. "Fucking hurts."

"Sorry about that."

"The pain sorta feels good, you know? I actually feel something besides the fucking emptiness in my heart."

Mason didn't know what to say.

"I won't go to prison," Kent stated, looking Mason in the eye again. "I can't. I've been in prison for twenty years."

"You don't know that will happen."

"Yes, I do. I killed that prostitute and set it up to look like you'd been there. I had to make it look brutal and angry. I wanted the scene to disturb you and everyone who looked at it."

"Did you take Jake's suitcase?"

Kent snorted. "Yeah, I was getting desperate. I was beginning to think I'd never get my hands on your son. I'd hoped to find something in the suitcase I could lure him with, but instead I found dirty laundry and a stuffed animal."

Mason eyed the growing pool of blood on Kent's left.

"We're in the back!" Mason yelled out to the SERT team. "He's down!"

"No!" Kent whispered. "Keep them away."

Mason reached to take the gun from Kent's hand on his chest. "Let me take this."

Kent shook his head, whipped the gun into his mouth, and fired.

• • •

Mason tried not to vomit as three members of the SERT team attempted to revive Kent Jopek.

Why didn't I grab the gun sooner?

Mason had fallen backward in shock as Kent swiftly shot himself, spraying blood on the wall behind him. He'd scooted away from the body, a split second before SERT swept into the back room. Now

Mason sat on the floor, his back against a stack of pallets. One heavily armored officer asked if he was injured, and Mason shook his head.

He couldn't speak. Shock locked his voice.

Mason hadn't seen Kent's suicide coming. There hadn't been time to assess any signs.

The officers shouted commands and acted like they'd practiced the resuscitation a hundred times. Mason stared as Kent's feet jerked with the officer's movements, knowing their attempts were futile. No one could survive that damage to the brain.

Jake sprinted from the far end of the cooler, two SERT members hot on his heels shouting for him to stop. "Dad!" he shrieked when he saw Mason on the ground.

Mason lifted a hand as Jake ran closer. "I'm not hurt."

"I heard a shot!" Jake fell to his knees, panting.

Mason pointed at the officers frantically working on Kent. "He shot himself."

Jake looked and jumped back to his feet. "Stop it!" he shouted at the officers. "Don't help him!" He lunged at an officer, but was grabbed around the waist by one who'd tailed him through the back room.

"Jake!" Mason leaped up, snatching his son away from the officer. "What are you doing?"

"Leave him alone! Stop them!"

Mason shook the boy, making Jake look him in the eye. "They're doing their job!"

"Don't let them save him," Jake pleaded as tears streaked down his face. "He'll come back and do this to us again!"

Mason pulled his son to his chest. "It's over," he said quietly in the boy's ear. "He's already gone. They can't save him. He won't come back."

Jake let out a shuddering sob and collapsed into his father.

27

Someone knocked at the hospital door and then pushed it open. Mason hopped up and tugged at the wrinkled shirt he'd worn all night, trying to sleep in the uncomfortable hospital chair.

ASAC Duncan peeked around the door and met Mason's gaze. "All right if I come in?"

Ava's boss was more than welcome because Mason wanted some answers. The agent practically tiptoed into the room, eyeing Ava sleeping in the bed. "How is she?"

"Good. They got her out of surgery at about midnight. She was awake in recovery for a while, but she slept all night long. No telling how doped up she is."

"Her surgery went fine?" Duncan asked.

Mason suspected he'd already had a full report from the surgeon himself. "Yes, her upper arm will be setting off metal detectors for the rest of her life, but she should recover nearly all range of use." *Over time. And after lots of therapy.*

"That's good." The two men stood in silence, watching the sleeping agent.

"We went through Kent Jopek's apartment overnight," Duncan stated.

Mason's listening skills shot to optimum. "And?"

Duncan shook his head. "He practically had a shrine to you."

"What?" Mason tasted bile in the back of his mouth. He eyed the plastic bowl on the table next to Ava's bed.

"He had a binder with every newspaper article you've ever been mentioned in. Printouts from the Internet and all his legal documents from his civil case and the inquiry into the shooting."

Dizziness swamped Mason. He sat down and rubbed his face.

"He had Jake's school schedule, and we found receipts for his plane tickets to North Carolina. A memory card full of pictures of Jake on campus, Henley at her bus stop, your home, and you on the job in various places. He also had a homemade kit for transferring fingerprints. I assume the ones we found in the kit will be yours. I don't think you'll be on leave much longer."

Holy shit. "He told me he killed Josie."

Duncan went on. "The stolen minivan was in his garage, and his Chevy sedan was in the Safeway parking lot."

"I can't believe this," Mason muttered.

"Besides you and Jake, he also had a ton of photos of Wyatt everywhere in the house. There was even a bedroom done up for a young boy. Kent lived in this place for three years, so Wyatt obviously never slept there. I'm wondering if it's a replica of his old room. It looks like Henley was kept in a small locked room down in his basement. We found some food, water, and bedding. Even some books."

Mason blew out a thankful breath. He'd imagined the girl had been kept in a much worse location.

"Sanford was there when Henley and her parents were reunited at the emergency room. He said there wasn't a dry eye in the hospital. All the nurses and cops included. Henley was just dehydrated from her ordeal. They didn't even keep her overnight." Duncan's expression turned grim. "And she wasn't sexually abused or abused at all. Everything checked out fine with her."

"Thank God. That could have gone so many different ways."

Duncan nodded. "Amen to that. Oh, and I'm supposed to tell you that the woman from Search and Rescue took your dog to her home until you can pick it up."

"Bingo," said Mason, remembering Henley's name for the dog. "I don't know if it's really my dog. I think it belongs with Henley," he said slowly, realizing he'd become quite attached to the furry black mutt.

"I don't think that's an option," Duncan said. "Sanford told me that Henley's mom started sneezing up a fit at the emergency room because the girl was covered in dog hair. The nurses were about to inject her with an antihistamine," he said with a smile. "Looks like you'll have your dog back."

Mason bit back a smile. Bingo had earned a place of honor in his home. He'd even buy him the expensive dog food.

"Jake says there's still law enforcement at the Fairbankses.'" Mason had been at the Safeway store for several hours after the shooting and then had gone straight to the hospital to sit in the waiting room while Ava had surgery. Now it was nearly 8 A.M.

"Yes, we still have a team in the house, and they'll stay there until all the chaos settles down. Probably a day or two."

Jake had texted him a few times last night, asking for Ava updates. Mason hadn't liked how impersonal the texts felt. He planned to get a phone that could do that video-calling thing. That way when he wanted to see his son, he could. And Mason would always know who was on the other end of the line.

"We also discovered that Kent had closed out his bank accounts. He also left a couple of farewell letters to his exes."

The man had been suicidal.

"I think we got real lucky that he didn't take anyone else down with him," said Duncan. "I believe that was his original plan. He was either going to take you or Jake out and then take his own life."

"He said he wanted to see his son," Mason stated. His brain whirled. *How close had he and Jake come to death yesterday?*

"Ava did a good job talking him down." Duncan looked at the woman sleeping in the bed.

"Yeah, and then I came in and pissed him off."

"It ended well."

"That depends on your definition of 'well,'" Mason argued.

"Henley's home safe and sound. So are Jake and you. Ava will be soon. I call that a damned good ending." Duncan stole another look at Ava. "I'm headed home to shower and then back to the office. Let me know later how she's doing." He strode to the door and opened it, stopping to smile back at Mason. "Merry Christmas."

Mason blinked. It *was* Christmas. "Same to you," he replied automatically.

Duncan vanished.

Mason pulled his chair up to the side of Ava's bed and clasped her good hand as he sat down. "Merry Christmas," he said softly.

The first of many to come, he decided. He wasn't letting Ava McLane walk out of his life any time soon. She'd pushed her way under his heart, and he intended to keep her there. Her eyes opened, and she looked directly at him, giving a small smile.

"Is he gone?" she whispered.

"Were you awake?"

"I woke up while he was talking. I didn't want to deal with bureau business," she said.

Mason chuckled. "You fooled both of us. I doubt he would have grilled you this morning."

"You don't know Ben Duncan very well. Being unconscious is the only way to avoid his questions." She yawned and flinched as the movement stretched her bandaged shoulder. "Am I in one piece?"

"Yes, thanks to the grace of God and Kent's poor aim. Now you're part cyborg. The surgeon seemed very pleased with himself, so I think you'll be in good shape."

"Sounds like I'll need some help for a while," she said, blue eyes staring straight into his.

"I'll give you whatever help you need. Getting dressed, bathing, eating."

"It could be a big job. I'm rather demanding," Ava stated.

He stared at her. "Why do I not believe you?"

"I can be difficult. I'm very particular about how I like things done."

Mason smiled and leaned closer. "Then I'm your man. Anyone who has discerning taste wants me to help them get dressed."

"What are you suggesting, detective?"

"I'm suggesting that you rely on me for a while," he said softly. "Catch your breath, heal, and see if you enjoy seeing me every day."

Her eyes widened as his words sank in.

Were they on the same page?

"Ava? Are you in here?" The door burst open without a knock, and Jayne swept into the hospital room, blond hair flowing behind her. She had two bandages on her face from her car accident, and her hand was in a fabric brace.

Mason shot to his feet and stepped in front of Ava's twin before she rushed the bed. "Slow down!"

"Jayne? What are you doing here?" Ava asked, surprise on her face.

"The hospital notified me. This is quite a switch," Jayne said with a wide smile. She scanned the bed, the room, the window, and Mason within two seconds. The woman seemed wired for a hospital visit at eight in the morning.

Her pupils were huge.

Shit. What's she on?

"Usually I'm the one in the hospital bed." Jayne laughed as if it were the cleverest joke in the world. "I'm so lucky that my injuries weren't too serious from that stupid car accident."

Mason kept one hand on the twin's good arm. Energy vibrated under his fingers. This wasn't espresso overload. Jayne was blinking too often, and a twitch shook her shoulders, painfully reminding him of Josie on his last visit before she was murdered.

Meth?

"Merry Christmas, darling!" Jayne squealed and tried to pull out of Mason's grasp to hug her sister. "Let go." She tugged at her arm, a scowl deepening the lines between her brows.

"No," said Mason. "Don't touch her shoulder. She's had surgery."

"I'll just give her a kiss on her forehead."

Mason slowly let go, and Jayne dropped a peck on Ava's forehead. Ava's expression didn't change. She simply watched her sister.

"I need to run. I could only spare a minute. I'll call you later." Jayne waved her bandaged hand at Mason and practically skipped to the door. "Ta-ta, darlings."

Silence filled the room.

• • •

Ava watched the door shut behind her twin. Tears burned at the back of her eyes. She blinked hard. *I won't let her make me cry.* She wiped her face.

Mason seemed dumbstruck. He turned brown eyes to her, his lips slightly open in shock. He shook his head, a scowl turning down the corners of his mouth. "And I thought I couldn't be any more surprised after meeting her the first time. She didn't ask a single question about your injuries."

Ava tried to shrug, and pain shot up the left side of her neck.

"She was on something," Mason stated.

"She usually is."

Mason carefully sat on the edge of her bed and took her good hand, rubbing her fingers in his grip. "You are nothing like her."

"I know." Ava fought to keep the tears back.

"No. Listen to me," Mason said, leaning forward and emphasizing each word. "You are plumb full of caring. Every damn cell in your body cares about the people around you. Even the ones who are crazy and treat you like crap. It makes you an amazing agent. When I heard you talking to Kent yesterday, I could hear genuine concern in your voice."

"I didn't want anyone to get hurt," Ava whispered.

"Do you think Jayne cares if anyone gets hurt?"

Ava rubbed her nose, searching for a different answer instead of the one that was screaming in her brain. "No," she finally admitted.

"That woman thinks only of herself. Maybe it's the drugs, but I believe they only enhance true character."

He's so right.

"She's always been like that," Ava said. "I'm surprised she didn't ask me where her Christmas present was."

Mason's eyes lit up as he smiled.

Ava's heart lurched at the handsome sight. Mason Callahan was very special. Honorable. Reliable. Steady. Caring. Definitely old-fashioned, but she loved that about him. She even loved that damn cowboy hat that was always within reach. His offer to stay with her while she recovered had made her nearly cry. Jayne had interrupted an important moment.

"You're very good for me," she said.

His smile grew broader. "I feel the same way."

"I was afraid he was going to shoot you if you came in the store yesterday. I didn't want to let you in."

His smile faltered. "Do you have any idea how hard it was for me to let you walk alone into that den with the lion? I wanted to throw up when the doors closed behind you. Duncan was about to handcuff me so I wouldn't rush the store when Kent started yelling at you."

"We have tough jobs," Ava said slowly. "Time-consuming. Sometimes dangerous."

Would he hear what she was asking?

Mason's gaze flickered from one of her eyes to the other. "I'm well aware of that."

"Can we do this?" she whispered, laying her heart open and bare for him to see. "Can we make it work?"

His hand tightened on hers. "Do you remember asking me if I've ever loved someone where the emotion was totally out of my control? Where someone physically feels the other person moving about in the world? That *exact* feeling is growing inside of me. I've felt precisely what you described, and I want to continue to experience it every day with you."

My words. He was listening to me. Her throat tightened.

"I'm willing to do my damnedest to make that happen between us. There was another motive behind my offer to stay with you while you healed. I was sorta hoping you'd get addicted to having me around," Mason continued. "You've dug out a whopping-sized piece of my heart, Agent McLane. I'd appreciate it if you handled it with care. And I promise to do the same."

Love for him surged through her.

"Kiss me," she begged. "And don't let me go, okay? Promise?"

"That's a deal I'll never back out on."

He kissed her.

ALONE BY KENDRA ELLIOT

If you liked *Vanished*, you might also like *Alone*, a dark and thrilling romantic suspense. Read on to follow forensic anthropologist Victoria Peres as she races to solve a horrific new case while confronting the secrets of her past.

"I won't miss this part of the job," Victoria heard Dr. James Campbell mutter as he held a blackberry vine out of the way for Lacey and Victoria to pass by.

A discovery of dead bodies had abruptly shortened their Italian dinner at Portland's fabulous Pazzo Ristorante. The trio of coworkers had been relaxing over a lovely Barbaresco when the medical examiner's phone buzzed. He'd taken the call at the table and raised a brow at the women, who'd nodded. Both forensic specialists wanted to accompany him to the crime scene.

Five teenagers were dead in the depths of Forest Park.

Time to go to work.

The guiding police officer who'd met them at the trailhead commented, "A hiker found the scene about four hours ago. Looks pretty fresh. One of the girls was still breathing and they rushed her to the hospital. She's not expected to make it." He paused to take a breath, and the volume of his voice dropped to where Victoria leaned forward to hear him. "I gotta say, this is one of the most disturbing sights I've ever seen." The tough cop looked rattled.

Who would kill so many teenage girls? Victoria Peres shook her head. It was a messed-up world. And working at the medical examiner's office as a forensic anthropologist showed her some of the darkest corners of that world. The indignities and atrocities that people inflicted on other human beings were mind-numbing. The kids were the hardest for her to stomach.

The three of them pointed their flashlights at the dirt path, choosing their footsteps carefully, following the police officer. Luckily the fall rains had paused for the moment, because tonight the forest was intimidating enough. Firs towered overhead, blocking all light from the full moon. Ferns sprouted from tree trunks, drawing nutrition from the bark and thick moss that draped the branches. Victoria had already given thanks that she'd worn her boots to dinner in honor of the fall chill. Still dressed for dinner, the three of them looked out of place for the two-mile hike in the damp woods. It was rare that she accompanied Dr. Campbell to a scene. Her job usually kept her inside the medical examiner's building.

But this was Dr. Campbell's last month on the job. Oregon's ME was ready to retire. And Victoria wanted to spend every working moment she could with him, soaking up his experience, wisdom, and wit. "I can't do anything about the death," Dr. Campbell once told her. "But I can do something about what happens after the death. I can speak for the victims, explain their injuries, and bring justice." It described exactly how Victoria felt about her job. There was a mutual respect between her and Dr. Campbell that made her cross her fingers, hoping she could achieve the same with the new medical examiner.

Dr. Campbell's daughter, Lacey, had told Victoria she'd miss working with her father. Lacey served as the ME's forensic odontologist. She and her father were very close.

Lacey was quiet behind Victoria as they trudged along the dark path. She didn't wonder out loud at the cause of the kids' deaths or bitch about the hike; she was professional. Victoria had worked with the petite forensic specialist for a few years, her respect growing every time one of their cases crossed paths. Only recently had they started using each other's first names.

A soft buzz of conversation touched Victoria's ears and the trail seemed to light up farther ahead. They were nearly there. She swallowed hard as the gnocchi she had eaten twisted in her stomach. Maybe she should have gone home after dinner and let the medical examiner do his job. But she'd be greeted by a lonely house. The evening had been so wonderful between the food and conversation, she'd hated for it to end. She'd decided to tramp a few miles through Portland's five-thousand-acre park to view dead teenagers.

Was something wrong with her?

The trail grew choppy with boot prints and small tire marks from the equipment hauled in to process the scene. They emerged into a clearing lit up with glaring lights, and the quiet hum of conversation stopped. The three of them halted and stared, scanning the surreal setting. Cops stood idle in small groups, observing, while crime-scene techs crawled through the display.

It looked straight out of a cheap horror film.

Off the path about ten yards, five young women lay motionless in a lush bed of ferns, arranged like a wagon wheel, their heads at the center, feet pointed out. The image was simultaneously beautiful and evil. One prong of the wheel was missing—the girl who'd been rushed to the hospital.

A cop thrust a log into Dr. Campbell's hands to sign. He barely glanced at it, his gaze locked on the eerie spectacle.

"Lead all souls to heaven," Lacey whispered.

Victoria Peres felt as if her hands were tied. These poor children still had the flesh covering their bones, unlike her usual subjects at work, but she still had a need to examine them to discover their story.

Five girls gracefully sprawled in the center of a clearing. Their skin harshly exposed by the lighting the crime scene team had brought in. Each girl had long dark hair and they all wore white dresses of different styles. Their hands were all crossed on their stomachs. There was neither blood nor immediate indicator of cause of death, just an unnatural grayness to their skin and lips.

Poison?

The girls looked asleep.

No kiss would wake them.

Victoria pushed her own long hair behind one ear, disturbed by the similarity between the girls' appearances. *Why did they look and dress the same?*

She didn't usually attend a fresh death scene. But she helped wherever her skills were needed. She'd definitely put in her share of hours over the flesh of the freshly deceased and the not-so-freshly deceased. Digging in the burial pits of the mass executions in Kosovo had desensitized her to most situations.

But when James had received the call, her instincts had kicked in. Death was her field. And she possessed a particular set of skills that could get answers for the questions the dead teens presented. She noticed the cops glanced their way, scoping out who'd arrived at the scene. None made eye contact with her. She'd busted enough balls at crime scenes to know they weren't her biggest fans. She didn't care. What mattered was that scenes were handled correctly. Mistakes weren't acceptable.

She looked away from the sorrow on Lacey's face. The odontologist had a big soft spot that she wasn't afraid to reveal. Victoria kept her own sensitivity hidden deep. It wasn't that she didn't feel the sadness of the situation; she simply didn't feel it was professional to show it. And she worked better when she tucked away the feelings.

"Who are they?" James muttered to the cop as he handed the log to Lacey to sign.

"We don't know yet, Dr. Campbell," he answered. "There's no ID with any of the girls. No cell phones, no purses."

"Parents will be looking for their daughters soon," said Lacey. "They can't be over eighteen."

Victoria eyed the stature and build of the bodies, silently agreeing with Lacey's assessment. Parents would expect these kids to be in bed by midnight. She followed Dr. Campbell as he carefully stepped to the closest body and squatted next to a female tech, pulling gloves out of his small kit. Up close, Victoria could see the first girl had applied makeup to cover acne on her chin and wore black liquid eyeliner to give the popular cat-eye look.

Someone's daughter.

Dr. Campbell bent the girl's arm. "Rigor has started. Not fully set yet. Can you roll her onto her side for me, Sarah?" he asked the middle-aged woman, who nodded and gently shifted the dead girl onto her side. He pressed at the purpling skin on her shoulder blades where gravity had guided the blood to settle once her heart had stopped pumping. It didn't blanch. "Livor is set. Have you noticed anything unusual?" Dr. Campbell asked the tech.

The tech grimaced. "Outside of this being a group of dead children? Not yet. It's a very clean site so far. The girls were cold when I got here, and they all look clean front and back. Frankly, it's like a sick fairy tale." Sarah frowned. "They're laid out so perfectly. I mean, even their hair is smoothed down. Someone must have arranged them."

"It's just wrong," Dr. Campbell said as he drew a syringe out of his equipment. Victoria didn't need to see the medical examiner extract the vitreous humor from the girl's eye to determine an accurate time of death. Very few things about the human body bothered her, but a needle in the eye was close to the top of the list. Victoria stood and walked back to where Lacey'd waited at the edge of the scene. Two men had joined Lacey. Victoria recognized them as Oregon State Police detectives from the Major Crimes division. The local police department must have called in the State Police for their help.

"Dr. Peres." The older detective, Mason Callahan, greeted Victoria. His partner, Ray Lusco, nodded at her. Both men had tired eyes and subtle slumps to their shoulders. She hadn't noticed that they'd been working the scene when she arrived. She'd been focused on the death wheel of beautiful girls. But obviously Mason and Ray had already spent several hours in the woods. She'd worked with the detectives several times, their opposite personalities making them perfect partners. Mason was the blunt-spoken salt-and-pepper-haired senior detective, rarely seen without his cowboy boots and hat. Ray was the younger family man, who looked like he should be coaching college football.

It wouldn't take long to get depressed or angry or frustrated at this scene. The absolute futileness of the death of these young women was like a gut punch. It was one of the quieter scenes Victoria had visited, not chatty like some. The tension was thick, and the anger from the cops and workers was palpable.

"No one has reported missing teens tonight?" Lacey was asking, surprise on her face.

Ray shook his head. "Not locally yet. Some males, but no females. It's only eleven. Calls will start coming in. This gives me the creeps. It's like the girls all lay down and fell asleep. No evidence of thrashing about or fighting back."

"What happened?" Lacey asked. "Do you think they drank something?"

Mason tugged on his ever-present cowboy hat. "Possible." He was tight-lipped. Victoria knew he wouldn't speculate out loud.

"No cups," stated Victoria. "Unless you already removed them?"

"Nothing's been removed," answered Ray. "Not by us."

"Ghosts took them," stated the cop with the log. Victoria shifted to read his name. *Dixon.*

The group simply stared at Dixon.

"What?" Dixon met their stares. "Don't you know where we are?"

Victoria saw a flicker of recognition on Lacey's face. The forensic odontologist had grown up in the area. Victoria was originally from a tiny coastal town; she didn't know about Mason and Ray, but judging by their faces, they were clueless about the cop's reference.

"This part of the woods is haunted," Dixon stated solemnly. "All the high-school kids around here avoid this area."

Mason looked disgusted.

Dixon's brows narrowed. "You do know this isn't the first ring of suicides here, right?"

The two Major Crimes detectives called for confirmation. Sure enough. In 1968, six female bodies had been found in Forest Park. Only three of the bodies had been identified. Three had remained unclaimed for decades. Victoria rubbed at her arms in the cold, hugging herself.

How come no one had missed them?

"How is that possible?" she asked the detectives. An hour at the scene hadn't answered any of her questions; it'd only raised more. "How can no one miss three women? I can understand one person who possibly moved here from out of state, living as a transient going unidentified, but three?"

"It was a different era," commented Mason. "I knew there'd been a mass suicide in Forest Park a long time ago, but didn't know where. This place is gigantic. You can believe we'll be looking into it again."

Dr. Campbell stepped up to the group. "I'm done here. It looks like I'll be seeing these young women again. With the air temperature here I'd estimate it's been six to eight hours since death, but I'll have a more accurate window tomorrow after the lab work."

Her heart ached at the regret on his face. She knew he didn't like seeing kids on his table.

"What a case to catch near the end of my career," he added. "I hope to get a clear answer on this one. Soon."

"I didn't realize you were retiring, doctor," Ray said, raising a brow at Mason, who looked stunned.

"I'm looking forward to sleeping in and not getting phone calls in the middle of the night. Or during my dinner."

Both detectives nodded in grim agreement. "Holidays are also bad," said Ray.

"I'll stick around to help transition in the new chief examiner. We've narrowed it down to two applicants. Either will be a good chief."

"You're not promoting from within?" Mason asked.

"Not this time. I've got fine deputy medical examiners, but none of them want the extra responsibility of the position." Dr. Campbell turned and looked over the young women in the ferns. "This case will stick with me for a while."

"Detective Callahan," came a different voice.

The group spun to see the new arrivals in the forest. Another Portland police officer had spoken as he led two men to the scene. One was a man in a dark green uniform with a baseball cap that read ranger, and the other was a tall civilian in jeans and a heavy jacket. The civilian's face was in the shadows, but Victoria stiffened at his approach. Something about the way he carried himself set off alarms in her head.

"This is Bud Rollins." The police officer gestured at the man in the ranger hat. "He's one of the park rangers and knows this forest inside and out. He's the first guy we call when we need help in here."

Mason shook hands with the slender man. "Sorry to get you out of bed."

"Not a problem. I like to know what's going on in my woods."

The weathered ranger spoke with a soft southern accent, making Victoria blink. The sound was a rarity in the Pacific Northwest. His eyes were kind, and she estimated his age to be in his early fifties. He scanned the scene ahead of him and paled. "Dear Lord. One of them lived?"

"So far," said Mason. "Doesn't look good for her, though."

The second man stepped forward and held his hand out to Detective Callahan.

Victoria couldn't breathe; her gaze locked on the man's face. Every coherent thought vanished from her brain.

"This is Seth Rutledge," said Dr. Campbell as he greeted the man. "Glad you could make it. Dr. Rutledge is one of the applicants for my position. I had the office call him to the scene," Dr. Campbell told Mason as the men shook hands.

Dr. Rutledge met Victoria's eyes. "Hello, Tori."

Everyone looked at Victoria.

Victoria pressed her lips together as she held Dr. Rutledge's gaze, her spine stiff, her hands crammed in her pockets, her ears ringing. "Seth."

Seth gave a half smile, and the shield around Victoria's heart started to crack.

"Been a while, Tori."

Victoria nodded and all ability to speak abandoned her brain.

ACKNOWLEDGMENTS

Kyron Horman, one of Oregon's still-missing children, was consistently present in my thoughts while I wrote this book. May his family find peace one day.

My readers often request stories for characters they have fallen in love with. Over and over I heard, "When will Mason get his book?" I'd always known I'd write about him, but I was surprised to discover that I needed more than one book to tell his and Ava's story. Keep an eye out for the next phase in their lives, and please let me know whom you want to read about in the future.

Thank you to Special Agent Pelath, Special Agent Rogers, and especially Special Agent Devinney, who took time out of their busy schedules to meet with a nosy writer and answer my ton of emails. Thank you to Angela Bell, who arranged for me to talk to these fabulous female agents. I got a big kick out of telling my kids, "I have a meeting with the FBI today."

I write fiction; these smart women gave me guidance, but authors have a tendency to write whatever makes their characters happy. Or miserable. Any mistakes are my own.

I have a dream team at Montlake. JoVon Sotak, Kelli Martin, and Jessica Poore keep me sane. As always, Charlotte Herscher wields her red pen with a master's touch to whip my stories into order.

My girls put up with a mom who stares at a computer screen all day and who loses her cool when they ask, "What's for dinner?" at 2 P.M. They share my love of reading, and I couldn't be prouder that I have such sharp cookies for kids. *How did I get so lucky?*

My husband understands my need to dissect serial killers' histories and buy books on poisons and criminal psychology. He gets me. Thank you, Dan.

ABOUT THE AUTHOR

Born and raised in the Pacific Northwest, Kendra Elliot has always been a voracious reader, cutting her teeth on classic female sleuths and heroines like Nancy Drew, Trixie Belden, and Laura Ingalls before proceeding to devour the works of Stephen King, Diana Gabaldon, and Nora Roberts. She has a degree in journalism from the University of Oregon. A Golden Heart, Daphne du Maurier, and Linda Howard Award of Excellence finalist, Elliot shares her love of suspense in *Hidden*, *Chilled*, *Buried*, *Alone*, and now *Vanished*. She lives and writes in the rainy Pacific Northwest with her husband, three daughters, and a Pomeranian, but dreams of living at the beach on Kauai. Keep in touch with Kendra at www.KendraElliot.com or through Facebook.